UNIVERSE OF LOST MESSAGES

Book 2: The Charismites

Janet Stilson

UNIVERSE OF LOST MESSAGES

Janet Stilson

IN MEMORY OF MY MOTHER, LETTIE

Paperback ISBN 978-1-77400-062-5
Ebook ISBN 978-1-77400-063-2

List Of Notable Characters

THE NARRATORS

Shakespear (Shake) Cardinale: A gifted young producer at the giant media conglomerate Nuhope. He is the adopted son of Petra Cardinale, who raised him as an Elite, but he was born into the lower Chav class. Shake's swagger and polished appearance mask some secret struggles.

Cheeta Lucida LaVera: A street-tough young woman who is fiercely tenacious. She was saved from homelessness by Senator Miles Morelli, who is like a father to her. Cheeta became Miles' assistant and has a keen aptitude for computers and robotics.

Tristan Ellington: The gentle, nature-boy son of Luscious and Jarat Ellington. Tristan is a Charismite, endowed with extraordinary powers of charisma. But unlike other Charismites, he can feel the physical and emotional pain of others as if they are his own.

Mercury Douglass: A metaverse designer whose career flamed out. Mercury likes to talk with his wife, Tavee, even though she's dead. All he really wants to do is retire and live an easy life. The Universe of Lost Messages puts the kibosh on that.

Luscious (Lush) Melada Ellington: A fun-loving country woman who knows no fear. When she was young, Lush was part of an experiment that transformed her into a Charismite and a mind-bending "tool." She rebelled against that and lives in seclusion with her family.

SECONDARY CHARACTERS

Petra Cardinale: CEO of a huge media company, Nuhope, and the mother of Shake and Izzie Cardinale. Her personal life choices have been messy and risky at times. Petra rose out of the Middles class with hard work and political savvy. She can be demanding but is kind.

Izabel (Izzie) Cardinale: Petra's rebellious daughter and Shakespear's kid sister. Izzie has used her gifts as a Charismite to become a mega-star performer, and her massive following is unrivaled. She can be maddening, reckless, and very perceptive.

Jarat Ellington: Once very active in the underground rebel group Theseus with almost wizardly skills as a technologist. He's intensely focused on the safety of two Charismites—his wife, Luscious, and son, Tristan—who could be used as weapons of thought control.

Miles Morelli: A leader of the Independent Alliance political party who is a senator and likened to Martin Luther King and John F. Kennedy. Miles' secret investigation pits him against powerful enemies. He is deeply humane and courageous.

Nadia Morelli: The temperamental wife of Miles Morelli, who was once a celebrated opera singer. After glottic cancer ruined her voice and her career, Nadia became a recluse filled with loathing and despair. But a passionate love for Miles burns in her soul.

Phineas: A daredevil racer who was once a fighter pilot for the Republic of Europe.

Octavie (Tavee) Douglass: A one-time hair designer to B-list celebrities around Los Angeles. Her husband, Mercury, is the love of her life. Tavee is no longer among the living, except in Mercury's mind.

Ginseng Childe: Nuhope's longtime head of news. Her North Star is the truth, even though it gets covered with clouds at times.

Celeste Sidhar: A cunning, beautiful tech entrepreneur. In addition to running a series of startup businesses that she's snapped up at a discount, Celeste has another secret agenda.

Asrushi and **Nintin Sidhar**: Celeste's parents.

Mikhail Toure: An FBI operative who was relegated to a desk job after a bad injury. Mikhail is a sleeper agent for the rebel group Theseus and Jarat Ellington's longtime friend.

Colin Steward: Senator Miles Morelli's chief of staff.

Petunia: The matronly, four-armed servant bot owned by Miles and Nadia Morelli.

Diana: A bot that Miles and Cheeta built together, and which takes off for parts unknown.

Geoff: Petra's bot, a jack of many trades who resembles an Aussie surfer.

Humbert Kwak: Inventor of a very curious device.

I. SHAKE

Startle-Eyed Sister

EVERYBODY'S BLIND IN their own way. But I was stupid blind on that morning, when the splintering, howling, thump-thump throbs of music from my sister's room ended. In the upside-down world that Izabel always created, sweet silence was my morning alarm.

Now, you could say that there was no way for me to guess what was about to happen—that I would drop into a vortex of devastation and the sublime. But fact is, I should have seen the signs. Not all of them, but some of them, *some of them* weren't that hard to grasp.

My cranky eyes let in the Los Angeles light, the savage heat ready to lunge like a tiger when I stepped outside. Stumbling into the bathroom, I peered in the mirror at my mottled brown and light face, shock of fine black hair. "Shakespear Cardinale, you talented son of a bitch," I told myself. "You can sleep while you're awake."

My sister was staying in one of my guest bedrooms for reasons that didn't make complete sense. The racket began every morning around 2 AM when she came home with her latest one-night stand. It lasted until well after sunrise.

There were usually a few nights a week of peace when I visited the women I was seeing at the time. They didn't need to be told why I was suddenly more willing to travel to their own turf—in Bangkok, Vancouver, and Ciudad de México. My sister's location was tracked by gossip newshounds, who screamed information about her at all times of the day and night —everything from when she lifted her left pinky to her latest acting gigs. My friends would have gladly suffered the excruciating music to get a glimpse of the most dazzling celebrity gracing Earth and all the outer colonies. But they didn't know who she really was: a Charismite, endowed at birth by extraordinary powers of charisma.

She was a freak of nature, and I wasn't about to tell them, or anyone.

Only a few of us knew what Izzie really was. When she trained her startled gray eyes on someone, they saw themselves differently than ever before. Her intense interest made them feel so clever, sensual, witty—more than anyone had ever made them feel. They didn't realize that she could shape what they believed and felt far beyond the normal levels of persuasion. Sure, other famous people were good at that, but they didn't come close to what Izzie could do.

I'd known about her special gifts ever since we were young and had some ability to resist her because I realized what she was. But it didn't come easy. Which was why I couldn't convince her to cut the sound. "Sleep is so overrated," she'd laugh when I complained, low voice drawing out each syllable between those delicious lips.

"Frickin' pain in the neck!" I grumbled to myself as a little shaving bot did its work along my jawline. The mobile device in my right contact lens triggered an air screen, which popped up next to the mirror. It launched into a report about some asteroid that had crashed outside the Phoenix Zone. Like Los Angeles, it was one of many Treasure Zones within United America—a nation that extended from the Arctic Circle region of North America down through most of South America. The asteroid landed three days before. A lot of rocks from outer space got deflected, but somehow this one got through. The news spot was just repeating what everybody already knew. Must be a slow news day.

The screen pinged softly, and I answered a call in private mode, hiding my naked state from the face that popped up. Phineas was one of my old drinking buddies and one helluva an air race jockey. He was in a show that I was producing for Nuhope, the largest media conglomerate in the world. I was a lead content producer, and this was my biggest production to date: *Space Ace.* In two weeks, Phin and four other speed demons would take off from Houston. Destination: dwarf planet Ceres. With a whole lot of guts and technical skill, they'd race from Ceres to Mars.

Phineas was an ex-fighter pilot for the Republic of Europe, another one of Earth's great super nations. He looked like a weathered elf—a giant one, that is, at over six feet. His brown hair was flying in some places and matted with sweat in others from the helmet that was now cradled under one arm, coiled air tubes dangling down to his knees.

"Hey Patch Man," he said, referring to my skin. His Irish brogue was comfortable as an old easy chair, even when he was agitated, like now. He'd been testing out his ship and spotted a malfunction. "You know I love you, but there's no way I'm going to fly in that."

"Hold on. I'm gonna get our top mechanic on this." I shrugged on a bespoke suit jacket. "Your ship will be fixed in a day. Better than ever."

"Give me a little bonus bump? I know you can make my girl fly faster."

"Fly fair, or don't fly at all, pal."

He laughed. "And *when* I win, we got to do a sake binge in Tokyo."

"Yeah, and it'll be all on you."

As we threw information back and forth about the ship's electrically accelerated ions system, I walked down the hall, trying to ignore the musky smell of sex and smoking sticks coming out of the guest room. Through the door crack, I could see Izzie's golden, slumbering face above black silk sheets. The hairy forearm of someone that pumped a lot of iron stretched across her middle. His shiny blue hair spilled down the sheet like water from a faucet.

The call with Phineas ended, and I dove into another with the head of advertising. A client wanted more of its branding on Ship5. "You know it's way too late for that, right?" I asked.

Mumble, frickin' ridiculous excuses from the exec.

"Beth, I get it. TigerBryte is an amazing sponsor. But can't you offer them something else?"

Her pleas went on as I stumbled toward the kitchen, craving my first sip of cappuccino. Nearly tripped three times. Water Man's leather jacket wrapped around my ankle. Food globules oozed between my toes. A half-eaten Indian feast and bottles of beer were strewn between the inevitable heap of guitars and keyboards that companies routinely sent Izzie with the faint hope that she'd use one during a performance. She had five whole rooms of them in her Sonoma mansion, which was undergoing a massive renovation.

Izzie had told me she was tired of sleeping in hotels, wasn't going to be here that long. But she'd already overstayed her welcome by two-and-a-half weeks. Something else was going on.

About the time Beth's call ended, I sliced my gooey toe on the metal edge of a racing air blade. I winced. "Fuck you, Izzie!"

"That's been taken care of." Izabel's husky voice held a vulnerable tremor. I turned to see her in the doorway, flexing her dancer's body, in black boxers and a cropped T-shirt. Hair stained copper and black, sticking out like the points of a wildfire. Sensual lips curled in a teasing smile. It was hard to ignore the electricity in the air, the feeling of being pulled toward her, but I'd learned to control that over the years.

"When did you say you're moving out?" I reached for a towel to take care of the gunk.

"Don't you remember? I said I was moving in permanently. Selling Sonoma after the reno. This space is so dope."

"Oh yeah?" Why was fear coiling out of those gray eyes? I was too annoyed to ask. Instead, I programmed the foodster for an Italian brew. "Not sure I'm going to hold onto it. Changing gigs."

"Wait. What? Not at Nuhope?" she asked.

"Some place new."

"Does Memere know that?" That's what we called our only living parent.

"Yeah." I was about to explain, but a bear-claw voice yelled out a "Hey" from down the hall. Water Man.

Want me to get rid of him? I asked Izzie silently. She nodded "no."

A heavyweight champion emerged behind her—at least, that's what he looked like, wearing my black silk bathrobe. The concentrated darkness of his eyes spoke of ancestors from the Indian subcontinent. He shifted under my chilly stare.

"Meet my big bad brother, Shake. This is …" Izzie snapped her fingers.

"Prill."

"Right. We met last night at the air blade race. He's super-fast. Beat me." He pressed the bulge under the robe into her butt. She flitted away, fiddling with the controls of my foodster.

Wasn't hard to imagine a scene from her previous night, the bunch of feral young things zooming on air blades a foot off the ground on pressurized air, weaving between trees and buildings, then across the desert in a mad dash for some Vegas goalpost.

The foodster spurted an espresso into her cup. "Hey. You should do a show on air blade races."

"Sure, if you star."

"No way."

She started to program a chocolate mousse, but Prill blocked her hand. "Hey. Fuck the machine, Babe. I'll make you some breakfast from scratch."

"No thanks."

"You're gonna need more energy—"

"No. Get dressed. It's time for you to blow out of here."

Prill's voice cracked. "You don't want that."

"Sorry. I've got rehearsals."

"Maybe tonight?"

"No. This would be it."

Tears welled in his eyes. "But can't we …?" *Be together forever? Make love every day and night?* I tried to hide a smirk. Seen it a million times.

"You know how I roll."

"Yeah." He fingered a stray guitar pick in a dried, sticky puddle of last night's beer on the counter and held it up. "Souvenir?"

Izzie took it from him, washed it off with soap and water, dried it and handed it back respectfully. "Yeah."

Prill pulled away and dragged himself back to the guest room.

She swished over to me and tamped down my hair with her fingers. "You know what the problem with you is?"

"Yeah, you."

"Beside that."

"What?"

She steered me over to a long mirror: her golden face, my

darker one, spotted like a frickin' riding-stable pony. "You don't realize what girls think about you. Sure, they're impressed by who you are. But that look of yours is raging."

"Uh-huh."

"I'm not kidding. That Chav-ness."

Chav. The massive lower social class I was born into. Izzie wasn't my biological sister. She was born an Elite—a class largely composed of super wealthy people who were genetically modified to emulate all different races on Earth blended together so that their skin tone was golden. Even the Middles class looked that way.

I'd never be a "natural fit," the way I looked. And yet I wasn't just any Elite; I was a prince. Our mother, Petra Cardinale, was CEO of the gargantuan media company where I worked, Nuhope. She'd wanted a kid so bad when I came along, a stray from the streets of the Boston Treasure Zone. An orphan. Hard to say who needed who more, Memere or me. Then a few years later she did the in-vitro-fertilization thing and had Izzie.

I finished college at the age of sixteen, worked for Nuhope's most talented producer, churning out ideas for shows and new games so fast nobody questioned my position. Not just nepotism. Wouldn't let that be true. And now here I was, a top producer at age twenty-three.

And yet. And yet. In the small hours of the morning when I stared out at dark blinking Los Angeles, I was disturbed by what I'd become. I hated myself for being an ungrateful wretch, but there was no denying that something was missing. This wasn't who I should be.

Izzie wrapped her arms around me from behind, her surging warmth so soothing. "Remember when you screwed the professor and then screwed his wife?"

"Izzie. That was you."

She laughed. "Really?"

"Why are we talking about this?"

She didn't respond. I peeled myself away and turned around. She was biting her pretty lip. "I singe you. Again and again."

"Silly duck. Think I can't take it?"

Her brows furrowed as she straightened my jacket, even though it was about as straight as it could get. Tears puddled her ghost gray eyes. "I just want you to know that I'm sorry. I didn't ask for any of this."

No, she didn't. Our mother had conceived Izzie by using the sperm of a Charismite that she'd fallen in love with. A guy named Dove Brown. After he died, she stored his sperm until she was ready. It was a big secret. Hardly anyone knew what she'd done.

And now here we were, with Izzie all teared up. Had to make her laugh. "Yes, you are the epitome of the term 'ill-conceived.'"

"Oh, shut up."

A booming voice sounded from the guest room. "Hey, Izz. Coming back?"

My sister rolled her eyes. "That one was totally not worth it."

"Why?"

"Something's off. And I ..."

"Izzie!"

"... was thinking it would be nice for you and me to grab some lunch. You know, talk."

It didn't hit me, that something was *really* wrong—that I should have drawn her out before anything else happened, yanked her out of there, down the hall, out of the building, get someplace where she could tell me, whatever it was. Even though I now realize that her eyes were like warning signals.

Like I said: blind spot. But at the time, Prill didn't seem that different than her other castoffs. And I really frickin' had to solve Phin's ship problem *right away*. So all I said was: "Yeah. We can do that. But you mean dinner, right?"

She walked toward the bedroom, calling over her shoulder, "Whatever you want to call it. Tonight around 7, at that Churrasco place you like on Wilshire." They had a private dining room. There would be a bit of a crazed scene with the other diners when Izzie walked in, but we'd get through it.

"I thought you were a vegetarian."

"Eh. You know they'll make anything for me."

The time readout on my air screen was scary. I was way late. It took an extra push to get my front door open. As usual, there was such a pile of bouquets and other gifts from Izzie's fans. The building's staff knew to just leave them at the door. It was easy to glide over the mess on my air shoes and then down the hall. I was calling up the *Space Ace* mechanic about Phineas' airship when…

BAM

The blast sent me flying. My head socked hard against a flower vase. The shards punctured my temple. Ears rang like a blistering siren. Green and yellow fireworks of light.

I crawled back in the apartment's blasted-open door, blood dripping. "Izzie!" The white door of her bedroom was black now. Why?

Strong arms helped me up. Two of the building's security guards. Max and Hank. "You okay, Mr. Cardinale?"

I babbled something about my sister, pointing at the awful door. They were spooked but dragged themselves toward it. Looking in, their mouths dropped. I stumbled through the debris, pushed past them. Furniture, mattress, all Izzie's personal belongings were charred. Where was she? And Prill?

Her thrilling aura was completely gone. Didn't have to look for body parts to figure out that there weren't any.

Nothing.

Disbelief clamped down on me. My utterly annoying, absolute best friend. From the time she was born. Just vaporized? I was in shock, couldn't trust my reactions at first.

No. Something else was going on. But what? Stumbling to the shattered window, I studied the pavement thirty floors below for any signs of a broken body. But there was no trace of her or the guy, just a crowd of people that got larger, larger, larger.

She isn't dead. There wasn't any reason why I should be so sure, but I could almost taste it. If that was really true, where the hell was she?

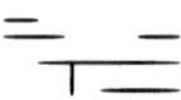

THAT WASN'T THE first explosion that ripped my mind to pieces.

When Petra adopted me, she had no experience with kids, let alone one who was messed up because a bomb had blown up his life. My whole family died. My birth mama, wide shadowed face, harsh love in a deep voice, papery hands. My squeaky sister, Lilya. My rebellious big brother, Deko.

When I was taken in by Petra, I wailed and wailed. She was beside herself, trying to figure out how to help me. Called in a whole battery of shrinks.

"You're not my mama! You're not!"

"Oh darling, I know. Never replace her. Never."

It took some time to figure out what I'd call her. And what came out was Memere, an old Creole word. That was my family's roots. Although when I was at Nuhope, I sometimes called her Petra. After all, she was the boss.

After a while, Memere and I became nearly inseparable. She

brought me to work all the time, and I was a little wandering cat that trailed after her. I could almost sense her nerve endings, knew how she felt about someone, or some situation, before she was even completely sure of it herself. And now that I was working at Nuhope as a producer, people seemed to think of me as her wunderkind sidekick.

Memere and I would arrive at some fly party in Paris, Sidney, Shanghai—all of them filled with celebs and assorted fat cats. We were the royalty that everyone wanted to talk with. She had a trademark look, with elegant silver hair that reminded me of old jewelry. A lock swooped down into a curl on her forehead. Her clothes were usually black and gave off an air of simplicity and gracefulness. More than a few of her staff acolytes had tried to copy it.

Most people didn't expect a powerful woman to be as feminine as Memere. She was the commander of Nuhope—with its legion of ten thousand employees all over the globe and on several of the most important satellite outposts. But there was no brittle edge to her. Her face was radiant and open. Hidden far below was the hot lava that surfaced during battles with Nuhope's board of directors and key corporate lieutenants. She had to call upon all her hard strength during the occasional rounds of layoffs when the economy dipped. How she hated that.

Memere was the person I needed to see now. I'd sat in my living room for hours as a battalion of detectives from first the LAPD and then the FBI grilled me, scanning every inch of the apartment. When they finally let me go, I jumped into my mag-lev car on the building's roof and crossed United America in ninety minutes flat with supercharge boosts from hyper-tubes in Denver and Indianapolis.

Nuhope's headquarters in the New York Treasure Zone

knifed up through the black sky over lower Broadway. It was lit by a carousel of promotional holograms that were each ten stories high. On any normal day, the promos would have been dedicated to upcoming shows, like *Space Ace.* We'd recorded jocular interviews featuring the five *Ace* pilots for those wallscapes and a ton of others, all over the world. Now their holos were nowhere in sight.

Instead, gigantic images of my sister were plastered all over the building: news stories from Nuhope's reporting team, with poignant closeups of Izzie's beguiling face as a voiceover reported on the mystery surrounding her presumed death; teasers for shows that she'd starred in; concert clips that featured her pipe-bright voice soaring up to the stars. The building had become a monument to Izzie. Buildings all over the city were like that. She was all that anyone wanted to think about or see.

I landed my ride on the roof, then glided down a private elevator to Petra's inner sanctum. The security bots recognized me immediately. Walls sparkled away, and I shot down a corridor that was entirely wrapped in a holo of crashing waves. Always made me feel like Moses parting the waters. It was a replica of an ocean bay in the El Central Treasure Zone, a place that used to be called El Salvador. Memere liked to go there every now and then.

Her private office wasn't exactly cramped. Rip it apart, and you got yourself the floor space for four basketball courts. As I came inside, the walls were a sea of holographic news feeds about Izzie from media outlets all over the world. My mother stood in the middle of it all, close to drowning.

"Hey."

Memere turned around abruptly, flicked a hand, and the images vanished. "Finally!" She came toward me quickly, arms spread wide; I fell into them. She seemed even more petite than usual, against my six-foot frame. We were locked together with howling terror. But for my mother, there was an added element of guilt. I pitied her for that.

A savage friction had developed over the years between Memere and Izzie. My sister blamed our mother for making her a monster whose powers of attraction and influence far exceeded what even the most naturally charming celebrities were capable of. If Izzie told people to jump off a tall building, they'd be sorely tempted, if they didn't actually do it. Because of that, Memere guarded her like a human weapon who *kind of* recognized her own power when she was young, but she was pretty reckless. Memere did the best she could by limiting Izz's appearances in the outside world to almost nothing, but the isolation was tough on Izz. And there was more to it.

My sister hated that Memere had used Dove Brown's sperm to conceive her. He was a legendary talk show host who had passed about twenty years before. "Fanatic" didn't begin to describe how people felt about him. His most obsessive fans could recite every line of his screen appearances backwards, they'd watched them so much. He was just about the first Charismite ever created. It wasn't a natural gift; he was cranked up on this substance called the Juice. It was a chemical concoction that amplified his human levels of charm way off the spectrum of what was normally possible.

Izzie didn't need the Juice at all. She was proof that, if there is a God, he has a very black sense of humor. Because somehow that frickin' Juice altered Dove's genes, his sperm, and she inherited all his extraordinary charm. No chems required! Charismite 2.0, you might say. Memere couldn't believe it.

When I was about sixteen and a much more cynical lad than I am now, I asked her how the hell she would take a chance like that, using a dead Charismite's sperm. How could anyone who ran a multi-trillion Americo business, who was a goddamned captain of industry, have such crappy personal judgement?

She let out a stream of air. "I don't expect you to understand this now. But as you get older, you become a different person. Things you think you'd never do right now may seem exactly right later on. And things you did a long time ago will seem utterly foreign, sometimes painfully ridiculous."

Her eyes shone into some far-off place filled with enchantments and nightmares. A long time ago, she'd agreed to take part in an experiment out of a desperate hope of finding the perfect mate. It allowed her to see visions of a child that she might conceive with the right guy. And the system said that man was Dove. She became addicted to him, like people were addicted to Izzie now After he passed, she was obsessed with that imaginary child the system had showed her she could conceive with Dove: a little startle-eyed girl. She hired genetic engineers to make sure Dove's sperm would actually do what she wanted.

It was clear almost from the get-go that Izzie was gifted. Memere was terrified of her own child's power. She wasn't affected by Izzie's charms as much as me—because I was naturally attracted to girls, and Memere went for guys. Although since I knew what Izzie was, I was able to resist her powers much more than an unsuspecting person. Took some mental concentration, but I could. Hardly anyone else was aware of why Izzie was like a goddamned love magnet. Memere wanted to keep it that way.

She only allowed two human helpers in her New York townhouse—a maid and a gardener for the courtyard in the back. It was a pretty lame decision. From the time she was three, Izzie screwed with their brains, making them do ridiculous things, like standing on their heads while eating a banana split.

(Yeah, it was pretty messy.) One day she had the gardener raid the bar; he was so plastered. Memere replaced them with bots, since machines are immune. Didn't help to yell at Izz or punish her. She just descended into tirades. Memere's guilt tore at her insides. Even when the fights ended, and everything was quiet, feelings bounced between them—guilt and rage, guilt and rage. It wasn't fun to be around.

Eventually, Izzie figured out how to escape and turned into a bad girl of epic proportions on the nightclub scene. Our mother's rage eventually caved in; she had to surrender. Long story short, Izz finally got herself under control, started taking performance classes, and turned into the biggest star in the celebrity firmament.

All of that history was zinging through Memere and me as we hugged each other in her office. She pulled away and surveyed my bandaged wounds, seeing deep down into me in a way that nobody else could. "Awful, awful, awful."

I knew what she was thinking: me witnessing another explosion. Another person I loved was gone, maybe forever. I managed to grin. "Hey. It didn't make me nuts, at least not in a meaningful way."

She rolled her eyes. "Let's raid the medicine cabinet." The door to her bathroom sparkled away and she disappeared inside. She had an assortment of the best pharmas known to humankind. "What'll it be?"

"Antacid."

She poked her head out the door, aghast. "That can't be all."

"Boring has its charms."

She foraged around to find some. "What did the detectives tell you? Do they have any ideas about what happened?"

"They're stumped."

"The wankers." It was hard to have much hope on those

fronts. The LAPD and the FBI were both hobbled by political bureaucracy and depleted resources. If they came up with much of anything, I'd be stunned. Didn't matter that Izz was the daughter of such a high-ranking Elite.

Memere handed me the pills, eyes blazing. "Izzie's alive. Has to be."

"Of course. Have you received any ransom demands?"

"No."

That meant they probably knew what she is. A Charismite. Someone who could convince anyone to do anything if she was forced. A massive number of humans all behaving, all thinking, in the way that some crackpot desired. How would they try to control her, if they actually knew what she was?

Or as Memere put it: "Why ask for a ransom when Izzie can get them all the money in the world?"

2. CHEETA

The Fallen Diva

THE FIRST TIME I got sent into the Universe of Lost Messages, it didn't make sense. I thought somebody had hacked my tech and sent me into some stupid game metaverse. There I was, free-floating in my old shorts and T-shirt in a kind of space-type place. But it was the color of a ripe papaya. The orange went on and on, like it didn't have no end.

Instead of stars and planets, there were these bubbles. Thousands, maybe millions. Up close, they were the size of soccer balls, and way off in the distance they were these sparkling dots, small as a grain of sand. The surface of the bubbles had colors glinting off them. And I could see a face in each one, jabbering away, although their voices were faint.

"Hey! Is this a joke? What is this place?" I shouted. There wasn't any answer, just the whispering voices.

Somehow, I knew to hold out a hand, and one of the bubbles floated right into it. I squeezed it. Just had to. There was a little pop, and out of it leaped a full-sized hologram of a woman with tight curls rolled like cigars and a splat of brown stuff on her face. She was holding a dirty white Pomeranian with black eyes and a long pink tongue.

"Jonas! Jonas!" she screeched. "Is this your idea of a joke? You dipped Frolly in the mud pond, didn't you?" The holo disappeared inside the bubble, then took off.

Another one came toward me. When I squeezed it a little,

there was another pop, and a slick man in a cowboy hat sprang out. He was standing in a desert. "Act now and act fast! You can get a sweet little home in Green Dream Estates for only …"

I tossed his bubble away and opened another, then another. Holo messages were one thing. They'd been around a long time. But I'd never seen them in bubbles. There were little readouts beside each one showing when they were sent. They all seemed to be about six weeks old.

"Excuse me," I yelled. "What's with you bubbleheads?"

Nothing.

"Is somebody going to tell me how to get out of here? Because Cheeta Lucida LaVera don't take no…"

There was a rumbling, and a mountain of bubbles appeared, way in the distance. It swooped toward me, and the spheres inside it grew larger and larger, voices calling "Cheeta, Cheeta!" I tumbled among them, flailing my arms around, trying to get out of that huge cluster, breaking bubbles left and right. The people that popped out shouted so loud I thought my ear drums would split.

Finally, I came out the other side, panting like crazy. Thought I was in the clear until this one bubble came right at me. Its light was piercing at first, but then softened enough for me to see a man inside, whispering "Cheeta Lucida LaVera."

At first, I didn't recognize him. But then I did. Someone I loved—that I'd seen almost every day for a bunch of years until he passed: Senator Miles Morelli. His face was so changed, so haggard and scared. His hair had always been so polished, but in the holo it was all frizzled out. And if the readout was true, he'd sent the message two days *after* everybody thought he'd been killed.

I was too messed up to even know if I screamed.

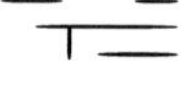

WHEN I THINK about what happened just before the senator's death was reported, I always come back to a song. I never would have heard it if Miles hadn't made a special request.

I'd gotten pretty messed up the day before—cause I heard Izabel Cardinale was gone. That girl was so hot! I slept long and hard after that. Heavy feet crawling across my belly finally woke me up. My two-foot-long Fire Salamander, all black with orange squiggles, looked down on me hungrily with these little black-ball eyes.

"LiZee, did you spring out again?!" The little princess glug-glugged as I carried her over to the big tank and set her inside with some worms.

I triggered the mobile unit in my contact lens to pull up a holographic screen and was shocked to find out it was almost 9:30. "Why didn't your alarm go off, *estupido*?" I asked the screen.

"Because you forgot to set me, *estupido*." Cheeky bish. "You had a message from the senator."

"Wha?"

"You're to report to his residence this morning, not the main office."

"Uh, okay." It was weird, but there was no time to think about that. I raced around my tiny studio getting ready, barely avoiding the jumble of furniture I'd found on the street. Gulped some leftover coffee. Threw on a black suit. Ran fingers through my dark hair that was thick as a goddamned shrub, willing it to look respectable.

When I slammed out the door, a paper fell on the hall floor. Frickin' landlord's eviction notice. I wadded it up and ran down the stairs out into the stew of people on the streets of Flushing, Queens.

Fifteen minutes later I was on the subway. There were a

bunch of shabby, tired buildings all along the track, but when we crossed the East River going straight into Manhattan, all these gleaming spires cut through the clouds. It was one of the most expensive places to live on planet Earth.

Three trains later, I made it to Sugar Hill, a section of Harlem. Gives you sort of a time-warp feel: four-story brownstones from a couple of centuries ago lining hilly streets. Old money Elites live there, the kind that gets off on an antique vibe.

The Morelli mansion was a lot bigger than most of them along Convent Avenue, separated from the pack by a wide lawn and gardens. I was almost up to the front walk when a blur shot out of the side door and across the garden. *Jesucristo!* That was a humanoid! Diana! The one that the senator and I had put together from a Build-a-Bot kit about a year before.

It looked like a replica of a buff, red-headed woman in a black body suit. Miles had used all his insider-government resources to give it a deep-data computational system that left most other bots in the dust. Why the hell was it running off that way? I started to yell "Hey!" but before the word got out of my mouth, Diana leaped over a high wall and disappeared. I messaged it like crazy, asking where the hell it was going. But I kept getting an error signal on my mobile.

"*Mierda!*" That was super weird. I tried again and again, but nothing.

Two plain-clothed Secret Service peeps were at the front door. They were drinking their morning *café con leche* and talking shit, backs turned on the garden area, so they didn't see nothing. But even so, something inside told me to keep my *boca* shut.

I shot them some *holas* as a four-armed bot, Petunia, opened the door. It was like a big ol' middle-aged mother type that pretty much ran everything in the mansion—a chef, housecleaner, healthcare worker all rolled into one. As soon as it let me into the huge entrance room, I could see Miles walking toward us from far down the hallway, distinguished as ever in a sharp-angled blue suit. But why was he was carrying a suitcase? Things were weirder on top of weirder.

His jaw was set hard, so determined, like something was pissing him off. But he tried for a smile when he saw me. “Hello, Mutt!” That’s what he called me. Sounded bad, but out of his mouth, it was like “love,” or “sweetie pie,” without the sicky sugar going on.

“Hey, Miles. Diana just—”

“Yes.” He said it in a way that told me not to ask more. “Petunia, is the car out front?”

“Yes, sir. Just coming around.”

“Great.” The troubles on Miles’ face seemed to blow away as he took me in with a deep, honest interest. He had this passion and kindness that made all the people around him reach for big goals. It must have been one of the reasons he’d been reelected three times to the U.A. Senate by the New York Treasure Zone. “I’ll tell you about Diana later.”

“Sure, no prob. But if you’re going someplace else, how come you want me here?”

The worried darkness came back over him. “I don’t know how long I’ll be away, and I can’t leave Nadia alone,” he said, speaking of his wife. “Just be here for her if she needs someone to talk to. And don’t upset her.”

I smirked. “You think that’s possible?”

Miles tweaked my cheek and gave me a laughing smile. “Set the intention and someday it just might come true. You’re really more alike than you know.”

Me and her? He had to be clowning me. I wanted to call him on that, but he was moving toward the front door real fast.

I had to pick my shots. "Um, Senator. When you get back. There's something I want to talk about."

He stopped in his tracks and turned back, eyes intent on me once again. "What is it?"

"Well, um. I like being your assistant and all. But I really want to go to school. Maybe Rutgers out in Jersey. There's this robotics program. Maybe if I took it, I could help you. At a higher level."

Miles dropped his suitcase, like I'd told him that God just gave me a high five or something.

"Are you okay?" Petunia asked him.

"I've been waiting for this girl to say something like that for ages," he said. "When do you want to start?"

"The fall. But. Well, um. I know you told me you'd help with tuition when I'm ready, but I'm kind of in the hole when it comes to living expenses."

"Cheeta Lucida. When are you going to learn how to budget?"

"I can work longer hours. Maybe get another job. I'm not asking for you to pay the whole nut. Just help me—"

"Pish posh. I'll take care of it. Just remember, watch over Nadia, okay?"

"Sure."

Then he was gone. Petunia led me down a hallway lined with holos of all this museum-quality artistic work. "Better watch out," it said. "That smile of yours is so big it'll crack your face in two."

"Yeah, I know. What's up with the Nadia thingy?"

"I don't know, but maybe it has something to do with this." Petunia opened a door that led to this room they called a salon. It looked like somebody had tried to destroy the place. Wine splats on the white stuffed furniture, broken glass and china everywhere. At least all the art on the walls was okay. "Holy crap," I said. "Who fired the first shot?"

"Her, of course."

"Wow." *What the hell was that about?*

We went past another stuffy salon, then Miles' huge study, which was filled with ancient books. At the very back of the first floor next to the kitchen was this tiny office where I was supposed to work. It was dank and sad looking, with piles of paper files that looked about a hundred years old and an office air screen. I'd only been there once before.

Petunia looked about as sympathetic as a bot could be. "Would you like a pot of tea?"

"Nah. I'll be okay."

Before long, I had shifted into work mode, pouring through the senator's database for a twelve-year-old tax return that had gone missing. It was such a lonely, cold place. How I missed his noisy headquarters on Third Avenue—always filled with shouts, cracked jokes and the occasional argument between staff peeps who were constantly coming and going, pumped up with passion for the various pieces of legislation Miles was promoting, the speeches he had yet to deliver on the Senate floor, the next election campaign. Didn't matter if all I did was this kind of low-level clerical stuff. The scene was da bomb, to me.

My mind kept coming back to what Miles had said about me and his wife. What the hell was he talking about? How could I ever be like Nadia Morelli? She was a famous opera star, what they call a contralto—a real big-time deal with the New York Metropolitan Opera. At least she had been. Now she was like some kind of exotic flower that was bruised and torn up, voice ruined by glottic cancer.

After they'd got the evil shit out of Nadia, she'd gone through a lot of plastic surgery in hopes of getting back the voice that made her famous. But it was impossible. I'd read this report once about the way she sang before. Frickin' critic called it "velvet, cascading peels of sound." Thought he was a poet or something.

I was about as far from being like Nadia as anything. Most people thought of me as one of Miles' poverty projects. Sometimes senators did shit for Chav people—the lowest of the low on the social totem pole. It was supposed to be goodwill gestures, to prove to the public they had a kind heart. But with Miles, it was genuine. He just did stuff like that.

Nadia sure didn't. As far as she was concerned, I was worthless as a dirty rag. She didn't have no right. Sure, I made it through two freezing winters in a smelly old coat living beneath a bridge in Central Park with my mama. I learned how to give people this "don't fuck with me" vibe when I walked down tough streets. But after Miles got hold of me, he kind of softened my edges. When Mama passed, he set me up with some foster parents, made sure I got into grade school—and eventually, the top tech high school in New York. Plus, he gave me the assistant gig in his office when I turned fifteen. That was two years ago.

I was way into some mental bishing about that sorry-ass office when a journalist called Miles' work number, and I answered. The woman that popped up on the holographic screen had this pinched-up face and a nasal voice. "I'd like to speak with Nadia Morelli's assistant, please."

"You got the wrong number, lady."

"I know that this is Senator Morelli's number, but I don't know how else to get through to her. Can you help? I want to do a warm, uplifting story." She struck a pose, like she was delivering a news spot. "One year after the great opera star Nadia Morelli disappeared from the spotlight—"

A hand swiped the air in front of the screen. The journalist disappeared. I swiveled around and faced Nadia. A blue velvet bathrobe with fur trim barely covered her fat belly. Her curly, acid-yellow hair was in snarls, surrounding a thick face and neck.

"What a delicious invitation," she said in a voice full of cut glass. "I'd just love to be on her freak show."

"Hey. That's not going to happen. Nobody's going to hear you, see you, nothing you don't want."

Nadia softened but couldn't hide a sharp look at my messed-up black hair and long face. "Thank you."

"Sure."

"I'm surprised you're working here," she said politely.

I shrugged. "Just doing what the senator says."

"He always tells you things. Where's he going?"

"Didn't say."

"Who's he seeing?"

"Dunno."

"Secret rendezvous with that humanoid? Miles' little sex toy." Her cheeks flamed with humiliation, fishing for intel about her husband from a Chav assistant she couldn't stand. It was pathetic.

"I don't know nothing about no sex toy." I swiveled back around and started going through files on the air screen.

"If you're going to lie, at least use proper English. You don't know *anything*."

It took all my control not to snap back. She went out and slammed the office door behind her. I tried to make the sting fade, but she pissed me off too much. After about an hour, I went to get some coffee in the kitchen.

Music came toward me, down the hall. The voices of a man and woman kind of laced around each other. That's the only way to put it. Each note seemed so tender, kind of warm and delicate. Later, I learned the song was "Parigi, o Cara" from Verdi's *La Traviata*. But right then, all I knew was that I needed to get closer, really hear it. I passed Miles' office, then came to the messed-up salon. The music was coming from inside.

Peering around the door, I saw the holo recording of a curvy woman brimming with ecstasy as she sang with a barrel-chested tenor. Then I realized: it was Nadia, from before I'd ever known her.

The real Nadia was standing before the holo. Her ugly face was lit up. She was reliving that night in the Metropolitan Opera. The audience was washing love back toward her younger self as she sang and sang, like her heart had fluttered out of her, touching each one of them.

I was shaken into a new sense of who and what she was. Sure, I'd known Nadia was famous. But seeing and hearing why was something else. All my resentment melted into pity, seeing how far she had fallen.

Nadia turned quickly and saw me in the doorway. Waving away the holo, she snarled, "How dare you spy me?"

Spy? It was ridic. "*Puta de madre*." I walked away from her, down the hall.

"What did you just say?"

"I said, if you didn't want people to pay attention, you shouldn't play that music so loud."

Her fury narrowed down to a sharp point. "Just because Miles has made you his little charity case doesn't mean you can walk around here saying things like you're a member of this family."

"Go stuff yourself," I mumbled under my breath.

"WHAT?"

"Nothin'"

"Get out. Get out!" she screeched. "You're fired."

"You can't do that! I work for Miles."

"If I say you're fired, you're bloody well fired! Petunia! Petunia!" The bot whisked in and took my arm.

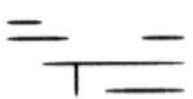

THERE WAS THIS skinny twerp down the hall in my apartment building that collected reptiles. He had hundreds. There was even a boa constrictor that wrapped around his toilet. How could he stick his dick out and pee with that thing there?

The guy kept to himself; hardly saw him at all. But one day, his downstairs neighbor carped to the super that there was water gushing out of her bathroom ceiling. Reptile Dude didn't answer his mobile, 'cause he was a doctor in the middle of a shift. (I know. A *doctor*!) The super bashed in his door and just about had a heart attack. An alligator in the tub had flipped on the water faucet with his tail, and the place was completely flooded. Bad-ass snakes and lizards stacked up in glass boxes, all over the place. There were some tarantulas, too.

The landlord called animal control, and the Wonderful World of Scary Shit was cleared out. I saw the whole evacuation. Only took about an hour. The pest-control bots had these big torsos like gigantic cans and eight limbs each. I must have seen them carry out about a hundred animals.

A few hours after it was all over, I came out of my apartment and almost stepped on LiZee. She was only about a foot long then, and I had no idea what she was. All I knew was that I was in love with those beady black eyes and bright orange streaks. So stinkin' ugly. Somehow, she must have streaked down the hall and around the corner before the bots saw her.

After a while, it seemed like LiZee was some kind of kindred spirit. We both knew what it was like to almost get trashed, to feel mentally stomped on by people without any hearts. We knew the saviors too. For me, it was the senator. If it wasn't for him, I probably would still be hunting through garbage in dumpsters trying to stay alive. And LiZee had me.

After I got fired by that loser diva, I spent most of the afternoon bishing to LiZee. I kept myself busy repairing this old IBM desktop. It was the very first model, from 1981. I'd spotted it next to the curb on Fred Doug Boulevard about two months before. Even had the original keyboard. Freaking blew my mind. There was a whole antique computer racket in the flea markets around New York, and if I just could get this sucker to work, I knew I could make some serious Americos. And I really needed them. Didn't know how long it would take to get things straightened out with the senator—or find another job. Most people hired bots to do the kind of office work I did.

While I worked at getting some gunk off the 8088 Intel microprocessor, I shot a look at LiZee, who was catching some rays on the windowsill. "Miles is going to take me back. He loves me."

Glug-glug.

"What the fuck business does she have firing me? She don't got no right. Don't run his fuckin' office. And I do so much. Never complain. Never ask for nothin'."

Glug.

"Okay. But not that much." He did say he'd help with Rutgers. And he gave me money for the down payment on this apartment. "But I'm pretty low maintenance."

PING. I always got alerts when the senator was in the news. Most times, it was stuff I already knew from being around him all the time. LiZee was staring at me harder now, the way she always did when she was hungry.

"You know we got to ration our food now, right?" I

imagined what was to come: me back to dumpster diving and digging through the park looking for worms. That would be a bitch, especially in the winter. Hellz, maybe there was money in that—selling worms to pet stores.

About fifty more pings came off my mobile, one on top of another. "Uh, I think you want to see this," my air screen said.

I flipped it on. Miles latest PR mug shot sprang up. A reporter said: "Senator Miles Morelli from the great New York Treasure Zone has been killed in a freak car accident."

That didn't make sense. He always used the national navigation grid, which controlled the movements of all vehicles so they would never collide, always stayed on course. The holo switched to a view of a huge fire with an angry cloud of black smoke. "The senator was traveling through the outskirts of the Chicago Treasure Zone when the explosive crash occurred. Investigators on the scene believe that the vehicle's controls malfunctioned. In addition to Senator Morelli, his two bodyguards …"

The report switched to the guards I'd seen just that morning outside the Morelli mansion. They were in the car with Miles. My knees gave out and I sat down hard. Dead too. I couldn't focus, couldn't stop wondering why the hell Miles was passing through Chicago.

I forced myself to listen. "A search is underway to find the three passengers' remains. But given the high-speed impact of the mag-lev into an empty school bus, it remains doubtful that anything will be found."

I sat around my apartment, a brainless mess, watching all the news tributes to Miles.

"A leader of the Independent Alliance party, Miles Morelli was considered to be the Martin Luther King of his generation, the John F. Kennedy …" It was hard to take in what the reports were saying. I kept switching from one to another to another. He'd been on the navigational grid when he made it to Chicago, but then the car just went off it. That's what they all said.

"Couldn't even do what you asked." I sobbed, looking at his holo. *Just be here for her if Nadia needs someone to talk to. And don't upset her.* Yeah, the bish threw tantrums left and right around Miles, and I hated on her fierce. But he loved her more than anything.

He loved me, too. And now there was nobody left to save me.

3. SHAKE

Boy in the Biodome

MEMERE AND I escaped to her townhouse and nearly wore holes in the old oriental carpets, pacing back and forth, trying to figure out what scumbag group had taken Izzie—and who could have found out about her special charismatic powers. By the day after my sister's disappearance, a massive crowd of reporters had parked outside—in-person and remotely through drones. The townhouse was off Fifth Avenue on East 86th. And the news hounds fanned out down the block in both directions and their drones swarmed the air.

Our bewildered panic blew up even higher after alerts popped up on our air screens about Miles Morelli's fatal accident. My mother wasn't a close friend of the senator, but they swam in the same circles around New York, and they'd spoken many times. Nuhope had been under the control of the Independent party for many years, when it was the ruling party in Washington. And Morelli was among its leading lights. He'd given her thoughts on the corporation's various strategies, and she'd told him her strong views about various pieces of legislation.

But things had changed. The Republican-Democratic Alliance, better known as the RDA, had unseated the Independents in the election that took place just the week before. And because the ruling party always controlled Nuhope—a government owned conglomerate—Memere's job was probably about to end. After all, she was an avid Independent party member. That meant my job was on the line—by extension, as it were.

"Reminds me of Andrew Massot," Memere said.

"What?"

"God. What did they teach you in school?"

Oh! She was talking about Miles Morelli, comparing his death to Andrew Massot's. "Of course I know about Massot." A senator from Minnesota, one-time presidential candidate who had been killed when his ship was attacked, just off Mars about twenty years ago. The group behind the assassination was still a mystery and subject to a lot of speculation. "Morelli wasn't assassinated though."

"That wasn't proven."

Her right-hand humanoid, Geoff, glided into the room. It was a blonde, buff surfer type with an Aussie accent that bugged me. Knew Memere and I well enough to figure out what we wanted before we said anything, which is why it said: "Double espresso, ma'am?"

"Yes please."

Geoff looked at me. "Iced cappuccino, mate?"

"Yes, but I am not your bloody mate."

Memere shot me some annoyance and placed a call. A holo of Ginseng Childe sprang up. She was Nuhope's longtime head of news, a trans woman with long crow-black hair shot through with silver, stony pock-marked face. After the hellos, Memere asked, "How's your security doing?"

"No bugs. Just checked. Things are fucked around here." We could tell from the background that Ginseng was in her Nuhope office.

"What kind of fucked?"

"I'm getting directives from the RDA to bury the news

about Morelli. They want us to turn us into the *All-Izabel Show*."

Memere was plenty rankled. No one should have undermined her authority as Nuhope's leader. But we both knew that it was a sign of the new times. And reports on the disappearance of Izzie would keep the audience levels extremely high. The idea of ignoring Morelli's death was about what we could expect from the RDA.

"So we keep doing this, right?" Ginseng asked.

"You'll have to." Memere shot a grateful look at Geoff as it arrived with our brew. "But we can't let that news about Morelli die away."

"What do you mean?"

"Keep a reporter on the Morelli story. And if they get any new information on that accident that doesn't get posted, feed it to other news organizations." Ginseng coughed in surprise at that. "We can't let this get buried. Do what it takes," Memere said.

The news chief grinned. "Right." Her holo disappeared.

Memere gazed at me above the rim of her cup. "Any word on what's happening in Pompey?"

"Yeah. They're getting ready for anything."

Pompey Hollow was about one hundred miles north of the New York Treasure Zone, home to Luscious Ellington and her son Tristan. They were the only other Charismites in the world, besides Izzie, and were under the loving protection of Jarat Ellington—Tristan's dad, Luscious' husband. Our two families were very close. Lush and Jarat were like an aunt and uncle to me.

"I've talked with Jarat three times about all this," I said. "When it comes to grilling, the FBI don't got nothin' on him." When there was a bone Jarat wanted to chew, he could gnaw it into pulp. Which was probably why he and Lush had actually managed to keep their son's existence a secret from just about everyone. Unlike Memere with Izzie. Although, in fairness, Tristan was a lot more docile.

I went back to pacing. "I really don't want to stay here."

Memere shot me a knowing look. "Geoff, can we escape the mob?" Her limo was on the roof, so the humans below weren't an issue, but the drones were another thing.

"No wuckas," the bot said. "You'll be in Pompey before you know it."

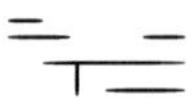

THE ELLINGTONS LIVED in their own realm; a compound that was encased in a biosphere stretching over seventy-five acres in diameter. When the car was ten miles away from it, the air became more crystalline. The plant life along the rolling foothills of the Catskill Mountains quivered with vibrancy, ever so subtly. And the sensation of being more alive, more vital, more thrilled washed over us. That's what Charismites did, especially when there were two of them in one place. Luscious and Tristan didn't make us insanely attracted, like the average person, because we knew what they were, as with Izzie, and knew how to focus our minds to guard against that. But still, there was a certain zing to contend with.

The compound was strange to look at—four old farmhouses that had been put together by the previous owner. It kind of worked, if you were into patchwork quilts. Which I wasn't. The biodome was on a dirt road off another dirt road off another—atop a hill that looked down on a glittering platter of water known as Mirror Lake. Our car flew about three feet off the ground, zipping up a tunnel of greenery toward towering walls that blocked any view of what was inside. The transparent dome covering it from above was made out of ZoneZel, a transparent substance that was harder than steel.

ZoneZel was something that Jarat had invented, with the help of some people at Silverton Enterprises. That was a well-known construction and design company that his father, Evander, had founded and run, until he passed. Jarat had had a really contentious relationship with his dad and was highly critical of huge corporate monoliths in general. So it wasn't a surprise when he spurned any notion that he should take over Silverton. But he did raise a few eyebrows when he said he wanted to run a certain division: the one that made biospheres. Needless to say, he had wanted one of those, and only the best. He operated the division remotely from Pompey, for the most part.

Jarat had a reputation, in the outer world, as an anti-establishment troublemaker, and a one-time leader of a group called Theseus, which was still largely thought of as a band of outlaws operating underground. I figured he was still a member, but he didn't invite discussion about that. At his heart, Jarat liked to invent stuff. He had this busy mind that never took a break. Thus, the ZoneZel.

His division at Silverton had become really lucrative. More and more biospheres were cropping up all over the planet as a growing number of Elites tried to control the air they breathed, the sunlight, and water—necessary for vegetation that the hotter planet was no longer able to support in a lot of places.

Whenever we'd approached the Ellingtons' biosphere in the past, there were always fans of Luscious milling about hoping to see her. Long ago, she was this starlet at Nuhope whose fame blew up like crazy because she was on the Juice and had become a Charismite.

Even though she hadn't been seen in about twenty years, she was still a legend. So it was kind of surprising when we reached the Ellington's front gate that none of her fans were around. Plus, the usual massive crush of bouquets next to the wall of steel was reduced to ash. Jarat had activated a strong field of electricity around it, with warning signs for people and sounds undetectable to the human ear, which kept wild animals away.

The gate recognized our limo and de-materialized. We shot through, and it grew solid again a nano-second later. Soaring up the steep drive, we passed trees and bushes sagging with plump berries, apples, peaches, figs, and pomegranates. A green ball of a tree looked like it was dotted with lemons, until the dots took off—yellow fly catchers that circled above, under the dome. God only knew how much wildlife was in there. Sometimes, they brought new animals in and released the ones that were there, just to keep the gene pool from getting too inbred. Yeah, it was kind of elaborate, but that's how they rolled.

As we approached, Jarat was leaning in the house's main doorway, craggy as ever, with glowering eyebrows, his silver-gray mane of hair brushed back, ancient plaid shirt, hands in his old jeans pockets. If a stranger saw him on the street, they'd probably think he was some kind of bum. Nuhope's casting directors would have loved him for unhinged character roles. In fact, he was a lot different than that. His dark eyes beamed at us, wheels in his mind churning in unfathomable ways.

A twinge of jealousy shot through me. To have *really done* something in life. On top of everything else, Jarat had rescued me long ago, when my family was blown to bits. It felt disloyal and small, that insecure feeling. I brushed it aside. We had a far larger problem on our hands than my little career crisis.

Memere's eyes laughed at Jarat. "You old thing. Your shirt's inside out."

He gave his shirt a comical look of dismay. Not that he'd change it. "You young thing!" Then he grew serious. "I can't quite scope it, how ridiculously painful this all is. I will do everything in my power to get Izzie back." He loved Izzie like his own child, almost—loved me that way, too.

Memere hugged him hard.

Lush came out of the front door. It felt like sunshine had just exploded all around us. "Well I'll be! Look who dropped into Ellington Land," she said, giving us a big gap-toothed grin. But knowing her so well, I could see dark unease beneath her surface. Her red-blonde hair was a series of childish tangles, and her thin frame was set off by a cotton dress that looked about as ancient as Jarat's shirt.

The country hayseed look made it hard for me to think of her as some kind of celestial being, like most people did. She had been part of a thought-control program hatched by a scientist within Nuhope—just like Dove Brown, the other early Charismite who was Izzie's biological father. People went crazy trying to do what they suggested in commercials—buy certain products, believe certain things.

Before the experiment, Lush had been a naïve small-town teen. She didn't realize what she was getting into when she started taking the Juice—until Jarat came along and set her straight. In her final message sent out to the world, Luscious told people to "Love everybody you can and pray for the rest." People said that line of hers for years and became kinder—helping the impoverished Chav much more than they had. But Lush's words had to compete for people's attention with a trillion other messages that came out later. The world was tougher, colder now.

At the time Lush sent out that love message, she outed herself and told everybody that she and Dove were Charismites, explaining what they did to people. At the time she did that, Dove had already OD'ed, taking too much Juice and passed away, and she nearly maxed out and died too. After that, she and Jarat moved to Pompey and led a secluded life. For Lush, it was all about regaining her health and raising a son with Jarat in the Pompey compound.

She only injected the scant amount of Juice necessary to keep herself alive. She would have died if she didn't take at least some of it. Nobody had access to the Juice now, except the Ellingtons. Jarat had committed the formula to memory and only made the concoction on an as-needed basis. The tiny amounts they had on hand at any given time were locked away in some secret safe.

When Lush wasn't thinking about her family, all her attention was focused downward, digging in the earth, planting seeds, pruning her garden. Not up at the stars that excited her so. She'd wanted to be a space dancer, way back when.

Now, she was peering at my face tenderly. "You strugglin'? Must have been awful."

"I'm okay."

She smiled sadly. Izzie's disappearance was hitting her hard; I could tell. We went into their huge living room, with the white quartz fireplace crackling at one end and cushy chairs. Jarat caught one of Luscious' hands in his, and she squeezed it as they sat down together on a sofa. It was hard for them not to touch each other, to stay connected physically in the smallest of ways.

"Where's the kid?" Memere asked.

"Upstairs packing," Jarat replied. "We have an underground bunker. He and Lush are gonna stay there for a while, until we know what we're dealing with—if anything."

"Keeping a seventeen-year-old in a bunker? That ought to be fun," Memere said.

"He knows what's up." Jarat looked at me. "Now tell me everything again, one more time."

It turned out to be three or four more times: me repeating what I could remember about the catastrophe in my L.A. apartment. I finally disappeared into the dining room to answer some urgent calls. One of the production assistants for *Space Ace* was trying to deal with the last-minute culinary demands of a racing jock. And a mechanic was still dealing with the malfunction problem with Phineas' ship. Weird, how it suddenly felt calming, to deal with those things. For a moment, I'd actually managed to stop thinking about Izzie.

When I came back into the living room, Lush was calling upstairs to Tristan. Everyone was silent, listening for some sound of him on the second floor. And so did I.

Nothing.

Jarat and I looked at each other, then bolted for the stairs. At the top, we both stopped. "You feel him?" Jarat asked.

Usually, I could sense Tristan's magnetic pull more than Jarat could, because I wasn't around him all the time. A current of fear shot through me. "No." Then I sensed it: a thrill from beyond the windows. "Outside."

Jarat barely controlled his explosive alarm. Tristan knew how dangerous that could be, despite all the extra defenses. *Why?* Jarat started to race downstairs. But I said, "Wait. I'll get him." Luscious needed his protection, too. We both knew that.

He glowered at me. "Watch out. Eyes everywhere."

I flew down the stairs and banged through the back door, hurtling past Lush's huge vegetable and herb garden. I felt a pull from an open field, dead ahead. Leaping over a split rail fence, I raced through hip-high dry grass, then crested a knoll. Tristan's head came into view above tall goldenrod.

His dark hair was airborne, an angel cloud shining with reflected light. There was usually a sense of openness and wonder about his dark eyes, which turned into an endless blue when he was tremendously excited. He could make even a city rat like me get all mushy about a bumbling beetle. A wet spider web in the forked branches of a tree became a bedazzled raindrop necklace when he talked about it. He saw everything in the woods and fields like a magic child—which I suppose, in a sense, he was.

Like Izz, Tristan didn't need the Juice to be a Charismite. He came by it through Lush's altered DNA. If he hadn't been gifted that way, I probably would have seen him as a scrawny naïve seventeen-year-old. In New York, his almost girlish body would have seemed ripe for scams or an attack. But as it was, he mesmerized any unsuspecting human around him—which was one reason why so few were allowed in the compound. My chest swelled with love at the sight of that head. Tris was the closest I'd ever come to a younger brother.

In earlier years, he'd galumph like a puppy through the fields on lazy summer days, excited to show me frogs in a far-off pond that were about to lay eggs. He took me to dens where foxes were nursing their cubs. They never ran away from Tristan. He had uncanny ability to understand when they were in pain.

Dr. Doo, that's what Izzie and I called him, short for that old storybook character, Dr. Doolittle. Izzie always said it like Tristan was a wimp. I said Dr. Doo because I loved teasing him in a gentle way.

Because of all that, my knees nearly buckled with relief when I spotted him in the field. But then anger welled up fast and hard. "What the hell? Tristan! Get back to the house!"

As he turned to me, his eyes were glassy with defeat. He didn't seem capable of moving.

Drawing nearer, I realized he was holding a baby rabbit, its belly ripped open, blood all over Tristan's arms. Dead. "I thought I could help it," he said hoarsely. "I didn't think it would take much time."

"Okay. But it's gone. So let's go."

He looked through the tall goldenrod. "Will you bury him?"

"Yes, of course," said a hushed voice. A light-haired young woman rose to her feet. She couldn't have been more than twenty-five, dressed simply, in loose brown trousers rolled up above her ankles, a big white blouse. Her eyes were so shiny-dark, from the Indian subcontinent, and I had the sensation that Tris and the woman were revolving together. *What the fuck?*

"Meet Geneva. Geneva, this is Shake."

"Yes, I know," she said.

"Really?" Tristan was incredulous.

"The Prince of Nuhope. That show you did, *Heaven Warriors*, it was like Nuhope's highest-rated drama ever, wasn't it?"

"Uh huh."

"I was totally hooked."

Her attempt at charming me was falling way flat. What the hell was she doing there?

"Gen helps me with the animals," Tristan said.

Right. "How did you get in here?" I asked coldly.

She shrugged innocently, eyes on Tris.

"That's our secret," Tristan said. A whirring sound battered the air, louder and louder above the dome. Terror shot through me. What was coming towards us? The ZoneZel was extraordinarily strong, but I wasn't going to take any chances.

"Let's go." I took Tristan's arm, pulling him toward the house. Another sound, a buzzing, louder and louder.

Tristan's face electrified. "Da."

Jarat tore through the field on his hoverbike, aiming straight for us. Overhead, there was an explosion as two aircraft broke the dome and dropped straight down, quick as a heartbeat. One of them landed right in front of the house—the other in the field beside us.

A stream of light shot out of the 'craft, blasting Jarat's bike. He was thrown across the field. Tristan screamed, started to rush toward him, but I yanked him away. *Where could we go?*

Three bots that looked like eight-foot metal spiders crawled out of the aircraft and raced toward us, much faster than we were running. I turned around just long enough to see one of them attack Jarat. *His brain. They want to extract the Juice formula from his brain.* Another spider bot grabbed my head in its tentacles, squeezing hard. The pain was so intense I was sure it was about to crack my skull.

Tristan screamed.

"Run!" I yelled, flailing around wildly, unable to get free.

The world reeled. I started to lose consciousness. Geneva gazed down on me, untouched by the bots. In a split second, I saw it: all the sympathy and cruelty in those dark eyes as I blacked out.

Sharp pain roiled my head, my brain. I opened my eyes to Memere, slapping me hard, furious with fear.

"I don't think you should do that!" said her bot, Geoff.

"Well, he's coming around!"

Fighting to ignore the hammering in my skull, I cranked my head over to one side. Geoff was a little way away trying to help Jarat. My dear friend was lifeless in the flattened grass with a huge gash in his skull. "Is he going to be okay?" I croaked.

"Yes. They didn't get very far before realizing they would never get past his memory lock—never get the Juice formula from him," Memere said. "Ransacked the house too. But didn't find anything. Lush is safe in the bunker."

Couldn't breathe a sigh of relief, not yet. "Tristan?"

Memere's sorrowful face said it all. Tristan had vanished. So had Geneva.

4. CHEETA

Mercury and the Hammer Girl

HONDURAS. I WAS ten years old. Mountains of angry-animal water beat the shore. Band of ink black at the Caribbean's horizon. Hurricane coming. Wind too hot. Knew four people that died from the heat over the last few years. Older people, weaker children. More death coming. Sweaty men, hair whipping around, eyes hollow, laughing too much. Uncle Franco and his friends hauled a boat out of the water onto a trailer behind his truck—the old kind with wheels.

Mama didn't like Uncle Franco. She told me to stay away from him. But he always gave me candy. Cinnamon-brown beard, chocolate eyes, fun grin like my stuffed toy bear. I ran through the sucking sand to his boat. "Where you taking it?" I asked.

"A secret place."

"Secret?"

"Um-hmm. You shouldn't be out here, *Chiquita*."

"I know." I started walking back toward the village.

"Come with me. It'll be faster." He looked up at the sky, like it was a clock he could read. "*Vamos*."

The skin around his eyes wrinkled with laughter, teasing me until I climbed into the truck beside him. It lurched down the road, boat behind. Warm metal smell, sweet tobacco. He gave me an accusing look. "Who told you to do that?"

"Do what?"

"Look so pretty."

My insides went all mushy. "I did!"

He laughed. Uncle Franco was the only one who saw me different, didn't think my hair was too messy, my face too long. His hand reached out and touched my arm like a close friend. Radio crackling a report, saying the storm would hit in a few hours.

We were getting close to the village. "I can walk from here." Mama would be so mad if she saw me in his truck.

"It's not safe." He yanked the truck off the main road and went down a small bumpy one through the marshes. Tall grass grazed the truck on either side. Out the rear window, I could see the nose of the boat bounce up and down as the wheels slammed into big ruts.

This wasn't right. "I want to get out."

"Don't you want to see my secret place?" He stroked my thigh.

"No." I tried to open the door, but I couldn't unlock it. "YOU LET ME OUT!" He hit the brakes and slammed me in the head so hard. I socked against the side of the truck. Tried not to cry. His face so mean, not like I ever seen it. He got out, grabbed me, threw me on the grass, ripped down my pants. Huge thing of his ramming and ramming.

Screamed so loud, throat burning. He punched me harder. I blacked out.

Somebody found me on the side of the main road when I was still unconscious. Don't know how they saw me; it was raining so hard then, just before the hurricane hit. They took me home.

Mama held me on the bathroom floor, our safe place, as the storm raged outside. Her eyes like liquid fire. Didn't need to ask me what had happened. I remembered all the times I'd seen bruises on her arms, her face, the huge gash on her leg.

Never understood before.

Papa had passed long ago, fighting in Venezuela for United America. Nobody to protect us except *mi abuelo*. So, when the hurricane went away, we went to see him. The tin roof of his general store had flown off down the street, and he was trying to find any stuff in the building that wasn't destroyed. Mama showed him my battered face, arms, and thighs, told him what his brother had done.

"Franco never hurt anybody!" my grandfather shouted. "How can you make up that shit now? People need help! You're lucky you still have a roof, a home. And all you can think to do is make up lies?"

Everybody was busy. People missing, some houses gone. My belly hurt. I curled up in the bathroom, couldn't talk no more. Mama was moving around in the other room. She called to me: "Stay inside. Don't let nobody in! Nobody!" Didn't know until later that she'd raided her father's house, taken his secret stash of Americos. Nobody saw us leave the village carrying our sacks.

So hot. Needed water. Nobody in the other towns had none that was good. Headed north, climbing over so many fallen trees blocking the roads, wading through deep water in flooded areas. More and more people on the same route, crying ones, determined ones, some with blank-eyed horror. We were a human river.

Mama started coughing. A little at first, then more. It took so long for us to get to Belize City, then Chetumal, then Tulum. Nobody in those places liked us. Some people on the road tried to steal our stuff, so many times. But Mama had a butcher knife.

We were caught a few times by patrols, but Mama paid them off. She argued so long with the boat people, but in the end she had to give them most of what we had left. Everybody trying to get on those boats. Some ready to kill. But we made it to the Tampa Treasure Zone.

Men that weren't scared of the knife wanted to jump Mama, but they backed off because she was coughing so bad. Everybody around us scared of what she might have. I pleaded with people we passed by for food. Just a little, something maybe they wanted to throw out? Most days, I had to dig through trashcans.

Somehow, we made it to New York. Tia Rosa lived there. Mama's sister. That's what we thought. But when we got to the address where she'd messaged Mama last, nobody had heard of her.

We were homeless for two winters, living under bridges when there was snow and sleet. Mama held on somehow. She couldn't eat much, spitting out phlegm with the honking coughs as she laid on our dirty blanket in Central Park. I was so scared.

One night, I was so sure she was going to die that I ran out of the park, straight to a big street, searching and searching the long line of cars hovering above the ground, filled with rich people piled up in a traffic jam. None of them liked the Chav. Swatted that thought away. Had to be *someone*. My eyes landed on a black car, not so large as most of them. It started to take off. I picked up an old boot lying by the curb and threw it hard. It hit a backseat window, and the car swerved to the side of the street and stopped. A side window sparkled away, and heaven gazed out at me. That's how Miles Morelli seemed, like heaven. And there was this luxurious scent from his pine cologne.

It was hard for me to speak English then, and I was crying in fear. All I could get out was "Mama! Mama! *Por favor*!"

Miles burst out of the car with two bodyguard bots.

"Senator! Curtain is in twenty minutes!" one of them

called. But Miles didn't pay no attention, charging with me toward Central Park, the guards just behind. I found out much later that he was on his way to Lincoln Center—opening night of *La Bohème,* and Nadia was the star of the show. But he didn't care. We crashed through some bushes toward Mama.

The sharp beam of searchlights on the bodyguards' foreheads scared the other homeless people, and they took off. Mama was lying under a tree. Miles talked to somebody on his screen, and before long, an air ambulance landed right in front of us.

I couldn't understand what Miles was telling the medics as they put Mama on a stretcher. I piled into the ambulance beside Mama. It made my stomach drop so hard as we whooshed up into the air, hurtling over Manhattan.

I stayed in the hospital hallway for hours and hours waiting for them to bring me to her. But they didn't, and I fell asleep in a chair. Jumped awake when someone touched my hand. Thought it was Uncle Franco. I was so scared. But it was Miles, smiling at me, still in his tuxedo. I couldn't believe he'd come to the hospital. He didn't speak much Spanish, but enough to make me realize the nurses were about to kick me out.

We got in his limo and before I knew it, I was in this pink frilly bedroom in his mansion. Nadia was talking outside the door. Didn't needed to know English to tell she thought he was crazy for bringing me home. But he soothed her, and then their voices grew dim as they walked away.

Mama passed the next morning before I got back to the hospital. Miles had his team help me. My new foster parents were okay—a couple of Middles that needed the foster care dough. The father never tried to do anything to me. But I had Mama's butcher knife if he ever did. Made a belt of rope to hold it, always on the inside, down my pants. Didn't take it off if I could help it, through all the years I was in foster care. So many nights, I dreamed about using it on my uncle.

AFTER MILES GOT caught in that explosion, I was doubled over on my pallet for days. Couldn't eat, even though the gnawing hunger was like a devil. "Fuck you," I told it. Sour stench of garbage that needed to be taken out. Couldn't pay the *maldito* rent. Didn't care about getting a job. I stared at the one picture I had of Mama, and a holo of the senator, side by side. The only people I ever knew who loved me.

LiZee's beady eyes begged me, throat working. Just got up long enough to feed her, and then crashed back down. Sleep took me over, more and more. Until …

CLICK.

I bolted up. Fear curled up my arms. It seemed like the sound came from my mobile air screen, hovering to the right side of my head, but maybe somebody was in the room. I grabbed the butcher knife off the table, scanned all my junk and stopped on the IBM desktop. Something was strange about it. *What?* I crept closer. There was a tiny speck of phosphorescent green light in one corner of the screen, like a cursor but just a tiny prick. Some asshole had hacked inside it; I was sure. They were watching me. Rage boiled through me. I tore out the wiring in the back of the screen. Then I took out my mobile lens and flushed it down the toilet. Nobody invaded my shit and got away with it.

So, in one pissed-off streak, all my tech and my one hope of making some cash with the IBM was gone. Plopping down in a chair, I cursed my stupid anger. It flipped around and pointed a finger at me. "You are *not* going to live on the streets again," I told myself. "You are going to find a job, no matter how lousy it is. And you better get some food, like, now."

I was down to half a box of crackers, and I was trying not to eat the whole thing at once when somebody pounded on my door. I froze, and it got louder and louder, like somebody was trying to knock the door down. "Open up!" My landlord's voice. "Now!" There was a scratching sound as a key fit in the main lock, but I'd put in three other ones. Nobody was getting in there. "Give me my money!"

LiZee looked plenty scared. "*Coraje, amiga*," I whispered, throwing on a jacket over the clothes I'd had on for a week. The pounding got even more savage. I opened the window and climbed down the fire escape. My feet broke through a rusted rung, scraping my right calf bad. Nearly fell down three floors. But I made it the rest of the way. The bald landlord came out the front door, wheezing beneath his dirty wife-beater shirt. I was too fast for him to chase.

Three blocks later I had to stop. World spinning around as I panted hard. Found an old tissue in my pocket to stop the bleeding on my leg. No tech, no family, no food—no home next?

There was only one person that might help me out of this. He worked in this flea market. You could get almost anything there if you weren't too picky about the condition. It was in a big ol' warehouse space in Jackson Heights. When I walked inside that place, my hunger doubled in size, seeing the crispy fish, thick sandwiches, and chocolate cake in some food stalls. I scraped through my jacket and found just enough Americos for a little *papusa*. I nibbled the meat pie in tiny bites, trying to make it last as I passed an old guy with blue false teeth selling super-fast freezer appliances. In the next booth, a tough old girl was hawking used air-chairs. They had these pressurized air streams that could hold a body about three feet off the ground in all the right places. Another table was filled with cooing baby doll bots.

Just beyond a booth full of religious stuff was a little section run by my friend Barston. He sold used computer parts. His pointed beard twitched as he haggled with this babe in tight pink pants clutching one of his motherboards.

"Forty Americos? What kind of chump do you think I am?" Barston said. He was kind of an actor specializing in outrage. But it turned out the woman was too. Talk about high drama.

While all that was going on, I straightened my clothes and smoothed down my mass of hair, hoping I didn't smell too much. The customer finally got him to agree on fifty Americos, and she took off with the merch. Barston grinned like a big stuffed cat—or somebody who had just got the price he was after all along.

As soon as he saw me, the smile washed away. "Hey, girl."

"Hey."

"Sorry to hear about the senator. That must hurt like hell."

"Yeah, well, I'll get over it." Not that I was fooling anybody. "I need a new mobile."

"I just sold you one!"

"It kind of had an accident."

He shot me a suspicious look, rummaged around a pile of stuff, pulled out a little case, and popped it open. Inside was a clear blue lens. "This little baby is real special. I'll cut you a deal. How much you got on you?"

"Well, actually, nothing."

"Nothing?"

"Well, you know, the senator's gone. I was kind of hoping maybe I could work for you. I'd pay you off in no time and make you so much more money."

Thump thump, thump, thump went my heart, waiting.

Sure enough, just like I feared, he said, "Sorry. No can do."

"Come on. I forgot more about tech than most people know. I'll make you a fortune."

A deeper "no" darkened Barston's face.

"Excuse me." I nearly jumped at the sight of a dark-skinned gramps type right beside me. He'd come up on us so quiet and seemed kind of shy. Barston looked over the stranger darkly. But he looked okay to me. Must have been a Middles, the way he was dressed in a pretty high quality shirt and pants, even though he didn't have yellowish skin.

"I've got this 2020 humanoid, and it needs a new lidar head," Gramps said. I gave the mounds of computer parts on the table a once-over.

"Nope. Don't have it," Barston said.

"You sure?"

Barston bristled. "That's what I said. Where's your partner, huh?"

"What?"

"The one working your con."

"There's—"

"Here's one." I pulled a disk-shaped lidar head from a heap. Barston looked surprised.

The old man pulled a pile of cash out of his wallet. My jaw dropped. "How much?" he asked.

Barston scanned the bills with his mobile lens. His air screen was in private mode, but he gave me a view. Turned out, the money was real. He got serious and pulled up an auction site that put the lidar head's value at about two-hundred Americos.

"It's worth about five-hundred," I said real innocent-like.

Barston's scowl didn't give away nothing, unless you knew him. I could tell he was impressed. Hell, maybe he'd give me a job after all. "Sure. I can do that."

The old man chuckled. "Well, I'll tell you what. My mama birthed a fool, but that was my brother." He walked away.

Barston smirked at me. It was a frickin' embarrassment. I caught up with Gramps three aisles away. "Why'd you give up so easy? We would have come down. You ought to go back there."

"Uh, no thanks."

"What will you take it for? Three-hundred?"

He stopped and stared at me with cloudy green eyes. "I thought the senator taught you better, Cheeta."

Cold fear ran through me. "What are you talking about?"

"He taught you to always be honest. That's what Miles Morelli was all about."

How the fuck did he know that—and my name? I was so freaking pissed. Before I could do anything, the old man went on, ever so casual-like: "At least, that's what he and I were talking about last week."

A guffaw burst out of me. "If you're going to lie, watch the goddamned news."

I started to stomp off, but he said, "There's a message he wants you to get. Just you. Nobody else."

My anger zoomed higher. Where was my fucking knife when I needed it? "You can take your spirit-world shit and stuff it up your butt hole!"

"I'm sorry. I really am. I know this all doesn't make any sense. But please just listen to me."

Something about his friendly, pleading face made me stop. I couldn't figure it out. He was either a spy, a con artist—or he was actually telling the truth. And the last idea was crazy. How come there was no liar stink coming off of him? I *always* smelled that.

"YOU!" A security guard with wet, liver-colored lips stormed toward us and put his face right up to the old man.

"YEAH, YOU! You're Mercury Douglass, aren't you?"

The old man went white as a brown man could get. "What if I am?"

"You're coming with us," said another guard, oily curls of chest hair sprouting from the top of his shirt. He grabbed the old man's arm.

That's when I caught on. I'd been around that flea market long enough to know what the regular security meat-wads looked like, and the uniforms these guys were wearing weren't right. The real ones would never show their chest rug, for one thing. They zip up all the way to the throat. The shield logo on their sleeves was a darker shade of blue. And they never wore knuckle guards like these creeps were sporting. Didn't take a lot of imagination to figure out what they wanted to do to this guy. But why?

Sure, the old man was really frickin' weird, but something told me that he was harmless. "HEY! Let him go!" I said.

Liver Lips burst out laughing. "What are you going to do to us, huh?"

The assholes tried to march Mercury down the aisle, but he put up a fight. THUNK! as Chest Rug slugged him over the head with his baton. Everything moved in slo-mo then. A mob of gawkers got larger and larger. I saw a table off to the left that was full of pipes, saws, nails—and an old hammer. I grabbed the wooden handle attached to the heavy steel block.

BAM! as I slammed it down on the pile of hardware. "Listen!" I yelled to the crowd. "Those aren't the real guards. Look at them!"

"Like hell we aren't!" shouted Liver Lips, but he and Chest Rug were starting to look nervous.

Somebody said, "No! She's right!" And other people echoed her words.

Barston pushed through the bodies, looking more outraged than ever. "Get the hell out," he roared at the fake guards. "That's my customer!" Three hulks forced their way through the throng of people. The real guards had arrived. The pseudo-ones took off.

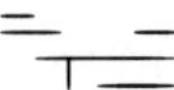

THE OLD MAN followed me along the cracked pavement of 77th Avenue. He kept side-glancing at the two-story brick buildings. "That was really something, what you did back there," he said.

Which, of course, was true. But the fact was, once I'd gotten saved by Miles, it made me want to do it for other innocent people, even when they seemed like demented goofballs. But there was a limit. "I got stuff to do, so why don't you take off someplace else."

"Can't we just talk?"

"No."

"Please! Please!"

I stopped and glared at him hard. "NO! Who the fuck do you think you are? Miles didn't talk to *nobody* last week, because he's dead. Stone dead. So keep your skanky ass away from me!"

I walked off, but he was right behind me. "Okay. Okay. I don't blame you. But I just want you to know that when the senator put you and your mother in that ambulance—well, he said it was one of the best things he'd ever done in his whole life."

Hated the wet coming out of my eyes. Hated how I had to stop. "Stop making up shit."

"I'm not. What can I say to make you listen? For just five minutes."

Mierda! I couldn't be mean to him. "Okay. Go."

Mercury scoped the sidewalks and all the windows around us, then fixed on an abandoned garage. "In there."

At one time, my mama and I would have gone in that place to stay out of the cold. Anybody could be living inside—junkies, thieves. "Forget it."

"C'mon, Hammer Girl. Don't tell me you're scared." He started for the garage. I followed him into the darkness, grumbling at myself for being such a goddamned softy. The old familiar smell hit me: rotting failure and rat turds. Light from narrow windows cut through the black, landing on a couple of abandoned cars that were covered with so much crud you couldn't tell what color they were.

Mercury looked like he was in freakin' nirvana. He walked to the middle of the space, beaming. "No security cameras." That was a pretty unusual situation.

"Spill it."

"I've got something for you." He pulled off his shaggy hair. Hadn't realized it was a wig. Then he picked something out of the white skullcap underneath: a little case. He opened it up. Inside was a purple lens that was filmy, like it hadn't been cleaned in ten years. *Yick!* He handed it to me with fever in his eyes. "This is how you get to the senator."

"No thanks." How did I ever get sucked into this?

"No, no. You need this. See, at first, I thought I'd just show you the message that the senator wanted you to get. But then I realized that you should go to the actual place where I found it."

I bolted for the door. But Mercury blocked me. "Please. Please. I can't do this alone anymore. And the more I looked into you, the more I've realized you could help me, even take over eventually. You've got guts."

Fury collected in me. Quietly, I said: "That was you. In

my tech. *This morning.*" I'd been so wrong about him—was so pissed at myself for not seeing it. "You fucking hack!" I threw the case. It bounced on the cement.

I was about to storm out of there, but he flitted in front of me again. "I'm sorry. I'm sorry. Didn't mean for you to find out and destroy your stuff. I won't do that again." I got past him, but he was so damned fast. Blocked again! "I just needed to be sure. That you're brave, somebody to trust, that knows tech enough to navigate through stuff."

"What the—?"

"Listen to me. Those fake guards, they'll probably find me again. And when they do, I don't know if I'll get away." The old man looked terrified, but there was also kindness in those hazy green eyes.

"Why do they want you?"

He picked up the case and held it out to me. "If you put this on, you'll go to a certain place. It'll seem scary at first. Christ, the first time I saw all the messages in there, I started shaking like a pregnant nun. But then I realized that most of them are lost. And some of them need to be delivered, like that one from the senator."

"You are one messed-up old man."

"Honest to God, this is for real. Please." He was so desperate that I took the lens. "You've got to go there as soon as you can. Just wait until you're alone. Put it on or just keep it close. Doesn't matter which. Just be very still. Say your name once you get there." I turned to go. "Promise me. Promise me you'll do this! And don't tell nobody about this you don't really trust. Nobody!"

Still didn't believe Miles was alive. But maybe the mobile contained some old message from him that got caught up in a spam folder, and this Gramps had somehow found it. My whole being craved to see the senator in any form, talking to me just one more time.

"Okay."

Mercury's grin went crazy. "Oh, girly girl. You're sure in for one sassy-molassy surprise." Before I could say anything, he raced off like those meat-wads were still on his tail. But I didn't see nobody suspicious when I left there.

That night, I washed that purple lens something good. Got some of the crud off, but it was still a little filmy. Needed a mobile something bad, since Barston didn't come through. But every time I thought about that old man telling me how Miles said those things, it pissed me off so bad. Yeah, some of it was true, and that part was spooky. Because Miles only talked about sticking to the truth when we were in private. And neither of us put it out on social media so it couldn't be researched. I knew on one level I should try to do that—never lie. But the fact of the matter was, honesty wasn't exactly dead in the worl', but it was lying on its back and smelling like a dumpster. My grandfather and Uncle Franco taught me that. And I learned it even more after Mama and I ran away. Other desperate people stealing our shit and pretending they didn't. Rich fuckers claiming on the news that the Chav didn't need any more help than they already got—which was hardly anything. They knew it wasn't true.

Even when the senator told me to be honest, and I told him I would, I knew inside that it didn't matter. Miles was living in a dream world. And I loved that dream. I did. But it wasn't real.

I shook off the thoughts. "Here goes nothin'," I said to LiZee as I put on the lens. Wasn't expecting much. Didn't think that I'd see the worl' clearly. But there was LiZee, looking sharp just like everything else in my pad. The mobile's air screen sputtered to life, and I watched some old episodes of my favorite mystery series, *Spooky Spooks, P.I.* It was kind of weird ass, and always helped me get sleepy. I lay back on my bed and grew still. That's when I hurtled down into bottomless black.

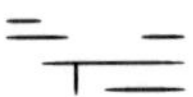

THAT FIRST TIME, when the black speckled away into that papaya colored outer space metaverse and I saw that crazy-ass guy selling funky real estate and the broad with the dirty dog, I was sure it was some kind of scam. But then that other bubble showed itself, the one with Miles' face inside. I was so afraid. He looked like he was in a nightmare.

When I finally got up the nerve to squeeze the bubble, out popped a holo of the senator. He was in the same suit he'd worn that last day I'd seen him, but it was torn and really dirty. Never seen him with a hair out of place, but now it was frizzled out, and there was a vicious cut on his left cheek that looked fresh. It stretched from his eye down to his mouth.

Miles turned his face away from the camera and balled himself up in the dirty corner of a tiny room.

A man said, "Talk to your wife."

"Bloody message in a bottle," Miles whispered hoarsely. I could barely hear him.

"Might not be another chance." It was Mercury's voice. Of course!

"Never believe me. No."

A silvery spray, like fireworks, wiped out everything. I held my breath, and after about thirty seconds, Miles reappeared, looking dead straight at me, full of fear and misery. "Cheeta Lucida LaVera, of Flushing, Queens. Send it to her. Cheeta will make my wife watch, somehow. I know it."

"Okay. So, tell her what you got to say."

His face softened, the way he always looked at me. "Cheeta, listen to me. I have been abducted by an organization called The Fist. I was on a secret mission that would have exposed their illegal activities when they took me."

I knew about The Fist already, just from working in Miles' office. He'd heard all these rumors that it was made up of a lot of corporate bigwigs. They supposedly had paid off a large number of congresspeople and a load of other government officials to pass certain laws, make certain court decisions. That's how so many huge companies had become so powerful they could get away with almost anything. And the peeps who ran them had almost endless wealth.

"They will kill me if I don't tell them where I've hidden all the intel I've collected about them. And I won't, no matter how much they torture me."

"Hurry up! I've got to leave!" Mercury said.

"Nadia knows who to trust, the people who will search for me. You've got to get this message to her. Make her believe it. Please!"

Miles vanished back inside the bubble, and it soared off, becoming a tiny speck among a gazillion specks, further and further away.

My mind reeled. I couldn't take that universe no more. Had to get out. Now! Looking around wildly, I saw three icons trailing behind me: a red dot and a black square—like record and stop buttons—and a white six-pointed star. I punched the black one, and my mind swooped back into my apartment.

I was shaking so bad I couldn't get the lens out at first. Didn't want to ever use it again, ever see the senator like that. Nothing had changed about my place, but everything had changed in my head. Was Miles really alive, in some private prison hell? Or was that message some kind of messed-up metaverse crap?

Who was that Mercury Douglass? Why had he been there with Miles, if this was something that was actually real?

"Fuck it." Had to put that lens back on my cornea to do any research, but I didn't want to go into that strange metaverse again. Mercury had told me to stay still in order to go into it, and that might be why I did. So I moved around a little, and the lens seemed to work like it was normal. The OuterNet gave me little info about him, but not much. He was retired; used to work as a security guard in some server farm outside Phoenix, AZ—the kind of place used to store and transmit massive amounts of computer data. No known home address, no contact deets.

Maybe the whole thing was a hoax. But maybe not. I got this urge to go back inside that orange Universe that was unstoppable. Maybe there was something in that place that would help me figure things out. I kept fighting that idea, but in the end I stretched out on my bed and went quiet again. Sure enough, the lens sent me back into the cosmos. That senator's bubble had only come after I said my name, so I did it again: "Cheeta Lucida LaVera!"

A gigundo cloud of bubbles collected in the distance, then rushed toward me, with one sphere among them more golden, its sheen almost piercing. As the others whizzed by, the bubble stopped suddenly, about three feet away, and there was the senator's miserable face. I jabbed the red circular icon behind me, hoping it would record what I was seeing.

"Do it. Do it!" I shouted.

S. TRISTAN

Twin Cousins

I KEPT MY eyes closed for several minutes after waking up. The vividness of the dream I'd just had was such a relief from where I really was, in a prison. If only I could get back to that fantasy and see Izzie's face, brimming with wonder that mirrored my own. We'd been deeply fixated on each other—her body next to mine in bed, faces so close that her breath feathered my cheeks. A sexual energy coiled out from my middle directly into her, and then spiraled back tightly from her to me. My cock was charged for what felt like hours.

It was weird, how the bad opinions that we'd always felt about each other had exploded into something so different in that dream. In real life, we were like two magnets that someone had tried to connect at the wrong ends, bouncing away from each other. Sure, we probably cared for each other on some deeply subconscious level. But Izzie hated on me whenever our two families were together. She made me feel like such a jerky wimp.

It got worse as we grew older, especially after Izzie rebelled against Petra's attempts to keep her hidden. By the time we were both fourteen, Izz had broken out in the world, always dressed like a ga-zillion Americos, so worldly. Guess it made sense that she thought I was some kind of wuss, happy to stay in the biodome. But it still hurt.

Ma told me a long time ago that Charismites were never

attracted to other Charismites. But that didn't mean they were repelled by each other. Before Izzie and I came along, Ma had only known one Charismite. And that one, Dove Brown, was like her older brother. From what she'd told me, it seemed like their feelings for each other were sweet, without any coldness or heat. So it was stunning to Ma that Izzie and I had such a bad relationship.

But in that dream, it was like some heavenly force had flipped around one of our magnets. We couldn't get close enough. Izzie had felt it too. "How did you switch yourself up so, Doo?" she asked.

Doo. Dr. Doo. I groaned. She crouched above my torso, face up to my own again, gray eyes more urgently vivid than anyone else's could ever be. "I'm sorry. I'm sorry I called you that. Tristan. Tris." The words dripped out of her mouth like rich strawberry jam.

My index finger swept from her breasts to her toned belly. She caught it in one hand. "Listen to me," she said. "You are going to be the one that gets us out of the prison."

I laughed. Where did that come from? "What are you, some kind of psychic now?"

"No. Don't need to be. Watch for it. The moment when you can do something."

Fat chance. "Okay. Got it. Now can we get back to …" I licked her breasts. She wanted me and she was afraid, all at the same time. I could sense it on her face, in her body as I trailed a hand down her stomach toward her vulva. Howling anguish torqued out of her into me. It was like a wolf was devouring her from the inside.

"NO!" She fell away.

Then nothing.

The dream was over, and here I was: lying on my back, eyes

still closed. It was just a twisted dream. And I suspected that it was manufactured—what they called a dreamisode—forced on me by whoever was in charge of this fucking prison. Not that anyone could completely control the subconscious. Otherwise, they never would have programmed Izzie's doppelganger to say the bit about breaking out.

Couldn't bear the idea of opening my eyes, seeing the walls smeared with my blood—from when the spider bots threw me over and over. Horror gripped me, remembering their tentacles squeezing pain through my nervous system. I could still feel the sharp and aching hurt in different places, all at once. But it had disappeared, in the dream.

Didn't know how long I'd been there, but it felt like maybe three days. I remembered being in the field behind our house, realizing I had to get down into the bunker with Ma. Just wanted to help that badly injured rabbit. Then Shakespear showed up, shocked at the sight of my girl, Geneva. *So what if I have someone who loves me?* That's what I wanted to say. Ma and Da had kept me away from almost every other human for years.

I understood why. But it was only natural, to crave a very sexual woman. So how could I turn away when Genny first showed up in the biosphere a few weeks before? Exotic-spice eyes framed by sunny hair, blossom-pink mouth, loose cotton clothing like a tease, not hiding the shape of her curves. Her voice reminded me of organ music, the way it vibrated as she explained that she'd stumbled upon an area of the wall in a wooded back section of the biosphere, far from the house. Some animal had dug a hole under it. That's how she got through. Somehow, the opening didn't trigger an alarm. I didn't understand why and might have been alarmed, myself, at the sight of this stranger. But Genny seemed so genuine. I grew more and more excited, to find someone whose tender thoughts about nature were so like my own.

That morning, before the attack, she messaged me. She was in the field with a badly hurt rabbit. She was so frightened it was going to die. An urgency spread through me, a need to help the rabbit and just to see Genny one last time before disappearing with Ma for who knew how long.

When the spider bots crashed down and dragged me to their 'craft, I fought back, kicking their legs, fat metallic bodies. Never treated anything like that before. Two of them went after Shake and Da. Geneva just standing there, helpless. That's all I saw before one of the spiders injected something in my neck, and I blacked out. When I came to, I was here. No matter how many times I asked, they wouldn't tell me what happened to Genny. Was she in this hell, too? What had they done to my father and Shake? Had they taken Ma, too? Were any of them alive?

Hate wasn't something I was used to, but how I hated whoever was doing this, could have murdered them without thinking, if there was ever a chance. Not that there would be one. Fantasy Izzie might think so, but that made no sense in real life. *It's too tiring, all the confusion and rage. Why feel anything? I'll never win against them, whoever they are.*

Fuck. Couldn't keep my eyes closed forever. Opening them, I jerked in surprise at the new surroundings. This room was larger, painted pale blue, with sunny yellow furniture covered with a red flower print. And the bed I was on was huge, and white, and … a body was beside me, the bed covers revealing curves, head turned away. I got up, wincing and walked around to the other side of the bed to see the face.

"Izzie!"

Her eyes flew open. "Doo?" Her voice was so disdainful and hoarse. Made me feel like a pile of horse manure. The idea

I'd dreamed of her actually *liking* me, let alone attracted to me, was a crazy joke. "So you're here too," she added, more to herself than me, like she'd thought that would happen.

I backed away from her and studied the room some more. "Fuck a goddamned duck."

Izzie smirked. "Your mother should teach you better swear language."

"Yeah, well. This room looks exactly like this place in a dream I just had."

She leaped out of bed in one athletic bound, flame-colored hair a crazy mess, bruises all over her arms and legs, too. God only knew what was under her torn black boxer shorts and shirt. Gray eyes looked at me, more startled than ever. "Jesus Christ. I was in here too." We went over what had happened in our separate dreamisodes and realized we'd had the exact same one.

"I guess it makes sense, that they'd do dreamisodes on us," Izzie said. "But I didn't know they could give people the same one. And how did it get in our heads?"

Usually, dreamisodes were delivered by mobile lenses in silent transmissions to the brain. You could order up dreams from media companies, and they were delivered in mobile transmissions. The dreams could be about living in a far-off time and place, or fantasies about adventures with certain friends. But what we'd dreamed was transmitted without any lens devices. They'd confiscated my mobile, and they must have done the same to her. The memory of how she'd looked at me in that fake dream—no longer seeing a clueless bore, but someone thrilling—seemed insane now.

"Don't you even think about touching me like that," Izzie said, remembering what I did. "God, so annoying."

"Not planning to. I guess they want to persuade us to have

sex in real life, whoever's behind this."

"Yup," she said, snapping the p. "Procreate. Like I'd ever do that with you." She crawled over to a wall and slammed her fist on it again and again. "I'm not going to bang him! I'll kill him if he tries!" she screamed at whoever might be monitoring us.

"Shove your asshole arachnids up your ass!" I roared at the wall.

"Arachnids?" Izzie said.

"Spiders."

Izzie laughed until she was doubled over. "Oh Dr. Doo. You are so fierce."

I resented her attempt to make me seem stupid. There was a little bathroom off the main room. I went in and banged shut the door. Stayed a lot longer than I needed to just to be away from her. When I came out, Izzie was standing by a little table, holding some kind of square cloth. She held it up, and the silky fabric unfolded like a shimmering waterfall, becoming a black kimono with orange flowers along the bottom edge. "There's two here." She peeled off her dirty shirt and pants. Gorgeous body.

Izzie kicked her dirty clothes into a corner, put on the robe, and slumped down the wall until she was sitting on the floor. Her fingers beat out a tune in her head. That's what she always did, to escape whatever was going on around her whenever she came to Pompey. I'd seen it so many times.

Once, when we were around twelve, she kicked up dirt in the garden, screaming in fury that Petra had taken her to our place. Didn't want to even play, completely ignored that I was standing there.

"Cut the crap!" Shakepear yelled at her. And just like that, she did. Her brother had that effect. Instead, she started humming and tearing the heads off a bunch of daisies.

Shakespear put his arm around my shoulder. "She won't stop doing that if she thinks it's annoying us. Let's get out of here." We walked off. "Tell me what you've been seeing." He was around sixteen then, tall and gangly, always happy to be with me. The exact opposite of Izzie.

There were animals all over the place to tell him about. We came upon a whole flock of turkeys, and when I held out a hand, the younger ones strutted to me. It was pretty clear they liked being inside our biosphere. There was plenty of room to roam, plenty of bugs and nuts to eat. Shakespear could never get enough when I explained stuff like that. If Izzie had been with us, she would have yawned and made some gobble-gobble joke.

Back then, she was just starting to sneak out of Petra's place in Manhattan and hit all the clubs. Didn't matter that she was so young. She could make the bouncers and bartenders do anything. A few years later, she gained some fame as a singer in a girl band. Then she switched gears and started to act in some two-hour, one-off dramas for small indie producers in fringe metaverses. That didn't last. Before long, she was barraged by producers clamoring to cast her in one show or another. And countless worshiping fans swarmed her wherever she went. After one blow-up after another, Petra had to call a truce with Izzie. Nuhope's board of directors was pressuring her to get her daughter signed to a talent contract. And she finally gave in and convinced Izzie to do it. After that, Izabel's fame as an actress rose to astounding levels. Nobody would miss diving into Nuhope's metaverse theaters to watch any show she was in. Nuhope made so much money off Izz. No other performer came close to attracting the kind of revenue she did, even though a lot of them had massive followings. Nobody knew why their reaction to Izzie's shows was so extreme, that she was a Charismite.

And me? I couldn't have been more of a recluse. Ma and Da

made sure that nobody even knew I existed, except for a few trusted souls like Petra, Shake, and Izz. Didn't want anyone to become fanatical about me.

A few months after Izzie was signed, Petra came alone to visit Ma and Da. I heard them talking from the balcony above the main living room. "We'll see how long this lasts," Petra said. "Izabel will get in some awful scandal or another. We'll see how happy the bloody board is then." But the moneymakers never cared. The scandals didn't faze them at all.

At least Petra had Shakespear as a counterbalance—the student who'd aced all his grades, then turned into a Nuhope producer laser-focused on his job, following in her wake every step of the way.

Ma and Da were silently critical about Izzie's exposure to the world, and Petra knew it. "What do you expect me to do with her?" she asked. "I can't keep her trapped somewhere."

"Tristan is so different. He never acts like we've put him in jail," Da said. "We're trying to give him some semblance of a normal life. Without goo-goo eyes on him nonstop like he's some kind of Second Coming."

Petra felt his judgmental tone and was about to fire something back when Ma said, "Pet, we know this isn't what you wanted. We're just lucky that Tris doesn't mind being here in isolation. We can't expect Izzie to be like him, or for him to be like her."

My mind came to the present as Izzie snapped, "Clean yourself up."

"What?"

"You stink."

I looked down at my clothes. My pants and shirt were a blood spattered, sweat soaked mess.

"Right." I stripped down and washed off. I ignored her

bored stare at my body, putting on the other black kimono. There was no design on mine, which was just fine.

"We'll get out," she said.

I smirked. "That simple."

"Of course not, but I meant what I said." In the dream. About me. Could tell by her knowing expression that's what she was thinking. Her gaze drifted away, like she didn't want me to remember the other part—how I'd felt that wolf inside, devouring her in the dreamisode.

A man's screams pierced through the wall behind Izzie, shrill and high. Izzie shot away from it, panting heavily, cowering behind one of those candy-colored chairs. The anguished shrieks went on and on. I could barely take it. But Izzie was even worse, the way she sobbed.

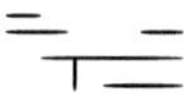

WE FELL ASLEEP after the screaming ended, but it took a long while. This time, a dreamisode didn't invade my head. We woke up several hours later to a scurrying sound. Izzie's eyes directed me toward the ceiling. She was right; it was coming from up above. A spider bot. Maybe a door would emerge somewhere.

It made me even more desperate and frightened than I already was. How long before they tortured us—or did something else? *What were they going to do?* The skittling sound moved down a side wall and disappeared. We waited, unable to breathe. Part of the wall sizzled. It was about to sparkle away into an opening, if this was like what usually happened. "Can we get past it?" Izzie whispered.

"Let's try." We moved to either side, waiting for a bot to emerge. If only we could slip through the opening before the wall went solid again.

The sizzling became a sparkling, then a round hole emerged. We were ready, crouching down, ready to spring. But a human form emerged, a man carrying a huge tray loaded with five silver domes, standing in the open doorway. He was golden skinned like us, full faced and hefty in size, wearing a simple tan uniform, like what an auto recharging station attendant would wear.

Izzie studied his small mouth and non-descript brown hair like he was the most beautiful man she'd ever met. When he glanced down shyly, she shot me a vulture's smile. He stepped through the hole too quickly for either of us to slip past. Delicious smells wafted out from under the silver domes, hitting my belly like a punch. I'd been living on stale biscuits and water ever since I got there, and Izzie must have too, given the craving on her face. Her gray eyes turned turquoise.

The man swallowed hard as he put the tray on a red-lacquered table. "Hi. I'm Darrel."

"I'm Izabel, and that's Tristan."

"Yes, I know. Sorry for the rude way you've been treated. Wasn't in the plan."

"Really?"

"They've been sent off for repairs, the bots that put you in those cells."

"Well, I'm certainly glad to hear that," I said as charmingly as possible.

Darrel pulled off a dome. Succulent Peking duck, crisp skin glazed, along with scallions, sweet brown sauce, and thin pancakes on the side. Another dome came off. Béarnaise sauce blanketed what looked to be a perfectly cooked tenderloin of beef adorned with caramelized shallots.

"Oh my God. You are an angel!" Izzie breathed. "But I'm vegetarian."

"No worries." Darrel lifted another lid, and steam billowed up from a large plate of green beans and mushrooms, along with another bowl of garlicky green salad. "And here's some rice and mashed potatoes."

Izzie clapped her hands in delight. "Oh, Darrel. This is amazing. You *have* to have some too. There's more than enough."

"Oh, no, I couldn't." Darrel backed away.

"But Darrel," I said. "We can't touch this food unless someone tries it first."

"Poison, you know," Izzie said confidentially.

"She said you'd ask that," Darrel said. *She?*

Izzie notched up her seductive look. "If you could just help us out by tasting these dishes. So we know they aren't laced with something … disagreeable."

"We've had such a tough time here. Couldn't you just do that?" I asked, going up to him, touching his arm, to feel what was inside. *Who do you like, asshole? Men? Women? Both?*

There was nothing to sense. Not a human; Darrel was a humanoid. Izzie read my disappointment. There was no way we could manipulate a bot.

Darrel backed toward the wall. "See you later."

"Bye bye," Izzie said gaily.

The wall sizzled again, and as it started to go through, Izzie pushed past the bot and started through the wall. But Darrel picked her up and threw her to the floor, kicking her hard over and over. She writhed in pain, sobbing.

Then it left.

6. SHAKE

Sitting Duck

SIX DAYS AFTER the two Charismites disappeared, the FBI was finally ready to speak with the two families together. And it was all I could do to get through the morning before the meeting took place. So far, they'd been as chatty as a sphinx.

I had started to recover from the trauma that the spider bots inflicted, thanks to the pharmas that Memere and her bot, Geoff, insisted I continue taking. My cluttered New York office at Nuhope dissolved as I entered a virtual chat room. The FBI sure didn't go in for metaverse décor, unless you were into a lot of gray. Holos of Lush, Jarat, Petra, and an FBI dude were already there.

During a minute of idle chit-chat, I focused on Jarat. Like the rest of us, his avatar was an exact reproduction of how he actually looked at that moment. There was a bandage wrapped around the top part of his head. And his left leg was under wraps, too, badly cut up and burned when they laser-hosed his bike. But whatever cocktail of pharmas Jarat was taking seemed to be working, judging by his alert expression.

I had some strange reasons for feeling relieved that those attacking spider bots weren't able to get past the locks implanted in Jarat's mind, making it impossible for anyone to steal his memories. It wasn't just a matter of keeping the Juice formula secret. There was more in his head that was really personal to me: my oldest brother's brain.

I was a baby when Jewles was killed so that Jarat could live. My brother had been sent away to jail for selling black-market merch on the Boston subway line. At that time, it was common practice to extract organs from convicted felons when Elites had a need for them. Which was a grotesque practice, if anybody asked me. Jarat thought so, too. But his parents felt differently. And when Jarat was a teen and got in a hoverbike accident that badly damaged his brain, his father arranged for an "organic" brain transplant rather than the synthetic kind. Jarat's relationship with his parents was already strained, but that little decision sent it right off a cliff.

I know that what I'm about to say might sound a little woo-hoo woo-hoo, but my brother's presence actually lived on inside Jarat, in more than a physical sense. Even though the content of Jewles' mind wasn't supposed to transfer, ghosts of his feelings and little memories passed through Jarat's consciousness—residue, of sorts. Some of them were really small, like Jarat's sudden craving for artificial chicken after the transplant. (Nasty stuff!) And there were big things too, like the day Jarat saw a tired-out Chav staring at him from across the street. The stranger was my real mama, who'd been following him. She'd found out where her son's brain was "living."

Though Jarat had no idea who Mama was when he first saw her, he felt such a jolt of love for her. A tiny fragment of Jewles was "talking." After that, Jarat and Mama became fast friends.

So yeah, Jarat's health was really important to me, for big and strange reasons. And his wife and son meant all the world, too. Lush was my aunt, for all intents and purposes. And Tris looked like a younger version of his dad. They had the same swirl of hair obscuring their eyes, lanky stance like a heron about to take flight, hands in their pockets when silently questioning something.

So while my little sister's disappearance crumpled me to my knees, the impact of that attack on Jarat and Lush—and Tris's disappearance—sunk me through the floor. Thank God those fucking spider bots never were able to find the bunker where Lush was hidden!

The FBI detective introduced himself as Sam Dredson. His black suit was tailored to show off his body-builder physique. From the neck down, the man could have been a retired wrestling star. His face was shaped like one of those old-timey map location icons: rounded up top and tapering down to a point. Bristly white hair and eyebrows, big saucer blue eyes, and a wrinkled upper lip. Nuhope's makeup department would have told him to get a moustache.

"Am I that pretty, Cardinale?" Dredson asked.

Hadn't realized my holo was staring. "Yeah. Gorgeous."

Dredson ignored my cynicism, turning to the others. "I want to thank all of you again for the recordings. They certainly helped." He was referring to the security footage that Jarat and Lush had provided of the field where we'd been attacked, and my recording of the hall and living room in my L.A. flat, just before the explosion. I hadn't put cameras in any of my bedrooms for reasons that seemed obvious at the time, but which now seemed like a really bad choice. If only we knew what happened in Izzie's!

"In what way did they help? What have you learned?" Memere asked.

"The two visitors, Geneva and Prill, don't exist."

The rest of us looked at each other. "Well that dude Prill wasn't a hologram, if that's what you're getting at. And Geneva wasn't either," I said. "I would have known." You could always tell a holo from a flesh-and-blood person—slightly rough edges, semi-transparent quality took care of that.

Jarat piped up: "Plus, Izzie and Tris had sex with them. So how could they be?" The Ellingtons had found old footage of Geneva during past visits getting all pornographic on their son in the fields. It just about killed Jarat when he realized the biodome had been breached without his detection. As for Prill, the sounds out of my guest bedroom when they first arrived home had been fairly graphic, even if I had no visual proof they'd actually had sex, in the traditional sense.

"Whatever they were, or are, isn't something we've seen," Dredson said. "We're still trying to figure this out."

Memere went into dragon lady mode. "Well, step up the bloody pace. I will call in every chip I have with your ultimate bosses if this isn't prioritized. Now."

Dredson could have called her bluff. He must have known that Memere had limited pull with the "ultimate bosses:" the new president and vice president of United America. But he looked like he didn't really care one way or another. "If that's what you want, you've got to give me more," he said.

"We have told you more and more and more."

"But not everything." His eyes scoured each one of us in turn. "Why, for example, have you kept Tristan Ellington's existence a secret? Why are you so adamant that we don't release any information about him?"

Oh yeah. There was that. Even now, while the FBI was aware of Tristan, the general public was still in the dark. Everyone knew there was an attack on the Ellington compound. It had been seen from a distance by several people whose property abutted the Ellington's. There was no hiding that part. But the news coverage ended when Lush and Jarat showed their faces in a public holo so that everyone knew they were okay. As far as most people knew, the attackers didn't do much damage at all. And there was no Tristan Ellington. Only a few insiders knew of his existence. And now the FBI. But even the agency didn't know that other thingy: that he was a Charismite—and Izzie, too.

No one was willing to give that up. Memere fixed on Dredson with a glare. "You can't figure this out? Tristan is the son of a legendary celebrity, Luscious Ellington. And Jarat is pretty damned famous too." Jarat snickered at that, making a smile come into Memere's eyes. "You know you are, as far as counterculture icons go. The point, Mr. Dredson, is that Luscious and Jarat just wanted their son to live a normal life, away from the public spotlight."

"It's been so important to us," Lush said, eyes turning from brown to molten gold—just enough for her holo to warm up Dredson without making him suspicious that something more was going on. "We want him to stay that way, if he's found, if he's …" A tear spilled down to those lips that looked so terribly afraid, thirsty for kisses, all at the same time. She still had a lot of pull, even though she was in avatar form.

Dredson was barely holding onto his self-control. "Yeah. I, uh, get it."

Jarat stepped in, softly casual but with knives underneath. "If word leaks out about Tristan, don't expect any more cooperation from us."

Dredson growled at that, but Lush cooed him into a better frame of mind. And we exited the FBI room pretty quickly. Before long, the two families had entered our own private chat room, which looked like the Ellingtons' comfy living room. Not that the comfy part helped any now.

Memere put a hand over her mouth and screamed in frustration.

"Does anybody here think those FBI numb nuts will actually find them?" Lush said.

The rest of us quickly murmured, "No." The U.A.'s security forces were so compromised with political bureaucracy and mismanagement; it was hard to have much confidence in them—including Dredson. Which was why we didn't divulge Tris and Izzie's special gifts.

"We need someone we can trust," Jarat said. "I'll take care of this." He was probably getting the semi-underground group Theseus involved. I exited the call and collapsed back into the air-chair in my cluttered office, dazed with frustration and a lack of good sleep.

A few minutes later, Memere poked her head in my door. "Don't get comfortable. Wanza wants us." I rolled my eyes. "And watch the bloody 'tude!"

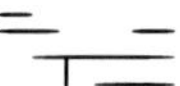

IT WAS HARD to choose which was better: an attack by giant spider bots or a meeting with Theowanza Newton—better known as Wanza. She had a swanky suite at Nuhope H.Q. on the top floor, just above Petra's office and about two hundred levels off the pavement. A few weeks before, Wanza was sworn into office as the vice president of United America, automatically becoming Nuhope's new chairwoman, and Memere's boss.

Wanza and the nation's new president, Tippi Pavlarona, had every right to do a victory dance. Just didn't like their rumba above our heads. They, along with the whole RDA party, had resoundingly defeated our own, the Independents—which put us both in a very shaky situation at Nuhope.

Decades before, when the U.A.'s leaders decided to take over the old PBS network and create Nuhope, they wanted to one-up the family-controlled media conglomerates, which were extremely dominant in the U.A. and most other nations on Earth. The family empires all backed one political party or another with the news and entertainment they transmitted. The opinions and conspiracy theories they spewed were supposed to help certain politicians grow their power base—and damage others. But they weren't completely reliable, when it came to abject loyalty. Plus, the vast amounts of revenue the companies raked in made some politicians drool. It took some doing, but when Nuhope was finally created, it cut out the middleman, so to speak. At least for the ruling party. It was so bloody lucrative.

Memere and I shot up the elevator to the top floor and walked down the long hallway past news-spot holograms reporting on my sister. I clamped down on my emotions. The vice president's first assistant, Gabby, was on her air screen in the reception area—looking like a sixty-year-old human version of a squirrel. Almost forty of Gabby's trips around the sun had been spent managing Wanza's affairs.

"I told you that yesterday! She's doing the D.C. one," she practically screamed at whomever she was speaking with—probably some underling asking about Senator Morelli's funeral services. One ceremony in New York's St. John the Divine would be followed by another in Washington's National Cathedral. Wanza needed to attend one of them for decorum's sake.

Gabby glared at us. "Don't outstay your welcome. Fifteen minutes max."

"Charming," Petra said acidly as we went down the long hall to Wanza's inner office. It was real cute. Even more palatial than Memere's, with transparent walls. Outside, thick clouds blanketed the teeming streets below, no doubt filled with the usual mishmash of joyous, furious, hilarious, famished, fatigued, stressed, serene, gob-smacked, sweaty, determined New Yorkers and assorted tourists. How I wished I was there instead of here.

The veep had looked like an athletic, dashing woman in all the political campaign hologram messages that swamped the OuterNet before the election. In reality Wanza was thin—in a weak, aging way. Her puffy yellow skin was set off by a glittering snarl of blonde hair, and she wore a billowy crimson caftan that swept down to cherry toenails that peeked out of air sandals. They accented the coiling red gleams deep down in her eyes, a mechanical corrective for poor eyesight.

At that moment her globes were trained on a holo screen of a Nuhope news segment, which I immediately recognized as something that ran before the election. A political commentator was discussing Wanza's bestie, President Tippi Pavlarona.

"I've never seen anyone so uncomfortable in their own skin—so apparently ill-at-ease with herself," the commentator said. "Everything Pavlarona says seems to be mannered and staged."

The veep stopped the recording and glided towards us. We let out an obligatory and somewhat reverential "Vice President Newton. So good to see you."

She gave us a chilly smile, voice high and thin. "You know, the first time I came to this office I was called in by …" she snapped her fingers in a what-was-his-name way. "Ten years back."

So we were in pretend mode. I stifled a smirk. "Vice President Glenoma?"

"Yes. Thought that he could bully me around."

"Now why would he do that?" Petra asked.

Wanza shrugged. "I org'ed some deep fakes to contradict all the Independent Alliance bullshit." Her pride was showing through. I knew enough not to look disgusted by that.

"Ah yes. You were in Congress then, as I recall," Petra said.

"Yeah. Glenoma told me it wasn't a good look. But now he's dead and look who's here."

She gestured for us to sit. We looked for yellow dots on the floor denoting where the invisible air chairs were located and settled in, allowing the pressurized air to support our seats and backs. Wanza slipped onto her invisible throne as Gabby scampered in with a cart of assorted teas, coffee, and treats. Memere declined, but I tried a sugar cookie, which had the texture of packed desert sand in the back of my throat. I stifled a cough and tried to wash it away with a gulp of Earl Grey. It nearly blistered my throat.

"I want to extend my personal sympathies about Izabel," the Veep said. "Who else knows about her *abilities*?" Wanza had been briefed about Izabel's charismatic gifts when she became chairman of Nuhope, since my sister was the most valuable member of Nuhope's exclusive talent pool, by far.

"A physician or two. Both paid off handsomely," Petra said.

"It's a shame about the Ellingtons—that Charismite boy, Tristan. So much like his mother, with those *talents*." I tried to hide my surprise. Didn't think she'd know about that. Wanza went on: "Makes sense, why they were hiding away in that biodome. Completely protected, or so they thought. Why wasn't Izzie shielded like that in her off hours?"

"You're kidding, right?" I blurted, showing what a complete idiot I can be at times. Wanza turned chilly at my disrespect. "Sorry. It's just that higher levels of protection weren't an option. My sister rebelled against all of them. And as we've seen, they didn't do Tristan much good."

Wanza grunted, toes curling up and releasing. "Contrary to what you might have expected, I didn't call you in here to fire you."

"Now why would we think that?" Memere said with a broad smile. She had a golden parachute in her contract with Nuhope that would net her a mountain of cash if she was let go. But my sister's incredible fame was probably the biggest reason why Memere and I weren't getting the boot right then. The public would shit its collective pants if that happened. Izzie, Memere, and I had showed up together all over the world for various functions that made a big splash on social news.

The veep waved a hand. "Eh. Disinformation is so easy. But enough about that. Let me ask you something, Petra. It has to do with the subliminal messaging at Nuhope. I like to think that your decision to do away with it all those years ago was well intentioned."

Petra lifted her chin. "Very much so." In fact, it was a fiercely held belief of hers, not to secretly plant ideas and opinions in people's brains. No more subliminal messages in dreamisodes and shows that would coax people to buy certain products, rage against certain people that the ruling government chose to hate, vote for certain candidates. My mother had made certain that they were removed shortly after she took over Nuhope as CEO, so many years ago.

Wanza scowled. "A rather unfortunate decision."

"In what way?"

"It's like we've gone back to bloody 2024, the freaking dark ages, with people warring with each other online, in the streets—violently different opinions and allegiances. This nation is falling apart at the seams!"

There was some truth in that. Without the subconscious propaganda, the chasm between various social and political factions was much deeper. Hate crimes had spiked over the last fifteen years. Propaganda had its upside—in a really twisted way. Petra's eyes flickered. Arguing would get her nowhere.

The Veep glided over to a window to stare at some clouds. "Nuhope has made a substantial fortune off Izabel's shows. But if she reemerges, I'll expect much more. You should never have blocked the ad sales department from using that girl in commercials."

"That didn't go so well in the past," I said. Wanza had to know the stories of what took place long ago. The Charismite Dove Brown, Izzie's biological father, had died in the process of delivering a warped political message at Nuhope—overdosed on the Juice that turned him into a Charismite. And Luscious nearly OD'ed, trying to un-do the chaos that Dove's message had provoked.

"But Izzie won't have those problems. She doesn't need any chems to do what she does—unlike Lush and Dove," Wanza said. "Now, let's move on. I'm stopping bullshit like this." She flipped to another holo recording. I immediately could tell from the time stamp that it had first run just after the election took place.

"The RDA party is not representative of the population," said a Washington wag.

The reporter sitting opposite him asked, "Are you saying the election was rigged?"

"Do the math. Even if you exclude the Chav—and I'm not saying you should—only thirty percent of the voting population are members of the RDA. The rest are largely Independents. So how could they have won in a landslide?" Wanza ended the clip.

"There were plenty of pro-RDA news stories," Petra said.

Wanza looked at my mother gently. "I want us to work together, Petra. I really think there's a way for me to keep you on. But things are going to change. Your 'jurisdiction' at Nuhope is now confined to reality shows. Any entertaining content with even a smidgeon of current events in them are now under my control, as well as all the news. You will have no further authority over those areas of the company."

Memere's jaw clenched. She'd just been stripped of about seventy-five percent of her content domain. "I've been told you've already started taking control of the news."

"By Ginseng Childe, no doubt."

"That's right."

"Clearly, her feelings about the news are different than my own. Which is why I'm asking her to resign."

Memere let out a short laugh. "I don't think you want to do that."

"Why not?"

"She could be more trouble outside this company than within it."

"I'll make it worth her while not to do that," Wanza said.

"Of course," Petra said sweetly.

Control Ginseng? The veep may have just shot herself in one of those cherry-red toenails.

MY REGULAR CIRCUIT within the gargantuan Nuhope building in New York involved three floors. One of them was packed with small offices and a hive of cubicles inhabited by producers and their support staff. Eight floors up, Petra had her vast office space. Ten floors down was the company canteen, where I usually ate lunch. That's where I heard about the massive layoffs underway.

Some staffers I talked to said that hundreds were gone. Others, thousands. This wasn't a downsizing. Replacements were showing up by the busload. I could see the new faces in the dining hall—freshly scrubbed young things. Wanted to bet they had campaigned for various Republican-Democratic Alliance candidates in the recent election and were now being rewarded with the gigs. Some of my friends had been tasked with onboarding the newcomers. They were none too happy about it.

I didn't see my mother for a few days after the Wanza visit. I was too immersed in various last-minute emergencies related to the upcoming live episode of *Space Ace* to think of anything else—other than the Charismite crisis, which was always on my mind, if not slamming me with dread. When I finally did see Memere, we were headed to Pompey in her car, with the bot, Geoff, monitoring the controls up front.

"I take it you didn't have anything to do with the firings," I said.

"Of course not. Kind of get the impression that Wanza wants to tip me over the edge so I'll walk out," Memere said. Of course, if she walked instead of getting pushed out, the golden parachute written into her contract would sustain heavy artillery fire from Nuhope's legal team. I had no doubt the parachute involved hundreds of millions of U.A. Americos, and if she bailed it would be severely reduced, if it didn't disappear completely.

But Memere was already an extremely wealthy woman. Which led me to ask: "Is it really worth it to stick around?"

She sighed, then grabbed my hand. "Believe me, I have no issue with the word 'enough' or even 'no.' And I'm not one to cling."

"Exactly."

"Someone has to bear witness. Someone up the ranks, who can really see what's going on. If anyone can do that, it's me."

I studied her knowing look. "What's going on? You're seeing something already, aren't you?"

"It's begun. Nuhope's servers are embedding propaganda in artificial dreams."

Yeah, we knew that was coming. But even so, a chill ran down my arms. Dreamisodes could be really fun. People were able to program their mobiles with certain information that would transmit subliminal messages to their brains, prompting certain storylines in dreams. Maybe they'd become a techno rock star or go on an adventurous trek through ancient Aztec ruins in the El Central Treasure Zone or have a funny dinner conversation with a dead brother. I'd always enjoyed them. Before.

Now, that dream adventure in El Central might include an exotic beauty wearing a diamond-studded necklace from Cartier. And when the dreamer woke up, she'd be obsessed with the idea of buying it, even if she didn't remember the dream itself.

"I've tipped off Ginseng," Memere said. "Now that she's on her own, she's started her own news feed. She'll make sure people know what's going on."

As the limo reached the long, green road leading to the Ellington compound, the air around the hovercraft crackled with electric currents—an even higher level of defense than what had been there before the attack. The gate recognized us and opened up, like always.

Jarat was waiting in front of the house. The bandage on his head was gone now, and the wound was healing in the place where the bots had attempted to get at the Juice intel in his brain, only to realize that was impossible. The house doors, which the bots had crashed through, were now reinforced, too.

Yeah, it was progress. But Jarat had good reason to look tense as he ushered us through the house and down into the bunker where Lush was living 24/7. He was there most of the time too. The living room looked cozy. No air chairs, just a traditional variety of well-worn overstuffed furniture that beckoned me to curl up and doze off. The earth-perfumed air was about ten degrees cooler than the outside temp.

Luscious emerged from an underground hothouse off to one side of the living room, overalls grimy at the knees, corkscrew whisps of hair crowning a flushed face that looked surprised. "Hells bells. You're here! Lost track of time. Be with you in a sec."

She darted off into the bedroom to change. Jarat gave us a tour. The bunker included five bedrooms and was completely equipped with everything Lush and Jarat might need. They'd turned one bedroom area into a studio, where Jarat could do his visual art and conduct various techno experiments. Lush's refuge was the greenhouse, crammed with all kinds of exotic plants. We exclaimed about it all.

Jarat smiled sadly. "It's still a prison. At least I can go outside, but my wild bird never does. She never complains, but she hates feeling trapped like this."

"Sure do, but that doesn't mean I'm not grateful," Lush said as she came through a door wearing the same kind of old cotton dress she always favored. "And I'm sure you'd all be grateful if we rustled up some drinks. What'll it be?"

We all settled on martinis. Lush started to mix up some, but Jarat hip-bumped her out of the way. Martinis were his specialty. She grinned, setting out some raw carrots and snap peas with garlicky dip, but an invisible force of barely controlled anger radiated off her. She wasn't one to sit back when there was any danger, and the disappearance of her son worked on her hard—along with Izabel.

Jarat put a hand to one ear, a reflexive gesture indicating that a message had just popped up on his private air screen. "Our last guest has arrived." That was a surprise. "Just a minute." Jarat left and came back shortly afterwards with a man of about sixty years, stocky and sagging inwardly. A slab of plain brown hair wandered across pasty yellow skin. His hands leaned forward awkwardly, a sign he was using an air cane to support himself. "Hey, everyone, meet Mikhail Toure," Jarat said.

"Pleased to meet you," Mikhail said in a reverberating voice.

We soon learned that Mikhail had been a field agent with the FBI for donkey's years. He was permanently injured about fifteen years before when some Asian thugs kneecapped him. The replacement joints were top of the line, but not good enough to keep him in the old gig, so he was relegated to a desk job in the bowels of the agency's sprawling headquarters in the Washington Treasure Zone. What the FBI didn't know was that Mikhail was a sleeper agent for the underground rebel group Theseus. Mikhail was little more than a file clerk now, largely unnoticed and forgotten by most everyone—which worked well for Theseus.

The bags under his eyes carried the weight of too many witnessed brutalities, but there was a flame of wicked-sharp intelligence on his face—and barely curbed desire as he gazed at Luscious, who was serving bowls of the seafood stew Cioppino and some crusty bread. Mikhail knew what she was: a Charismite—how he needed to guard against her mentally. The flame grew more fervent when Jarat explained that Mikhail was going to conduct his own investigation of the young Charismites' disappearances.

I tested out how far they'd go. "So, you and Jarat work within the same Theseus unit?"

Mikhail stopped his spoon in mid-air, stealing a look at Jarat.

"We can't answer much about Theseus's inner workings with outsiders," Jarat said. "But I'll give you this: we weren't in the same cell until recently. There was some shuffling around. My own unit has always been very small, and in recent years it got … reduced."

He grew sad, and Lush reached across the table to hold his hand. I remembered that he had told me confidentially, sometime ago, that he had two close friends who passed away. Jarat didn't say much more, but something about the way he said it made me think the pals were part of Theseus.

Mikhail pushed away his bowl. "That was an outrageously fine meal. Thank you kindly. I hope you don't mind my asking a few questions of my own.

"It will be an even finer meal if you do," Memere said.

"The detectives on the case probably questioned you about most of what I'm about to ask. But if even one of the agents assigned is somehow connected to the attacks, then the reports within the FBI's database are compromised. I'm not saying they are, just that they might be. So I want you to repeat yourselves one more time."

"We'll talk until your ear falls off," Lush said.

Mikhail used a soft conversational tone as he proceeded. It would have been easily mistaken as polite and casual under other circumstances. After a while, we retired to the living room, and I helped Lush bring in dessert: Stilton cheese, dried cranberries and pecans over pear and apple slices.

"The FBI agent we met with seemed to think that Geneva and Prill weren't human—that they were some form of technology, but that doesn't make sense," I said.

"Why do you say that?" Mikhail asked.

"Izzie went to bed with the dude Prill, so it's a pretty good bet that she'd know if he had a cock. Could technology fake that well enough?"

"I think they were human, but somehow masked," Mikhail said. "Humans in camouflage."

"There's something else," Memere said. "Why would the group that took them need to have Prill or Geneva there on the ground, as it were? Exactly what function did they serve?"

"I wondered the same thing," Mikhail said. "I've looked at the recordings of the attacks that are in the FBI files, and I don't think the detective quite caught everything. At least not at the Ellington compound. It looked to me like that hot young thing with Tristan was signaling when to attack, at just the right moment."

"It makes me insane, that any signal could slip past my detection system!" Jarat said.

Mikhail shot him some sympathy. "There's more. If you look really closely at the movements of Geneva's hands, she seems to be communicating with the bots. She was directing their movements as the attack was in progress."

Jarat's face hardened even more. "Let's get back to the masking. How did they do it?"

"It's a mystery at this point," Mikhail said. "I'd like your own copies of the recordings, if you don't mind. But unless they give me really big clues, we're going to need something more."

Lush looked into his eyes deeply. "Tell us. We'll do anything."

Mikhail dropped his love-sick eyes, regaining composure in a couple of seconds. "I believe that this is going to take desperate measures …"

"For desperate times," Memere finished softly.

"I want to see this masking phenomenon in real time, up as close as I can get. That might give us the information that's really critical to understanding what it is. We need to lure the abductor out of hiding. I have to have a better image."

An idea had been flitting around inside me like a girl all dressed up with no place to go. Had just seemed like idyll mind chatter, something that came to me when Lush and I were talking in the kitchen. After Mikhail said those words, I couldn't hold back. "What if my mother decided to throw a party and Luscious was one of the guests?"

"Absolutely not!" Memere said. "We can't turn Lush into some kind of sitting duck! After what's already happened? How could you even suggest that!"

Jarat was dangerously calm. "Luscious?"

"Yessir!" his wife said.

"What have you been persuading that poor boy to say?"

"Hells bells Jarat Ellington! How dare you accuse me of that!" Lush said, seemingly outraged, until she broke into hilarious laughter punctuated with little snorts that were actually pretty adorable. By the time she caught her breath, her brown eyes were flecked with gold, as they always were when she was determined, energized. "The boy's fucking brilliant all on his own."

"Brilliant my eye! That idea is awful," Memere said.

"Just hear me out," I said. "This party would be in a closed, heavily guarded environment. But someone might be tempted to try and capture Lush. I'm betting that they use the same camouflage to make an appearance."

"And I stand a chance of figuring out what the hell it is, and who the hell they are," Mikhail said. "But we'd have to keep Luscious protected."

Memere rolled her eyes. "I can't believe you actually think that's possible, after what's already happened."

Lush put her headlight eyes on Memere and Jarat. "This is my life, and my choice. And this duck says we do it."

Jarat gazed at his wife with pleading eyes, like she was on the ledge of a building and there was no way to stop her from jumping. We were all powerless when Lush's energy worked on us.

"I love you all. I do," Lush said. "I know you care. But if we can't get those kids back, I don't give a flying fig what becomes of me. If you were in my shoes, I know you'd do it too." Her eyes glowed with defiance and excitement as she directed them on her husband, who seemed to be silently exploding as he gazed back.

"Since you're pressing the point, there may be a way to do this," Jarat said.

7. CHEETA

Fierce as Fuck

JUST AFTER I hit the red dot in that screwy Universe, I hit the black square too. And bam. Just like that, I was back in my apartment. My head was reeling, couldn't think straight. Not at first. When I finally got steady, I searched through my mobile. There was the message from Miles, the one that nearly killed me to listen to. The red button had recorded it!

Energy surged through me. Wasn't any doubt in my head now: that really was the senator. He was being tortured, about to die, and I was the only one who could save him. Didn't like what my mind was telling me to do now. LiZee glug-glugged, like she was saying, "You my girl. You can do anything."

That was so wrong. "Why did he ask me to do that one thing?"

"Nadia knows who to trust, the people who will search for me. You've got to get this message to her. Make her believe it. Please!"

I hated the idea of seeing that bish again. It was bad enough that I still was going up and down the fire escape so I wouldn't run into my landlord. Now I had to deal with *her*?

But I loved Miles. And whatever crazy-ass thing she said to me didn't matter. She had the fame, guts, and off-the-hook rage to get to the right people—the ones that might find Miles and weren't part of The Fist. Maybe. All I knew was, if anyone could pull the right strings to get Miles back, it was her.

When I showed up at the Morelli mansion, there were

soldiers all over the place, including snipers on the building rooftops all down the friggin' block. I was in the middle of arguing with two hulking meat wads at the front gate when Petunia banged open the front door.

"Back off!" the bot roared at them. Worked like a charm.

I followed it inside. "You got the touch," I said.

"Somebody's got to take charge here." The bot hugged me with all four arms, even though it wasn't exactly kosher for humans and humanoids to do that. "Come on to the kitchen and I'll get you some tea. Taking you the back way so *she* doesn't see you."

"Um, actually, I need to talk to her."

Petunia stopped dead in its tracks. "You don't want to do that."

"I've got to. Please."

"She'll send me to the junkyard!"

"Not when she hears what I got to say."

The bot was way smart enough to sense how I had this storm inside me. So, it sputtered out some mechanical tsk tsks and led me down the hall.

When we reached Miles' study, Petunia whisked away like it was running from a hurricane. Like I said, it was way smart. Nadia was at the senator's giant desk, looking so small, like she'd crumble to dust with the smallest poof of air. Never seen her like that. The senator's chief of staff, Colin Steward, was standing over her shoulder. He was kind of this good ol' boy in a big-boned body. Sometimes he seemed self-conscious, as if he'd forgotten that he was all grown up. But that hid these deep wheels churning inside that I'd seen in action, when he and Miles were strategizing all kinds of political shit.

Nadia's eyes looked so tired listening to Colin talk about the funeral services. "We've got eight speakers for Saint John the Divine and another nine for the National Cathedral," he said, showing her something on his air screen. "Here's the program for St. John."

"I'm sure it's fine." Nadia got up, as if she couldn't get away from the screen fast enough. She stumbled a little, like she was going to faint, and Colin grabbed her. It was too personal, that touch. She moved away from him. "I can't do any of this!"

"Hey, hey, hey, hey. Of course, you can. Nobody's tougher than you."

"I just don't understand why they haven't found any remains at the accident site, not even a bone with his DNA."

"That's what happens with high-speed explosions."

Nadia looked like she was going to be sick, clutching the edge of the desk for support. Colin walked off to take a call, talking softly for a few seconds. Then he came back up to Nadia. "*The Times*' White House correspondent would really like a talk with you."

"No."

"Just five minutes."

"I can't."

"It won't be a good look if you—"

"She said 'no!'" I yelled.

They both jumped. My cheeks felt way too hot. Why couldn't I keep my *boca* shut?

"Get out," Nadia said, voice even more scratchy than usual.

"I can't."

"Talk about sorry timing," Colin said.

"Please. I'm sorry, but I got to talk to you!"

Nadia screeched, "Petunia!"

Colin tried to be kind. "We're making some serious decisions here, kid."

"Yeah, but what I've got to say could change them."

Petunia whisked in. If the bot had had a tail, it would have been between its legs.

"Take that Chav away," Nadia said.

"For the love of Miles," I cried. "Please let me talk to you. Just this one last time."

Nadia hated me so much, but she couldn't help backing down. She turned to Colin. "Christ. Let's take this up later.

"Of course," he said, then took off.

Nadia's eyes went into me like stakes. "I hope this is the last two minutes I ever lay eyes on you."

Fucking *puta.* "I have a message from Miles. He's alive."

Nadia grew even paler than she already was. "Whatever drug you're—"

"He's in some kind of prison."

"That's outrageous. How dare you!"

"I couldn't send the message to you. The signals aren't secure enough. You need to see this."

"Ha! You think you can tell me what to do."

"They're probably gonna kill him, really soon."

Nadia turned back to Petunia. "Take out that trash!"

The bot grabbed me. I shouted: "If you don't watch that message, I'll show it to some journos. And you'll regret it. Like, forever."

Didn't really know if I'd get any reporters to listen, but I was freaking desperate. Nadia looked like she wanted to kill me, but she calmed down a little and let me transfer the holo message to her mobile using her private, super secure line.

"If you just infected my device, I will damage you. Permanently," she said.

I was dying to give her some lip, but kept my mouth shut. I'd done what Miles wanted. Didn't need to feel guilty anymore.

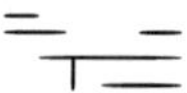

SEEMED LIKE A joke, that I could ever get another job. Even though I'd been an office assistant to a U.A. senator, nobody wanted anybody that hadn't been to college for gigs like that. Plus, my dark Chav skin was a problem for a lot of people. So I knocked on a ton of restaurant doors, hoping to wait tables. Most of them used bots. They didn't need me.

The whole time, I couldn't stop thinking about Miles in that prison. There was no sign that Nadia had looked at the message I gave her—nothing on the news about Miles being alive, or in prison. Maybe there was a secret rescue operation underway, and I wouldn't know about it till later. That's what I kept thinking. But she probably never bothered to watch the message. I called her bot, Petunia. But it didn't know anything.

On the third day after I went to the mansion, my anxiety level was maxed out. I decided to wait until 3 PM. And if there wasn't some kind of clue that Nadia was doing something, I'd reach out to some journalists. Or maybe one of the senator's colleagues—somebody that I didn't think would be connected to The Fist. But how could I tell? Would anybody listen to a Chav like me?

By 2:30 I was getting really tense. Still no sign that Nadia had done anything, and I'd run out of leads for a new gig. I tried to reach Diana, the humanoid that had raced out of the senator's mansion just before the accident. What the hell happened to it? I'd already tried to reach it a bunch of times, but no response. Just like now.

There was a soft knock on my apartment door. I cursed the landlord. Wasn't no way I'd let him in. "I said I'd pay you next week!"

Another knock came, this time louder. Then another, and another. I was too pissed to race down the fire escape. Throwing open the door, I came face-to-face with Nadia. She was wearing a long dramatic cape, like she was still queen of the frickin' worl'. It was a shock—to see somebody that I hated, let alone a celebrity diva—gliding past me on little golden air slippers into my shabby place.

She pulled a box of green tea from her purse, the kind that's super expensive.

"I don't need your handouts," I said.

"You have a guest. Make some."

Her lip curled at the sight of my girl LiZee. Good. I put the salamander on my shoulder to drive the bish crazy and boiled a pot of water on the stove. The diva flared her nostrils in distaste, making me smile, then swept her gaze over the junky furniture.

"What a ridiculous piece of theater," she said.

"This isn't no stage."

"Not *here*. God no. That recording! Who created it? Did you have a co-conspirator?" She drew out that last word like she was in some goddamned performance.

I slammed a cracked mug on the table and made her jump. "You wouldn't know the truth if it slapped you in the face."

"That *supposed* message is six days old. If it's real, why did you wait? Too busy figuring out how to torment me?"

"I've got better things to do."

"Liar!" she cried.

Anybody would get mad, if somebody called them that. But "mad" was a lot weaker than what I was feeling. There wasn't a word strong enough. The whole reason Mama and I had gone through so much was because my grandfather didn't believe us back in Honduras. So many people didn't believe me all through my life—except for the two people who were gone.

And now this Elite bish was doing it to me again. But it wouldn't do no good to yell.

"You're right," I said. "Who am I fooling? The truth never

wins. Or if it does, it's about once in a fucking century."

"That's what you believe?"

"I believe your husband is gonna be killed. And all you can do is waste time telling me I'm a liar. Why the fuck did I even try?" That's when I saw that her eyeliner was squiggly, like it had been put on with trembling hands. And she was teary. "I don't blame you," I said as kindly as I could. "Of course, you'd think that way. But I gave it to you as soon as I found it. You have to do something!"

Her eyes narrowed; it was like she was scanning every pore on my face. "You know something more. What aren't you telling me?"

I couldn't look at her, focused on pouring the tea. "Not really."

"Where? Where did you find that message?"

"In a junk folder."

"No you didn't."

I turned my back and started washing the dishes that had piled up in the sink.

There was a soft thunk. "Here. Is this what you want?" she asked. I turned back around. Hard cash. Hundreds of Americo dollars were on the table, maybe thousands. My stomach churned, just thinking how it would help me buy dinner—so many dinners—and pay the rent. Maybe she'd believe me if I told her more. Probably not.

"Please! Tell me!" she pleaded. I didn't want to. She'd just keep thinking I was scamming her. But she kept working at me and finally said, "I swear to God, if you don't tell me, I'll make sure that everybody who hears that message will think it's counterfeit nonsense."

No reporter would believe me if she did that. My toughness crumbled.

"It was in this virtual place," I said.

"What place?"

"It looks kind of like a universe. Only not."

"Show me! IF THIS IS REALLY TRUE THEN YOU'LL SHOW ME. NOW."

I was trapped. There was only one way to make her believe, and I wasn't sure I could even do it. "This probably won't work. But maybe I could take you there if we lie on the bed together and were connected in some way—maybe hold hands."

"You've got to be—"

"Do you think I want to do this?" I snapped.

It creeped me out, even to think about touching her. Nadia was even worse, so revolted. But she finally got on my pallet, so disgusted, as if it was covered in slimy dirt. I lay down beside her. The faint scent of flowers coming off her hand-embroidered silk cape warmed my nose.

"Don't move." I took her boney hand. And holy crap! It worked!

AS WE FREE floated in the orange Universe among the gazillion bubbles, Nadia jerked around, shrieking like a crazy person. She gripped my hand so tight.

"If you don't calm the hell down, I'll let you go!" I yelled.

She screamed, so frightened by the endless void full of all those damned bubbles. "I'll be good. I'm sorry. I'm sorry I called you a Chav."

That bish would have said anything. "You think I'm embarrassed by what I am?"

"I don't know."

"You're the one that should be embarrassed. A spoiled old

priss. A coward. That's all you are."

"Get me out of here! Get me—"

A mountain-sized cluster of bubbles rushed toward us. I tried to swim-float us out of the way, but it wasn't no use. We tumbled over and over among the bubbles.

The voices inside were whispering, "Out of here… the hell… get me!" And there was also a bunch of screams, 'cause that's what the bish was doing. And other holos saying "STOP IT!" 'cause of what I was saying. We fought our way out of there. But no matter how far we floated away, there was this one bubble that kept trailing after us, a little brighter and larger than the rest.

At first, I thought maybe it was the senator. But peering inside, we could see the face of a guy, just a little older than a kid, dressed in the green triangle cap of a U.A. soldier. He looked so desperate, and there was a huge gash with half-dried blood all over the side of his forehead and cheek. He was saying, "Just a baby boy. He ain't got no one. How am I ever going to get out of here? Somebody help me! Help me find a place for him!"

I don't know who was more shook up, Nadia or me. "Maybe… maybe we should hear the whole message?" I asked. "I could pop it open."

"No! No! Please." She looked around at the other bubbles as if afraid she'd start another avalanche. "Where is Miles' message? If you really found it here, show me.

So I called out my name again and again until it finally came. Nadia cupped it in her free hand, wrenched with torment and fear as she stared at her husband's miserable face. It seemed as if every flake of doubt had fallen away from her. It was more real to her than *real* could ever be. Just like for me.

IT WAS NIGHT by the time we got back. Sitting across from each other at my little table, we clutched cups of cold tea. Nadia was stunned and exhausted. "I don't understand why that place exists. How did you get in there?"

"This man gave me the lens I have on. Mercury Douglass. He was tired out. I think he... What do they say?... He kind of passed the baton. But I want to find him again. I got so many questions about all this."

Nadia thought that through. "I keep thinking about that poor soldier. I wish we'd heard what he wanted to say. Should have."

"I know what you mean."

"There have to be other messages in that place that need to get out. Not the nonsense ones. Clearly, there are a lot of those. But maybe there are others that could mean so much to the right people. They might be trapped."

"I think so. That's why I call it the Universe of Lost Messages."

Nadia grunted at that, mouth set in an iron straight line. "Well, we need to deal with our own lost message." She swung the cape around her, as if imagining an awful fight ahead, then looked at me accusingly. "You think I'm a coward. Well, I'm not!"

It was there in her glare, what Miles had told me long ago—how Nadia had done everything in her power, as a young singer, to train her voice with the dedication of an Olympic athlete, so it was more pure and exciting than just about anyone else's. So many sacrifices along the way to achieve that—no time for friends or family, now long gone. Eating ugly-tasting nutritional supplements to achieve the stamina she needed. Sometimes they made her ill. No one tougher than her. So, yeah. I'd call her a lot of things, but not a coward. Not never.

She blazed with pride and made for the door. "Hey!" I

called after her. "Want to hear something weird?" She turned back. "Miles told me that you and I are more alike than I know. What a laugh, right?"

She didn't even smile, thinking about it seriously. "Well, we're both fierce as fuck." Then she added softly, "And we have him."

We gleamed at each other, almost like friends, but that couldn't be. She got all bossy again. "Are you going to help me with this or what?"

8. MERCURY

Hard Johnson

"WOO WEE. LOOK at that," I said. Not that any words came out of my mouth. The room I was peering into had three rounded walls that buzzed with blue-black light coming off three rows of screens. Underneath was a blank white desk. Tall cases of equipment flanked it on either side.

"The command center!" said my dead wife, Tavee.

"Gotta be it, Hon."

In my head, her spirit peered at me through a magnifier. She was in her ratty old easy chair in our ranch house in Cucamonga, in the L.A. Treasure Zone. That was the way she looked before every good part of my life got trashed. Tavee's thick dark hair was sprayed out and covered with tiny colored gemstones, just like always. She was so excited her metal nail file froze in mid-stroke.

Finally, weeks after I was thrown into a goddamned prison and then figured out a way to escape my room, I'd located its nerve center. Thank Gawd nobody was around.

"Get in there," Tavee said. "Work your mojo on that shit."

All the bruises on my body throbbed with terror. What would happen if I did? Would some security alarm get set off? "Can't. There's only four minutes left."

"Then get out of there, Babes."

I beat it back towards my room, following the tiny dents in the rubbery walls that I'd made with my fingernails to find my way back. It was some real Hansel and Gretel bread crumb kind of crazy, but that was the best I could do. If I was counting right, four weeks had gone by since I made the message with the senator, and three weeks since I got the lens to that Cheeta girl.

Just after I gave it to her, the damned bots that looked like arachnids found me in a dive hotel in Newark. They exploded through the side of my tiny room, knocked me out, and when I came to, I was in this hellhole.

That first day, Tavee and I listened hard. Things were scurrying around outside my room. Then the monster bots dissolved a wall and came inside—bloated, fat, about nine feet high, maybe four feet across—and the wall re-materialized behind them.

"Hello, Mercury," purred a disembodied female voice that I knew only too well. Seemed to come from everywhere. "You do realize that all this will end when you tell me where it is?"

When I didn't say anything, the bots picked me up by the shoulders and heaved me against every surface in that little room. All the goose eggs they gave me hurt bad. Cut my leg something awful when I landed against the metal rim of the toilet. After a while, my blood was on the walls. The arachnids kept coming back—sometimes with dry cereal and some moldy other stuff that made me hurl, sometimes to mess me up some more. But I didn't give up what they wanted.

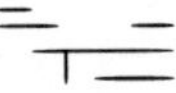

ABOUT SIX YEARS before, I had a decent job as a 3D designer in a metaverse creation firm. And Tavee was a queen of the hair design business. Her business attracted B-list celebrities in Los Angeles. Everybody loved her way-tall 'dos. Tavee called 'em towers. You could find shit about her all over the OuterNet in special holos about glamor. Had a wig business going on, too.

Anyhoo, I was in awe of Octavie, right from the start. That's Tavee's full name: Octavie. She had what they call perfect posture. You'd think she was royalty when she walked into a room. And talk about reading between the lines! We'd go to some places and have these little conversations with people we knew. And afterwards, she'd sum up the stuff they never said. If she knew somebody a little, she could tell a lot. And nobody could play her; nobody could hide nothin' around my girl.

Yeah, I was pretty proud. We were saving up so Tavee could expand her line of signature beauty products and I could start my own metaverse biz. Wanted to help people get away from the prefab metaverses that corporations offered up, which never really understood who people were or what they wanted to do, despite all the algorithms.

But then Tavee was diagnosed with terminal bone cancer, and we stopped talking about the future. Got so the only thing she did was watch old reruns on the air screen—shows she saw when she was a kid. Six months later, she was gone.

I felt robbed and got really pissed off. Hit the enhancer drugs too hard, wrecked my mag-lev, got "sick" a few too many times for my boss, and then got fired. Screwed up my rep as a designer with other folks too, and I ended up in a recovery joint to dry out. When I finally got released, the only gig I could land was working as a night shift maintenance guy at an outdated server farm called Cloud Forest in the Sonoran Desert, twenty miles outside Phoenix. It was a kind of relay station. Messages people sent came in, got boosted by the servers and then were retransmitted back out into the world, making it to the people who were supposed to receive them

Yeah, the job sucked at first. But then a weird thing happened. I started falling in love with those tired-ass servers.

The lines of them went through that cloud farm for nearly a mile. They didn't need a lot of maintenance. And I had better things to do than take a hike up and down those aisles all night long. Especially since one of my knee joints was acting up. So, I put microscopic cameras in some clear paint and brushed the servers with it in just the right places. They were all black, and I matched the surface finish pretty good. Nobody ever called me on it. The guy that owned the place wasn't too bright.

I spent most of my time in this little closet-space office they gave me and worked on my own project: a brand new virtual universe. It was a tangerine-colored version of outer space. And private. Wasn't connected to the other metaverse platforms at all. I floated around in there without a care in the worl'. And sometimes it even gave me this happy feeling I'd had back in the good days, when Tavee and I settled into a tub of water full of special minerals on a Saturday night. We shared a glass of bourbon on the rocks and talk about all the shit that bugged us, and the good times we were planning.

My universe was like a blank canvas. There was a bunch of stuff I had in mind to do. But even then, I had a good time in there. Already had an exit function, a record button just in case something happened in there I wanted to remember, and another icon for creating stuff when it sprang to mind. It made me forget about my real life. I lived for the paycheck and the day I could get the hell out of there and retire.

About five years into the gig, I had enough money saved up to do that. And just in time because one of my knees needed replacing. With all that on my mind, I didn't pay attention to the news reports saying that an asteroid was headed to Earth and would land somewhere around the Phoenix Treasure Zone. The world was full of destruction—tornados, wildfires, hurricanes, floods, you name it. Gotta admit I was kind of blasé about it all. Besides, if I died, would it be so bad? Me and Tavee would be spirits together, *maybe*.

Turned out, the asteroid was the size of a doghouse, and it hit the cloud farm about a quarter of a mile from my office. I was zoned out in my universe at the time. So I didn't really know what was happening. I found out later that a massive electro-magnetic pulse had hit the servers. Long, snaking coils of energy shot through the building. It threw my body up in the air and slammed me against the ceiling.

I ended up in the Phoenix Medical Center, treated for a severe concussion and abrasions. They never took my mobile lens out, 'cause I fought them off tooth and nail every time they tried. Lot of thieving went on in places like that.

My lens started triggering these weird spitting sounds in my ears. And the next time I went in the Universe, I sure got a shocker. My blank orange space was suddenly filled with millions of transparent balls, each one throwing off colored lights, like bubbles. And inside each one, there was these holographic faces, each one blabbering away at low volume.

Made my skin crawl. I tried to get away from them, arms going round like a windmill. "How the hell did you get in my space!?"

The balls started shifting around, some coming forward, others drifting away. "My space! … Hell! … Did, did, did you?"

I thought I'd have a heart attack if I didn't get out of there. Reached behind me for the exit button real fast. But my arm bumped into one of the bubbles, and out sprang the holo of an old Elite dude with cloudy eyes that looked about one-hundred and fifty years old. He was shaking a finger. "Don't let Archibald in my space after I'm gone. He'll rob you blind."

I reeled backwards, panting hard. And the old guy sucked back into his sphere. "No, no, no!" I said, reaching around to hit the black stop button again. But another bubble hit my forehead.

Three little boys in matching blue sequin suits popped out doing this jiggly dance. They was singing: "No, no, no, no, no she don't love me. No more squeezin' and huggin', no more Saturday night lovin'." A sign swished up in front of the boys: "On sale today! The latest tunes from The Vishy Brothers!" I swatted the holo away. Damned spam! But a mess of other bubbles came at me with whispering people inside.

The whole thing freaked me out. But the feeling went away when I rejoined the living in the hospital and the jackhammer in my skull returned. Hadn't realized it disappeared when I was in my secret cosmos. It was so painful, feeling like that in real life. I got real curious. Had I just hallucinated all those bubbles, moving around like stars and planets? Only one way to know.

Sure enough, when I went back into the Universe, the people balls were still there. A theory started to hit me: somehow, that strange coil of energy that shot through me and the cloud farm had transferred a bunch of messages out of the servers and into my metaverse! Never seen anything like it, but then again, who knew what was going on with that energy field coming off a space rock? I started having fun, popping them open. Most of them were nothing but junk. But there was this one that stopped me. Inside was a holo of a middle-aged man that looked so upset; I just had to open it up. He had these sleepy, heavy-lidded eyes, and his lower lip was trembling, just a bit. A flowery scarf curled around his neck, falling over a royal blue uniform. "Randall Heatherscape! Have some compassion, Randall Heatherscape!" he said.

When I got back to consciousness, a worl' of pain squeezed me so tight that I cried out. It was like there were brutal pinchers around my head. "He needs another dose," said a nurse humanoid.

"No, please don't do that. He must think clearly," a woman said. *What*? She was behind me; I couldn't see who the fuck she was.

"His cognitive abilities will be fine. And they will improve," the nurse bot said. It injected some chems in my arm. The agony eased up within seconds. I smelled something like cloves and cinnamon, which was a big improvement over the usual chlorine and piss blend.

The stranger glided into view. She was one helluva looker, with these candy pink lips puffing at a diamond-studded smoking tube, sending out that smell. The skin on her smooth cheeks glistened, so golden, accenting honey-colored hair that swooped into the kind of towering twist that Tavee specialized in. Her black eyes turned up coyly in the outer corners, but there was a deadening sorrow way back inside them. A crazy thought whispered in my head, that she'd never learned to laugh.

"Mr. Douglass!" she breathed. "Thank God you're finally awake."

One of the bot nurse's limbs wound around my wrist like a fabric band and took my pulse. "All vitals are approaching normalcy. He's going to be just fine, Ms. Sidhar."

"Sidhar?" Tavee said, looking down from her magnifier. "Never heard of her."

I coughed out a huge wad of phlegm and spit it in the little sink beside the bed, wheezing badly. "Sorry."

"That's normal. He needed to clear things out," the nurse said.

"Of course," the woman said, looking relieved. "Please call me Celeste. After what you've been through, I dare say that first names are in order."

"Sure. I'm Mercury. But I guess you know that."

Celeste smiled like I was a child. "I certainly do."

Tavee snorted. "She's the kind of woman that's going to piss down your back and tell you it's raining.

Celeste kept talking. "It is a miracle that you lived through that catastrophe. I am certainly glad that I was called in to help with things."

"Called in?"

As the nurse bot gave me a cup of water and warned me to take small sips, the Sidhar woman brought me up to speed. After the asteroid destroyed most of the server farm, the U.A. government bought out the owner. Like I said, he was pretty clueless. Nobody liked to deal with him. Hell, I barely could. The asteroid had screwed up that place in ways that nobody could understand, and NASA wanted to keep a close eye on it. Then the Pentagon got involved. So that's why the government took it over.

Because Celeste was friendly with a lot of government peeps, they asked her to step in and manage the place from a business perspective. She had a tech company that specialized in startups called Sidhar Enterprises.

"Sorry you have to deal with that," I said.

"Oh, no, no. I do love a good challenge. But what happened to you is so distressing. The value of human capital can't be minimized. And you! *You!* Your talents were drastically underestimated. I'd like to make amends by offering you something that I think you'll find quite exciting."

"Watch out," Tavee said.

"What's that?"

Celeste's face lit up. "Well, it has to do with that asteroid. I will personally make sure that you're handsomely compensated for your valuable expertise and time."

"Well, I'd definitely like to talk about it." This might make up for all my bad luck. Maybe it would make sense to hold off retiring so soon. Although I would need to deal with the bum knee.

She reached over and took my hand, eyes so anxious and warm.

"What the hell does she think she's doing!" Tavee said.

I wasn't crazy about it either. Touching wasn't done unless you were really close to someone. I inched my hand away, but Celeste held fast. She turned to the nurse. "Why aren't you feeding him? He must be famished."

"It's coming."

"I sure would like to get a look at that asteroid," I said.

A dim light of annoyance glimmered in those black eyes. "Maybe at some point. First, I need you to focus on one thing."

"What's that?"

"It has to do with the gibberish you spill when you're apparently sleeping."

"Gibberish?"

"Things like, 'Damned spam' and 'What are you a bunch of half-assed messages?'"

It was real funny, to hear 'half-assed' come out of those uppity lips. But Tavee didn't think so. "Don't tell her nothin'!"

Figured she was right. "Just a bad dream, I guess."

Celeste beamed like we were both in on the same joke. "You do know what the cloud farm was used for—before the destruction."

"Transmitting messages, yeah."

"Well, as it happens, several million have gone missing. I think you might know where they are."

"Me?"

I thought my innocent old man look was pretty good, but Celeste laughed without any sense of humor. "Oh, Mr.

Douglass. You are a sneaky one. Do you think I didn't find the cameras you painted on the servers? Or the lapses when you were in some kind of, well, fantasy world, there in your office? Naturally, I've gone through a lot of security footage."

"Oh. Well, I did all my work."

"Yes, but I have reason to believe that you were creating a metaverse—given your specialty before. And that metaverse just might contain all my messages."

"*Your* messages?"

"They are now part of what I oversee. So yes, as far as you're concerned, they are mine. And you have stolen property in that metaverse."

I didn't trust her. Not one bit. "That's some leap of imagination you got going on there."

"I would think that someone your age would be better at masking the truth."

I shrugged. She could believe what she wanted. "I'm really sorry that the cloud farm is so messed up—"

"Destroyed. Largely."

"Right. And I'm sorry all those messages are gone. But I—"

"Let's not quibble. What if fifty-thousand Americos were transferred directly into your bank account? Assuming you hand me your lens, and it has what I'm looking for."

"Wait. What? You'd take my lens?" It was a disgusting thing to ask of anybody, giving up their lens.

"I know, I know. But think about it. All that money. And then, after you've worked a little longer for me, you'll be free. Retire. Go on some big adventure!" I swallowed hard. She was scaring me for reasons I didn't completely get. Her hand patted the bed. "Don't answer now. Let's get to know each other a little more, shall we?"

Celeste came back several times more, making chitchat

without pressuring me. But the blankness of her black eyes were devouring me, silently asking me to give in. I kept getting stronger, thinking and thinking about what I should do.

Every night, when the pain kicked in harder, there was a squeak, squeak, squeaking down the hall that got louder. Light from the hallway beamed through a window in my door. I crept out of bed and got closer to the glass. A bot rolled a body bag on a gurney down the hall. I soon discovered there was about one bag a night, with a small white box on top of each one. Personal belongings, I guessed.

"Why do you think she wants those messages so bad?" I asked Tavee.

"Well, Baby, I'm guessing it's the usual bullshit: information is power. And she wants more. Did you see her hands the last time she was here?"

"Hmmm. Kind of boney looking. Hadn't noticed that before."

"That's 'cause they weren't that way."

I knew what my wife was getting at. It was almost like Celeste had digitally layered some kind of camouflage on top of her body but didn't get the fingers part quite right. Which was whacked because most people that didn't like their bodies just got an enhancement surgery. Why do the digital stuff? "I've never seen anything like that before."

"There's some kind of evil crap going on with her," Tavee said.

"Yeah, but I like her money. Maybe she isn't so bad. Maybe she just feels responsible and wants to get the messages to the people that are supposed to receive them."

Tavee looked at me out of the tops of her eyes. "Did she say anything like that?"

"Nope."

My wife drew a little closer from up there in her heaven spot. She always did that when she was real serious. "You got to do what's right. Go back into that jacked-up metaverse and release all the messages so they get to people."

"Oh hellz. It's nothing but spam."

"Did you see that guy looking for Randall what's-his-face? That wasn't spam."

I'm not a do-gooder by nature. But what Tavee said kept eating at me. What if there was stuff in that Universe that would make a worl' of difference to people? And when push came to shove, I didn't need much money to be happy. That wasn't my style. Then again… I was kind of torn.

Two nights before they were going to release me from that hospital, I decided what to do. By then, I could move around pretty good, and they'd weaned me off most of the pain meds. When I heard the squeaking sound, and the bot with a body bag went past my door, I crept out of bed and followed after it down the hall.

The bot was waiting for an elevator by the time I reached it. About seven feet tall, super thin with a big oval head. I tried to look frail and begged for some drugs—said I needed to relieve the pain right away. It had big black eyes in a permanent state of sympathy, and I pleaded a few times until it read my chart in its database, gave in, and swished away to run my errand.

My heart was beating like crazy as I looked around. No one was visible down the six white hallways spanning out from the elevator bank. I grabbed the white box on the body bag and pried open the lid. The dead woman's possessions were sorry-looking—fake flowers, cheap jewelry, picture frame with a holo of some grandkids. Couldn't find what I wanted. A far-off swishing began again. In a few seconds, the bot would round a corner and see everything. Then I felt it, way down in the bottom: a little clear box, and inside was the cadaver's mobile lens. I pocketed it, closed up the box softly, just in time to give the bot a shiny smile as it came in sight with the pills.

Over the next day, I spent every waking minute deleting the dead woman's files and populating her lens with some meaningless stuff, including another metaverse I'd made a while back that didn't quite work right. About two hours before I was scheduled for release, Celeste dropped by, and I gave her the lens. She gushed out some thanks and left.

Two things seemed possible when Celeste tested it out. Either she'd just figure she'd gone down a false trail and I was innocent, or that I'd conned her. She was crafty, so it was a good bet it would be the con option. But I was counting on buying a little time.

As soon as they let me out, I took all my retirement money out of the bank and converted it to cash so nobody could track my payments. Figured it would be a good idea to have some extra lenses, so I made a quick stop at a tech store and got two. One of them was just normal, what I could use every day. I gave the other new lens the same functionality as the old one, so it could be used to get in the Universe. Then I hid that one and my old purple lens under the wig that Tavee had customized for me. She had this special hair-making technique that made it impossible for anybody to tell it was a fake afro. Even when my hair was parted, you couldn't see the cap. Completely invisible. After that, I went to a place to hole-up for a spell: this cabin up in the Sierras that my cousin Archie owned.

I went back inside that Universe again and again. The more I spent time in there, the more I realized that even though most of the trapped messages were trash, there were some that just seemed to beg for a delivery.

Like that one from the sleepy-lidded guy. Took me a while

to remember the full name he'd been calling out, which I needed because the bubbles responded when I called out certain words or names, and I couldn't remember exactly what I'd said when it came my way.

Sure enough, when I called out "Randall Heatherscape!" a few times, his message came right to me. He was some kind of social worker at the Tan Tock Seng Hospital in Singapore and wanted to tell Randall that his spouse had been rushed to the emergency ward after he suffered a massive stroke. It was easy enough for me to find Randall in Spokane. He had been sure his husband had left him for another man and nearly collapsed when he watched the holo. At first, he thought I was a con man, but then he called the hospital in Singapore and found out his husband was still in rehab and hardly knew his own name.

"Why didn't I ever get this message?" Randall asked.

"I don't know. It just came to me by mistake somehow." If I gave him the whole asteroid story, he would have thought I was nuts. But Randall was so overjoyed to find his guy that he didn't spend a lot of time questioning me.

Upshot was, I came to realize that one little message could turn somebody's life around. And it seemed like there had to be more like that. Sure enough, I found one from a young woman that had sent out some deep-source info to a news reporter. She wanted to blow the whistle on a test lab that was secretly engaged in a lot of animal cruelty. Everybody thought it was on the up-and-up.

Then there was one from a half-demented woman in Pasadena. She'd sent a message to her daughter, because she was afraid she'd forget where she'd hidden the diamond ankle bracelet she wore when she won the U.S. Open about sixty years ago. That daughter sure was glad to find out it was buried under a rosemary bush.

"You know what?" I said to Tavee. "This message-delivery business is the best thing I've ever done in my whole lousy life."

"Except for meeting me."

"Oh yeah. That's in a higher stratosphere, Hon."

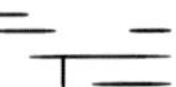

LATER ON, AFTER I found the senator and got him to make that message to put in my metaverse—and after I got the lens to Cheeta LaVera—those arachnid monsters attacked me in the Newark hotel. And they threw me in Celeste Sidhar's damned prison. They made me take the regular lens off my eyeball. Hadn't found the special one, under my wig. I was dizzy with pain. It didn't help that they hardly gave me any food or water. But then my brain started to pick up things. There were times when the bots' scurrying sound outside my room seemed to intensify a little, then drop off. When that happened, the soft purr of a vent in my ceiling went silent, and the lights dimmed. It was a mystery, when those little quiet stretches would come.

After a while, I started counting off the seconds to figure out how long the quiet periods lasted. Every time, I got all the way up to nine-hundred before the sounds reemerged. Fifteen minutes. Every time, almost exactly fifteen minutes.

Okay. So now what? It was just useless information. I was so depressed.

Tavee tried to make me feel better. "This place is not where you're going to die."

"Don't know that."

"Mercury C. Douglass. Calm down, pay attention and remember."

"What?"

"What it's like to go on a cruise. That's what you're going to do when this whole thing is over. *You're retired*. You're gonna get on with it."

"Cruise, huh."

"Um-hmm. Tropical beach, not too hot."

"Lord, no."

"Maybe—maybe better make it Nordic."

"Nordic? What the fuck do I want with a place like that?"

"It's beautiful there!" I wasn't going to argue. We didn't say nothing more for a while.

I gave her a teasing chuckle. "Remember when we took that cruise up to the Anchorage Treasure Zone? Back a ways now."

"Watch it." She'd got so mad at me on that trip about some fool thing that she almost leaped off the side.

"Never would have jumped in after you."

"You lie like a ratty rug." Her eyes widened. "Wow. Did you feel that?"

I did. It had to do with my balance, and the floor. It felt like we were in a boat. Big solid building on water. "I'm probably hallucinating, 'cause of the cruise talk."

"I don't think so."

If it was true, it sure wasn't good. Maybe I was in the intestines of some huge vessel, cruising through an ocean. Or was I in space? Didn't think it would feel like this. But if either scenario was true, and I managed to get out, I'd be royally screwed—without any oxygen (if we were in space) or solid ground (if we were in the middle of the ocean). Unless there was something inside this prison to steal, some kind of mini spacecraft or a raft or—who the hell knew what I needed or how I was going to get it! Christ, I couldn't even get out of the damned prison cell at that point. And the arachnid bots kept coming in and throwing me against the wall. Couldn't stop weeping, no matter what Tavee said. And I just wouldn't give up the lens. Just wouldn't. Which might seem nuts, but I just knew that evil bitch was up to no good.

After a while, I calmed down and started to formulate a theory. Maybe when everything went silent, the ship was recharging, and it needed to be in certain locations with access to power sources in order to do that—places it couldn't stay in for long.

If that was the case, the water theory didn't make sense, because every boat I'd ever seen was either wind or solar powered. And both of those energy sources were all over the ocean's surface. So maybe that meant I was in space. Sometimes the ship must be near the sun, sometimes blocked from it by some planet.

I talked it over with Tavee. "I don't know what the hell to think, Hon."

She got out of her chair and came closer, so her face was peering right up against the magnifier. "We both know there's a tired-ass word you gotta pull out and use on yourself. Hope. *Hope*!"

I sighed hard. "There's a mountain of questions I want to get answered. And there's only one way to chip away at it: get out of this cell and explore the prison somehow. All they can do is beat me up some more."

"That sure-as-hell isn't all! She can snuff you!"

The trick was not to get scared all the time. I focused on how to get out of the room when things went quiet. Whenever the bots came in to beat me up or give me food, I studied what they did, how they moved their toes. Each tentacle had five of them, like a hand.

It took a lot of study, because they made the movements so fast. But I finally caught the pattern. Fork between the middle and second toe, circle with the fourth and fifth ones, three quick taps on the wall with the first toe on two separate tentacles, first one then the other. I did it with my fingers and… I'll be damned if it didn't work!

The first time I dissolved the wall of my room, I nearly collapsed in terror, looking out at the green tunnel-like hall going in both directions. Holding my breath, I waited for the bots to show up and kill me. Nothing. It was too scary, right then, to even think about walking down the dim corridor. And how the hell was I going to get the wall to close back up again? I shot back inside my room in total panic mode, hyperventilating like crazy.

"What the fuck was I thinking!"

"Calm down!" Tavee said.

"I can't! I can't!" Five minutes left. Three minutes. Two. One. Why the hell hadn't I studied what the bots did to close the wall?

"Wait. What if you did the exact opposite sequence?"

"That's too easy."

"Goddamnit, Mercury. Try it!"

So I fumbled through the hand movements in reverse order, and the wall solidified. It was such a close call that it took a long time for my heart beats to stabilize. Waited a long while before another quiet period came. I got up the guts to dissolve the wall and took a few steps outside. Nothing happened. So, every time the place was silent, I went further through the maze of hallways, limping a little because of all the bruising and my bum knee. The floor kind of bounced under my steps. I counted down the nine-hundred seconds so I'd get back to my room in time, using my fingernails to put little dents in the rubbery walls way down at the bottom where they were less likely to be seen, as a way of figuring out where I was, where I'd been. No alarms went off, and no bots attacked. Which was a little crazy. Didn't they have security cameras? Or maybe they were there, and this was just some kind of rat's-maze game for them, watching me. But there were no signs of that. I came to believe that in those quiet periods, no one was watching.

One day, about five-hundred seconds in, I heard somebody moaning on the other side of a hall wall. I did the secret code thing so fast. Sure enough, a hole opened up. Inside the little room was the man I'd suspected might be there: Senator Morelli. He was a lot worse than when I'd seen him before, at the time we'd made the message.

If I was counting right, a whole month had gone by since then. And he wasn't no more than a stick now. His filthy blue suit looked three sizes too big, dried blood on his temple, bruised hands folded over his stomach, eyes closed as he moaned.

"Senator! Senator!" I whispered.

His eyes popped open, alarmed. "You too?"

"Can't stay."

"Not the same place."

"Yeah. Different. Trying to figure out where we are."

"The message!"

"It's out. Cheeta. She might find it." Couldn't lie. Didn't really know if she'd get in my metaverse. Had to rush back to my room after that.

"That man's gonna die soon if somebody don' help him," Tavee said.

"I know, Hon."

I saved up some cereal and put it in a pocket, even though I didn't get much. And every time it went quiet again, I went back through the halls until I found the "X" that I'd pressed in the wall showing where he was. It was too hard for him to eat much, but I got some of it inside him.

"You gotta try harder," I told him. "Keep up your strength. If the time comes to escape, it'll be better if you can move on your own."

Morelli turned his head toward me, tight skin over bones, dim eyes pouring out sad amusement.

IT TOOK A lot of trips going down all kinds of new tube directions to find the command center. When I did, there wasn't a lot of time to do much of anything. The blue-black lines of monitors above the smooth white shelf were daunting.

In the past, I'd tried to find a signal in the hallways, pulling my lens out of the secret place under my wig to test for one. But nothing. If there was any spot that might have that capability, it was in that command center. I was going to need a signal if I was going to make another message and get it into my metaverse. If Cheeta went in that Universe, maybe she'd find it!

The second time I made it to the nerve center, I only had a few minutes left before I needed to get the hell back to my room. I pulled the lens out, settled the little disc onto my cornea and pulled up the settings screen. A surging line of green shot across it, ending in crackling red static. A signal was in here! I could do this. But it was freaking scary. What if someone picked up on what I was doing?

"Don't get hung up in your underwear," Tavee said. "You found this room. It's a start. A really big start."

"Right." Wanted to let the senator know about this place. But there wasn't enough time to do that right away. When there was another quiet period and I finally went down the halls toward his room, something happened that made me forget everything. "Shit!"

"Uh-huh," Tavee said. "Mind telling me why your johnson just got hard?"

9. TRISTAN

Geezer in Our Midst

IZZIE KICKED THE stones in our yard a lot. When we were young, she threw tantrums when she came to our biodome outside Pompey Hollow. "Why do we have to be here?" she screamed at her mother.

Didn't make sense to me, because I never grew tired of roaming the fields around our home. I loved discovering things, like the papery gray architecture of a hornet's nest. And in the winter, when Da opened the top of the dome to let the snow in, we'd toboggan down the side of a snowy hill, swerving to avoid the trees, with Ma shout-giggling behind me. In spring, there was the watery aroma of living plants and animals too tiny for the eye to see.

I felt sorry for Izzie, mostly confined to the fifteen-room Ellington townhouse in Manhattan—when she wasn't at her mother's places in Paris or Los Angeles. Sure, she owned every possible toy and gadget a kid could ever hope for. But she could be so mean to her mother, who was just trying to protect her.

Izzie never had a chance to go outside when she was home, except for little gardens walled off from the outside world. I didn't get it. She should have loved coming to see us in the country, where there was a lot more space, so many living creatures. There was so much inside our dome to see and do.

Izzie didn't just loathe the biosphere; she also hated me—mostly because I didn't care that I was sheltered away. Didn't matter how much I tried to make her like me. Once, I showed her a treehouse that I had built high up in an oak in the woods. I scrambled up a ladder, looking down on her from above. "Come on up. It's a secret. Nobody else knows about it yet."

"No." She kicked the ladder away. "Let's see what you're made of! Jump!" It was about a twelve-foot drop. My chest clenched, imagining the pain of a broken arm or leg. Her gray eyes laughed at me. "Jump, jump, jump, jump!"

"Come on, Izz. Don't be that way."

"Such a scared little bunny," she yelled, then ran away.

Later on, I learned that when Izzie got back to the house, Ma asked where I was. She said she didn't know. Hours passed in that tree. I stared longingly at the fallen ladder, willing it to magically rise up on the straight trunk, which had no notches, nothing to put my weight on and ease down slowly. Couldn't shimmy down it without slipping and falling; I was sure.

Far away, Shakespear called for me. So did Da. They never heard my shouts back. I sobbed angrily, knowing Izzie was right about one thing: I was a coward—a wimpy, stupid kid. But then, after I was too tired to cry anymore, the floor began rocking. The treehouse, cradled between two outstretched branches, was swaying in a soft wind that carried the scent of dry leaves.

I looked out over a swirling long stretch of yellow and orangey-red tree crowns. There was a gap in the leaves. Through the transparent upper walls of our world, I could see silvery Mirror Lake. Beyond that was the little village of Pompey Hollow. White clapboard houses sprinkled around a long brick school filled with kids I'd never met and probably never would. There was the whisper-roar of a crowd coming from the long green playing field next to the school. A real, live soccer game—not something in a metaverse! I could barely make out the specks on the field that were boys and girls running back and forth, and a bleacher of people. I imagined myself kicking the ball, racing down the field faster than anyone. Everybody in the stands shouting in excitement.

A pang of loneliness swelled inside, but I squeezed it down hard. How I hated Izzie then.

The sun traipsed down. The town went hush. Tiny lines of curling smoke from chimneys. My stomach rumbled. Dinners were cooking. What was Ma making? Maybe a stew, or fried catfish, or chicken and mashed potatoes swirled all over with gravy. A fresh round of fury at Izzie rose up with my hunger. Waves and waves of it.

I felt a sharp pain in my leg. Didn't know what it was. Shouldn't have been there. Hadn't done anything to make it hurt. Down below, on the shadowy ground, there was something light colored in the tawny leaves. Looked like gray fur. As the minutes passed, it very slowly crawled forward, and the hurt in my leg grew sharper. It twitched, head looking around. I filled up with terror that wasn't my own; it was coming from the gray creature. A mouse? Too large. A squirrel? Was it sensing a coyote on the prowl?

It's going to die.

How could I save it? I had to get down. Not only would I break something if I jumped, but I'd probably scare the wild thing even more than it already was. But there *was* a way to do this. Maybe.

I stepped out of the treehouse, gingerly walking along a branch as my hands clutched another branch overhead, making it to the wide trunk. Crouching down, I weaved back and forth on the limb before finding my balance, then put my arms around the trunk's bark and flung my legs out into the air momentarily. They hit the trunk and hugged it on either side. I shimmied gingerly, slowly down the tree. R-r-r-rip! My T-shirt tore all up and down the front side. The bark clawed into my belly and chest as I tried to keep track of the animal below. The strange pain in my leg grew even sharper as the little being watched me in terror. I could see now that it was a squirrel, and it was desperately trying to crawl away.

I finally reached the ground and limped toward it, trying to send out soothing vibes. Its right back leg stuck out at a painful angle. I picked it up carefully, not touching the damaged limb and cradled it in my arms, carrying it home.

By then, Petra, Shake, and Izzie were long gone. Ma had convinced Da that I'd come home—to just wait. But they both looked incredibly relieved when I turned up, still limping badly.

As we made a little dried-leaf nest for the squirrel in the shed, Da shot me a quizzical look. "What do you mean, you didn't hurt your leg?"

"It's the squirrel's leg. That's what I'm feeling. A-a-and there's something wrong inside its belly." I rubbed my own stomach, where I had started to feel an ache just after reaching home. I could see Da didn't think I was crazy. It was more like he was leery. We found some walnuts in the house, cracked open the shells and left little pieces of the meat next to the squirrel.

Da looked skeptical. "Probably won't eat it."

"Is it going to be okay?"

"Let's ask the Country Pumpkin." Da turned to Ma, standing in the doorway.

"That's Queen of the Country Pumpkins to you, Bub." The frizzes in her yellow hair glowed in the light from the house beyond, her caramel eyes hidden by the shadows.

"Okay, Queenie. Should we call in a vet?" Da asked. A look passed between them. They didn't like other people in the biodome, how they got so obsessed with Ma and me.

"I honestly don't think a vet can help at this point," Ma said. "And those nuts probably have too much of a human smell on them for the squirrel to take to."

"But we've got to try," I said.

"Course. But the two of you are going to scare it to death even sooner if you don't leave it the heck alone. Besides, your da tried his hand at fish chowder, and for some strange reason it's not too salty this time. So come and git it."

I didn't say anything about what Izzie had done, but Ma figured it out. After I went to bed that night, she sat down on the edge beside me. "You know what my gram said to me once? She's in the grave out in the pasture."

"I know where she is."

"That's good. Anyway, she said, 'Love everybody you can and pray for the rest.'"

"I try to."

Ma took my hand. "Tris, how long you been able to feel the insides of animals?"

"Just with that squirrel."

"Hmmm. We'll see what happens with that. Reminds me of something else Gram said."

"That thing about you playing with a strange deck 'o cards?"

"That's the one." Ma gave me one of her gap-tooth smiles and tweaked my nose. "You got a stranger deck than my own, God help you."

"Yeah, but you stopped using yours." I'd heard the stories, about how she used her powers to get people to buy stuff, think certain things, when she was at Nuhope—how she'd confessed to everything in a message spread all over the worl'. That seemed to have done some good, getting everyone to think more kindly about poor folk, swaying them to love more, hate less. But that was a long time ago, and that old message didn't affect people the way it once did. It was buried under a gazillion other messages.

She looked at me with a wise sadness. "It's no good, twisting up people's heads, even if it seems to be for the right thing. Do you get that?"

"Yes, Ma."

"It's important."

"I know." We let the darkness sink into us a little more, happy to just be quiet together. She finally patted the bed like she always did when she was about to leave. "Anyway, what I really came in here to say is, don't hate on Izzie."

Fact was, I didn't. But I sure didn't understand her.

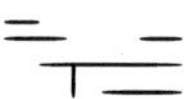

THE PALE BLUE room lurched into view as I opened my eyes. Rolled over. Izzie was beside me, golden eyelids closed. The sheet was pulled back to her waist, and the skin of her breasts looked tender as rose petals, moving with her breath. There was a tiny "O" opening between her lips, letting out warm puffs. Gentle, serene. So different than the way she'd been as a kid.

There had been another dreamisode. I danced with her, holding her loosely.

The word "crave" didn't begin to describe how much we both wanted me inside of her. She peeled away from me, walking to the syncopated beat of airy music through a wide field. I followed after her.

My mind reeled, dick so big I thought it would explode. She looked kind of rocked by me, too. I tried to hold her. She pulled away, picked up a buttercup, and brought it to her face. Shiny patch of yellow on her nose.

"Listen, Tris. I'm older than you, so I'm gonna take the lead here."

I laughed. Older by two months. "Right."

She tore off some of the flower's petals. "What I said before, about how you could get us out of here? I know that might not happen. But here's the thing …"

"What?"

"You're stronger than me. You don't see it. Maybe that's why I was always such a pain. When we were kids. Because not only did you not see it, but you were too timid to ever break out of that dome."

"I wanted to be there."

"Because you were afraid."

"You are so good at being annoying. It's really quite impressive."

"The point is, maybe I'm wrong. But maybe the time will come when we actually *do* find a way to get out. And you'll be the one to …" She couldn't go on. I was stroking her wide mouth with my thumb, teasing her slowly, luxuriously. There was no point in having that conversation. We were never going to be saved, never going to escape. So why not just enjoy the moment? I could sense her vagina opening wider, see the "oh" in her eyes. Something snapped in her. "Be serious!"

I tried not to laugh but it burst out of me. Then I straightened up. "Okay. Serious and strong. Got it."

The dream disintegrated after that. And there she was, beside me in bed. Above the red sheets a bad bruise was visible on her temple. The pain of it was shooting through me, and the other ones below the sheets where Darrel had kicked her.

Izzie turned over and gazed at me. "You danced a lot better in dreams than you do in real life." Her voice was tough and dull. Thunder cloud shadows under her eyes.

"You never saw me dance."

"Just one time. With Lush." Intense ache cracked open in me. "Sorry," Izzie croaked. "I know better than to mention them." Our families.

"S'okay. I was already thinking about them." Still, actually *talking* about them meant thinking more about them—wondering what happened to Shake and Da—Ma and Petra in the house. Izzie and I would go crazy if we thought about all that too much, let alone everything else.

I sat up and put my head in hands. "Crap."

Izzie stared at me. Don't know what sparked it exactly, but she couldn't contain all her frustration, screaming long and hard like a freaking amplified eagle. It stopped so quickly, I was jolted. My ears were ringing.

"That must have felt good."

"Yeah. Give me my clothes."

I followed her gaze to a chair, where some silky stuff was neatly folded, and passed her some shorts and the short boxy top. Threw on some drawstring pants myself. As she dressed, I saw more of her bruises. As casually as possible, I started to memorize them like a map: one on the left thigh, left midriff, right forearm, and ankle. Might come in handy later on, recognizing any new damage from what was already there if she tried to get out again.

Izzie didn't notice what I was doing, too busy singing to keep the anguish and boredom away. It was a kind of hip-hop. "Doo-duh. Doo-duh." Sounded like she was making fun of me with the Dr. Doo thing, but then the song started to morph: "Be boop ee doop ee doo pee doppy."

She danced between the chairs, then sprang up on one and took off, in a high arabesque through the air, voice rising in full-throated melody as she sang, "Trissee, Trissee, Triss-ee. Sing it, sing it, sing it, sing it."

And I did, silly non-word after another. "Krall pop! Bah pip!" Until Izzie hooked into some lines, and my rhythm became the base for her wave to ride on: "Haze of bliss, haze of bliss. Can't fight the trance. Should we die, or just dance? Sing it to me, Strong Man!"

I looked at her hard. There it was again: the strong thing. Had she really meant that? Something shuffled behind us. Felt like somebody had sliced my leg. And my right knee hurt something wicked.

We wheeled around and found an old man with bright eyes, reeking of sweat and a history of fear. He was dark-skinned, but the slim cut of his soiled pants and plaid shirt made me guess he'd risen up from the lower class into the Middles. He was dazzled by Izzie as if she were a miracle, a phenomenon, which of course she was.

Were the cries that we'd heard before *his*?

"Hello," I said.

"Don't got much time," he croaked. "Ten minutes before they come back. Fifteen altogether."

The bots. Must be.

"They can fucking hear you!" Izzie whispered.

"No. Don't think so. They're around, but way, way back in another part of the prison. I can hear them moving, far away, when I'm outside sometimes," he said. "And if they've been watching me on security cams, I would have gotten punished, or they would have changed the lock code." A long, inflamed scab showed through a rip in his pants.

"Please," I said. "Will you let me look at your leg?" He tore his eyes away from Izzie, giving me a curious stare. "Sit, sit!"

He walked backwards and nearly fell into one of the plush chairs, feeling the bright fabric with one hand. I knelt before him and rolled up the pant leg, my hand hovering above the wound. He flinched. "Don't worry."

He kept looking around. "You got it better than me in here."

"Yeah?" His pain coiled into me, sharper now. One of his knees was a mess inside. Joint pain. Sure, he could walk, but it was costing him.

I didn't know a lot about medicine, just stuff that I'd found on the OuterNet. But maybe I could help him, a little anyway. In the tiny bathroom, I opened up the medicine cabinet. Nothing. So I wet a sponge and washed the man's surface wound. "You've got to keep it clean. You have something to do that with?"

"Yeah." He looked back and forth between Izz and me. "What is it with you two?"

"We're Charismites," Izzie said, trying to pour a sobering look into him with her gaze. But she wasn't good at it.

"Charis-who?"

"Supercharged charmers." She glanced at me. "That's Tristan. He's older than you might think, not that it matters. He can feel what's going on inside you in ways people normally can't. My name's Izzie. We were born with genes that magnify our normal abilities, what would have been normal. That's why we're in here. To be used."

He breathed hard, adjusting to that idea, looking like he wanted to dive right into those silver eyes of hers. "I know you. You're famous."

"Not because of natural talent."

"Bullshit. Give yourself some credit," I said.

She sounded like she was rolling sand around in her mouth. "Gee, thanks."

"What's your name?" I asked the man.

"You can't know that. If she found out—"

"She?" Izzie asked. Silence. It was costing him, to fight

against her eyes, which were turning deep green, focused so intently on him. "C'mon. We know how to keep our mouths zipped—for frickin' decades."

He struggled not to say anything, but that was too tough, with Izzie working on him that way. "I'm Mercury."

"Mercury. So why are you in here?"

A prideful courage came into his jaw line. "'Cause of a place she ain't gonna git."

There it was again: *she*. And what place? Izzie was on to other things as she drew closer to him. She brushed his arm with one hand, and his face grew fire bright. "Are we the only prisoners? Can you tell us that?"

"One more I know of." He stepped back from Izzie, trying to get out from under her spell.

"Who's that?"

"Getting late."

"But..."

He vanished through the wall in a split second. The hole sealed up again. *How did he do that?* We waited, breathlessly. Would he get caught? Did he know how to get out of the prison? Not likely. Otherwise, wouldn't he be gone?

A couple minutes later, a skittering sounded from up above, over our ceiling. Izzie and I gazed at each other. Had the geezer figured out the rhythm, when they weren't around?

"Shit." Izzie collapsed in a chair, overwhelmed by it all.

There was a howl from somewhere. A man stretched beyond all levels of pain endurance. He descended into beseeching cries. The words were impossible to make out. Was that Mercury, or the other prisoner?

BANG.

Silence. What had those bots done?

Turning around, I realized that Izzie was balled up in a

corner, trembling in terror. Never thought I'd see her like that.

"Hey." I crouched down beside her. She flinched away, didn't want me to feel inside her as she wept. "We will not let them win, won't, won't."

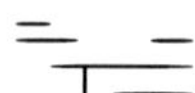

AFTER THAT, I ate everything they gave us, unlike Izzie, who largely ignored it. I became obsessed with exercise—pushups, lifting furniture, running in place. Needed to get ready to fight, run, do anything that might help us if the time came to escape. The sexy foreplay dreams continued, but as soon as we woke up, Izzie and I moved away from each other, off the bed. It was our way of rebelling against what our captors apparently wanted us to do: copulate, conceive other Charismites. At least, that was our guess.

We kept waiting for Mercury to show up again, but our next visitor was someone else. At the time, Izzie was picking at a yogurt parfait, propped up in bed, and I was at the little table devouring a mushroom and cheese omelet with toast.

"Hello there." It was a lilting floral voice, someone from the European Republic's British Treasure Zone, but spiced by the Indian subcontinent. We spun around. The woman before us looked like my sweetheart, Geneva, but with the settled face of someone older, maybe by fifteen or twenty years. A dark brown waterfall of hair nearly touched her waist. There was no mistaking those black Indian eyes. How had she changed herself that way? *The fucking monster!* Hadn't wanted to believe she was behind all this.

She lifted a smoking stick to the mouth that I'd kissed so many times, stained red now, corroded somehow. The burning smell of cloves, and something else (cinnamon?) radiated toward us.

"Prill," Izzie said. I looked at her sharply. What was she talking about? "You're a *woman*?" The woman shrugged, like Izz was an idiot to ask.

"And you are…?" I asked.

"Celeste. Celeste Sidhar." She looked at us boldly, like it didn't matter if we knew that or not.

"That thing, that thing of yours wasn't real?" Izzie asked.

"Ah yes. Tricky piece of camouflage, that penis," said Celeste. "So convenient that you don't let men get inside you. Didn't have to put it to the ultimate test."

I managed not to look at Izzie incredulously. She didn't let anyone enter her? All the people she bedded down, and not *one* got that far? Wow. Izzie stood up as we glared at the festering pile of garbage in the shape of a woman. "Nothing you do will make that change," Izzie said. "No matter what dreams you give us, we will not be banging. We are not your fucking Charismite baby factory."

"Oh, dear ones, that won't be necessary. Not anymore."

"What do you mean by that?" I asked.

"You've been tested. Your chemical coding has been analyzed. We know now that incubation outside the womb will work perfectly fine with creatures like you."

There was a tiny cut on my testes. I hadn't paid any attention to it, given all the other wounds. But now… was that where they'd done the test? Had they numbed the area so I wouldn't feel it? Izzie was clutching her middle. She must have one too.

The smoking stick went in and out of that rust-red mouth. "A shame you didn't give in. You could have had so much more fun. I can tell you that Tristan here is quite lovely when you get him inside. Inexperienced, but inventive."

"How about you give me a dream where I strangle you to

death? I'd be ecstatic," Izzie said.

The woman smiled gently. This wasn't getting us anywhere. I came closer to her. Her lilting black eyes widened, waiting expectantly, as if excited by approaching prey. So hard to fix on her as Genny, as someone sweet. But maybe if I pretended, just bent her mind, a little.

"She doesn't mean that." I reached out to cup Celeste's face.

Lust came over her like a hurricane. How she wanted me. But then a bar of hot voltage bored through my belly. I socked against the wall. She lowered a little e-pistol to her side, tilting her head with curiosity at my writhing face.

"You pile of hot scum!" Izzie shouted.

CRASH.

A spider bot fell through a newly formed hole in the ceiling and landed. Its eight limbs surrounded Izzie like bars in a cage. We both screamed as it tightened its grip, squeezing her. There was no way I could stop the bot as it leaped through the hole again with Izzie and was gone. I whisked around, ready to lay into the woman, but she had disappeared.

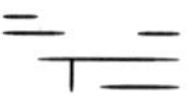

IT FELT LIKE a day went by, though there was no way to tell. No Izzie. The old man didn't come back. Hard to sleep, but I did. And whenever I woke up, a tray of fresh food was always there—cereal, soups, roasted meat, piles of vegetables. My appetite was gone.

Very faintly, far away, I heard a scream. Izzie? The pitch was so high it might have been an animal. After that, muffled groans filtered through the walls. Male? Female? Couldn't tell.

Hours and hours of tortuous worry. Sleep overtook me more and more. Finally, someone whispered, "Doo."

Izzie was back, and very dizzy. I was feeling it. She crawled toward me across the floor. I rushed to her as she collapsed on her belly. Her black emotions shot into me. She was in a whole new level of terror and despair. No more bruises or cuts. At least there was that. We lay there on the floor, side by side, for a long time. I put my arm around her shoulders, waiting for her to throw me off, but she didn't.

"Tell me," I said.

Nothing at first. Then, "I didn't want to."

"What?"

"You are going to hate me, forever. And you should."

"Never."

She wouldn't open up, no matter how I coaxed. Exhaustion roiled out of her. What could I do? Then it came to me. In a broken voice, I sang, "Haze of bliss, haze of bliss. Can't fight the …" What came next? "Crap."

The speck of a smile warmed her eyes. And then she gave in to sleep.

10. CHEETA

Bombshell Presser

NOTHING WAS HAPPENING. Nadia hadn't pinged me about helping her somehow. A week had gone by since she came by my place. I tried to stay positive. Maybe she was busting some balls. Maybe a search was launched to find the senator and crack open that Fist org. I wanted to throw every single member in a vat of boiling oil. Wasn't no bottom to my hate for them, whoever they were.

I couldn't stop imagining the senator in some torture chamber or dead now. And what happened to that weird old dude, Mercury? I had so many questions about him and the Universe.

The only way to stay sane was to do what I could, like paying my back rent with some of the money Nadia had given me. Then I laid in an order of freeze-dried worms for my girl LiZee and had some decent meals (some with actual chicken; none of that fake shit). Plus, I worked on fixing the IBM desktop by replacing a bunch of wiring. When I went back to the flea market, Barston had just what I needed. Man, was he ever surprised I didn't beg for free stuff and actually laid down some Americos.

I soon realized that old lens from Mercury did a lot more than I expected.

It answered questions, like: "Is anybody out there saying Miles is alive?"

"No," the air screen squeaked. "The two memorial services are still scheduled."

I made a mental note to adjust the voice. "Are you sure?"

"It's 98.043% certain. All available data on the OuterNet has been analyzed."

"What about Izzie Cardinale?" She was still on my mind, even though I was so worried about Miles. I'd fantasized a bunch of times about getting in her pants. There was this one show where she played this evil bish queen of an intergalactic empire that was going to nuke this planet of cuddly little animals that never did nothin' to nobody. Only it turned out she was in some kind of trance, and it actually was her mother making her think that way. And the queen breaks out of the brain daze and kills herself and her mama.

I'm not telling it right. I mean, there's a lot more to it and everything. But point is, I'm right inside that Izzie girl's skin, every time I watch her. No other actor ever does that to me. And sing! Voice like a frickin' black angel.

The air screen told me there wasn't no news about her, and then trilled with an incoming call. Up popped a holo of Nadia. "Where the hell have you been?" she asked.

"What are you talking about? I was waiting for—"

"Meet me at the office."

"Oh c'mon. *There*?"

Nadia looked at me imperiously. "If you're serious about assisting me, then I expect you to arrive in exactly one hour." She ended the call before I could say anything else.

Miles' New York headquarters was about the last place I wanted to go. Riding the creaky old subway, I was torn between bishing about going there and the thrill that something was finally happening, even though it might end up being stupid. The office was in this low-rise building on Third Avenue, only twenty floors high, all blue horizontal lines like one of those antique cruise ships.

It was freezing. Even my eyeballs were cold. Leaning against the building, I pulled the hood of my thin jacket so it almost covered my face. Ten minutes later, Ms. Thing showed up. She stepped out of the mag-lev up to her thick dark glasses and furs, black turban clamped over her head. Even though her eyes were hidden, I could feel acid pouring out of them as she looked me over. She waved a hand like I was a hopeless, miserable slug. But there was a tiny bit of fondness growing in her; I could sense it. This slug had her back, and she knew it.

As she walked through the circular doors, I gave her backside the finger, then followed behind.

Up on the third floor, the big main room was deserted. In the dim light, we could make out the stuff that the noisy, cocky staffers left behind when they moved out. An old "Vote for Morelli" bumper sticker, flower skeletons in dingy vases, cracked mugs with rings of brown mung inside, stacks of old books. The senator insisted that his peeps look stuff up in paper books sometimes. He claimed that some info in the digital copies had been deleted, important legal decisions that were controversial in some way. He used the deleted stuff to prove certain points on the Senate floor, to the amazed joy or rage of the other senators, depending on what side of a debate they happened to be on.

My heartbeat started going like I was in the middle of some cyclone when my little desk came into view. Almost looked like a child's—from the distant past even though it hadn't been that long since I was there. It was just outside Miles' office. I hadn't picked up any of my stuff after he disappeared, 'cause I couldn't face the memories. A petrified half-eaten candy bar, a cartoony goat toy Miles give me once to remind me not to be so stubborn, dusty picture of Mama in a little frame.

I stuffed the photo in my pocket and faced the most terrible part: Miles' space, stripped nearly bare, door wide open. Looked weird without his huge wooden desk. A holo of his wife on stage at the Met had always hovered off to one side of it. Nadia must have had his stuff packed up—before she found out he was alive. *Maybe* alive.

Nadia caught her breath. His scent was still there—woodsy pine. Just for a second, and then it was gone.

We kept walking, rounding a corner. Light streaked out of Colin's glassed-in office. Miles former chief of staff was moving around inside. Nadia rapped lightly on the doorframe. He glanced up from the box he was packing, glasses sliding down his nose. "Do I really deserve *silence*?" she asked.

Usually, he had this not-so-secret devotion thing going on for Nadia, but that day, it was edged over with nervousness. His eyes tracked to me like a big question mark.

Yeah. I don't know why the fuck I'm here either.

"Sorry I didn't respond to your calls," he said to Nadia. "But I've been trying to think of something to say that wouldn't make you spit tacks."

"Did you look at it?" Nadia asked.

Oh. So, she'd showed him the recording.

"Yes."

"And? What do you know about The Fist?"

He threw some trophies in the box from some of those yacht races that he and Miles always loved to talk about. "Just rumors. Supposedly a group of corporate fat cats that secretly control about half the U.S. Congress. Puppet-master hoo-ha."

"So you don't believe it exists."

"Haven't seen any evidence."

"Miles had some. Surely, you are aware that he was

investigating them."

"That wasn't in my department."

"I didn't know there was anything that wasn't your department."

The wrinkles in his face deepened. "I'm sorry. But he compartmentalized some things."

"Is that right?" Nadia's harsh voice grew corroded with sarcasm. "Your outrage, your amazement, that all of this has happened is truly extraordinary."

"Uh-huh. And what's Cheeta's part in this?"

"She's seen the message. Found it, in fact." Nadia said defiantly.

Colin scoured my face. "Where?"

"Um. I can't say," I mumbled. Sure, I trusted him. But I didn't *really, really* trust him.

He smirked.

Nadia didn't like that. "Cheeta knows when something's been faked, and that message was not. She's far more sophisticated about technology than most of us."

"A refugee Chav? Someone who hasn't even gone to college?"

"Anyone who would say that about this girl, *this girl*, is a fucking Neanderthal."

Shit! *That* blew me away. An impatient sigh burst out of Colin. "Well, if you really, truly believe that message is for real, you need to give it to the Secret Service or the FBI. They have equipment that is far more powerful than whatever Cheeta—"

"They have it. The FBI has opened an investigation into whether or not Miles is dead—where The Fist might be holding him." She looked at my thrilled grin. "Sorry dear. Didn't have a chance to divulge."

A hose of anger shot out of Colin. "You're just telling me about this *now*?"

"If you'd returned my calls… Anyway, there's a press conference this afternoon at FBI headquarters. I've canceled the memorial services."

"Do you know how many dignitaries you just pissed off? Do you have any idea how much time and—"

"There's no evidence that Miles was in that accident."

"I told you! I've gone over the surveillance footage. That was his car!"

"Doesn't mean he was in it," I said.

Colin shot me some deep annoyance. "She's making such a fool of you," Colin told Nadia. He picked up the box and walked past all the empty desks, disappearing through the outer door. *Was he part of The Fist? Is that why he was pushing back so hard?* Then again, a lot of people might be skeptical.

Nadia had enough on her mind. Wasn't going to bring it up. Tired lines darkened her eyes. "Well, then. That's that," she said.

I grabbed the goat. Don't think either of us wanted to see that place again.

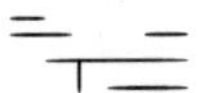

"FIND SOMETHING FOR Cheeta to wear," Nadia rasped out to Petunia when we got to the Sugar Hill mansion. "She can't go like that."

"On the double." The bot bustled upstairs.

"Go where?" I asked.

"To the press conference! Jesus! Keep up!"

I rolled my eyes.

Nadia's old stuff was way too big for me, but Petunia's tailoring skills were superfast and very exact. Before long, I had on this velvety green suit that cut in at my waistline and had a skirt that was too short. Wasn't used to seeing my legs bare out in public. Nadia thought it was posh, but I felt like I was in some historic costume.

Her eyes sliced into me. "Are you capable of combing your hair?"

As I managed to get the springy mess into a ponytail, I could hear Nadia in the salon, working her crippled voice up and down some scales. Her eyes were glassy with defeat as we got in the mag-lev, then floated down Broadway from 145th Street past shabby-plastic Times Square with all the amusement rides, then the ancient Flatiron Building, closer and closer to Foley Square, near Manhattan's bottom tip. I was so busy looking out the window that I didn't realize Nadia was staring at me until she said, "You should tell them. About the place."

Her limo had been scrubbed of surveillance cams just before we took off, but still, talking about "the place" made me twitchy. "It doesn't feel right. I mean, I think you did okay, telling them what you did. But…" Members of The Fist could be anywhere, including the FBI. If they knew about the Universe, there was no telling what they'd do with it. We both knew that.

"Alright. It's your secret." She gazed at me so soft. "I'm sorry, Cheeta. About so many things. When you hate yourself, it's hard to like anyone. Even when you love …" Tears threatened to spill from her eyes. It came back to me, that salon she'd destroyed in some big fight with Miles the night before he disappeared. I knew there had been others. Many others. But he always stuck by her, knew who she really was underneath it all. Her truest self. She'd shown him that, too. I could feel that now.

She gave me a fierce look. "What do you want, Cheeta, when all this is over—when Miles is found?"

Maybe dead but found. That's what she was getting at. "I don't know."

"Tell me." She searched my eyes. We were so close to FBI headquarters, it didn't seem like the right time. "Cheeta! Speak!"

My dream came out in a burst. "I want to go back in there. Again and again. To find messages that matter, the ones that people really need."

"Like that soldier."

The wounded soldier, so desperate and close to death. With a baby. Somewhere. "Yes. Like him. And maybe other ones from Miles." And Mercury, if I could ever find them.

"Would you take me in there again if I helped you? If I made sure you had enough money?"

"I thought it … I don't know, maybe scared you."

"The whole bloody world scares me. The point is, if I want to someday, would you?"

I grinned. Of course I would.

Mesh-like white walls loomed up before us: the Jacob K. Javits Federal Building, which towered into the sky. There was a swarm of news hounds outside clamoring to reach Nadia's limo, but they were held back by a ton of FBI security guards. Kind of a barely controlled chaos situation.

Nadia just sat there, looking out the window sadly. She put on her sunglasses and pulled her fur coat tight. Two guards opened the door. They cleared a path for us, and we walked toward the massive front door.

"What's this about?" somebody shouted.

"Speak to us, Nadia! Let's hear that voice!"

"How do you feel, after the death—"

We got inside the stone-lined lobby, footsteps echoing in the silence. As an elevator shot up the floors, I could almost hear Nadia thinking, *How can I do this?*

"Fuck them," I said. She looked at me in surprise. "So your voice sounds different. It's what you say that counts."

"But the truth doesn't win. Right?"

It was like she transported us back to my place, right before I took her into the Universe, when I said that. "I guess it does sometimes. I mean you believed me, in the end. We got to try for it. We've got to fight for Miles. Right?"

She hid her nervousness below a layer of determination as the elevator doors sparkled open.

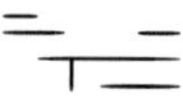

I'D BEEN TO a few pressers with the senator, and as far as I could tell, Nadia's went about as good as it gets. She sat front and center at a table with the FBI deputy director. Yeah, her voice was snarly and broken. The reporters went crazy over it at first, until Nadia gave them something that made their jaws drop. She and the FBI guy just let out some sketchy facts: Senator Morelli was believed to have been abducted, not killed, and an investigation was underway. Anyone with even a nanobyte of information about what happened should contact the FBI immediately. She left out the part about The Fist, at least for the time being, although the FBI did know. The agency peeps thought it might make the search harder, if The Fist knew they were on to them. That's what they said, anyway.

The reporters were hungry for a lot more, couldn't ask enough questions. They were still shouting them out when the FBI deputy director led her offstage.

It was a crazy scene when we made it back down to the street. Journalists were like dogs foaming at the mouth, harassing Nadia with shouts for more answers. The guards made a human wall, pushing them back, threatening to fire their guns at the news drones hovering around our heads.

We were only a couple of yards from the car when I saw a guard reach into his pocket. He was inches from Nadia. Just a small plastic tube was visible in his hand. Could have been nothing. But there was a deadness on his face as he looked at her. He raised it just enough for me to realize that it was an injector.

I shoved Nadia as liquid shot out of the tube, thin as a needle. Fiery heat exploded through my chest. I fell. My head socked onto the cement.

11. SHAKE

Luscious in the Limelight

IT WAS ONE thing for me to produce a show about a dangerous space race. It was another to actually be in a situation similar to those risk-crazed jocks, hurtling toward Ceres and then on to Mars. I wasn't in space, but that thrill was there as a car dropped me in front of a baroquely decorated apartment building across from the Museum of Natural History. How this evening would end was anybody's guess, but it could be death defying. So I'd rehearsed my role in the potential fiasco with Jarat about fifty times.

The street was bristling with cops. Two of them read the I.D. data in the air around me and cleared the way as I headed toward the building. It was the main home of my mother's bestie, the pop star Sosha, along with her private-investor husband, Chris.

Memere had told Sosha what was going on shortly after the meeting between Mikhail and the *due famiglie*—as I was starting to call the Cardinale and Ellington clans. The two women confided just about everything to each other. Sosha had learned long before about Charismites, and she was devastated when Tristan and Izzie disappeared.

My mother had complained to Sosh about the party idea I'd suggested back at the Ellington compound. Jarat had made it a lot more elaborate. The whole thing was based on our certainty that Tristan and Izzie had been abducted, not killed—that they could be used as powerful mind-control tools. The attackers had already tried to take Lush once, when they attacked the Ellington biodome and snatched Tristan. So now, we were serving her up as bait.

Needless to say, the trick was to make sure they didn't get her. Instead, when they tried to do it, we'd get some very important intel about who they were, and their ability to mask their identity. It was the first step in rescuing Izz and Tris.

Memere's vehement objections had been completely outvoted. She was horrified that Sosha not only was excited by the plan but wanted to host the party. Memere argued that this would be a high-security risk. Who knew what would happen to the extraordinarily valuable penthouse where Sosh and Chris lived for a large part of the year? Luscious was making a public appearance for the first time in decades.

But in the upside-down world of famous Elites, the whole idea was sexy to Sosha. Her life was so pampered, so cushioned from any kind of danger. It would be the most thrilling event of the season, if not the decade. Besides, we'd make sure the place was armed to the gills, right? After repeated arguments, the pop star wore my mother down and she finally relented.

Sosha had an excuse for the party in mind: a celebration of Petra's twentieth anniversary as head of Nuhope—a major feat for any media executive. Didn't matter if Memere was about to get kicked out, along with yours truly. Didn't matter that we were about six months shy of that anniversary date.

It wasn't lost on any of us that Sosh and Chris's luxurious pad would lend the party a super-privileged insider glitz. Aside from the massive security, the key to it all was a carefully disseminated rumor that Luscious and Jarat Ellington would be there. We still didn't know who the enemy was. Yes, we'd all heard Nadia Morelli's announcement and accusations about

The Fist. But there were all kinds of bad actors out there. The Fist was just one of them—if it actually existed. Maybe the opera diva was delusional. Hard to say.

The lobby was teeming with security guards, who cross checked the guest list with my I.D. data again, and I zoomed up an elevator. A bot servant greeted me with champagne in the foyer, which had a very high glass ceiling. I'd been a frequent guest there as a kid, when Sosh and Chris's two boys were my playmates. The twins were a few years older than me, and great fun. Now they were off on their own.

I passed through a couple of rooms that were usually filled with some of the finest musical instruments and recording equipment known to humankind. Scattered among them were climate-controlled transparent cases containing memorabilia from Sosha's heroes: Jay-Z's first Grammy award, a John Coltrane sax, and even more precious: a violin from the early 1700s once owned by Antonio Vivaldi. That evening, they had all been stored away elsewhere in anticipation of the possible havoc.

I remembered my sister at age five, staring in wonder at them all. Seeing her entrancement, Sosh helped train Izzie—how to use her voice, how to play various stringed instruments. They were inseparable in those early years. Memere got a tad ticked when Sosha backed up Izzie's idea of going out into the world and performing professionally, Charismite magnetism be damned.

In the end, the two friends loved each other too much to stay angry. You never would have known the feud had even happened. Now I found them in Sosha's dressing room. My mother was far from pleased, looking at herself in the mirror. Her glittering silver hair was accented by a deep red gown. The bodice was made out velvety rose petals, frozen in time by a preservative. And the holographic skirt sprayed down her like a red waterfall, hiding and exposing her legs and stiletto silver air slippers flirtatiously.

Not to be outdone, Sosh was wearing an evening gown with holographic fabric in a heavenly lapis lazuli blue design shot through with veins of white and gold. The pop star's hair was an old-brass color, sweeping up two feet into the air above long black eyes that were lined with Kohl. The skin of her fingers and arms rippled with holographic tattoos in a lacey, zig-zag pattern.

Now in their sixties, the two women hadn't beaten back the effects of aging completely. Sosha was more Rubenesque than she'd been in earlier years, and Petra was slighter, more delicate now. Watching them together, pecking out little words of encouragement and jittery dismay made my heart swell up.

"This dress was a bad idea. I don't want to fuck anyone," Memere said.

"So what?" Sosha said in a voice that always had a little snarl underneath.

Memere gave my tuxedo an approving once-over before asking, "Should I change?"

"Nah. You're stunning."

Memere brushed back some hair that had fallen across my forehead to see if any trace of my wound remained. But it was gone. If she lost another kid, she'd probably go completely bug nuts. I grinned at her with a look of rock-solid confidence. She shot me some cynicism.

When I reached the huge main living room, Chris was welcoming the guests. Waiting in the receiving line, I admired his European elegance, standing there in his pewter-colored tuxedo, curly black hair artfully arranged on top, Swiss-German accent tinging his words. He was physically smaller than his wife but could hold his own in any debate with her—usually by laughing. Which is why I gave him a sotto voce "Thank you for agreeing to this." At the unspoken reference to his wife's insistence, his eyes brightened. "Why fight it?" He glanced around at their elegant belongings. "Besides, none of this really matters, when you stack things up on the priority list of life. I love you guys."

A crush of rare fragrances intensified as the room filled with a mishmash of guests: well-loved megastars that owed their fortunes to my mother in no small part, glamorous socialites, Nuhope's most senior executives who were still loyal to her, and techno rock geniuses who were Sosha's personal friends. They chatted away, casual and lighthearted as they watched the doors expectantly to see who would come in next.

The walls were usually noisy with multi-billion-Americo-dollar holographic masterpieces of streaming color. Audio components triggered when someone came near them—everything from dogs barking on a rainy day to the piercing screeches of steel wheels. Now, they had been removed, just like the musical museum pieces.

"All set?" I murmured into my mobile.

"Yes," Mikhail replied from his hiding place. He was in a guest bedroom, watching everything from micro cameras and other sensory devices brushed into a layer of transparent paint in the rooms where the guests were now milling about.

I traded hellos with various people, making sure that everyone knew I was there before my real work began. Across the room, a cluster of people swarmed around Jarat, excited at his rare appearance. I found a quiet corner of the room to take in everything a little more clearly, wondering which guests might be connected to the abduction.

Ginseng Childe came up to me. "Here's someone who

will give me a straight answer." Nuhope's former head of news was wearing a sleek tux that brought out her chiseled, Native American features. She was now flying solo as a journalist, putting out her own reports on the OuterNet whenever she got a hot story.

"What do you want to know?"

"Are they part of the militia?" She directed my gaze to three humanoid waiters refilling everyone's glasses as soon as they emptied. They were dressed like old-fashioned butlers, in white bolero jackets with black bow ties, but their seven-foot height and bodybuilder physiques were not the usual party-staff-support sort.

In fact, the waiters were part of the highly trained FBI security detail that Mikhail had provided. There were several other members of his crack team of humanoids crowding some adjacent rooms, ready to burst in at a second's notice. Mikhail had forgotten to inform his superiors they'd gone missing from the Washington H.Q. (Oopsie!)

"You can never be too careful at an event like this," I said.

"Uh-huh. Don't bother to tell me she isn't here already." There was no doubt who she meant by "she." Ginseng knew what Luscious felt like, having been on the "inside" at Nuhope when the Charismite nearly died of a Juice overdose about twenty years before. She was probably the only one alive who could remember what really happened behind the scenes, other than family members. "I'm not here to blow anyone's cover. Just looking for a little off-the-record info."

"Yeah, you're right." Luscious had actually arrived a few hours before and was secreted away on the top floor, carefully guarded in a little room away from the hubbub as she awaited the time to appear.

"Why would she do this after staying away so long?"

I shrugged. "My mother means a lot to her."

"And your sister."

"Sure." I didn't like the direction this was headed in. I started to take off.

Ginseng blocked my path. "Why don't you tell me what's really going on?"

"She'll appear before you—"

"The other part," Ginseng whispered in my ear. "That Izabel is a Charismite—or *was* one, if she's no longer… you know."

A cold trickle ran down my spine. "Who told you that?"

"No one."

"Tell me."

"It's just a very well-educated guess."

"That would be a very dangerous rumor to spread around."

"I'm not going to. Come on. Your mother has trusted me for years. I thought you did too."

Yeah, but that trust only went so far. "Gotta go."

It took a lot of effort to tamp down my annoyance as I crossed the floor, trying to look happy and relaxed as I traded a few "hellos." Three minutes later, I was in Chris's mahogany-paneled study. The murmurs of guests below were so faint I could hear the sound of my pounding heart. Chris had a piece of art on the wall in front of his desk that he hadn't bothered to clear out. Admiring it now was steadying: two young white stallions on a white sand beach, front legs raised high, whinnying in ferocious play-fight—a brilliant blue sky behind them. I was ready to rumble in a much more serious way.

Jarat strode in, frowning in concentration. "You ready for this?"

"Yeah."

I'd never seen him look so posh. The man I loved like a father was born an Elite, knew all the graces that went into a social event like this—so he was wearing a classy suit that accented his athletic build. But his rugged face seemed out of place—the look of a man who'd spent years living in the country in self-imposed isolation—not polished by the skin enhancements favored by most Elites.

"Here you go," he said, handing me a little plastic box, about an inch in length and half an inch in width and thickness. It was what he called his doohickey, a device he'd inherited from a genius friend named Thom, who passed away long ago. It could make people become invisible. Without any form of instruction to go by, it had taken Jarat time to learn how to use it—and then a lot more time to figure out how to make a duplicate copy. I'd cajoled him into finally letting me use the dupe that evening—reasoning that two invisible people were actually needed. But even now, standing with him there in the study, he looked like this might be a big mistake.

We'd practiced so many times. It took lots of trial and error for me to get down the hand gestures that triggered the device to unleash a combination of quantum tunneling and reverse electron imaging. That caused me to not only become completely transparent but also pass through objects. However, I was under strict orders from Jarat not to go through any walls or bump into people if I could help it. When that happened, the device let out a strange slurping sound that startled unsuspecting people nearby.

"Just stick to the periphery of the rooms. That's the best way not to collide with anyone, needless to say," he said.

"Got it. About that other thing… How hard do I need to grasp somebody to make them go invisible too?"

"Not that hard. But firmly. Proceed with caution on that front."

"*Ai, ai, mi capitán*!"

Jarat gave my humor the stink eye, then we went through the elaborate hand gestures needed to become transparent and descended to the main living room. The reddish hue on several faces signaled that the guests were now on a multi-cocktail high.

My eyes gravitated to a young star whose auburn curls were piled above her head. She searched the room carefully like a queen contemplating which country she should conquer next. Only a month before, I'd overseen the production of a romantic comedy that she was starring in, and we nearly kissed after the last take. The heat between us had made me think about her repeatedly ever since. Was she looking for me now? Was her attraction to me solely motivated by the quest for a new leading role that would add to her already formidable list of credits? Why did I even need to ask myself that?

Her eyes alighted on a producer that I knew vaguely. His liquid brown eyes turned down a little at the outer corners, and he moved across the floor with a dancer's grace in his hand-tailored black suit. He glanced at Aurora, then moved on. Her eyes were gemstone bright as she kept searching.

My mother and Sosha sashayed through the wide main door arm in arm. They weren't the most dazzling, among all those gathered there. Too seasoned for that, but bad-ass to the core. They owned that evening. A cheer went up at the sight of them. Memere looked gay and confident. No one could detect the traces of anguish I'd seen that morning, brought on by long nights of trembling hysteria, imagining what was going on with Izz and Tris. It seemed like everyone was waiting to pry her open with questions, and I could sense her girding for that. She was immediately surrounded by a crush of well-wishers.

A short distance away, a woman with a jumble of stained teeth scarfed down a mound of canopies on a little white plate. A sticky sweet odor came off her stuffy business suit. She was dressed like she had imagined this would be some kind of office party, and flicked back yellow corkscrew curls from her tiny eyes as she gave Sosha a worshiping gaze.

Most everyone invited had asset portfolios worth at least ten billion, or they were well on their way to that. The odd duck was probably an assistant standing in for her boss. I watched her flit from waiter to waiter, taking food off their trays with a tiny fat smile. She bumped into one of the bots. A wine glass on its tray fell. Its reflexes were lightning fast, but while it caught the glass mid-air, red wine splashed on her white blouse. She dabbed at the stain with a napkin vigorously as the waiter dashed off to find some cleaner.

I dipped behind a little partition separating the service kitchen from the main room and tossed back a flute of champagne on the waiter's abandoned tray. Coming back out, I spotted Memere talking to a thin man with a polished face, brown hair gelled back, dark eyes devouring her. I recognized him in an instant, though we'd never met: Hans Larssen, Petra's ex-husband from long ago, before my time. He'd gained enormous fame as a space tumbler, someone who danced in various places around the Solar System, his acrobatic, graceful moves attracting huge audiences.

Memere had a thing for space dancers. She'd raked in billions of advertising bucks off their acts. But Hans had *really* gotten to her. And he didn't like whatever she was saying now.

As she walked away, Hans gave her an "I'm not through with you" look. But Memere was pointedly oblivious, filtering through the guests, air kissing more than a few. Were any of them behind the Charismites' disappearance? I studied each one in turn, looking for some expression, some clue about that. *Nada*.

The room filled with more gorgeous, artfully dressed

guests. A few worked at Victory Star, Nuhope's main media rival. Would any of them hire me? Might be fun, to produce shows there—flipping ol' Wanza the finger whenever my shows bested her own. Then again, did I really want the same old gig?

"How you doing?" Jarat whispered, voice coming out of thin air.

"How did you know where I was?"

"When you picked up the champagne."

"Shit."

"My bride is on her way."

Though Luscious was nowhere in sight, the air tingled even more than before, on my fingers, my lips. Everything sharpened. The guests grew livelier, stimulated by the Charismite's energy as she got closer—maybe in the elevator now, maybe crossing the hallway floor.

"Ready for anything," I whispered back.

"See you around." I sensed Jarat drifting off.

Sosha glided gracefully through the crowd, the train of her glowing blue dress shimmering behind as she made her way toward the long line of windows framed with silky white drapes. A musical chime played a series of chords from Sosha's latest hit tune. And the guests began to clap excitedly.

Everybody went hush as the pop star stared out at them from the center stage area. "Hello! I see we all got our glam game on," she said in her trademark snarl. Everyone laughed. She waited for it to die down. "Long, long time ago, there was this girl I knew. She was starving most of the time—needed enough money to eat one day, hungry for recognition another, feeling like a shit-head pretender all the time. She scratched out a living in clubs, couch surfed like crazy all across Europe, sang, sang, sang herself into a new style, a new sound. Most people she met thought she was nothing but rich U.A. trash.

Even though her parents kicked her out without an Americo long time before. Then this skinny kid talent scout came up to her in a Berlin club about 3 AM one Sunday, strung out on too little sleep. The scout saw deep into the singer, through all the rawness, all her awkward crap. And she changed the singer's whole damned life. So they grew up together, and held fast to each other no matter what happened, no matter who else came or went in their lives."

Tears were on the verge of spilling out of Memere as Chris hugged her, and everyone clapped.

"But here's the thing," Sosh continued. "Even though I'm throwing this bash to celebrate that kid's twenty years at Nuhope, I don't think any of us believe that she stands a chance of staying there. So, this celebration is also about what's up ahead for her, after she leaves Nuhope. Whatever that might be. Because she won't fade away. You can bet your sorry asses that I wouldn't let that happen. The world needs her; we need her. Because she has a nose for talent and entertainment like nobody else. And what really turns her on is getting to the core of what's true for all humans. So pay attention, all you media types. Get ready to line up if you want this mega-power in the shape of a very sexy woman. Because she's all about studying her options. And if she don't join any of you, she just might grab everyone's attention with a brand new venture."

Memere laughed. "What?!"

"Well, you should think about that, if you haven't already," her bestie said.

"Oh c'mon!" someone groaned. "Do we really need another media company?"

"Yes, we do!" Lush's voice rang out. Everyone gasped as she walked across the room toward Petra and Sosha with a gap-toothed smile. Her countrywoman look that I'd only ever known was gone. No more heavy boots for gardening and hikes, no more rain slickers and faded shirts. She glided through the crowd in a flowing green gown, matching air shoes, honey-fire hair circling her head and shoulders, skin glittering. Shit. She had always been like an aunt to me. But now even *I* wanted to get her in bed. She'd definitely taken a lot more Juice than the usual amount.

"I think we all know what's going on at Nuhope, now that the RDA is in charge." The Charismite looked at the guest who had groaned. "You don't want another media company? Fine. Let this nation go back to the way things were. Let your children and your children's children get their info and all their entertainment from a company that twists their dreams. No other media company can ever become more powerful than Nuhope. We all know that. Unless somebody shows up who really knows how to fight against it."

I could see it in their shining faces, how everyone was remembering what Lush had once done—a starlet working at Nuhope who had riveted the whole world by explaining in a holo transmission how Nuhope was controlling their opinions, and what they did. She'd even confessed that she herself had been shaping their thoughts because of her extraordinary charms, thanks to some chems.

So yeah, they knew what Lush was, even though no one put it together that Izzie was a Charismite, too—except for Ginseng, Sosh, and Chris, who were on the inside, and maybe members of the group who'd snatched Izzie, if they were there. Charismites created a kind of blind spot in most people; they just couldn't "detect" them unless they were told.

Questions were on everyone's faces. Was Lush manipulating them in some way now? She was reading that too. "Oh, fuck a goddamned duck," she said. "Yes, I'm hepped up on chems.

But only to help you to see what's going on, and what Petra Cardinale just might be able to do. Maybe that's a brand new company."

Chris was riveted by what Lush was saying. Sosha watched him closely. She was no slouch in the glamor department. And yet. Chris squeezed her hand reassuringly, then called out to Memere: "You do what you want. But if you were to start a company—well, I'll be the first to invest in it."

Petra's cheeks flamed with a new energy I hadn't seen in a long time. Everyone clapped madly, captivated by this new-business idea. Off in the corner, the assistant with the big teeth was pulling at her curly hair.

CRASH.

The windows exploded as a small army of bots blasted into the room, brandishing DirecWep guns, which emitted heat-sensitive infrared beams that could slice through Jarat and me. The invaders were around ten feet high and resembled giant spiders that had extremely powerful tentacles—like the ones that took Tristan. Four of them raced toward Lush, while the others brandished their weapons at anyone who even thought of intercepting them. But the guests were confused and too frightened to do much of anything.

Lush stood up gracefully, with a fearless, mocking smile. Her powers didn't work on humanoids; she couldn't do anything to control them. Not that it mattered, because as they lunged for her, Lush vanished. Everyone screamed—amazed and spooked.

I exhaled in relief. Jarat had reached her and made her invisible. If all was going according to plan, they were racing to a side door. Whatever slurping sounds they made, passing through guests, went unnoticed amid the shrieks. Everyone stampeded toward the exits. The infrared laser sights on the bots' guns searched the crowd wildly, trying to find the

Charismite. But Jarat and Lush managed to elude them.

"NOBODY MOVE!" one of them roared. As frightening as it was, I nearly laughed. Whoever programmed them was clearly into old crime shows. Everyone else froze. The bots pushed their way through the crowd. "WHERE IS SHE? WHERE IS LUSCIOUS ELLINGTON?" I made my way toward Memere as the waiters and Mikhail's other twenty bots poured into the room with their own guns.

One of them shouted, "Get on the floor!" The partygoers bumped into each other as they quickly lay down. DirecWep laser fire ripped the air. I got closer to Memere, sticking to the room's outer edge. I had no intention of getting fried—or detected. I made a note of as many faces as possible. Which of them was behind this? Hopefully Mikhail's cameras were picking up clues.

I'd almost made it to Memere, who was sprawled on the floor—nearly an arm's grasp away. Her head was turned on its side, and one of the invading bots kicked her hard in the face. There was a crack, and her nose was suddenly bent in a way that left no doubt it was broken, maybe her left jaw as well, given the point of impact. Blood streamed out of her nostrils and from her sliced cheek.

"Where is she?" the bot screamed.

I'd never seen hate spew out of my mother. Scared as she must have been, she managed to get out: "Fucking slime tech." The bot tried to kick her again, but in the second that took, I reached Memere, and she disappeared. I clutched her in my arms, racing out the door and into the stairwell. People stampeded down the stairs in front, behind and through us—guests along with residents from other apartments in the building who'd felt and heard the blast—everyone screaming in terror and confusion.

Outside, honking mag-levs, screaming police cars, and firetrucks descended on the building. A crowd gawked at the huge hole in the side of the building's top floors. I walked straight through the mayhem to Memere's limo, parked two blocks away. Her bot, Geoff, was waiting beside it. "Okay, now," I said. At the sound of my voice, the bot opened the door. Half a minute later we were flying down Central Park West, watching a small army of NYPD mag-levs tear through the air toward the mayhem.

I let go of Memere and she re-materialized, as did I. "Crikey!" said Geoff, looking at her bloodied face from the front seat.

"How bad do I look?" She pulled up her air screen and put it in mirror mode.

"Like a bunch of kindergartners got at you with Halloween makeup," I said.

"Geoff? Are you going to be able to patch me up?"

"You may look like dog's breakfast now, but nothing I can't handle."

Had to wonder if Geoff would need to crack her nose in the other direction to get it straight again. That sure would hurt. She reached for a first aid kit in the back seat compartment, and I helped her apply some spray to stop the bleeding and keep the swelling from getting any worse. The more her face emerged from beneath the red, the more I realized that she was exhilarated. This was a woman who had masterminded ten-thousand action and suspense productions behind the scenes over her career, and she was now a star in a real-live production.

"We did it. We really *did* something!" she said.

I was thrilled, too. We weren't just victims, weren't just biting our nails waiting for any new move by the attackers or the FBI. Who knew how effective this whole fiasco might be. Who knew how long it would take Mikhail to analyze his recordings—and maybe find some clues—or if this would help us save Tris and Izz. But right now, Memere and I were on fire with excitement.

"At least no one was killed," she said.

"You do know how to give things a positive spin." She let out a laugh but then grimaced at the pain. "How about we get your face fixed and head off to the beach house for a week or two?" I asked, referring to her place in the El Central Treasure Zone. A little surfing for me, massages with hunky dudes for her, lots of super fresh fish, time to heal.

"Oh no! We can't leave now," Memere said. "The publicity is going to be frickin' phenomenal."

12. CHEETA

Rocked by the Rak

MY BRAIN WAS a marshmallow. Nadia's fuzzy voice: "Back here… Now." Opening my eyes was an awful idea. Numbness all over. Slippery fabric under my fingers. A sheet? Not mine. Where…

Nothing.

Cold metal BING, BING, BING. "She's coming around," a man said.

Light. Ceiling. Nadia's face lurched in front of me, surprised and relieved. She shot a stink eye at somebody I couldn't see. "She looks awful."

"If you think you hired God, you're sadly mistaken, dear."

"Given your gargantuan fee, I expect God. And don't fucking 'dear' me!"

"Apologies. But this requires patience."

Fingers felt my right wrist, lifting it up. Pain like a knife sinking into my skull. Groaned.

"Petunia, another one," the man said.

Stinging heat in my neck. "*Hijo de puta!*" I rasped. Sudden pain in my throat when I talked.

"That's right. Let it out." Must be a doc. "Just needs a second to kick in." Piercing bright eyes probed my own coming from computerized pupils. Allowed him to magnify everything. I wanted some of those someday. "Get your bearings. Then try moving your head again."

Didn't want to. Squeezed my eyes shut.

Sniffling, howls of fear. Nadia. Couldn't let her be that way. Not hurting so much now. Shit, the drug they gave me worked fast. I opened up and saw Nadia again, frightened about me—*me*! Petunia was there too, looking pretty worried, for a bot.

The man's eyes dimmed, and I could make out more of his face. Reddish beard, warm brown eyes. Like Uncle Franco. I felt like puking. An Elite. Not my uncle's voice. But still, it was too close. I couldn't stand him. Couldn't stay focused. Down, down—and out.

Nadia was the first thing I saw when I woke up again. Her mouth curved up in an unsure smile. Because smiling was a foreign idea for both of us. Ever since what happened with Miles. Once we'd been tigers ready to tear each other apart, but now we wanted to tear apart everything between us and him.

"Anything?" I asked.

She knew what I meant: after she made that press announcement, did anybody come forward, were there any tips about Miles and that frickin' prison? She shook her head "no."

Nothing. Here I was, feeling like a building had landed on me, and we were still at square one. That hurt more than anything. The smell of roses made a pang well up in my throat. Only one place I knew smelled like that. The bedroom where I stayed just after Miles rescued Mama and me—until Nadia made Miles kick me out of their house. Pink upholstery, pink rug, pink drapes. Probably still had Goddamned pink toilet paper in the bathroom. Jesus! I wanted my beat-up, dirty place in Queens so bad.

"You almost died. You almost died saving a has-been star with a voice like a pathetic clown," Nadia said.

A has-been who knew how to get whatever she wanted better than anyone. No one wanted Miles back more, not even me. I didn't need to say it out loud. We both knew. So all I said was "Crazy." My voice came out in a croak. "Wow. I sound worse than you."

"That's saying something." Now we really were smiling. "You had tubes down your throat for a while. That's why."

I moved my head and realized the doctor wasn't there no more. Pain exploded in my skull. As soon as I groaned, Petunia rushed over and hit me with some stuff in an injector. The chems shot out of the tube. Stabbing heat in my neck. Only took about thirty seconds for the World War Four in my head to disappear. "There, there, there. Right as rain," it said.

"How long have I been here?" I asked.

"Six days."

Jesucristo! Was LiZee still alive? Maybe she broke out of her tank and ate the flies buzzing around the window. But it wouldn't be enough. "Got to get home."

"Oh, no you don't." Petunia went over to a table and picked up my big orange and black girl, desperate to slither free.

"LiZee!" She scrambled out of Petunia's arms and jumped on my belly with all fours. "Ooosh!" She was so heavy.

"Ms. Nadia found your apartment keys in a pocket and retrieved her," Petunia said.

"You're kidding me."

Had a suspicion that Petunia did the carrying. But I wasn't going to call Nadia on it. Ms. Thing was too busy adjusting a feather boa on her shoulders with a flourish. "Couldn't let the ugly thing starve."

"Starve? She looks like a little pig."

"I've been feeding her live bloodworms," Petunia said.

They were so damned expensive. LiZee had always got the cheap freeze-dried kind. "Looks like a whole lot of them."

"She kept staring at me with those beady eyes."

"You got played, Petun—" Couldn't go on, because my eyes spotted another surprise: my old IBM on a little wooden table.

"You see? Absolutely no reason to leave." Nadia was so damned smug.

"How did you know to bring that?"

"The way you looked at it when I visited," Nadia said. *Visited?* More like an invasion, the way I remembered it. With tea instead of guns. And I took her into the Universe. Now, her eyes were so warm and teary. "Stupid fool! You should never have saved me like that. All those years, I had you so wrong. Had Miles so wrong. I really thought he was betraying me with that… that thing." A whore. A sex toy. That's what she thought about Diana—the red-headed bot that raced out of the house. The one Miles and I built together in the basement.

"Not what you think."

"Is that right? Then what's it for?"

"I don't know. I thought we were just having fun building it—giving it all these super computing skills." Now that fun idea seemed lame. *What had Miles been up to?*

"So where is it? I'd like to have a chat."

"Yeah, well so would I. It just took off. On the day." I told her about Diana jumping over the garden wall like a frickin' pole vaulter without the pole.

"Since when does a humanoid just leave?"

"I know. The only way it makes sense is if Miles told it to do that." *Why? Where was it?* The same questions were on Nadia's face.

I blinked my eyes a few times to see if Mercury's mobile lens was there. A screen popped up, but it wasn't the usual welcome page with the picture of LiZee I'd put on it. "It's a new one," Nadia said quickly. A wave of panic rose up in me. "Don't worry." She pulled something out of a pocket and handed it to me: the old lens case. "We needed to throw inquiring minds off the scent," she whispered, like we were in some kind of spy thriller.

Everything was so trippy: Nadia and Petunia grabbing LiZee and the IBM out of my pad, then taking a lens off my eyeball while I was comatose and putting in another one. My mind backed up a few steps. "What do you mean by 'inquiring minds'? Who are you talking about?"

"Some detectives keep dropping by. Very government issue," she said sourly. "They want to know where you found that message. I gave them a song and dance about spam in your junk folder."

"Did they buy the act?"

"Well! I am known for certain abilities," she said proudly. I pumped her for some information about my little near-death experience. She told me that the slimeball that blew that poison stream into me had been killed just after I went down. The FBI ID'ed him as a small-time hood. No connections with any underground organizations like The Fist—not that anybody knew anything about it but rumors, supposedly.

Over the next few days, I asked Nadia about Dr. Bright Eyes. Turned out, he was one of the world's foremost authorities on poison substances. Nadia had him flown in from Dubai to take care of me. That did it. I had to stop thinking that he was like Uncle Franco. When he came by again, I tried to get past it by asking him about what had made me so sick.

"You were rocked by the Rak, as I call it—Raktonium-348."

"What's that?"

"Similar to Polonium-210." *Whatever that was.* He saw me roll my eyes. "It's an extremely rare substance. A type of radioactive isotope. Alpha particles were released in your body."

"So, I got radioactive poisoning."

"That's right. Almost did you in. There are only faint traces of it in you now, and you should continue to recover completely. My work is done. But!" His face darkened. "You have to take it easy. Give your body time to recover."

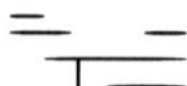

I FINALLY FELT good enough to walk around, but going downstairs was a painful experience—painful to my ears. Nadia was always playing the piano, trying to run her ground-glass voice up and down scales. I stayed in the awful pink bedroom and did some research. First, I tried to figure out where Diana the humanoid had gone, tapping into government surveillance recordings. I had Miles' passcodes for that, so it wasn't too hard. But *nada.*

Next up: Mercury. It didn't take me too long to hack into the security system at the flea market where I'd met him. I downloaded holo images of the two of us talking together about the lidar head, then his terror when he got accosted by those meat-wad pseudo guards—Liver Lips and the other one with all the chest hair.

It came back to me, what Mercury said about them in that old garage: "They'll probably find me. And if they do, I don't know if I can get away."

Who the hell was Mercury, anyway? I'd found a little on him before, but not much. I blew up the flea market security camera's view of his face and tried to do a facial recognition search. Same stuff on his last position at Cloud Forest, the server farm. But then the screen pulled up a few holos of Mercury standing beside his wife, a big old girl named Octavie. Her hair was all sprayed out around her head and glittery. The snap was about ten years old, off the BlueAngel social platform, where a lot of middle-aged women yakked. Turns out, everybody that was friends with Octavie called her Tavee for short. She was some kind of hair specialist based near L.A. Mercury had this kind of far-off look of happiness. At that point in time, he had this high-end tech design gig—sort of like what I wanted to get one day. But then Octavie passed and Mercury kind of dropped out of sight for a while.

I came to a news item about Mercury from a few months back. It was on the AZCentral news site based in the Phoenix Treasure Zone: a picture of him in some hospital bed. I've seen dying homeless men that looked better than he did then.

The story said that there was an explosion at the server farm that banged him up something good. An asteroid landed on it. I kind of remembered something about that. Talk about crazy-ass bad luck! Apparently, after Mercury was in the hospital for a few days, he disappeared.

I called up an aerial view of the server farm. It was kind of a boring white building that spread out about a mile through parched, tan desert. Looked like someone had used the east end of it for bombing practice.

"That's some strange shit," I told LiZee. She glug-glugged like she totally agreed. Seemed about time for me to do some strange shit of my own. I put on Mercury's lens, got really still, and was sucked into the Universe of Lost Messages.

There was no reason to think I'd actually find anything useful. There must have been millions of bubbles in there, and everything that came at me was old spam, or boring messages from strangers sent to other strangers that didn't mean much. "Mercury Douglass!" I shouted out over and over. Nothing. So I tried "Senator Miles Morelli!" Again, *nada.*

"Cheeta Lucida LaVera!" A few bubbles swerved by that I'd seen before. An old one from my flea market friend Barston that

I never got. A bunch of spam from tacky clothing companies. (Why the hell had they targeted me with *that*?) I shortened my name to "Cheeta LaVera" just in case the "Lucida" was throwing stuff off. Way, way off a pinprick light moved, not in the regular straight line like the others, but spiraling, getting closer and closer. It looked all fiery, like something terrible was inside. My heart was banging like a hammer as the bubble stopped right in front of me. I cupped it in my hands, afraid it might burn me. But the flames disappeared. And… and… I gasped. Finally. This was really something!

13. SHAKE

Scraggily Ball of Fury

NEWS ABOUT THE attack at Sosha and Chris's penthouse didn't let up for days. It was the stuff of gossip-hound dreams since it involved some of the world's most posh gazillionaires and celebs. The appearance of a reclusive legend, Luscious—who seemed to miraculously disappear just as some hulking bots tried to grab her—heaped a whole lot of spice on the sensational platter. So did shots of the apartment building. Looked like somebody bored a black cave into its top floors.

Did that extremely expensive and destructive party trap actually yield any clues? Our inside-FBI man, Mikhail Toure, wasn't answering his mobile. Which drove me bug nuts.

I tried to keep my head down and tend to *Space Ace*, but my thoughts were constantly cut through with a zing of fear about where my sister was now. And Tristan. The possibilities, of what the abductors wanted the Charismites to do made for sleepless nights. Where the hell were they? We had to find them!

I tried to clear my mind one Saturday with a long hard run along the Hudson. Caught my breath on a pier jutting out into the pewter mass of water filling the deep fjord—which was what the Hudson really is, not a river. That's where I was when a twittering on my mobile announced an incoming message from Mikhail. About time! He was calling a virtual meeting, which included everyone in the *due famiglie*. Everyone, that is, except the two members that had been snatched.

I made a dash for my apartment and entered the metaverse chat room. My holo was the last to arrive. The excitement in my mother's eyes was striking, and a bit odd. I hadn't spoken with her in a while, and something seemed to be going on there. Mikhail looked shaggier than before, with a stormy cast to the folds under his eyes. He stood before us, leaning on his air cane, in a replica of his living room, which was filled with plastic boxes and tired suitcases.

"Jeez Louise. It's been twenty years. When do you plan to unpack?" Jarat asked.

"I just do it on a need-to-use basis," Mikhail said. Guess he didn't need to use a lot. "Sit! Sit!"

Our holos settled into chairs, and Mikhail told us that he'd been working well into the nights, analyzing the recordings of the party. He pulled up a view of it. "Take a look at this person." He enlarged the dorky young woman that seemed like somebody's assistant. "Keep your eye on her."

He zoomed out for a wider view. The dork pulled on her curly hair as Chris said to Petra: "You do what you want. But if you were to start a company …"

The invading bots exploded through the windows. And we could see the dork motioning to them, directing them to take Luscious and then attack my mother—similar to what we'd seen with Geneva in the Ellingtons' field.

Memere was stunned. "Who the hell is she?"

Mikhail froze the recording on the woman's face. "According to the party records, she is Sophie Devereaux, a niece of Simone Burgess."

"Okay. Well, I did invite Simone. Is this intruder really who she said?"

"No."

"The planning team should have caught this!"

"Don't blame them. She covered her tracks quite well. Chose a disguise that exactly duplicates what the real Sophie Devereaux looks like. Had some bang-up fake I.D. data points swirling around her."

Mikhail reversed the recording, then zoomed way in on the Sophie impersonator, down, down, down to a magnified view of her skin. Like gangly golden strings woven together, set against the darkest black, like the void between stars. "If the skin cells were normal, they'd look vaguely like the froth on whipped milk—interconnected translucent beads, but oblong in shape."

"So what are we seeing?" I asked.

"Some kind of technological layering, camouflaging the person's actual skin. I can't dig down past it to the real human. I figured I might find the same thing if I examined the footage of that Geneva person in the field with Tristan—and Izabel's friend, Prill. The recordings of them aren't high rez enough for me to tell, but I want to bet it's the same masking." He zoomed back out to the dork's full body, and we watched as she raced for the elevator and took off.

"Sounds like you don't know what the tech is," Lush said.

"No. Not yet. And that's not the only mystery." He showed us a recording of the exterior of Sosh and Chris's building. The Sophie impersonator dashed out and disappeared in a crowd of people in the aftermath of the blast. "There is no surveillance footage that shows where she went—or who she became when the mask came off."

"But you will. Find her," Memere said, voice smooth on the surface, enraged beneath.

"That's the plan."

"And there's no connection with what happened to Miles Morelli?" I asked.

"Not finding any, so far. We can't make that assumption. Plots to abduct well known people happen more frequently than the general public knows, and there are a lot of bad actors out there."

Sure, I knew that. But my gut was getting more and more suspicious that whoever snatched the senator had also taken Izzie and Tris. *Maybe*.

"Let's get back to the camouflage. There's got to be more we can find out about it," Jarat said.

"I'm with you on that, my friend," Mikhail said. "Drop by my place, have a look at what I've got."

Jarat said he'd be right over like a dog greedy to gnaw on a meaty bone. And with that, we all dispersed.

Memere called me directly thereafter. There was that excited look on her face again. "I checked in with Sosha several times. The building's coop board is off-the-charts with outrage. But she and Chris are fine. They were ready for anything before it happened."

"Including *that*?"

"Well, all bets were off. They knew that. Anyway, whatever repairs their insurance won't cover I plan to pay for."

"If they let you."

"Listen, I've been thinking…" she said, the light in her eyes growing brighter.

"Uh-huh?"

"That ludicrous idea someone suggested. The one about starting my own media venture."

"Yeah. Ridic."

"Yes. Too much work. Makes me tired just to imagine it."

"With you on that. And like somebody said: how could you get enough funding?"

"Yes, Chris was very kind to offer some. But that would

only go so far. Still, it could be amusing to chat up a few people, see what they think. Before we bury the idea completely."

I could have pointed out that this discussion had quickly evolved from "I" to "we." But why quibble? Besides, asking a few questions on her behalf didn't mean that I was going to get involved in the long run. The restlessness I'd been feeling about what to do with my life might not ever be satisfied if I just rode shotgun beside her at some new company. Not that I knew what to do.

What would it hurt, to help her a little? And maybe, just maybe, I'd find some clue about Izzie and Tris when I talked with a few people. It would make us feel like we were moving forward, instead of waiting for Wanza to bitch-slap us some more.

Memere went on: "I'm thinking we lead with the idea of an independent production house that would provide content to various media companies. So, we wouldn't compete with them—just help them."

"Yeah, but … Do Nuhope and Victory Star actually need indie producers? I thought they did everything in-house."

"Exceptions can be made if the shows are compelling enough." And if the indie producer happened to be someone like Memere, with a powerful track record and connections, no doubt.

After the call ended, I took a shower, knocked back a fruit smoothie, and contacted a few people to set up some coffees and dinners. Then I had a long meeting with my *Space Ace* team. To the untrained eye, it was a typical Saturday.

I had an immediate response to one of my invites from an old family friend: Patience Dubois, who ended up being my "date" for that evening. She hadn't been at the party and was eager for a first-hand report. Patience was an octogenarian who was once a celebrated beauty. She was crowned Miss America over half a century ago and married one of the wealthiest men in the U.A. If anyone would back Memere's possible newco other than Chris, it would be her.

When we entered the four-star eatery, La Poire D'Or I had to deal with something new. I was used to triggering sour reactions when I stepped into high-end places, with my blotched Chav skin—until people realized who I was. It had taken some time, when I was younger, not to feel cowed by that. But I developed an arrogant swagger and sense of humor to counteract it. After all, I was just as smart, just as well educated as the lot of them, if not more so. But the stares in that restaurant were full of questions and the thrill of scandal. Patience and I both enjoyed it as I navigated her fragile body past the tables and aroma of truffles.

We entered a private dining room, and a thick red velvet curtain dropped in place, separating us from the crowd. "Well!" Patience said in her smoky voice. "That was certainly stimulating. I haven't had looks like that in decades."

Just then, all hell broke loose at the restaurant's entrance. "M'am. M'am! You cannot go in there!" said a raised voice.

"SHAKESPEAR CARDINALE! WHERE IS HE? NOW!"

Patience chuckled in delight.

"Excuse me a moment," I said. The diners looked aghast and secretly amused as I made my way toward the entrance. My cheeks would not obey a mental command to stop flushing. A scraggily ball of fury struggled against a couple of waiters as I reached the maître'd.

"Do you know this person?" he asked.

"No."

The angry mess became a scrawny girl-woman, who lunged in my direction. But an oversized busboy did an intercept, locking the stranger under one arm like a gorilla with a football and headed for the restaurant's foyer.

"*Hijo de puta*! Put me down!" The stranger kicked and beat at the busboy, knocking a few chairs in the process. The sweating hulk heaved her out the door.

By the time I made it outside, she was in a heap on the sidewalk. She forced her trembling arms to lift her torso up and shoved back scratchy dark hair from her face, staring at me defiantly.

I'd been trained to look at people clinically, to assess how they might come off on screen. And that affected all my first impressions in general. Even the most statuesque, sexually charged beings had ceased to make my heart bounce about like a ping-pong ball. I tried to think of them as commodities, a way for Nuhope to attract attention, and ultimately revenue.

The raw creature before me couldn't hold a candle, not even the spindly birthday-cake kind, when judged against the average showgirl. There was no doubt she had been born a Chav, given that dusky skin, bitten-off fingernails, and hungry edge. But I could also tell that she knew how to swim in the Elite "pool," given the cut of her suit and what looked like a new pair of air slippers. As she took in my cold expression, the similarities in our Chav/Elite backgrounds seemed to slide back and forth between us. If she wasn't such an annoyance, I might have been curious.

"What's this about?" I snapped.

"Do you want Izzie and Tristan back or what?"

My world went still, soundless. *Tristan?* Izzie was one thing. There were all sorts of cons who claimed to know where she was, looking for a finder's fee from Memere and me. But hardly anyone on the outside knew about Tristan.

"If you really know something, then of course. But making

a scene in a restaurant like this is not the way to do it!"

"If you accepted my frickin' messages, none of this would have happened," she yelled.

I winced. People near the front of the dining room were probably enjoying the street theater. "For God's sake, cut the volume," I said.

Tears shone in her eyes as she returned to a normal voice. "The damned doorman in your building wouldn't even let me leave a note."

No sense getting into my spam filters and security protocol back at the apartment. "And you are…?"

"Cheeta LaVera. I used to work for Senator Morelli."

The skin on the back of my neck prickled. "Okay." I did a quick data search on my invisible air screen. The mug shot of her checked out. Morelli's former assistant. Got in a kerfuffle outside the FBI's New York H.Q. after that press conference about the senator. She'd nearly died.

Maybe she was in camouflage, like that corkscrew Sophie imposter. And Prill. And Geneva. But my instinct was telling me "no." I zinged with the possibility that there actually was a connection between the senator's abduction and the Charismites.

I desperately needed to know whatever this Cheeta person had to say, but I needed to get back to Patience. "Can you give me a minute?"

Someone coughed. Patience was in the doorway, weaving a little. "Don't worry. I'm leaving." The excitement was taking a toll. And I could tell by the softly determined look of her jawline that there was no sense trying to save our dinner.

I took Patience's arm and gently guided her down the steps. "I'm so sorry. This idiot's behavior is completely—"

"Call me tomorrow, darling. I expect a very, very good story."

Some kind of soothing reply came out of me, with a vague hope that a *good* story would actually be possible. Still wanted to talk to her about Memere's production company idea. Her limo swooshed to the curb. "Are you going to be alright?" I asked.

"Of course."

As Patience flew off, I managed a stiff smile for the Cheeta person. To her credit, she looked embarrassed. "Well then. Let's go across the street," I said, nodding toward the ever reliable if somewhat gritty Old Towne Bar.

"No way." She let out a piercing whistle and a swank Mercedes pulled up.

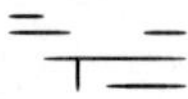

I'D BEEN TO a fair share of old-money New York homes. But I'd never been to the Morelli extravaganza. There were only a few dim lights in the massive brownstone's windows. A blue and white U.A. flag hung limply on a tall silver flagpole in the front yard. Two lethal-looking secret service agents stood before the front door. And snipers on the rooftops of nearby buildings gave the scene some added bristle.

Cheeta got out and headed straight for the house like she'd been there a million times. I trailed behind. The door sprang open and a matronly four-armed bot emerged, tsk tsking at Cheeta. "There are very tall waves coming ashore right now," it warned as we stepped into the foyer.

Cheeta looked up the massive staircase, shouting "I didn't have no choice!"

"Do not EVER steal my ride again!" rasped a disembodied voice.

"Jesus. I just borrowed it. Are you going to come down here?"

"NO!"

"Fucking bish," Cheeta said softly.

"WHAT DID YOU JUST SAY?"

"That I love you. Bish."

"HA!"

Cheeta turned back to the humanoid and me. "Shakespear, this is Petunia. Petunia, meet Shakespear Cardinale."

"Pleased to meet you," the bot said. "Care for something to drink? I'm afraid there's no Châteauneuf-du-Pape in the cellar, but we have a lovely 2023 Bordeaux."

So my tastes been researched. And probably a lot more. Right. "That's fine."

Petunia ushered us down the hallway to a massive sitting room dripping with masterpieces: weird, fanciful characters on a blue background, which I recognized as a Kandinsky, the purple-blue tornado of a Mitchell, next to the swarming black and red splatters of a Pollack. On and on the paintings marched along the walls, extraordinary work from another time.

This was the home of a man who stood for principles more associated with another age as well, someone devoted to maintaining a humane government. It was a place for heady conversations. It was easy to imagine Morelli talking with dignitaries sitting on those white cushy chairs before the massive stone fireplace, strategizing ways to push their agendas forward on the Senate floor, all of them glancing at the door from time to time like children waiting for a fairy princess. I envisioned a young, sprightly Nadia Morelli emerging in the doorway, ready to entertain them all with a song, or amuse them with stories about her latest theatrical escapades.

The one peculiarity in the room was Cheeta, who stood out like a scratch on the skin. She glared at me, then moved to a bar in the corner, pouring herself some water and downing three glasses in quick succession.

Petunia glided in with a bottle and poured me a glass. At another time, I would have enjoyed the ruby liquid, but the circumstances were so strange it might as well have been weak tea.

"There's something you got to see," Cheeta said. She activated an air screen in public-viewing mode and pulled up a holo shaped like a sphere. Inside was the thin face of an older man with bushy black hair. Like someone homeless. Or a prisoner, which he clearly was.

The misery in his wet-bright eyes made me die inside. Senator Morelli. "Oh God."

"Watch." Cheeta swiped the holo screen. The view widened, and Morelli began to move as the camera revealed his whole ragged body, which couldn't have weighed more than ninety pounds. Nearly everything about him contradicted the countless images I'd seen of the senator over the years, always so robust, with a hero's sheen. Now he looked around his cramped cell, terrified. The walls were streaked with brown matter that may well have been dried blood.

"This gotta be fast," said somebody else in the holo. Sounded like an older man, off camera.

"Cheeta," Morelli said in a broken voice. "This message needs to reach Cheeta LaVera." A wave of pain seemed to hit him, the way he doubled over, panting hard.

"Easy now. Easy now," said the other man.

The senator looked in the camera, mouth opening and closing with dry little clicks. "There's four of us, far as we know. Izabel Cardinale—you probably know who she is—plus a friend of hers, a guy about eighteen or so. Name's Tristan."

"They got this powerful gift. Call themselves super charmers," the other one said.

My heart was pounding.

"This place is run by…" The senator gave a quizzical look at whomever was behind the camera. "What's her name again?"

"Celeste. Celeste Sidhar."

"That's who you need. She's part of them…"

His expression filled with horror. Then the holo message evaporated.

"Play it again, please," I said. So she did, then played it three more times when I asked her to.

"Who's the 'them' he mentioned?"

"The Fist."

A chill ran through me. The Fist was a powerful and vicious group, if rumors were true. Closely tied to the RDA. It wasn't mentioned during Nadia's press conference. They must have held that part back. "Who's the guy behind the camera?"

"Mercury. Mercury Douglass."

"How do you know?"

"It's a long story."

"For crying out loud. Show him the other one," a harsh voice said. Nadia Morelli stood in the doorway, looking markedly different than she had at the FBI press conference, when she was a bit ravaged but presentable. Now her hair was pulled up into a ratty French twist, black velvet robe reminiscent of hag characters that showed up in cheesy metaverse games. But there was no denying the sanity in her harsh eyes. "Show him!"

Cheeta pulled up another holo: Miles Morelli again, telling his wife that he was alive, that he had failed to tell her about the secret intelligence he'd gathered against The Fist. The group was trying to pry info out of him about where he'd hidden it.

It felt like someone had twisted my stomach and stomped on it. What incriminating evidence did the senator have on them? Would they kill him for it? Looked like he was already at death's door. Was that what Izz and Tris looked like now? *Where the hell were they all being kept?*

Nadia Morelli's eyes were so black, trained on me. So were Cheeta's. Like two crows.

Cheeta pulled up another holo, of a woman with long, lilting eyes. Someone of East Indian heritage, I guessed. "That's the bish. Celeste Sidhar." Was she the body-masked person that impersonated that Geneva person? Maybe Prill, too? The Sophie imposter at the party? There was something secretive and taunting about her. A snake's head in the undergrowth.

"Now that we've laid so much bare, perhaps you could open up a little," Nadia said.

"What do you want to know?" I asked innocently, although I had a good idea what was coming.

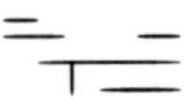

AFTER I GOT back to my place in Hudson Yards, I couldn't sleep all night. Finally sent an urgent chat room invite at 7:30 AM the next day, which was as long as I could wait. By the looks of her holo, I'd jarred Memere out of a dead sleep. But Mikhail, Lush, and Jarat were alert. I told them everything, and then got to Nadia's big ask: she wanted to know why Mercury said that Tristan and Izabel had a "powerful gift"—that they were "super charmers."

Nadia and Cheeta refused to give me a copy of the messages—or any new ones that emerged—unless there was some kind of explanation.

"I can't make up some kind of story," I said.

"No, lying isn't a great way to start a relationship," Memere said.

"They clearly know how to keep a secret, but that's no

guarantee," I said.

Everyone agreed we had to take the risk. By the time we exited the chat room, I was tasked with inviting the Morelli duo to a gathering as soon as they could make it up to Pompey.

A black sleep took me over about 9 AM. Would have been out for a long time, if it weren't for the sound of my sister laughing. At first, it seemed like just another one of my dreams about her. Had them so frequently. But no. My eyes flew open. I shot up and looked out the window, which was fifty floors above the pavement. It gave a view of the gray Hudson and the strip of park down its side. People were coming out of the park in droves, nearly getting killed as they evaded traffic along the old West Side Highway. I quickly realized they were running toward the sound of Izzie saying, "Hey! Sorry to drop out of sight like that and cause such a fuss."

I raced to the other side of the apartment and looked out the long line of living room windows, facing east across Midtown and Chelsea. Izzie was on wallscapes covering the sides of at least twenty-five buildings. It was unusual to see such a wide wallscape "roadblock" in one area of a city.

Izzie was sitting in a white room wearing a white dress, looking weirdly demure. She hugged one knee. Her gray astonished eyes stared directly out, as if she could see each person who was watching. "It was totally jacked up for me to disappear like that for so long. So first off, I want to apologize—and also let you know that I'm okay. Nothing happened to me. Nobody took me anyplace I didn't want to go. I'm living the sweet life, my people! Yeah, I was a bit dramatic about it, but you know how I roll."

I flipped on my air screen and looked at a remote view of the Nuhope News control room, which included a whole mosaic of newsfeeds. Each one showed people on the streets in New York, Los Angeles, Paris, Nairobi, Shanghai—every major market across the globe, it seemed—all of them gazing with goo-goo eyes at Izzie's holo. Later I found out that the roadblock involved ten-thousand wallscapes. Data researchers estimated that seven-hundred million people saw them in the first half hour alone—people who couldn't look away, couldn't focus on anything else.

Izzie went on, "I had to get away because of my mother. Petra Cardinale is part of a political party that I can't believe in. Just can't! Yeah, I know that sounds harsh, but the Independents have been devastating to the U.A. over so many years."

Izzie would never say that.

"My mother just doesn't see it. She doesn't get that I have to think for myself now, not just blindly believe whatever she says. And as much as I love her, I just had to break away from her—break away from everybody and really think about what I believe in."

The camera view flipped to a holo of the U.A. president, Tippi Pavlarona, sitting with Izzie in a modest room, surrounded by smiling children—so wholesome. Tippi's hair was tightly curled against her skull, tall frame set off by a crisp red shirt and blue pants. The veep, Theowanza Newton, came into the room with a plate of cookies, wearing an electric blue suit. She sure loved cookies. As the veep handed out the sweets, my sister laughed at something she said. Usually, Izzie made a barfing sound when she talked about those two politicians. All we could hear was her voiceover: "I'm so thankful that the Independents lost the presidential election—that Tippi Pavlarona and Theowanza Newton are in charge of the U.A. now."

The view flipped back to Izzie in the white room. She leaned forward, hand on chin, like she was confiding something to a close friend. "We really need them. Because there are signs—

big, big signs—that the Earth is about to be attacked by an exoplanet. It's called Kepler-22b. I know that sounds ludicrous. Like some cheesy sci-fi. But believe me, this is real. That asteroid that fell out near the Phoenix Treasure Zone? It was sent by Kepler-22b. An exploratory mission. NASA and the Department of Defense know a helluva lot more than they're able to say right now." A tear glittered down Izzie's cheek. "I'm so scared! The world needs strong leaders to protect us, to lead us through this. We are so, so lucky that Tippi and Theawanza are in charge now!"

The holo went back to the little room with the kids. Wanza stepped out of view as Tippi and Izzie continued talking without sound. Izzie's voiceover continued: "And frankly, we don't need to be dragged down by the Chav any longer—the way they're constantly looking for more handouts they don't deserve. Tippi and her good friends in Congress will keep them in check."

Yeah, I'm sure they'll do that.

The camera focused on Tippi, who looked straight into the camera. "I'm so pleased to have the support of Izabel Cardinale. I intend to help our great nation, our precious world, protect itself from any possible invasion. We must move forward together, as peacefully as we can."

Izzie reached out and took the president's hand. "Helping the whole world! I love that." She cast her gaze directly at the audience again. "Well, that's about it. Again, I'm so sorry about the disappearing act. I'll come back."

The holo vanished from all the buildings.

So the RDA wanted to stick it to the Chav, disrespect Memere, and protect us from an alien invasion? I didn't even know there was an exoplanet where life had been discovered in any form other than what amounted to gelatinous algae. And some quick data searches on Kepler-22b turned up "no known life forms" again and again.

I had the strength to resist Izzie's powers of persuasion, to see how ludicrous this was. But other people watching couldn't do that. Down in the streets, the crowds looked chaotic, their cheers full of patriotic terror.

Someone was on a megaphone, shouting: "Fight back! Prepare to fight the invaders!" More and more voices joined in. "Fight back!" "Izzie! Izzie! Tippi! Wanza! Tippi! Wanza!"

My knees nearly buckled. "Oh God, Izzie. What did they do to you?"

14. MERCURY

The Hydra Head

EVERY TIME I got back to that prison's command center, I was so scared that my heart nearly knocked out of my chest. Didn't want to know what would happen if I got caught. It took about ninety seconds to get there if I really booked it. And that wasn't easy, because it felt like I'd been sideswiped by a hover truck—limping real bad, bruised up by those arachnid bots. Plus, I was fuzzy-headed from a lack of enough water and food.

Even so, I'd been there a few times and made some progress trying to figure things out. For instance, I figured out how to access a signal in that place. So I made a second recording of the senator. Then as soon as it got quiet again, I speed-limped my way to the control room and uploaded it, all in fifteen minutes. Took me days to recover.

Sure, that was progress. But not enough. The three rows of blue-black rectangles in that room seemed to pulse with secrets. I just wanted to rattle them, get them to cough up the answers to all my questions about how to get out before the senator died and the rest of us got messed-up even more than we already were. They were torturing Morelli something wicked, a lot more than the wall banging that those spider bots were giving me. The senator was in such bad shape, he could hardly talk.

At least the young ones—what'd they call themselves?

Charis-who?—didn't look that bad off. But I had a suspicion that some kind of mental ju-jitsu shit was being used on them.

I just had to figure out how to access more stuff in that nerve center! My mind wasn't in a great place, lots of times. "It's just not going to happen. Can't do this!" I told Tavee in my head one day.

"Mercury C. Douglass! Don't piss in my face and call it ginger-ale. You've always been a show-off in the tech department. Get moving!"

Didn't say nothing back but felt like crying. Eventually, a kind of numb, laser-focused courage set in. Crazy fear will do that to you.

The next time I made it to the command center, I stared at everything, thinking real hard. Seemed like the long counter under the blue-black rectangles would be the control panel, but there weren't any buttons or switches. Just smooth whiteness. Only one red chair in front of it. I brushed my hand across the counter surface—heart beating like crazy, waiting for some alarm to go off. No reaction. Used a firmer touch. Nothing.

I ran my hand around the monitors, other pieces of equipment. Didn't do a damned thing. Without thinking, I sat down in the chair, and my knee bumped the counter's bottom edge. Light flashed into my eyes. Nearly fell off the seat. The rectangles on the bottom row had turned into windows. My mind did a double flip. Outside, creatures floated—huge fish that looked gelatinous, all gray with some pink and blue around the rippling edges. Black button eyes, series of round dents above their mouths. Weren't showing any teeth, which was just fine by me.

"I hate to state the obvious, but those are crazy ass!" Tavee said.

"Uh huh." I was busy looking at one of them that was

swimming upward so I could see its topside. Looked like a tadpole turned monster.

"Stay focused. What's this place run on?" Tavee asked.

I tore my eyes away from the fish and studied the slim oval shaped boxes along one part of the wall. I'd been thinking about that some. Over the years I'd read a whole lot about cases that looked like that. Seen some of them too. "I'm gonna go with quantum computing. Powering a combo of AI, navigation, and communication. This is a giant submersible."

"Wowza!"

I fooled around some more with the counter's underside. A lighted panel bloomed to life across the top surface. I got one of the monitors to show a rendering of the facility's exterior. Looked like a man-made version of a humongous manta ray but covered with tiny glowing dots. "Bet those lights are acoustic sensors, telling the controls what the hell is out there that might stage an attack, or just get nosy," I said.

Before she could say anything more, I had to beat it back to my room, only a few ticks away from the fifteen minute mark. After that, Tavee and I kept talking. "We're on the ocean floor," she said. The monitors had shown a sandy surface just below, and rocks that didn't move. "And, we're stationary."

"Yep. I figure those dots on the sub's exterior probably help it navigate."

"If this place wasn't run by an evil sociopath, I bet you'd just love to hang out here."

She sure knew me. Next time I got back to the control center, I fumbled around, and finally got one of the monitors to pull up all kinds of grid lines. Numbers rolled by on one screen, changing really fast—from zero all the way to 4,252. As in meters? I did a quick calculation. That would be over 2.5 miles below sea level. If that was the case, there would be no way to swim to the surface without lethal damage—even if I could find some scuba gear in this place.

A huge shape shot by one of the windows. *Holy crap!*

"Is that a shark?" Tavee asked.

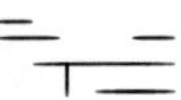

SOMETIMES I THOUGHT back a ways—before I went to New York to find Cheeta LaVera and got sent into the damned prison. One time I remembered a lot took place just after I escaped from that hospital and high-tailed it to my cousin Archie's cabin up in the Sierras. He hadn't been there in a long spell, ever since they put him in a nursing facility. Didn't have any other relatives. It was pretty safe to stay there.

I couldn't get enough of that damned Universe—finding the messages that seemed to really matter. Not just that message from the social worker in Singapore and the demented old broad with the tennis bracelet. There were three sets of lovers that wanted to get back together. And a thief on death row sent a message that gave the location of stolen art from a museum in Seattle. When I got it to the right people, the message completely absolved this museum curator whose life had been destroyed when he was accused of the theft, even though nobody ever proved he did anything.

For every decent message I found, there were thousands of junky ones. Not everyone I sought out was happy to see me. Some people thought I was a con artist and got really pissed off.

There were times I just wanted to quit the whole thing and get on with my version of normal retirement—kicking back with Tavee's spirit, doing crossword puzzles, drinking beer, watching the games—even though I was hiding. But I'd wake up the next morning and hear birds outside cheeping stuff at me. “Don’t give up!” they’d twitter. “You can help more people stop hurting from bad stuff that happened and never made sense! Or maybe you’d make them happy in other ways.” Which was pretty elaborate personification shit on my part. But you get my drift.

“There’s only one way to get this whole thing done. Release the messages all at once,” I told Tavee.

She put her hands on her hips. “How the hell are you gonna do that?”

“Get them back in the server farm and blast them out to wherever they were supposed to go.”

“You can’t go back to that jacked-up place. It’s a death trap.”

She had the description right, but I just had to try. It would involve staying away from that dragon lady, Celeste Sidhar, who I met in the hospital, and finding servers that weren’t fried by the asteroid. Plus, I’d done some research and found out that the cloud farm’s various parts were going to be scrapped in just a month. So, it was either act fast, or don’t do it at all.

In the end, the idiot angel on my shoulder won out over Tavee’s objections. I went back into the Universe over and over, recording about fifty-thousand messages at random over a two-week period. There was no time to sort out the good from the spam, and there was only time enough to record a fraction, but it was something.

I got into a dusty old Ford mag-lev that I’d bought real cheap and zoomed out of the Sierras. Made it to the server farm by 11 PM on a Saturday night. Seemed like that would be the easiest time to break in.

I cut the headlights a few miles shy of the building, zooming the Ford above the cold desert surface, with half-dead vegetation and moon-like rocks. When I got about a quarter of a mile away, I glided over a knoll and saw the huge facility glittering in the distance. Something weird was going on. The lights pouring out of it were too bright, and kind of green. *What the hellz?*

I put the Ford in reverse and went back down the little hill. Then I climbed up on foot, trying not to brush the organ pipe cacti, looming like ghouls. I hid behind a boulder, looking at the mile-long building through my telescopic air screen lens. Nothing made sense.

Ten SUV mag-levs were parked outside. Activating the magnifier even more, I could make out a U.A. military emblem on the side of one. Two dark figures walked from around the side of the building. They were patrolling the outside, and as the lights picked them up, I could see that they were military-grade humanoids wearing grey uniforms and carrying DirecWep rifles. The more I looked, the more bots I saw. There must have been about a hundred of them, all around the building. Their eyes gleamed as they looked in all directions, probably using magnifier scopes just like me. One of them swept its gaze directly towards me. I ducked behind the rock just in time.

It was too creepy. I beat a retreat and took a room in a dive motel far away, in Los Angeles, to think things over.

"You know how to find out what's really happening," Tavee said.

"Yep." Had to do with my network of microscopic cameras in the paint on the old servers. I could access them remotely and soon discovered that most had been destroyed by the asteroid. But some hadn't. Slowly but surely, I used them to look through one section of the building after another. Nothing at all interesting, just servers upended and thrown around by that blast. It was like a giant kid had thrown a tantrum in there.

The place was deserted. And one section was still intact. Hardly damaged at all. Looked like there were hundreds of servers that might be operational. All I had to do was get in there, embed the messages, and get them sent out in one giant transmission. If I could get past the security bots. I was shaking like crazy, just thinking about it. But I was determined.

Then I saw it: a scaly blue-eyed humanoid carrying a tray with a dome over it, like hotel room service. The bot whisked around one corner after another. Didn't have enough micro cameras to track it. Tried one after another after another, until I found the bot again, gliding past this big black glob that looked to be about four feet in diameter.

The bot stopped at a door that I remembered well; it led into a little room where old server parts were stored. With a few hand gestures, the humanoid dissolved the doorway, and I could see a glimpse of someone inside, huddled in a corner. Then the door sparkled shut. After a few minutes, the humanoid came back out with an empty tray.

A prisoner was in there? That proved true around 10 AM the next morning when the black ball uncurled, becoming a giant arachnid bot. That was the very first time I ever saw one of those mofos. It scurried inside the storage room. There were beseeching cries of pain for a long time, and then the monster reemerged and crawled into its corner, curling back up again.

I tried to calm down, but it was tough. Over the next five days, my mind was split. Couldn't stop thinking about that poor prisoner. Sure didn't want to end up like them! At the same time, I couldn't stop trying to figure out the answer to the question that brought me there in the first place: how the hell was I going to get the messages back in the servers?

"I may be sneaky as shit, but full-blown espionage ain't my thing. And neither is pain," I told Tavee. Maybe there was a way to get inside without getting caught and tortured by that monster bot, but damned if I knew how.

"Just keep watching," she said.

The spider bot uncurled at the same time each morning, skittering across the floor, and then it disappeared into that little room. The prisoner's weeping sounds grew weaker and weaker as the days went by.

Around 2 AM each day, a delivery truck pulled up to the facility's front door. The blue-eyed humanoid walked outside, took a box from the driver, and disappeared back inside. Shortly thereafter, it unpacked canisters of evil-looking soup and bread, put them on the domed tray, and carried it into the little room like it was the fucking Ritz Carlton. The bot went in and left so quickly I couldn't pick up much of anything inside.

Finally, one night it opened the door wide enough for me to get a split-second view of the prisoner's face. I saved an image, enlarged it as much as possible. Once it was enhanced and color corrected, there was no doubt that I was staring at someone I'd seen on newsfeeds a million times: Senator Miles Morelli—barely alive.

"Jesus H. Christ. Isn't he dead?" Tavee asked.

"Supposed to be." I sighed long and hard. "Always admired that man."

"We got a whole new game goin' on now, Hon."

"Sure do. Saving him is worth more than a million of those messages."

There was only one thing to do, as far as I could figure out: come out of hiding and pay a visit to an old tech friend in Venice Beach that was way into espionage.

The more I had studied that cloud farm, the more I'd realized that the green lights around the server farm were connected to tech that would recognize and destroy suspicious matter that was as small as a mosquito. So my friend made me a customized drone that was small as a gnat's wing.

Tech wasn't perfect, but it was good enough to fool the facility's alarm system. It didn't pick up my tiny drone when it landed on the food-delivery box the following Monday. Before long, the drone attached itself to the underside of the food tray that the blue-eyed humanoid carried into Senator Morelli's prison room.

In my sleazy motel hangout, I watched the senator's body lying in a heap in one corner as my drone surveyed the space from all angles. All the server equipment had been cleared out. It looked cold and empty, except for the senator. I made the drone land on the outer rounded surface of the senator's ear and started to talk to him, very softly. Just a little at first, to make sure that damned arachnid bot didn't detect the sound and burst in. The senator didn't react, so I made the audio a little louder. It took a full thirty-three minutes before the senator said, "Why, why, why, why? No hallucinations! No!"

"This isn't in your head. It's real," I said.

"How do I know that?"

I flew the drone to his right index finger so that he could see it, if he looked really closely. Then I told him what I knew—how the worl' thought he'd died in that car accident, how so many people were in deep mourning, how he was in a cloud farm that was about to be dismantled. But he still didn't buy that I was real.

"Even if that's the case, what do you have to lose, talking to me?" I asked.

His hacking laugh sounded like somebody scraping the bottom of a garbage can. "Point," he said. "But why bother coming here?"

"What if I make a recording, a message, and hide it someplace where nobody can access it, except the people you trust?"

"Now I know I'm crazy."

"No, you're not."

Three more horrifying days went by. Whenever the monster bot entered, its black sensor eyes flooded the room with light, minutely studying every surface, flat black tongue slithering in and out of its mouth, licking the walls for information. But it never found the drone. I watched its vicious attacks on Morelli, trying to get him to give up some secrets. But Morelli didn't give in.

I finally convinced him to let me do the recording. He wanted it to go to somebody named Cheeta Lucida LaVera. We were almost done when the spider bot burst in, grabbed Morelli, and shook him hard. "Who were you talking to? Where is she?" it asked in a metallic voice.

The senator put on a dementia act, talking back in gibberish as the bot scanned the room again. There were lights on its tentacles that glittered, and I got the sense it was communicating with someone. It knew that something was up, even if it hadn't found me. Decisions were being made; I could sense it, watching from a cracker crumb in a corner.

The bot yanked the senator out of the room, down the halls, and through the front door. My drone followed behind at a safe distance, and before it could land on him again without being detected, Morrelli was thrown into a large truck. It tore out of the server farm's parking lot. There was no way to keep up with it. And the surveillance footage I could access didn't help.

A few hours later, huge hover trucks arrived and started tearing apart the facility's interior. Thousands of servers were dragged away. Gawd only knew where they were now. Some junk heap? My whole plan to get the messages in them went bust. There wasn't no other cloud farm I knew of that used the same kind of old servers and would "talk" the same techno lingo, allowing me to dump the contents of the Universe inside them.

I was exhausted and full of despair. But after a while I started triangulating a few things with Tavee back in the dive motel. The senator had said in his message to Cheeta LaVera that The Fist was behind his abduction and he was hiding some damaging evidence about them. I'd heard rumors about that group. If it was real, it was involved in some malicious RDA subterfuge. Nobody had ever been able to prove its existence, until now.

"Here's what I think happened," I said to Tavee. "The asteroid hits the server farm. The U.A. government gets real interested in the asteroid and takes over the place so they can do some investigations without outside interference. They put Celeste Sidhar in charge of it, because she's somebody they can count on, and she knows her tech shit."

"Okay."

"Then, on a completely separate track, The Fist finds out Morelli's got a mess of information that's going to mung up their operation something good—and destroy the reputations of some powerful people. So they nab him, faking his death so that no one will try and find him. But there's a problem. They need a place to stash him where no one will look. So they take him to the server farm."

"So do you think Celeste Sidhar is part of The Fist?"

"It makes sense."

Tavee got out of her old chair and started pacing. "It's too dangerous for you to try and find where they took the senator."

"Point. But I can get that message to the Cheeta girl."

"Mercury C. Douglass! If you come out of hiding again, they'll chop you into mincemeat. I just know it!"

Maybe so, but I couldn't stop thinking that Cheeta LaVera

needed to know the senator was alive, that he could be saved. Maybe The Fist could be driven to its knees. Or maybe that was a dimwitted dream and I was ready to go on a suicide mission. Either way, saving the senator meant so much. He was a helluva lot more important to the worl' than my sorry ass. How could I *not* do this?

I'd found the Cheeta girl in Flushing, this section of Queens. It wasn't too hard to infiltrate her old IBM desktop and mobile. Kid was out of work, and her apartment looked real sad. Lost her gig. No food in the fridge. No work prospects. All she cared about was her ugly salamander, working on the IBM, and grieving for Senator Morelli. I got the sense Cheeta was plenty brave and sharp as a laser knife.

A new idea glimmered up in my mind. Maybe she not only had the guts to raise the alarm about the senator—maybe someday I could retire, and this girl could pick up where I left off and deliver all the important messages.

But my life went to hell in a hand basket after I gave her the lens in an abandoned garage and took off. An aircraft of spider bots captured me in Newark, outside the hotel where I was staying. I was knocked unconscious, and they brought me to this sunken hell.

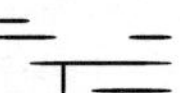

TAVEE WAS RIGHT: the thing approaching the submersible looked like a shark. But when it got closer to the outside cameras, I could see that it was transparent, with the silhouettes of people inside. So it must be a mini sub. It glided past, and there was a loud bump, like it was hitting the side of the prison. I nearly lost my balance and accidentally swiped my hand under the far right section of the white counter that I hadn't touched before. Instantly, one of the dormant, black monitors sprang to life, showing long strings of numbers and letters, one set after another, after another. It looked so random, but that couldn't be.

Were they some kind of coded message—the answer to everything I needed to know about how to get out of this place? Knew I had to get going, but my brain was on fire with ideas about how to crack into whatever the gobbledygook was saying. Tavee shouted at me, but I didn't make out her words. What the hell was I looking at? It wasn't longitude and latitude coordinates. Something el—

Cloves and cinnamon bloomed in my nose. Bald-wire fear bristled through me. Celeste's smoking stick.

"Hide your ass!" Tavee shouted. Marching feet from down the hall, and faint voices. There was no escape route. Celeste was talking to someone, a woman. Never heard that voice in this place, but I knew it somehow. The military footsteps grew louder and louder.

In a few seconds, they'd round a corner and see that someone had triggered those numbers and letters on the screen. And way worse than that, they'd see me. I touched the same part of the desk surface and thank Gawd the gobbledygook disappeared. But there were no closets, no big furniture for me to hide under.

I backed into a corner, girding for Celeste's fury and violence from the arachnid goons. The smoking clove odor was so strong now I almost choked. Through watery eyes, I spotted a small crawl space between the control panel and the wall, just below the bank of monitors. There was only about ten inches to fit into. How the hell was I going to do that? Then again, I was close to starving, so maybe, just maybe.

I got down on my knees, pushed one heel into the floor, the other into the wall, blew out all the air in my lungs, and managed to wedge into the long area, dragging myself across coils of cords and somehow managing not to unplug anything. My ribs felt like they were going to crack.

The pounding feet grew even louder. "Halt!" said the stranger. "There's hardly any room in here."

"Yes, we don't need much for the core of the operation," said Celeste, voice so near. I tried not to breathe, arms crammed into my belly. "The entire facility is state-of-the-art. We are completely invisible to the outside world, unless we want to be seen, that is."

"This place can go invisible?"

"Not literally. We do, of course, occasionally surface to collect supplies and solar energy from ships—as you just witnessed. The bots can get everything loaded in about fifteen minutes. But what I mean by invisible is that no one is monitoring this particular area underwater. Of course, if some intruder were to happen by, we do have some defenses."

What? Torpedos? Other kinds of explosives? If they were there, I had to find them. That might come in real handy one day.

"It's all very impressive," the other woman said. "But this whole operation is several million Americos beyond the allotted budget. I don't know why we had to resort to this."

"I'm sorry about that, Madame Vice President." *Holy shit! Wanza Newton! Of course, that was the other voice. I'd heard her on the news so many times.* "But you know that the server farm was only a temporary solution, until this facility was optimized. That drone intrusion made us hurry everything along, unfortunately. And there still is one annoying glitch."

"What?"

"Whenever we start to surface, the surveillance system shuts down. But we're working on it. I'm sure it won't take terribly long to fix."

"I certainly hope not."

"Excuse me," It was Darrel's voice. "Would you like some coffee or tea?"

Both women opted for coffee, and as Darrel poured, the smell of it mixed in with the cloves made me want to hurl. Somehow, I barely held everything down.

"That message from Izabel turned out quite well, I thought," Wanza said.

"Why thank you."

"I've taken the liberty of scripting the next one."

"Excellent! I was hoping we might discuss a timetable."

"I want to let one week go by and then release the new one."

"That sounds fine. But actually, I was thinking of another timetable—when I'll start the new position. Doesn't have to be an exact day. Maybe a target week, or month?"

Wanza snorted. "Don't put on your diamond tiara quite yet, my dear."

"Is there an issue?"

"Make no mistake, Celeste. We have every intention of installing you eventually. The president has been informed that you are my choice to become the next CEO of Nuhope, and there's been no pushback. But this isn't the time to schedule anything on that front."

I sensed that Celeste was leaning against the wall, just inches from me. The smoke from her stick curled through my nostrils like claws. I clenched my throat, my nose. "But that recording with Izabel is beyond viral. Off the charts! President Pavlarona's approval ratings are at an all-time high—and so are yours. The fear of an invasion from that exoplanet is electric!"

"Yes, that's a start. But I need much more."

"What would you like?"

"Well, perhaps you can explain why the two Charismites

aren't copulating?"

"That's no longer necessary. I have their eggs and sperm."

"Well, don't waste time."

"Yes, Madame Vice President."

"And how is that asinine Morelli? Still isn't talking?"

"That's right."

"Jesus Christ! Why didn't you just extract his brain? You should have done that to Jarat Ellington, too. We need that Juice formula!"

"That proved impossible. They both have memory locks."

"If you'd just found that chemical substance none of this would have been necessary! Tippi and I could have become overpoweringly magnetic ourselves!"

"I'm sorry. We searched everywhere in that Ellington house. Nothing was in storage. They must make up a batch as needed. And we couldn't find Luscious Ellington."

"Such a nuisance! How do you intend to get Morelli to talk? What's next?"

"Satan's Bed may be the answer to our prayers."

No one said anything for a minute. The coffee smell intensified. "Then there's the matter of the leak, isn't there? Somehow, Nadia Morelli found out about her husband. How did that happen?"

"That drone in the cloud farm, I believe."

"Who sent it?"

"A doddering fool named Mercury Douglass."

"Fool my ass!" Tavee said.

"He worked for the server farm. But I've captured him. He's here. See?"

Sweat dripped off me like water from a shower. They must be looking at a monitor view of my room. Thank Gawd I'd put some junk under a blanket on my pallet to make it look like I was asleep.

Celeste went on: "I have reason to believe that he knows something about all the data that went missing from that server farm. He created some kind of metaverse—a secret hiding spot where he might be keeping messages that went missing after the asteroid landed. And maybe some that he's created himself. He was spotted in Queens talking to Morelli's assistant, Cheeta LaVera."

"Did he give her anything?"

"Nothing physical, as far as we could see, but I think he showed her how to get into the metaverse. That could explain how Nadia Morelli knows so much. I intend to put a stop to any future damages."

"Brilliant. If you actually manage to do that, Celeste, then Nuhope is yours."

15. TRISTAN

Skin of His Teeth

AFTER IZZIE WAS dropped back in our prison room, she slept for a long, long time. She was completely out of energy and hope. That's how she felt when I ran my hand over her head, her chest. *What had they done to her?*

It felt like there was an enormous, bruised sky between us, filled with her secrets. Then again, we'd always been distant. Waiting for her to wake up, I remembered about how things had been a year or two after Izzie stranded me in the treehouse. She turned into a full-blown rebel, defying her mother so hard. Petra and Shake had to yank her drugged-out body from skanky dens where she had been singing with one band or another, huge crowds gathered around her passed-out body. And they brought her home from the hospital one night when the mag-lev she was racing smashed into a store. Broke one of her ribs and left forearm.

If Petra made a list of everything Izz did that drove her crazy, it would have stretched into infinity. At least, that's what it seemed like. Finally, Petra just gave up. Izzie blew up into a mega-star, started acting, got in and out of crazy scrapes. The tabloid newsers were in constant overdrive, trying to keep up.

Life for me was almost the exact opposite. I was focused downward, on what was going on in the biodome that no one else perceived. My mind and body mirrored the emotional and physical conditions of animals with greater clarity—creatures that were close by, and those I was able to touch.

Ma and Izz—the only other Charismites alive—weren't able sense what was going on inside animals. Nobody knew why I had that gift, but I didn't want to waste it. It wasn't easy; sometimes it hurt so much. But I could take it. If only I could help them heal! That became my passion.

I couldn't learn enough about medicine, visiting all kinds of health platforms on the OuterNet, although a lot of it was too advanced for me to fully grasp. I dreamed about speaking for humans that couldn't talk properly: babies and the mentally challenged. If only doctors knew what was really going on inside them.

It was clear that to get the best medical training, I should go out into the world. Remote learning could only go so far. Realizing that, I wanted to leave the dome so bad. At the same time, that idea was awful. I didn't want to attract crowds of people rabidly worshipping me, like they did Izzie. How would I ever get anything done that way? How could I *live* like that?

"You're okay in here. You're doing a lot, even if you don't realize it," Da told me. Ma thought so too. I tried to remember that. But life seemed more lonely and confusing, the older I got. Shake rarely visited anymore—first studying like mad in college and then working long hours at Nuhope. Izzie didn't come either, and even though she was a major pain, I kind of missed her. Plus, my hormones were in overdrive.

Then Celeste showed up, pretending to be Geneva. When we had sex, it was staggeringly addictive—me experiencing her orgasms as well as my own. And she was captivated with nature and how I could feel inside animals. She showed me how she got inside the biosphere, climbing through a wall crack in the furthest section away from the house. But still, I never found the courage to go away with her, no matter how she tempted me. Guess that's why she called in the spider bots.

Now, everything was upside down. I detested Geneva-Celeste with a passion. Izzie, once so wild and fierce, was a mess. I could feel her ache the strongest in the bottom of my throat. She wanted to find a way to die, I knew. But there was a tiny, quivering feather of hope underneath that kept her from that. If it had been someone else in that deeply depressed state, it would have made sense. But Izzie? She's always had so much fight.

A skill Da had taught me, how to memorize quickly, had kicked in with Mercury's visit. I'd watched the way he configured his hands when he opened the wall; it was so clear in my head. When Darrel brought us meals, it used hand codes too, but I could never catch them—the bot always had its back turned away from me.

As I watched Izzie sleep, I pulled up Mercury's movements in my mind, going over them again and again to make sure I had the memory right. Outside in the corridor, the scurrying of the bots came and went. The hours limped by. Days. There were passages of time when everything was completely silent. I began to time them, counting out the seconds and minutes in whispers: "One thousand one, one thousand two…" Usually about fifteen minutes of silence, just like Mercury had said.

Excitement and terror tore through me. What would happen if I tested the signals and opened the wall? Would those spider bots attack me like they had Izzie—bursting through the ceiling, eight legs caging her in, then snatching her away? What if Celeste actually wanted us to figure out how to get outside, to study us like mice in a maze? Maybe not. What was out there? Maybe I'd figure how to get out of the prison! Wished Mercury would come back so I could ask a bunch of questions about all this. But he didn't.

One day, I knew it was time. My heart thumped loudly as Izzie made little puffing sleep breaths. "One thousand one, one thousand two, one thousand three…" I counted to sixty, five times. No sounds outside.

Now! My fingers moved in a "Y" symbol, then an "O," three taps on the wall with first the right little finger then the left. Didn't work. I cursed myself. I must not have the memory right! Tried over and over as the minutes passed, and then it was too late. The scuttling outside returned.

It felt like a few days had gone by before the next silent period began. I tried again, using different fingers for the "Y" and the "O." Nothing. I tried to tap differently—shorter, lighter. And finally the wall vanished in one place. There was a hole right in front of me. I nearly fell over in thrilled fear. Stepping through the opening into a giant green tunnel made me feel like I was balanced on a cliff. Exposed. I listened carefully. A very, very faint scurrying, from far away. Had to keep listening, to make sure the bots didn't come closer.

How could I get the opening closed? I slipped back in the room and desperately tried the finger sequence again and again, heart thumping like crazy. It took a long time, too long, to figure out I needed to reverse the sequence. The wall solidified. I collapsed to the floor in relief, but the tension soon returned. What if some surveillance camera had seen me out there? What if they came and beat up Izzie some more? She was in awful shape. Didn't care as much about me. It was so foolish, to have risked that.

I waited, listening to Izzie sleep-breathing. Nothing. No one came to punish either of us.

Time passed. I planned my next trip outside. Izzie woke up now and then, moving around listlessly. Telling her seemed like a bad idea. When the silence came again, she was asleep. The time was right. I opened the wall and walked down the corridor, listening for the faint scurrying from very far away, counting out the paces so I'd know how many it would take to reach the wall of our room again. I reached an intersection. There were two directions I could go in, and either option led to even more intersections; I could see them up ahead, either way. Each one looked exactly the same. How would I find our room again if I went any further? Sure, I could keep counting paces or the seconds that I was out there, but would it be accurate enough?

Back in the room, my eyes landed on Izzie's largely untouched bowl of black bean soup. I could use that! Hopefully, whatever they fed us before the next silent period emerged would be dark enough to mark the walls well.

It was. I walked through the dissolved entrance with a cup of tepid tomato bisque. Dipping my finger into it, I marked the wall down by the floor in a short, straight line. As I turned left at a corner, I counted first the seconds, then the minutes in my head. During the next trip outside, I did ten minutes out and back. Then longer, fourteen. Each time I turned a corner, I drew thin arrows with some soup to show the direction back. And each time I returned to our room I erased the soup streaks by spitting in my hand and using the saliva as an eraser. Each time, I traveled a little further, girding myself for an attack, wondering if I'd see Mercury.

On the next trip outside, I reached a tube hall I'd never been in before. Electric pain shot through every part of my body. It was barely endurable. A vomit stream of words wanted to explode out of my mouth. Every secret I had was on the verge of tumbling out of me. And yet whoever was actually experiencing the pain, whose sensations I was feeling, seemed insanely stubborn. They wouldn't give in. Didn't want to die.

I tore myself away, first crawling, then stumbling down the

hall. But then I stopped.

How could I live with myself if I didn't try to do something to help that person—even though there wasn't much hope I could do much of anything. Eight minutes left. I could at least *see*.

I went back. The closer I came, the more suffering I felt, but something had changed. The overwhelming, electric shock was gone. But that prisoner was covered with festering wounds, at least that's what it felt like. And more pain inside the belly, like there was an animal gnawing at the stomach's lining.

Would not let fear rule me. Would. Not.

I dissolved the wall. The smell of rot and decay rushed out, even before I saw the ice blue, flat cloud in the air, surrounding a man's body, suspended four feet off the floor. The light from the cloud reflected off his ancient face. He was skeletal, with a long brown-gray beard, stringy hair and ragged clothes.

"Hello," I whispered, forcing myself not to react to his stench.

The man turned his head, eyes boring into me. My chest clenched up with his excitement. "Rrrr. Rrrr." I'd never felt inside a demented person before, but that's what he seemed to be. What skin I could see, on his arms and legs, was covered with sores. *Not Mercury. But who?* He raised an arm and pointed at me, excitement surging through both of us: "Ruh, ruh, ruh, ruh."

I tested the blue cloud with one hand. Nothing happened. So I reached out and touched his hand. A hollowing, burning sensation coiled out of him and gripped me hard. I looked around wildly. The squalid room was so small, and the walls were caked with blood and dirt. If only there was a sink with a rag or sponge, for starters. But there was nothing like that, only a hole in the floor with caked waste all around it.

The need to vomit was almost overwhelming. I held out the bowl of tomato soup that I used to mark the walls. "Can you drink this?" He shook his head no. The animal in his belly gnawed at him harder. "My name is Tristan. Tristan Ellington. I'm a prisoner too." Five minutes left. Had to go. Maybe just a few more seconds here.

"Ruh, ruh, ruh, ruh," he chanted.

Three minutes. "I'll come back."

"Ruh ruh!" he yelled. And suddenly the electric bed sent a charge through every bone, every muscle, every blood vessel in his body. I was filled with the violence, couldn't move or think. Something was scouring my mind. I wanted to scream long and hard. But I was frozen.

Something gripped my free arm and yanked me away from the cloud bed. Saw Mercury's terrified face as he pushed me through a wall hole.

BAM. A spider bot must have landed. Couldn't see it.

BAM, BAM. I could imagine the monstrous tentacles racing toward me.

BAM, BAM, BAM. Just around a corner. I was dizzy, couldn't see straight. Wanted to hurl. What about the soup markings? Would the bots see them? Tried to say something about it, but Mercury threw me through a hole into my room. And then he hobbled off.

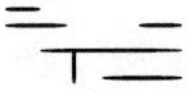

IZZIE WAS WIDE awake and furious. This from the woman who had done so many outrageous things over so many years without bothering to think about anyone else.

"What the hell?" she screamed.

"I had to. How else am I going to find a way to get out of

here?" I whispered. "You told me I'd be the one."

"Well, I was fucking wrong. Okay?"

Izzie went silvery with tears, collapsing to the floor. How the hell had they broken her that way? I reached out and touched her. A tornado of ferocious despair surged into me. She yanked away. We didn't speak again all that day, and I couldn't talk to her in a dreamisode when we both fell asleep later on. They never seemed to happen, anymore—like it didn't matter if we wanted to… A chill went down my back. Checking my testes, I could see the cut had never healed. No way of telling exactly how much time had gone by. They'd gone in there again when we were unconscious? Yes. I was suddenly sure of it. Probably into Izzie too. Though her middle was covered, no specific pain telling me if that was true. She was too upset to ask.

Mercury showed up the next time things went quiet, even more angry than Izzie had been. Which was saying a lot. "You steal a code from me and use it? And what's with the soup? Stupid ass idea." He'd found my markings and wiped them out. Luckily, no one else had noticed.

Apologies didn't do any good, or thanks for saving me by the skin of his teeth. He didn't want to hear it. "I know what I did seems idiotic. I get it," I said. "But do you know who that man is—why he's here? And why the hell are *you* here?"

Mercury sighed and sat down heavily on one of the flowered chairs. His shoulders looked caved in. I wouldn't let up: "If you don't tell me anything, then I've got to go back out there and see if there's something I can do to help him."

"Don't you dare!" Izzie said.

"It won't do any good," Mercury said.

"How do you know?"

"Because he needs more than any of us can get."

"Jesus. Calm down!" Izzie said, looking around wildly,

so frightened.

"Can't you tell us what the hell is going on?" I asked. "You know a lot more than we do. Don't you?"

That's when the old man gave in. He explained that he'd worked for a server farm in the Sonoran Desert. A place that Celeste was now managing for the government. How he had been thrown into a vast metaverse filled with lost messages after an asteroid explosion. How the partially destroyed cloud farm had turned into a prison for a very important person—whom Mercury had found and tried to help. But he was moved to this prison, and then Mercury was snatched.

"The man is a senator," he said.

"What?"

"Miles Morelli."

"Fuck," Izzie and I whispered at once. Even in my isolated Pompey world, I'd known about the great senator from New York, despised by the Republican-Democratic Alliance and revered by my parents and their friends. When Morelli was reported dead, Da had been beside himself. It was hard to match up in my head: that miserable, emaciated man in the other room and the pictures I'd seen of Morelli. "Does anyone on the outside know he's alive?"

"Maybe. I got a message out through the metaverse to somebody that worked for him. The she-devil that runs this place says she'll tear me from limb to limb unless I get her into that Universe and show her how I use it. But I won't do it. And the senator won't give up his own secrets that The Fist wants. Found out just the other day that they put him on that Satan's Bed."

"Satan's Bed?" Izzie said.

"So that's what they call it." I gave Izzie a description of the blue cloud, what it did.

"I'm probably next," Mercury said. "And she's creating little super-charmers out of your reproductive stuff to fuck up the worl' even more than it already is." The cut on my scrotum prickled suddenly.

"Yeah. I kind of got that," Izzie said. *So she'd figured it out too.*

"This is high level crazy," Mercury said. "Wanza Newton was here the other day."

Izzie got up suddenly, bedhead of charred red hair flaming out. "They aren't waiting for babies to do their shit. They drugged me, put words in my mouth to spread their awful garbage in a recording. I had no control over what I was saying, what I was doing!"

"Uh huh. They said something about that," Mercury said.

My chest filled up with Izzie's shame and guilt. That's what she hadn't told me. She couldn't look at me; there was no use asking for more info. Not now. I tried to stay focused. "If you've got something better than soup to mark the walls, I'd sure like to know about it," I said.

Mercury held up a thumb. The nail on it was long, at least an inch above the tip of his skin. He showed us how he made grooves in the rubbery surface, then smoothed them out.

"Wow." Why hadn't I thought of that? "Listen. The senator, he was trying to tell me something. He kept saying, 'Ruh, ruh.'"

Mercury's tired wrinkles deepened, thinking that over.

"What?" I asked.

The old man didn't say anything. Just left.

16. LUSCIOUS

The Chameleon's Skin

WHEN MY FACE hit the outdoors air it felt like swimming into a cold spring in Mirror Lake—warm one minute and then cold, all back and forth. Weeks had gone by since I started living in the bunker, the rooms that were below the ground floor of our house. Last time out was when I went to Petra's shindig in New York and nearly got attacked and taken away by the monster militia—the one that stole my son and the girl that was like a niece. It wrung my heart out, just thinking about them, but I had too much angry fight to give into it.

Jarat walked up the long grassy hill toward me, a lean silver-black wolf of a man. He had the steady, top-of-the-worl' gaze of someone born Elite, but he was different. "Jeez Louise. Look at that." He was looking dead ahead, but his eyes had picked up something way off to the side: a passel of little chickadees mobbing a red tailed hawk in mid-flight. Jarat's peripheral vision was much stronger than the average human's. He'd "inherited" that talent from a kid named Jewles, whose brain was transplanted into his head long ago.

"Maybe you better round up some of the hawks and get them out of the dome. I mean, I love it when the little guys win and all, but that's the third gang-up in three weeks." I'd been watching the fields through the monitors down below, in the bunker.

"Yeah, well I'm about to round up *little you* and get you to safety." He didn't like me outside, even though the security level of our ZoneZel-protected biodome was bristling with electric force. More powerful than it ever had been before, which was saying a lot.

"I promise. If they're not here in five minutes, I'll go back down." Had wanted to welcome the visitors we were expecting but causing him so much worry wasn't worth it.

We had enough to deal with already. Izzie's love-letter holo with Wanza and Tippi was a big clue about what had been done to her, what might come next for Tristan, too. Could tell nobody had manipulated Izzie's image in some fake recording. Her magnetism wouldn't have been that strong, if it was just a hack. That message had to be real, the way people replayed it rabidly on social channels for weeks and weeks. Usually they were on to the next piece of gossip or news in a couple of hours. Attention spans were way short. But Izzie's transmission created an endless feedback loop, and not just socially. There was an explosion of fearful news and talk show chat about an impending attack from that exoplanet, Kepler-22b, and everything else that was said by Izzie, President Pavlarona, and Veep Newton.

Tippi and Wanza's popularity spiked up to astronomical levels. Even people in the other regional superpowers—the Commonwealth of Asia, Supreme Africa-Mideast Federation, and European Republic—were crazy about the U.A.'s prez and veep now—when they weren't shaking in their boots about the freaking asteroid scare.

"Here they come," Jarat said. Way down at the end of our long drive, the biosphere's massive gate was sparkling away. Pet's limo shot up the hill and glided to a stop in front of us. The mag-lev looked like a rainbow trout to me, but my old friend wouldn't like the fish thing, so I always kept my trap shut about that.

Geoff climbed out. The bot looked like it'd just come back from about a month on a surfboard. "G'day, mates!" it said, helping Petra out. To a stranger, she would have looked like one well-kept sixty-something broad—not a strand of silver hair out of place, flaring black pants and a turtleneck made out of video fabric showing a night-sky. She had this energy that always seemed to throw off sparks of new ideas, lots of enthusiasm, and possibility. Captain of industry kind of hoo-ha. But now those sparks were smoldering inside her. Izzie had said such hateful things about her in that freaky message that it tweaked the mindset of Nuhope board members. The ones that still had a soft spot for Petra were turning against her completely now.

I gave her a hug, sending some of my Charismite glow into her muscles. "Oh my God. I needed that," she whispered.

Shake climbed out of the mag-lev. I hugged him too, feeling his heart beat rise.

A giant groan came from the car. Geoff helped out a queenly mess, the one-time opera goddess Nadia Morelli. Her black clothes made her look like a burnt-up house. And the fierce glow coming out of her eyes made it clear she could either eat somebody for breakfast or love them till they were dust in the Earth.

A twig-like girl-woman came out after Nadia. A long dark braid hung down over her baggy suit. I bet she put herself together in about three seconds flat. Had to be the Cheeta person Shake had told us about. Looked like she was trying to get her balance on a floating surface, the way she stared at me. She had a fluid sexuality vibe. Right now, I was tilting her toward the female persuasion, but it looked like she was trying to resist.

"So, you told them about Charismites," I said softly to Petra.

"We'd never make much headway if they don't know what we're dealing with."

Shake looked darkly at Cheeta and said something quiet. Her eyes peeled away from my face, a little guilty. Some energy was zinging back and forth between those two, but I couldn't tell exactly what. Hoped I wasn't wrecking anything.

Nadia glided up to me, looking like she was just a wee bit jealous of the Charismite thingy. "The world has missed you," she said.

"Guess we got that in common."

She smiled darkly, then grew cold and sharp, heading toward the house. "Let's get going." Jarat choked back a laugh as he held the front door open. She sailed through regally, and the rest of us trooped in behind.

Down in the bunker, everybody ooo-ed and ahhh-ed about how large it was. The main room was surrounded by huge holos showing everything that was going on in real time in various parts of the biodome. Black and gold koi gliding under the pond's surface. Barn swallows swooping over a tree-topped hill. The sound of wind through the leaves whished like ocean waves. It helped me breathe, to see and hear all that.

Before long, Jarat and I had served up some veggie stew with pomegranate seeds, alongside thick country bread. Everybody got in a convo about how street life was changing in New York, and a lot of other places too. Crowds of Elites and Middles were attacking Chavs—another side effect of Izzie's awful message. RDA politicos were clamping down, too. Local clinics and government offices that were meant to help poor folk were closing at a steady clip.

The Chav were my peeps. Always would be. How could they survive the next violent hurricane or wildfire, let alone all these attacks from other people? How would they pay for medical treatments when their little babies and grandpas got sick, or some poor kid took a bad fall? Seemed like there was only one way for them to make much money: join the military. Same thing that happened to some of my friends a long time ago.

"Izzie would never say what she did in that message unless she was forced to, somehow," Petra said. Which was true. Sure, Izz was wild. But the few of us that had watched her grow up knew that she would have died rather than deliver a message like that. "How did they make her do it? Any clues?"

"Not so far," Jarat said. Mikhail was trying to figure that out. In fact, our FBI friend was listening in on our conversation from the safety of his own home. Needed to be more sure of these newcomers before we revealed his involvement.

"Izzie *hates* the RDA, including Wanza and Tippi," Shake said.

"So why the hell didn't she use her charm firehose to make statements against those bishes before they were elected?" Cheeta asked.

"She doesn't have a political bone in her body," Shake said.

Cheeta snickered. "She's sure paying for that now."

Shake was ready to snipe something back, but Jarat cut him off. "Hey, hey, hey. Fact is, none of us who love Izzie wanted her to get involved with the election. We all wanted it to be fair, without underhanded mind control."

Cheeta's face went fire hot. I got up to clear off the empty plates and brushed her shoulder softly. Nobody usually touched anyone unless they were super close, but when I did it, people tended to forget that little social rule. Jarat gave me a look. He didn't miss much. Cheeta followed me into the kitchen. Together we put plates in the quick wash and slabs of my extra rich carrot cake on plates.

I gave her a short version of the love story between me and Jarat. How he'd spied on me long ago at Nuhope. How my pissed-off state about that—and his disgust at how my Charismite powers were being used by Nuhope—eventually sparked into a kind of love fire. Cheeta caught my drift and lost hope that she could ever start anything with me.

"So where you from, girlfrien'?" I asked. "I'm getting a tropics kind of vibe."

"Yeah. A long time ago. El Central Zone. Honduras." Her face had an ache to it, so I asked some soft questions to open her up more. She told me about living on the streets of New York with her mother and what Senator Morelli meant to her.

All the heart in her voice made me open up, too. "I thought things were bad when my gram died. And before that, my dad and mom. Everybody said a lot of sympathy stuff. But now—having people you love just stolen away?" Too tough to go on. Couldn't help tearing up.

Cheeta clawed at her hair, pulling strands out of the braid. "Yeah."

"Nothing I wouldn't do to get them back. I don't care if I die. I don't."

"Me too."

"And you almost did."

She took in the respect on my face. "Fuck fear."

"You're my kind of people." I held out a spoon with a little cloud of cream cheese frosting on it. "It'd be a sin to let this go to waste." As she moved in to lick it, she couldn't stop looking into my eyes, which grew more golden. It was what I called a warming of my whole system, a kind of caressing. "I gotta say, there's something about you I don't get."

"What?"

"Why not tell other people how you got those messages from the senator and Mercury? I mean, I got the sense they didn't just jump into your inbox." The girl's eyelids drooped, like someone easing into a hot bath, but she was resisting me. I kept going: "More minds on this can only help. There isn't one person here you can't trust."

My powers were weaker than they used to be, but I could still do things gently—coax people into saying things, doing things that they normally never would. All it took was a little of my sunshine on their tight little flower heads. Cheeta probably wouldn't realize what I was doing with the warming at first. Might take days before anything changed in her. But I was there, inside her now.

We went back into the other room balancing plates of cake on our hands and arms, passing them around. As everyone dug into the spicy sweetness, Shake darted a silent question at me. I shot back a "mission accomplished" smile.

Jarat cleared his throat. "I'd like us to be a team now. One team. With one goal."

"You will have our complete cooperation," Nadia said, as if she was in the cast of some kind of law-and-order show. She flicked a questioning glance at Cheeta. The girl nodded yes. "I assume that FBI detectives are assigned to Tristan and Izabel's case?"

"Yes, of course," Petra said. I could almost feel Mikhail smiling at that as he watched through our camera.

"Cheeta? What can we tell them?" Nadia asked.

The girl just paused for a tick, then pulled up a holo of a man, maybe sixty years old or so. Like Cheeta, he seemed like a kind of cross between a Chav and a Middle—sporting a kind of pressed-clothes, worker-bee tech look. He was too dark-skinned to have been born into the Middles class.

"This is Mercury Douglass. The one who made the messages." She gave us a little background on Mercury but dug in her heels when Petra asked her where the messages had been found.

My warming still hadn't quite caught hold. Petra was about to say something to Cheeta, but she caught the look on my face. Wasn't going to do no good. She could see I had something up my sleeve.

"Well now, is it time for your portion of the show and tell?" Nadia asked, a little too brightly.

"Yeah. I've been doing some research," Jarat said, pulling up a holo of Celeste Sidhar. She had the kind of heavy eyebrows that could either look super ugly or hot. And hers were on the sexy end of the spectrum. High cheekbones and eyes turned up at the corners made her look like an old-time glamour girl. So did her long dress, made of some chiffony pink substance that fit loosely yet showed off her graceful body.

Even so, "She looks sad, underneath it all," I said.

"Probably is. She grew up in the Republic of Europe's state of England. Parents died when she was twelve. Apparently, some kind of nasty food poisoning they contracted while vacationing in Phuket."

"Yeah, I found out about that," Cheeta said. "Convenient that she wasn't there when they died."

"Well, she was only twelve," Jarat said. Cheeta shrugged, as if that didn't mean much. Shake smiled. Jarat kept going, using a lot of intel he'd gotten from Mikhail, and some stuff he'd found out on his own. "She inherited about fifty billion Americos, which was in a trust until she turned twenty-one. She went to the London School of Economics and eventually used all the family money to invest in a bunch of startups."

"Siblings?" Nadia asked.

“Only child.”

“Is she a member of the RDA?”

“No. An Independent.”

“Really? Don’t remember seeing her at any Nuhope functions,” Petra said. “Usually, Independents with a high net worth showed up sooner or later, before the RDA took over. And if Celeste was there, I would have remembered her face.”

“Not active. And there’s nothing on the social channels to suggest she’s an ardent supporter of any particular cause or candidate,” Jarat said.

“A good sleeper agent for the RDA and The Fist!” I said.

The caption underneath the holo of Celeste told us that the picture had been taken in Èze, in Europe’s French republic, at a social event organized by Keystone. That’s a very exclusive club for fat cat technology entrepreneurs. Some people try to get in for years before they’re accepted. The only reason I knew about it was because my father-in-law, Evander Ellington, had been one of Keystone’s board members. But then he passed away.

“And you think that she masked herself to look like the hunky guy that went home with Izzie, and then she turned herself into a sexy nature girl that went after Tristan,” Petra said.

“I don’t think; I know.” Jarat threw up a holo of Tristan’s squeeze, Geneva, in the field just before the abduction. Beside it, he put another holo of Izzie’s hot friend, Prill, then another holo of Celeste as she normally appeared. “Look at the eyes.” They all had a lucid, black Indian-ancestor thing going on.

“So what? A lot of people look like that,” Nadia said. I was thinking the same thing.

“She’s got a bit of a birth defect.” Jarat enlarged the right eye in all three images so that we could see something more: a tiny white fleck on the cornea.

“So, the digital masking didn’t cover that part,” Petra said.

"Bit of a gaff, I'd say," Nadia said.

"Unless she purposely wanted us to see—like a signature. A kind of arrogant taunt," Jarat said.

Shake looked a little perplexed. And I knew why. Prill went to bed with his sister. Was it possible for whatever masking technology Celeste was using to make it seem like she had a real wanger, not some kind of strap on? There was so much we didn't know.

It looked like Shake was about to ask a question when Nadia said, "Did you come across any indication of a masked presence near my husband before he was taken?"

"No. But I'm guessing there was. There was a lot of confusion around that accident site. They could have been obscured," Jarat said gently. Nadia looked like she was drowning at the bottom of a pool.

"We've got to find out more about that digital masking technology," she said.

"There's a lead on that front," Jarat said. "One of the startups Celeste invested in was experimenting with ultrasound projections—volumetric display."

"What the hell is that?" I asked.

"Extremely advanced holograms that encase a real human. It makes them look completely different than what they actually are. Here's the guy that led the startup." Jarat waved his air screen and pulled up the holo of a balding man with light brown hair, bland plaid shirt, eyes that didn't look at the camera lens but instead stared off in a distracted way. Guys like that always melted my heart a little; they seemed so adorbs.

"Who's that?" Cheeta asked.

"Doctor Kwak. Humbert Kwak."

"What an unfortunate name," Nadia said dryly. "Where does he live?"

"Dunno. He disappeared."

"Any indication that he was killed?" Shake asked.

"Nope."

"Maybe Celeste made him really uncomfortable," Shake said. "Maybe he thought he was in danger. He could have used the digital masking to disguise himself and take off."

"There might be some truth to that. But we just don't know."

Later that night, after everybody went to bed, I tapped on Nadia's guest room door. Her muffled, harsh voice told me to come in. She was sitting on the edge of the bed, in a satiny rose robe. Her large breasts heaved—the chest that had sung thousands of arias, bringing her audiences to tears, flying them into ecstasy. And now she was a broken horror doll.

I sat on the bed and held her hand, surging soft warmth in her system so she wouldn't pull away. "There was a party once at Nuhope where I saw your husband. I mean, of course I'd seen him on the news, but in person was another thing."

"What do you mean?"

"He was with a bunch of other government types talking about this bill that would help Chav, the ones that had migrated out of regions that turned into deserts. It would give them a way to start little businesses—mom-and-pop groceries, cleaning services—just a way to survive. And they'd all pay back the loans when they got on their feet.

"Oh yes, I remember that bill."

"Looked like your husband didn't want to talk about it at the party. But people kind of picked at him, dissing the whole idea that Chav would pay anything back. And he kept ribbing them about their sorry golf games and asking after their families. All the while, the whole pack of them was looking around, trying to figure out why they were getting so excited in a sexy way. The senator definitely wasn't doing it. Then they saw me. Nobody really knew who I was then, why I was like fly paper."

"What's fly paper?"

"An old country thing. Kind of a sticky trap."

"I think you're a little more than that." She squeezed my hand, and I spread a little more of my heated honey into her so she'd feel stronger. It looked like she understood that I was doing something but not exactly what. And she didn't care.

"Yeah. Well. Anyways. I came up to Miles and asked him if he really thought the bill would pass. And his eyes kind of laughed at me. I got the sense that he loved it when there were really stiff odds stacked up against him."

"Yes, he was like that," Nadia whispered. It was so easy to imagine them together, Nadia and Miles.

"Have enough blankets?" I asked.

"Yes."

I made for the door.

"Wait. Tell me about your son." She pounded a few pillows into shape and lay back on the bed, motioning me to rest beside her. I swung my feet up on the bed and settled in. "When did you know he was gifted?"

"That chubby little thing was working people right from the time he was a month. He had this sneezy way of laughing." I felt for her hand again, zinging more energy into her, silently telling her we could find them. If we just fought like hell.

17. CHEETA

She Red

WE ALL HAVE ghosts in our heads. Angels, too. Ghost memories of people like Miles. And angels that turn up when there's no hope.

My brain was thrumming with the heavenly kind after that trip to the Ellingtons' place. That Luscious had sent vibrations through my whole body—like silent music and the stunned wonder when you first realize you're in love. All the negative thoughts about never getting Miles back were shaken out of me. And Mercury. And the two other Charismites.

I wasn't the only one who changed. When we got back to Sugar Hill, Nadia warbled and screeched for hours, practicing scales, trying to sing.

"*Jesuscristo*! She's like an exterminator. If there were any rats or roaches around this place, she's either killed them with that voice or they've split," I said to LiZee. Girlfriend was glug-glugging up on my shoulder, tail flicking hard. She could barely stand it either.

The noise drove me up to the third floor of the mansion. Could hardly hear the awful sounds up there. Looked like nobody had walked around there for a long, long time. Nadia didn't want Petunia to clean any of the bedrooms on that floor. All the stiff, antique furniture and velvet drapes were coated in black.

Even if the squawking hadn't been so bad, I probably

would have nosed around up there sooner or later. That fluffy pink bedroom gave me the hives. It had this sticky rose smell that stuffed up my nose. If only I could go back to my place in Queens! But I had to take care of Nadia. That's what the senator wanted. Plus, The Fist would probably love to finish me off, even if I wasn't the one they were originally aiming for with that attack outside the FBI office.

"I don't know," I said to LiZee after we went through all the third-floor rooms. "Even if one of these was cleaned up, it still wouldn't feel right." Not for me.

We went up the creaking wooden steps to the fourth floor. All the electricity was cut off. Light from a long, narrow window at the end of the hall punched through the black, filled with dust motes whirling in lazy circles.

LiZee dug her claws into my shoulder. "Watch it!" I said. She gave a door we were passing a freaked-out stare. Nothing different from the three other ones on either side of the hall, as far as I could tell. The music that Lush put in my blood told me to turn the knob. Soon as I did, the salamander leaped off my shoulder and shot down the stairs. The coward.

At first, I didn't know what the fuck was going on in there. Twenty tall, dome-topped tubular things stood across the floor like crud-covered goblins, each one about four feet in diameter. Walking over to the nearest tube, my right foot crunched something: a dirty broken wine glass. Looking around I spotted three other broken glasses covered with thick dust. Nadia must have had a drunken fit in there.

I brushed off some of the dirt on one of the tube things. Turned out, it was a transparent case. And inside there was a mannequin dressed in an old opera costume. Smearing away dirt on the other tubes, I found out they were all like that.

Little labels at each mannequin's feet explained what

performances the costumes were from. There was this glittering eggplant-purple gown with a sign that read: "Juliette, *Roméo et Juliette*, Gounod." Another dome beside it contained a yellow-white satiny number with gewgaw embroidery around the hem and a short orange-red jacket with the same cray-cray trim. "Rosina, *Barbiere di Siviglia*, Rossini" read its sign. Two domes over, there was a pale-pink dress with a wasp waist and full, long skirt. "Gilda, *Rigoletto*, Verdi."

They were Nadia's ghosts—memories of her greatest performances, the awfulness of what she'd lost. LiZee was right; it was pretty freaky. I got out of there.

Climbing up some more stairs, I came to an attic room, with rough beams across the slanted ceiling and one round window. Two spindly rocking chairs stood before a simple fireplace. There was a bed made of metal, too. Everything was too plain to be Nadia's castoffs. And the senator never paid a lot of attention to what he was sitting or lying on. But he'd told me about his parents and grandparents—Middles that ran a family business, a hardware store in the Bronx. Maybe this stuff had been theirs.

Cool, fresh air mixed with old soot came down the fireplace chimney. When I smeared away the window dirt, it turned out that I was at eye level with the sharp shooters on a building across the street. It was so fly!

Some of the soldiers out there were bots, but not all. Through the cold rain, I could see them stomping their feet to keep the circulation going—even though their puffy, sand-colored uniforms looked way warm.

It took some doing, but Nadia finally let me stay up there. She even had Petunia help clean it up. The bot found a table with a busted leg, off in a dark corner. After a little work, the table was good as new. Before I knew it, everything was gleaming. Petunia replaced the dirt-crusted mattress on the metal bed with another one, adding clean sheets and blankets with green and white stripes.

I spend a lot of time looking out that round window. The sharp shooters made me think about that dying soldier in the bubble. The one with the baby boy that didn't have nobody to take him in. If that man's luck had been better, he might have been out there on that roof, looking out over the rich-people townhouses on Sugar Hill. And his baby would be safe.

No way anybody would let me go meet the soldiers. But I had Petunia deliver coffee to them every morning, and a couple more cups to the plain-clothed cops that were parked on either side of the front door from 5 AM until mid-afternoon. The bot asked the human snipers some Q's and found out that they were all Chavs, and fans of the senator. They knew Nadia was the only person with big enough *cajones* to get the U.A. government to find him—and that I was the one that almost got killed outside the FBI building. There wasn't nothing they wouldn't do to keep us safe.

I dove back into the Universe again and again, trying to find more clues, but nothing. What was I supposed to do with all this super dope energy that Lush put in me?

One gray morning, when I was toasting the sharp shooters with my *café con leche,* a blaring backfire sound made me look down. The soldiers trained their DirecWeps on a bright colored hovercraft that looked like it belonged in a circus. It was weaving back and forth between the curbs. Didn't seem dangerous, just stupid. Then I saw it: a child-sized humanoid with a cloud of red-blonde hair on the sidewalk looking directly at me with tiny black eyes.

"*Hijo de puta!*" I nearly fell down four flights of stairs in about twenty seconds. It was Diana—the red-headed bot that disappeared just before the senator was abducted. The humanoid wasn't just designed to look like an athletic adult; it could shrink down into this little-girl type. The adult part fit over the child part like a case. It had been super complex to build. At the time, I didn't understand why the senator wanted the double look.

What the hell was it up to? I banged open the front door ready to fly down the steps. But the cops held me back. "You got a death wish?" one of them said. Down the street, Diana's little eyes seemed to gleam brighter, then it raced off. I struggled to get free as the bot zig-zagged between all the other people out there and disappeared around the corner.

"*Mierda!*"

I stormed back into the house and went to find Ms. Thing and give her some lip. Knew she'd ordered those cops not to let me outside. It had taken weeks for that humanoid to show up, and who knew when it would do it again. I went towards the salon where Nadia tended to hang, but the sound of her voice stopped me cold. She wasn't a Screaming Mimi anymore. Pain was firing out of her in a ragged velvet stream. She was singing out the corner of her mouth as her fingers rippled down the piano. But it sure wasn't opera.

The song was, well, buttery—the kind of stuff that old dudes played on the street. I was so caught up in her tough ache that it took me a minute to realize she actually sounded decent. Not oh-wow-that's-the-best-sound-I-ever-heard. But still, it kind of worked. She wasn't trying to get back to what she'd had: clear and over-the-top passionate. She stuck to lower octaves, smoldering with a deep honest pain. Even so, after the song ended, she bowed her head in failure.

I coughed. "That's a lot better."

She snorted. "Yeah. Now I'm up to the level of hot trash.

Why did you just burst out the front door?"

So she heard that. "Diana."

Her eyes melted with regret. She knew I was pissed and why. And I knew she couldn't afford to lose another person by letting me go out after the bot. She clenched her fists. "Shit."

"Yeah."

"Isn't there a way for that *thing* to communicate without you running off somewhere?"

"I don't know what's up with it. Just like I don't know why it ran away. But I think Miles programmed stuff I don't know about—or told it stuff." Didn't need to tell her that it probably had to do with The Fist, or that a long time might go by before Diana showed its face again.

"I fucking hate this!" She crumpled into a chair, head in her hands. How could I stay mad?

Back in the attic, LiZee was curled up on the green tiles in front of the fireplace, probably dreaming about fat worms and bugs. I made some green tea—the same kind that Nadia brought to my pad back about a million years ago. Plumping down on one of the old rocking chairs, I put my feet up on the fireplace's iron grate, loving the sooty air. The chair beside me looked really empty. I had this growing urge lately to tell Shake about Diana. Every day the volume pumped up on that mind chatter. Even wanted to tell him about the Universe. I fought off the temptation. Couldn't go against Mercury's wishes not to tell anybody about it that I didn't really trust. What would Shake do, if he knew? What if he got the old man in even more trouble somehow? Or maybe it would somehow hurt the senator. Even so, Shake seemed like somebody that I could tell, and there might be something more going on inside him, too.

Like when we were riding in the limo up to Pompey, he'd said, "Mind if I ask you something?"

"No."

"You go for girls?" The way he looked at me was like he was mentally stripping me. He'd never done that before. The sex thing came and went in an instant. His mother was watching from another corner of the limo, which was kind of embarrassing.

"I'm flexible."

"Okay, then you really need to pay attention to what I'm about to say." That's when he laid it straight down the line about Charismites, and how if you were attracted to girls, the female kind could really pull you in. "The magnetism is always stronger when you meet one for the first time. You only get used to it if you're around them a while and know what you're dealing with."

"There will be this tug, like you can't look at anything or anyone else," Petra added. She was one chill broad, even though she made a really whacked-out decision to conceive Izzie from a dead Charismite's sperm. Shake had told me about that when she wasn't around.

When I met Luscious, I kind of understood what Shake had gone through most of his life, being around Charismites. But even so, it pissed me off thinking about how he defended his sister. I mean, I was a huge fan and all. But she should have helped the Independents win the last election. Fuck her lack of politics. Nobody could afford to be neutral. The RDA fought too dirty for that. Look what happened to her! Look who was running the Goddamned nation!

Yeah, Shake could be a pain in the ass. Wasn't gonna tell him nothing he wasn't supposed to know. The only thing that made total sense was to go back into the Universe. I picked Mercury's lens out of its little case and slipped it on, going into stillness mode. This time, I had to do it different. This time I was determined to find something.

I SWOOPED AROUND in the endless orange-ness, moving faster, farther than I ever had before. Felt like a wicked rollercoaster ride, like zinging metal coins down my spine. Murmuring faces in the glassy balls hurtled by. Some trailed after me, even though I didn't say nothing, as if the holos inside were searching for ways to break out.

Man with quivering jowls was saying, "She's going to get torn up like mincemeat…"

Honey pie with eyelashes long as a ski slope: "Lost all his money. Got to find him…"

"Baby doll's got the hots for…"

Couldn't waste time. "Nadia Morelli! Nadia Morelli!" I shouted. A sizzling purple bubble spun toward me with a slick face inside. I held the bubble and squeezed. Out popped a skinny holo, saying, "That reclusive hag Nadia Morelli couldn't sing her way out of hell."

"Piss off!" I sent the holo flying, then yelled, "Luscious Ellington!" Once, twice, ten times. *Nada.*

"Jarat Ellington!" Again and again. *Nada.*

"Cheeta LaVera!" Nothing. *Jesucristo!*

"Cheeta Lucida Rivera!" Silence. I didn't have no patience for this. Who the hell was I fooling? This wasn't going to lead to nothing. Mercury was probably dead. And Miles. *Both* Charismites were probably turned into zombie mouthpieces by now.

How could we go up against The Fist? Just had to stop this. It was hard to keep from crying. But I still had a skinny thread of hope that Lush put in me. I went further and further into the endless space. "Cheeta Lucida Lavera!"

Something sparkled strangely about a million miles away. It was just a pinpoint, but it almost seemed shy and unsure. Blinked my eyes. Must be hallucinating. But I kept watching. It became a bubble, glimmering within a huge clump of bubbles. I yelled my name louder and louder. It peeled off from the pack and came toward me, so slow—almost lazy.

"Cheeta Lucida LaVera!" I cried. *Come to Mama. Come to Mama, you goddamned weird-ass!* The sphere grew larger, more steady, throwing off glistening power. It flew right up to me, hovering in place. Inside, an old guy saying very faintly: "You gotta get this." Mercury! He was boney and gray-tinged. "Cheeta Lucida LaVera," he whispered. I jabbed at the red record icon, then squeezed the bubble.

Silvery water-like static covered his face. Something was wrong. "No! No!" I cried. And then it cleared. Mercury hovered before me, leaning one hand on a wall for support. Looked like he was in some kind of control room. All these monitors were behind him, with shadowy images I couldn't make out. But one of them was different: there was a stream of nonsense moving down it: **%&allegra…cattablok***rogella.%^70@@@ periodita$4…Q. Must have been some kind of code, whirring by so fast. He was breathing hard, "Miles Morelli is really bad off. And they're making more Charismites. And something else."

Mercury's lips were silently counting. What was that about? He swiveled around, like he was afraid of getting caught, then looked back, talking more quickly. "There's one thing about this Universe place you got to know about. Downtown. I didn't make that part right. Needs a lot of work. But it might be the answer to everything, if it doesn't eat you up alive." More waves of watery static washed him away. And then Mercury came back, really frightened now. "Shoulda tol' you that before." He came closer to the screen. "Don't for—"

The holo disappeared back in the bubble and sailed away. I hit the red button to stop the recording, and then I realized it had never started. I'd messed up! Shouted out my name, again and again, hoping I could get the bubble back, but it never came. I cursed in Spanish, then English, then Spanish again, raging and raging.

Okay. Okay. Breathe. Think. That only went so far.

I was so damned tired. Just couldn't stop, blabbering, "Cheeta, Cheeta, Cheeta." A sapphire-tinged bubble came towards me, with that sweet face I missed so bad. "Miles!" I cried out. "Oh, Miles!"

His fingers stretched out before him to the edges of the bubble, as if peering out a window. I cradled the ball in my two hands, thrilled and destroyed. He was a skeleton tightly covered with flesh, insane glint in his black eyes. "Chee, Chee, Cheeta," he mumbled. Could barely make that out. "Ruh, ruh, ruh. She red. Red! She red!" This time, I made the record button work. Kept recording and recording the little "Ruh, red" message.

It started to make some kind of *chingando* sense.

18. SHAKE

Hamburger Snip Snaps

SPICEY SKIN ROSE and fell on a woman's breasts—the old friend I'd stayed with overnight. Even in sleep she was deeply seductive. A caramel arm extended down the white sheet. Outside, sounds of street sweepers, faint bird calls. A gray tabby with fiery green eyes peered at me from a sheer-curtained window. Mexico City. *Stay here for a few days. Forget everything for a while.*

No. Couldn't do that, as much as I wanted to. I forced myself to sit up and face the long day ahead. Historical drama about life in London circa 2019 needed my attention. All kinds of squabbles on the Santa Monica set. Would have made more sense to bed down in L.A., but I still couldn't bring myself to go back to my apartment there, even though it was completely renovated, all evidence of the explosion and Izzie's abduction gone.

That awful morning came back to me, just before she was taken. Izzie was with me in my kitchen talking about Prill—that vicious Celeste Sidhar in camouflage.

"That one was totally not worth it."

"Why?"

"The way he holds me. Something's off."

What was off? What had Izzie realized? I got up from the pillowy bed, stepping between two boxes of rescued stray kittens.

"You know what the problem with you is?"

"Yeah, you."

"Beside that."

"What?"

"You don't realize what girls think about that look of yours."

Izzie was always seeing what nobody else did, getting at the truth in people that she chose to focus on. Which wasn't something to necessarily expect, since she had to be among the most self-absorbed people on the planet.

There was an ache in my chest, an overpowering need to see Izzie. While I'd grown mostly resistant to her magnetism, being away from my sister for so long felt almost crippling at times.

A few minutes later, I walked toward my mag-lev in the Coyacán neighborhood, past electric blue, marigold, and watermelon colored buildings. A holo message popped up on my air screen. Wanza was requesting my presence in her New York offices. Memere was wanted, too.

There was barely a minute to spare if I was going to get there in time. I directed the mag-lev's controls to jump from Mexico to hyper-tubes in Denver, Indianapolis, and Philly. That would put me in Nuhope's Manhattan H.Q. in about two hours. With the mag-lev on auto-pilot, I tried to distract myself from the meeting ahead with the latest news.

A holo of Ginseng Childe's chiseled, Native American face popped up. When she was fired from her gig as Nuhope's news chief, it lit a fire in her belly. The journo had gone back to her roots as a kickass correspondent and launched her own newsfeed. The time stamp in one corner showed that the spot had dropped about six hours ago.

"How can anyone believe, even for a nano second, that Izabel Cardinale would align herself with the Wanza Frickin' Newton and Tippi the Terrible? Speaking of which, if the president and vice president of United America made a message with Izzie, they probably know where she is. Why did they leave us in the dark?"

Good point. "My advice is, don't watch that video of Izzie. Even if you freaking love her. Especially if you do," she said. "You know how magnetic she is, how she's always charmed us to no end. Don't let her twist your thinking now!" Ginseng was walking a thin rope—not betraying the secret that Izabel was a Charismite. Not that I'd actually confessed to that, at that party. But I wasn't fooling her. And she was too loyal to Memere to let that intel out.

"And by the way," Ginseng said, "where's the evidence that Keplar-22b is about to invade? My sources at NASA say that there is no proof that asteroid that dropped near Phoenix was in any way the prequel to an invasion!"

I hoped that she was protecting herself. Those were dangerous views. The news hound could get attacked for them. She had a whole following of journalists who revered her work. Hopefully more of them would follow her lead in how they reported all this. If they dared.

I flipped to another feed, this one featuring Nuhope's top anchor. He was interviewing Tippi, who was lobbing back a reaction to Ginseng's report. "When Izabel contacted me out of the blue, I was astounded," the president said.

"So you didn't know where she was before then?"

"No. And I still don't. She was very clear that she wanted to make a message to get the word out about what the world was facing, why she'd disappeared. But she would only do it if we arranged a virtual recording."

"But you're sure she's safe wherever she is?"

"As safe as any of us, with Kepler-22b staring down its guns at us."

What had The Fist done to Izzie so that she'd say what they wanted? The question haunted me every waking hour and burned into my dreams. I pulled up another report. This time, the same anchor was interviewing a military commander with so many medals on his chest it looked like a glittering tossed salad.

"General, a lot of people are skeptical there's any sentient life in the universe that is in any way meaningful. What do you say to them?" the anchor asked.

"We've known for a long, long time that the mathematical probability of some life form out there is good. It's been a matter of when we'd find it. Now we have. And it's on Keplar 22-b."

"How long do you think it will take for the alien invaders to show themselves?"

"That's not something I can talk about," the commander said. "But we've got to get fully prepared. There needs to be a coalition of the world's great superpowers, with one strong leader to guide us."

Blah, blah, RDA crap. The last person I wanted to talk to now was Wanza. As my ride swooped toward Nuhope's shining spire, I could see a gigantic crowd on the sidewalk watching a towering wallscape on the side of the building: the recording of Izzie. "That asteroid that fell out near the Phoenix Treasure Zone? It was sent by Kepler-22b. An exploratory mission… I'm so scared!"

It didn't matter how many reports emerged to contradict what Izzie said. She was too riveting, her affect too powerful. I parked my ride on the roof and rode the elevator to Memere's floor. She stepped in beside me, and we shot up one floor.

"Ohm fucking shanti, and all that," she said, prompting both of us to take a deep breath. Wasn't any doubt we were about to lose our jobs.

"I feel like I've been waiting for somebody to birth a really ugly baby that's five weeks overdue." The metaphor was pretty lame, but that's all I could think of right then. Good of Memere not to call me on it.

Instead, she squeezed my hand. This was coming after weeks and weeks of anticipation—after two decades of passionate leadership. But as excruciating as this was, Memere's eyes zinged with defiance. She hadn't sat still during those weeks of waiting for the axe: she'd spent it with some prized employees, drawing them out in conversations, figuring out if they would fit into the new company she might create. The company idea was starting to feel like an inevitability.

"You are some kind of mother," I said in admiration.

She fell out of her thoughts, surprised. "Why thank you, darling."

When we reached Wanza's colossal inner sanctum, the veep feigned deep regret. "I really wanted this… this *alliance* to work out. It could have been brilliant, to have an RDA chairwoman and Independent CEO of Nuhope, running the company together, balancing each other—"

"Oh, for fuck's sake. Let's just get this over with," Petra said.

The red coils in Wanza's eyes drilled into her. "It is my duty to inform you why this is happening. The board members who were supporting you seem to have changed their minds." *You handled that quite deftly. With some Izzie twisting.* "There was also a fair amount of displeasure concerning that anniversary party disaster and how the two of you used it as a launchpad to raise capital for a new company."

No sense correcting her. Petra just shrugged. "What did you expect?"

"That you'd be smart enough to realize that violates the terms of your contract…"

"No, it doesn't."

"… as does your unfortunate decision to spread falsehoods about me and the president through that loser Ginseng Childe."

I smirked. "Really? She's spreading falsehoods?"

Wanza glared at me, then launched into Memere again. "You can kiss that golden parachute good-bye."

Petra let out a bright little laugh. "I've always enjoyed a good court fight."

Wanza turned a glower on me. "And Boy Wonder here can expect no more than two week's severance pay." I loved being likened to an antiquated DC Comics character.

"He has gotten better numbers out of Nuhope shows than any other producer in the company. You don't deserve him," Petra said quietly.

Thanks, Ma.

"You've got half an hour to collect your belongings. Guards will toss you out of the building if you take any longer." We made for the door. Wanza called after us: "And Petra, I do hope you realize that if and when your daughter surfaces, she is still under contract here."

Petra smiled back as if to say, "Fat chance." But she wisely kept her mouth shut.

We boarded the elevator. "Invigorating! Got everything?" Memere asked.

"Yeah." I'd packed up the important stuff in my L.A. and New York offices weeks before. Memere had done the same. The elevator shot down to the lobby. Memere gripped my arm as if she were losing balance. The reality sunk in: we were never coming back to this place. I'd walked down Nuhope's corridors from the time Petra adopted me as a four-year-old orphan. She'd put all her passion in the place, launched so many careers, greenlighted a long and storied cascade of top shows and new tech ventures.

As soon as the elevator doors sparkled away, we were greeted by a stunning sight. There must have been a thousand Nuhope staffers in the vast lobby. Was this an emergency drill? Was the building on fire? A loud wave of cheers and applause came at us. Holos of Nuhope's top celebrities, based all over the world and even distant space ships, floated above the crowd, clapping and whistling for both Petra and me.

Word had certainly traveled fast. We were frozen, looking at everyone as the sound solidified into "Petra! Petra! Petra!" Then "Shake, Shake, Shake!" Raised arms of salute spiked the air above the wave, which parted just enough for us to pass through.

Memere swallowed hard, fist wiping away incredulous tears. She had never been a pushover as a boss. There had been firings, layoffs, brutally frank demands when people needed to get a lot better at what they were doing. But she played fair, didn't put up with any crap. And everyone I'd ever met at Nuhope was extremely proud that she'd done away with subliminal mind-control practices, like embedding messages in dreamisodes. They knew she hadn't been the one to bring them back. To most people there, Petra was a guiding star always pointing people toward the truth—though that had become a tattered goal of late.

We went outside. An even larger crowd had collected in front of the building, outnumbering the crowd of *turista* gawkers. I strained to look over the heads. Yep: thankfully, Memere's bot Geoff was waiting at the curb with the limo.

A chant rose up: "Speech! Speech! Speech!"

We kept going, but as the cries grew louder, we finally stopped. I could sense Petra pushing aside all the turmoil in her mind, finding the calm she needed before calling out:

"Okay, Okay! I guess there's too many of you out here to be fired for insubordination by you know who." Everyone laughed at that. "Thank you, all of you, for making this company as strong, as purposeful, as I ever could have hoped. You may be losing me—and Shake here, too. But don't lose sight of each other. When things seem confusing as hell and you're about to lose..." She swallowed hard. "... lose what really matters, turn to your tribe. Get their support. Kick yourself into making a new plan. And move the fuck on."

Cheers and whistles rang out, powerful and shrill. News drone cameras captured footage of the celebrity holos, the massive crowd, as we made our way toward Memere's car. I traded a few air-fist bumps along the way.

"Tell us where you end up, man."

"We want to know!"

"You got it," I yelled back.

Cruising away in the limo, it gave me pleasure to know that even though the sound of what was happening on the ground wouldn't make it all the way up to Wanza's 200-story suite, she would most certainly see the paparazzi news holos. And for once, just this once, I didn't mind those damned newshound gnats at all.

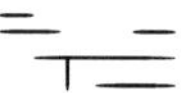

I WOULD HAVE been a nitwit to spend any more time thinking about Nuhope. But I'd be lying if I didn't admit that it took some doing, not to obsess about shows like *Space Ace* at first. Even though I'd been in Hamlet mode, not knowing what "to be," juggling all the show complexities had become part of my nature. But it didn't take me long to double down on the catastrophe at hand, finding the four prisoners before somebody got killed—or more of those messed-up messages from Izzie dropped.

A meeting with the *due famiglie* and Mikhail made that easy. It took place in a virtual rendering of his FBI office, which had all the ambiance of a storage closet. He'd been downgraded even further by the FBI since they found out he'd "borrowed" some operatives for Petra's party. Four of the bots had been badly damaged.

Jarat opened with an obvious question: "Have you figured out where the prison is?"

"I'm eating away at the edges of that," Mikhail said. "Here's what I know: Celeste Sidhar has seven domiciles all over the world. Not your typical sprawling estates on prime beaches and mountains. She favors condos in large buildings. Stays at each one on an extremely random basis. She may enter a building looking like herself, but I have reason to believe that she sometimes exits in disguise. Can't trace her then."

"Fuck a Goddamned duck," Luscious said.

A laugh registered in Mikhail's eyes. "I've been studying another angle." He pointed at the wall behind him. Up popped a corporate flowchart filled with a mosaic of oblong tiles. A big block at the top was labeled Sidhar Enterprises. "What we've got here is a classic Russian Doll set-up for a private enterprise."

The second-tier row had tiles for five companies. Two or three offshoot companies were below each one. The chart cascaded down like that, a "doll" leading to a "doll" leading to a "doll," seven layers deep. "There's hardly any info about some of these businesses, but the ones near the top are pretty well known," Mikhail added.

I peered at some of the names. Cloud Forest, the name of the server farm where Mercury worked, was on the fourth level, designated as "no ownership – management only." Looked a little forlorn, off on a far end of the row with no offshoot companies underneath it. Five rows down was MasterBlab and BlackCream Central. "Can't say she's got a gift for branding," I said.

"She didn't do the naming. Most of the companies were acquired. She's snapped up a lot of startups at drastic discounts. The owners were in strapped-for-cash situations."

"Is this setup a tax dodge?" Jarat said.

"Could be." Mikhail pointed at a tile for Dry Rain Enterprises on the second row down. Up popped a view of an oblong white building. "This is the one to focus on."

"Why?" Memere asked.

"She goes there almost every Wednesday morning. It's the only place she seems to visit with any regularity."

"Guess it's time for me to burnish a newly acquired skillset," I said, looking pointedly at Jarat.

"No. Oh no!" he said. We argued about why I should go into ghost mode again, this time as a solo act. Jarat insisted it was too dangerous. Of course, he wanted to do the espionage work himself like he'd once done at Nuhope in the bad old days.

I had to get all guilt-trippy. "I hate to tell you, but you just aren't as fast and strong as you once were."

"You're not exactly an action hero," he said acidly.

"Nope. But I'm more like them than you."

"Come on. Give the kid one of your doohickeys again," Lush said. It took a little more debate, but Jarat finally threw up his hands in growling surrender.

Mikhail's eyes bored into me. "Play it safe. We need you alive and well."

The next day, I left my mobile lens in my New York penthouse so nobody could track me, went into ghost mode, and speed-walked through a hammer-cold rain from Hudson

Yards up to Penn Station on 34th Street. The water went right through my invisible body like nothing. I could get used to that.

A mag-lev train took me to Washington, then the city's cranky old subway system delivered me at a stop a few blocks East of Dry Rain's Arlington office. It was as captivating to look at as a giant bar of tofu. Maybe that's what the architectural geniuses behind it were aiming for.

According to Mikhail's intel, Celeste Sidhar almost always appeared there at around 8:15 AM on Wednesdays. I arrived a little ahead of that, leaning against the wall of a decaying, one-time sugar processing plant across the street.

A scattering of office workers used their umbrellas to fight off the windy, very wet rain before passing into Dry Rain. Not your happy camper types. At 8:17, a snub-nosed 38-94 mag-lev—the hottest Tseng model on the market—soared up to the entrance. A bot raced out of the front seat and opened up the back, helping Celeste climb out. She was encased in a dry human-sized cube of air that protected her from the water.

I was in danger of falling down, just looking at her. Sure, I hated her to the bottom of my soul, and I'd seen pictures of her. But in the flesh, it was even more apparent that was the kind of woman that I tended to go for. Tall and lean as a sailing cutter. Straight black hair waterfalling down the back of a shell-pink cashmere coat. Oval face with pronounced straight eyebrows. Her nose was a little too sharp, a little too big to be ideal, at least for someone who was genetically tweaked—as most Elites were. I longed to get close enough to see the defect in her eye, to put my hands around her neck and break every bone in there. But not now. She was too valuable for the intel she could give us, alive.

"Ten hours. Don't keep me waiting," she told the bot gently.

"Yes, ma'am."

I followed close behind her as the front door sparkled open, barely making it inside before it solidified again. She was in old school mode, walking (not gliding) up the stairs (not the elevator), hips swinging back and forth rhythmically under the luxurious pink. At the top, a door dissolved, and we walked into a gigantic space lit by a transparent ceiling. I held my breath, waiting for a shrill blast or any other clues I'd been detected. Didn't know what security was in place, or if it could spot me. But nothing.

Her staff was wearing pretty dope gear, angular and trendy. But there was one slob in the bunch with stringy hair. A bushy-furred golden Labradoodle dozed at his feet. A box poked out of a half-open drawer beside him. I recognized the brand logo for Hamburger Snip Snaps dog treats.

Celeste walked up a center aisle between long rows of work tables, calling out hellos, only stopping when she got to Stringy Hair. Her nostrils flared, probably at his faint body odor.

"How's it going, Scott?" she asked.

He gave her a begrudgingly bleary look. "Okay."

"Your project doesn't look much different than it did last month."

"It's not like I'm making toilet paper, Celeste. This is entirely new stuff."

She stared at his arrogance. "When I acquired your company, you said you'd have this developed by… What was it? Last spring?"

"You want this fast, or you want this right?" he seethed.

The room went dead. Celeste absorbed him with a tiny smile, then waltzed off, stopping at a winsome-looking lass three table rows away. Scott reached down to pet his dog's belly. "Vagina from hell. Can't make shit herself," he said softly. But not soft enough.

A thrill came over Celeste's face for an instant, then she walked to her office, which took up the entire left side of the room. There was a retro door on it—wooden, on brass hinges. I whisked in before she shut it tight, avoiding the squelching sound my ghost state would have made.

Her office was very minimalist, with a coolly dated look: a long red-lacquer desk, sleek black cabinet against pearly walls, couple of steel and black leather chairs. Celeste peeled off her coat, uncovering a heaven-blue dress, then picked up an oblong gold box on one of its shelves next to some picture frames. I came up close enough to smell the soap on her butter-smooth skin. She opened the box. Inside were two lines of small vials, each one labeled with a different essential oil. Can't say I shared her taste in scents: tomato leaf, fresh-cut grass, martini. I didn't catch all of them. She selected one called snowfall, put some drops in an air diffuser, then picked out another bottle, this one without label.

She sat down at her desk and pulled up an air screen view of the office's main room, rolling and rolling the vial in one hand, focusing in closely on Scott. He was staring intently at his screen, one hand dangling down to massage his dog behind one ear.

I leaned on the wall behind her, watching, waiting. She swiveled around, facing my invisible body, crossing her legs, and kicking the top one impatiently. I jumped back. Last thing I wanted was to make a slurp. She uncrossed, crossed, and uncrossed her legs again.

One project after another emerged on her air screen. Arcane technical schemas flew by. As the day progressed, she met with various staffers to review their projects. They were all focused on products that were in the test phase. One was designing biospheres that were several miles in diameter, with air currents and other conditions capable of supporting a wide variety of species—far more advanced than the biospheres currently in use, and much larger than the Ellingtons' dome. They'd give Jarat's business at Silverton a run for its money, if they ever became operational.

Another person was working on something called the Shroom. The prototype looked like a mushroom cap which fit over the head. It was supposed to calm the wearer down, bring them joy, playfulness, a charge of excitement—whatever they needed—by emitting sensory experiences based on the user's memories. The smell of a freshly peeled orange, sounds of little children playing in the waves, image of a seductive woman belly dancing—that sort of thing. I really wanted to give it a test drive.

By 5 PM, Scott was the only employee she hadn't called in her office. Celeste watched him on her screen, how he kept looking toward her door, dejected and resentful. Everyone else wrapped up their work and filtered out. He finally slumped out with his pooch.

When the main room was empty, Celeste sat still. Sadness mixed with an old horror took over her face. Opening a drawer in the cabinet, she pulled out some thick transparent gloves, put them on, and slipped out into the main room. Scott's drawer was still half open. She removed the box of Snip Snaps, fingers trailing over the happy Spaniel puppy on the box's front side. Opening it, she dumped the dog treats on the desk. They looked like yellow checkers. Then she pulled the unmarked vial out of her pocket and sprinkled a clear liquid on each treat. Blowing on them with her full lips, she helped them to dry. Fifteen minutes later, they were back in the box, and it was poking out of the drawer again. Swinging on her pink coat, Celeste dropped the unlabeled vial in her purse and swept out of the office.

I spent the next few hours breaking into her cabinet's doors and drawers with some locksmith tools and went through the contents. There wasn't much to speak of. My eyes kept drifting back to three pictures on a shelf—the old-fashioned paper sort, each in a heavy pewter frame. A round-faced older Indian gent and petit woman looked out from them with younger versions of Celeste. Nice touch of loving parental remembrance. The Snip Snaps maneuver was making the idea that she'd offed them even more likely.

Walking up to Scott's desk, I snatched the box of Snip Snaps and dumped the treats in the trash. Then I wrote a tiny message on the box lid: "Your dog's not safe here." I put the empty box back in the drawer. It was a big risk, but I had to take it.

I went back to Dry Rain a few times and was pleased to find that the Labradoodle was no longer at his master's feet. Scott was just as messy as before, but tightly wound, on constant guard.

On my third visit, I hit pay dirt. It came in the form of a call Celeste placed one night after everyone left for the day. The holo of a young woman with hopeful, nervous eyes emerged on her air screen. Looked like her jaw was permanently clenched. Her tennis shirt was emblazoned with the oval logo for NASA.

"Hello Sarah," Celeste said.

"Sorry ma'am. I didn't want this to take so long. But I finally have what you want."

A document popped up on Celeste's air screen, and she read through it swiftly—and so did I. It was about the asteroid that had dropped outside Phoenix. The report showed that it was composed of a crystalline alloy that was a new discovery, completely unknown on Earth or any planets that had been surveyed. Geologists on NASA's staff had named the alloy Sonorite—with a tip of the scientific hat to where it had been found: the Sonoran Desert.

X-ray diffraction and radiochemical analyses revealed that the rock was in no way harmful to humans. But when subjected to any kind of force, it sent out strange currents of electro-magnetic energy that completely destabilized any form of nearby technology.

"Like the servers in Cloud Forest," Celeste mused.

"Yeah. Turn to page fifty-two. See what the asteroid's currents do to mobiles?" I read behind Celeste's back some more. The researcher who wrote the document reported that he started picking up messages in Mandarin. He did a language translation and discovered they were from a mother in Miami communicating with her daughter in Beijing.

"I see. Simple random messages transmitting to far-flung areas of the globe."

"Yeah. They all passed through a server near Cape Canaveral."

"Near the researcher."

"Correct. Did that happen to that server maintenance guy, Douglass?" Sarah asked. "I mean, the impact of that asteroid crashing to Earth must have been about a hundred times more intense than what the researcher simulated. Maybe what he went through was a little different. Nobody here seems to know. Why did he just disappear like that?"

"I have no idea," Celeste said smoothly. "Let's move on. What has NASA learned about the sentient beings that apparently sent that asteroid to Earth?"

"I… don't know."

"But you did see a lot of green colored deposits in your banking account?" Silence. A friendly glimmer came over Celeste, verging on intimate. "I hate it when you make me turn into a hard ass."

"It's just so…" Sarah looked scared. "What they could do, if they found out what I'm…"

"Sarah. Please trust me! No one will ever know. Ever! Just tell me. Is there any sign of an impending attack on Earth?" Still more silence from Sarah. Celeste tried again: "I'm making you a very wealthy woman."

Sarah stared at Celeste's warmth, then said so softly I could barely make out: "There's no evidence."

"Of what?"

"No life detected on Kepler-22b. No connection between the exoplanet and the asteroid."

Celeste smiled broadly. The call ended shortly after that. As she started to put on her coat, Celeste stopped, looking far into the distance, as if climbing up a rope ladder of strategic moves. "Lovely. Absolutely lovely."

The next Wednesday, Celeste received another call that sent an electrified jolt through my system.

"Oh, hello, Madame Vice President," she said as Wanza's holo came into view. "Congratulations on getting rid of Cardinale and her adopted spawn." I swallowed a guffaw. "So glad Nuhope's reluctant board members finally came around."

Wanza smiled crisply. "That holo with Izabel turned out to be just the right leverage."

"Anything to help clear the way. Just about ready to record the next one. And I've started to collect ideas about how I can make Nuhope a much more effective tool for the RDA."

"I look forward to hearing all about them, after a few outstanding matters are taken care of."

"I have an update. About my most distinguished guest."

Wanza sat forward, all ears. A buzzing sound distracted me. A fly zoomed through Celeste's office.

"I'm sorry to say that Morelli still isn't responding. In fact, he's beyond the point of no return, Madame Vice President. Physically. Mentally. We did everything we could."

"Then remove his goddamned brain. There must be *somebody* that can get past the locks and extract the memory."

"I'm sorry. I would have found them, if there were. And now, he's so far gone." The fly landed on Celeste's bare arm. She flicked it away in annoyance. "But I wouldn't worry. His secret files are probably lost forever. And no one will ever know where they are."

"You don't know that! This is unacceptable. You can forget about taking over Nuhope, Celeste. That door is now closed."

"I really don't think so."

"Oh, don't you?"

"No. Unless you'd like me to drop word about the lack of any connection between that asteroid and Kepler-22b."

"You don't—"

"But I do. There is no impending invasion. I have proof of that." The fly sailed toward Celeste again. She swatted it with triumphant glee, sending it straight into my invisible body.

SLURP!

An AI voice rang out: "Warning. Warning. Security has been compromised."

"Fuck!" the veep said. The conversation cut off.

Fuck, indeed.

19. TRISTAN

Upside-Down Freefall

IT DIDN'T MAKE sense, how the room was revolving. I was too dizzy to sit up. Izzie was in my face. There was a glass in her hand, like she wanted me to drink something. The idea was disgusting.

Chest vacuumed clean of air. Gasping. Sucking in. Izzie was furious with terror. "Don't you do it. Don't you dare leave me here alone!"

Won't. Won't. In, out, in, out. Yes, air now.

Whining and scuttling sounds in a far-away field. Were we back in Pompey? No, not a field. In the hall. Spider bots traveling, crawling, flying by this room. Not stopping.

Izzie pounded on the wall. "HEY! SOMEBODY! GET IN HERE! YOU GOT TO HELP HIM. SOMEBODY!" Had to tell her something, but I couldn't remember what it was or how to speak.

Everything collapsed… Nothing.

Time was a strange concept. Fear and anxiety, too, as I lifted into elation. Up, up, into endless calm. Where had this been all my life? Laughing inside at myself, because of course, this couldn't be *life.* This was –

WHACK. Whack, whack. Was somebody hitting something? Hitting me? "Tristan Ellington, you goddamned sack of shit. Get back here!"

WHACK.

Huge jolt of electricity socked my chest. BAM. BAM. Tried to say, "Leave me alone. Get away from me." But I couldn't.

Wide-mouth howls out of Izzie.

Numbness dissolving into a hum. Prickles trickled down my arms and legs. Then stronger. Opening my eyes, a fizzle of light turned into Izzie's red, wet face, then the room. Our awful prison room.

How had this happened? The last thing I remembered was coaxing her to eat. What was it? Soup, of course. Something orange. Squash maybe. We'd both had the same meal. Maybe my bowl was poisoned. But no. What I'd felt wasn't something that happened to me. I remembered the sensations: raw pain in my back, arms, and legs. Burning in my stomach. I realized it then: someone had died. Knew him.

Darrel, the round-faced humanoid, poked into view. "Vitals are normalizing," it said. I felt a tug and suddenly realized that a tube was poking out of my chest, and now the bot was removing it. The other end of it was coming out of its belly. Then Darrel left.

We waited a long time, not saying much. Finally there weren't any sounds outside. The fifteen-minute countdown began. "Why didn't that fucking bot get here sooner?" Izzie asked.

"It couldn't." I whispered. "Morelli died. It must have been working on him."

Izzie stared, not believing at first. Then she collapsed in a chair. "Oh my God. You're sure? Not Mercury?"

I nodded yes. "The pain was the same I'd felt from the senator before, but it got so much worse until…" It was hard to parse, the more I thought about it. This was new.

"What?" Izzie said.

"Morelli died, but his pain was so excruciating in my body

it didn't just go away. Darrell had to get me on the other side of it. I've never been through something that intense."

"But… Morelli's room is so far away. You never felt him from here, in our room."

"Yeah. Maybe because it was so excruciating, or maybe they moved him closer. Who knows?" It started to really sink in: the great Miles Morelli was gone forever. "Shit. I hate this place." *Yeah, right. Talk about stating the obvious.*

Determination gleamed on Izzie's face. "We've got to get you out."

"What do you mean, *me* out?" I could almost feel the wheels in her head churning in a bad direction. "Izzie, are you nuts? If you don't get out, how many more messages are they going to make you—"

"That won't happen." There was a sense of finality about her, and I did not need to cast a hand near her belly to know that it was roiling with darkness, that it would lunge out at me, howling. Of course she could kill herself, in a quiet moment. There were ways to do that, even though they did pre-cut our meats and didn't give us sharp knives. But how could she give up like that? She really pissed me off. If I wasn't so weak, I would have destroyed something.

She read that in me. Her eyes went soft, like silver powder. "Tristan, listen to me. If I get out, they'll just find me again. They tried to get me before they actually did, several times. I don't know how many!"

"Tell me," I said, trying to control my anger.

"Hot guys, sometimes hot women, would… insinuate themselves into my world. That's the only word for it, insinuate. A director, a producer, a friend of a friend. They looked so real. Some of them I really liked."

"How did you know what they were doing?"

"I'd see a kind of fuzziness on their hands or another part of their body when they moved sometimes. Just a little. And I knew they had some kind of digital shit going on."

"You knew that about Prill?"

"Not until it was too late."

"Why didn't you tell someone?"

"I didn't think it was malicious. Fans can be so weird-ass. Plus, if I told Memere, she'd force me into some kind of ridiculous seclusion. I thought if I just stayed with Shake it would be okay. You know, his building in L.A. has such high protection. But the way those digital jerks started to be so regular was too strange. That last day I was all set to tell him." She sighed. "The point is, even if I get out of here, they'll take me again."

"That doesn't have to be. Come to Pompey. Stay with us."

She snickered. "That worked out really well for you."

"You don't think my father hasn't put on all sorts of new protections? We'll be safe! We will. Izzie!" She rolled her eyes. Why wasn't she seeing this? "You'd be with people who care about you. There's so much you can do from in there virtually."

"What? Little songs? Stupid actor pretend games? Why the hell would I want to do *that* anymore?"

"So find something new."

Izzie didn't argue back. Nothing had changed. Suicide was still right there, on her face. And she knew she couldn't convince me why that made any kind of sense. She saw my fear and took one of my hands, sandwiching it between her own like I was some kind of delicate child. "Tris. Forget about me for a second. I want to talk about *you*. Here's what could happen: After this, you go back home. Your parents will be so fucking glad to see you, they'll do anything for you as long as they think you're safe. So you get some doctors to come to the biodome and teach you whatever you need to learn in a hands-on, in-person way."

"That's not—"

"Stop it. You'll find the people that are strong enough and smart enough to be there without turning into sex-crazed jelly. Maybe your Da will even figure out a way to inoculate people so they aren't affected by Charismites. I mean, he hasn't yet. But you never know."

"We couldn't just bring in patients!"

"Of course you will, Doodlehead." Now I was the one doing an eye roll. She smiled. "I didn't say Dr. Doo. I said Doodlehead. It's better."

"Right." She was not going to make me laugh.

"Anyway, like I said. You'll figure things out. Because you and the doctors need to set up a hospital in there. And you'll work on cases that no one's ever been able to solve. But you will. You are going to be beyond fucking brilliant. You'll go down in history, forever."

It was nuts. A fairy tale sprinkled with freaking Disneyland pixie dust. And yet, ridiculous as it might be, she charged my mind with this crazy hope, her eyes shining fiercely right into my own. It wasn't the same kind of seductive thing that she and I could do to other people. It was just one human energizing another human, like anybody could do, but with the kind of vision that was pure Izabel Cardinale… the one that I never really knew, until we were thrown in this hellhole.

Reason rushed back to me, and I tossed the excitement away. We were never getting out. Why hope for something that could never happen? It would just crash me into even deeper despair when the truth finally hit home.

Izzie grabbed my shirt and yanked. "Stop it. Just stop it. You've got more inside you than me, Tris. And you're going to use it. To get out of here. And you will."

"That's just stupid."

"Why do you think I hated you so much?"

Before. When we were kids. "Because I was a happy wimp."

"Point. But when we got older, and I could see what you did, I was so fucking jealous."

I snickered. Didn't believe that.

"Tristan. Awe doesn't come easy to me. But you have all my awe. And I know you can turn that bitch Celeste. You can twist her mind. You can." The tenderness on her face, the way she searched my eyes, was riveting. Her palms, still on either side of my hand, were so smooth, like delicate flowers. They fit around me so perfectly.

We loved each other. The realization was so clear, so sudden. If I'd been standing up, I would have toppled over. I could see she was hit by the same avalanche.

That was all the more reason why I had to make her change her mind. "I heard you say it, when I was in all that pain. You told me not to leave you here. And I didn't die. So now you can't do it, not here, not anywhere."

Izzie pulled away, still so dark. This was asking a lot. Maybe there was something else I could do to flip her mind. "I want to show you something."

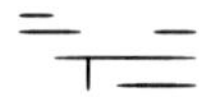

DARREL MONITORED MY heart area with one human-looking hand that was full of sensors, then it put it on my stomach, up to my temple—just to make sure I was totally on the mend. All the while, the bot's careful eyes shone into my own, monitoring my mood. I managed an innocent smile. And apparently the ploy worked, because it looked satisfied as it left.

Izz and I waited. When the silence finally came, I taught her the hand movements: "Y" symbol, then an "O," three taps on the wall with first the right little finger then the left.

Didn't work when she did it.

"Lighter than light," I said. It took five tries before the door de-materialized. Her mouth went into a silent scream of amazement. I took her by the hand and led her through the opening. We didn't go far that first day. And when we went out a second time, there were no revelations. I didn't pick up any clues that another human was anywhere near us, alive or dead.

The last time we'd seen Mercury, he hadn't been in good shape. Maybe they'd killed him. Maybe he had escaped without us, but somehow I didn't think so. My whole being was intent on sensing him.

"He'll come to us," Izz said, trying to convince herself as well as me.

She was right. The old guy eventually showed. He was even more ragged and dirty—with inflamed gashes on his head and chest. Izzie went spongy with pent-tears at his misery.

I wet down a washcloth. "Let's get you—"

"No."

"Those infections are bad."

"They'll know." He de-materialized the door and motioned for us to follow, feeling for the indentations he'd made with his nail. He took my hand, gliding it over the wall near the intersection with another tube corridor. A long, straight indentation. "Corner marker."

"Got it."

We turned down the new hall, and he picked up his pace. A dozen turns down corridors that were entirely new to me. I'd never gone so far. The minutes were ticking by. I grabbed his arm, motioning wildly that it was time to get back. But he seemed possessed, kept urging us on.

Two hallways later, he stopped at a wall. And then I smelled cat piss.

It hit me like an upside-down freefall—what I imagine that would be like. Charismites smelled like cat piss, for the tiniest of moments when you first came near them, until the olfactory senses acclimated. Only this odor was mixed with an animal scent, milky and teeming with the energy of new cells multiplying at an incredibly rapid rate. Softly babbling coos came from beyond the wall. Izzie's eyes were twin worlds of terror. "No, no, no, no," she whispered.

"You're as yellow as your skin," Mercury growled.

"Yeah, well why wouldn't I be?" Izz said.

"Because you *can't*. Because they're *yours*."

Izz and I clutched hands, couldn't move. The old man dissolved the door. The room beyond was glaringly red. It was hard to see anything at first, but the cries of newborns were distinct now, and not just one or two. As our eyes adjusted, we could see transparent, rectangular boxes, six in all. In each one was an infant. *We have six kids?*

We drew closer, peering inside first one box and then another, ready to think of them as horrible little creatures. But they were the most stunningly gorgeous babies that ever existed, with chubby cheeks just waiting to be kissed. Curly amber hair, spikey raven, and fine-haired fuzz-heads. Some had startled eyes, like Izzie. And every single one had the magnetism of a Charismite, which would only get stronger as they matured.

I tore my eyes to Izzie. She was glowing, just like I must be. How could we keep ourselves from reaching in, picking them up, giving each one cuddling whispers of love, brushing our lips on their warm, silky skin, telling them how we would care for them our whole lives, each and every one.

And at the same time, I wanted to kill them—even though I'd never murdered anything in my life. What would that Fist organization do with them? How would they be used?

Izzie was the same way: beyond the extreme end of the furious spectrum, and absolutely in love with them. There was no time to think about the contradiction. We were going to get caught if the three of us didn't race back to our rooms, and I wasn't even sure we could do it at this point. I'd completely lost track of the time. Mercury and Izzie didn't look like they were counting down the minutes either, completely mesmerized.

"Let's go!" I said.

"No." Izzie's voice was shot through with titanium. She looked at Mercury. "Pull it out. Whatever you got that makes messages, we need to do it now!"

"We'll come back," Mercury said.

"No. What I've got to say won't take more than a minute." She wouldn't let go of his infatuated eyes—magnetizing him. He pulled something out from under his wig, a lens, and stuck it on his eye.

WHISH. Black blur out of the ceiling. THUMP as three spider bots landed, tentacles stretching out. No time to run, but we made for the door anyway. Their snake-like limbs grabbed us. I screamed as a pincer squeezed my head. It seemed like my skull would splinter.

I saw Mercury's baggy pants flailing around as he was tossed off the ground and then bashed again and again into the wall and the sharp edge of a metal table. Izzie was hitting the bulging head of another spider as it wrapped a tentacle around her neck—but that didn't do a thing.

I felt like I was about to black out when a delicate voice said, "Oh no, no, no, no. Not yet." The spider loosened its hold on my head. Two of its other tentacles snaked around my middle. Izzie struggled against the bot holding her.

Swish of a long skirt. Royal colors swirling—ruby, emerald, sapphire. A whispering fragrance of clove. Geneva. Celeste. Above the dress, a graceful oval face with a delicate glow, the pronounced dark eyebrows.

Her long mouth curled up playfully. A spider bot groveled before her. She took something from it. A small transparent disk balanced on her finger. I looked at Mercury in horror. One of his eyes streamed with blood.

She laughed, at first faintly, then harder and harder. When the awful sound ended, she wiped away tears. "Bravo. Bravo, Mr. Douglass. If only you'd given me this in that hospital. Think how much effort that would have saved us both. You could have gone back to your life, such as it was—after you told me everything that you're going to tell me now."

Mercury's gory face was like a horrifying boulder that would never budge. Celeste glided back and forth before him. "This is what you used, isn't it? This is where you keep the messages."

Hatred streamed from Mercury.

"Last chance."

He girded himself. Celeste nodded ever so slightly. Bot tentacles wrapped around Mercury's throat and squeezed hard, harder.

"No! No!" Izzie and I screamed. It didn't make a difference. The bot kept crushing Mercury, then finally stopped. His broken body crumpled to the floor. They dragged him away.

"YOU," Celeste blazed at Izzie and me. "Let me be clear. This lens is picking up stolen data from my facility. And I will find out how it's used, every secret within it. What did he tell you? I need *everything*!"

Izzie cleared her throat, as if trying to figure out how to speak. Celeste motioned the bot holding her to loosen its grip.

Izzie whispered hoarsely, garbled words. Celeste drew nearer, right up to her face. In one rapid move Izzie lurched her head forward and bit Celeste's nose, wouldn't let go. The spider bot socked her hard in the temple. Her jaws released, and the bot threw her against the wall. She slid down, twitching, laughing like someone who wanted to die. Which, of course, she did.

Babies wailed. When did that begin? Darrel rushed in and tried to examine Celeste, but she pushed him away, radiating rage. "Why are these prisoners in here? How did they get the code?"

"I-I don't know."

"Change it!" Her fury landed on each and every bot. "Make sure that never happens again!"

They all cowered. Celeste focused her wrath on the spider holding Izzie. "Take her to the pen. Prep her for the next message."

Time stopped. Watching Izzie was like seeing a holo of an iceberg about to disintegrate. Beneath her tremoring face were memories I didn't know. She was crumbling. What had the world heard her say? Her breath too short, face too fragile—really would kill herself if they pushed her off this cliff.

In that frozen moment, a memory of my mother came from out of the blue. We were sitting on the cracked wooden steps that led up to the back porch. Back when I was about twelve, long before Celeste ever showed up. Ma was shelling peas, dropping the little tender balls in the skirt of her stained work dress, hair frizzed out in the July heat. She was plain, not a Charismite legend to me. But her caramel eyes held a fierce light. "When God made you, she didn't add the fight stuff. The normal boy kind. That's not in you. But you got something better than that. Do you know how to use it?"

Sometimes I'd done that. In front of the bathroom mirror,

when no one was around. Making my eyes change, from hazel to deep, brilliant blue. Knew what that could do. "Yeah," I told her. "But. Do you want me to?"

"Someday, you might not have a choice."

I came back to the present. Izzie was staring at me. What she'd said before, about turning Celeste, twisting her mind was right there.

"Wait. Geneva," I said. Celeste whipped around ready to lash out at me, but then she saw my eyes. I could feel my spiral of energy warming her, making it impossible for her to move. Hadn't done anything this forceful in the past. This energy was different, this was way stronger than what I'd done to her before, back in the field or when she used that e-pistol on me. Couldn't let her do that again. "I don't mean any disrespect, calling you Geneva. It's just how I think of you—of *us*."

Her eyelids drooped, voice slowed. "Do you think I don't know what you're doing?"

"Just trying to calm things down, y'know? Just stop things for a little bit. You want Izzie to make a message? Sure, she could do that. But I could do something a whole lot better."

Celeste marveled at me. I didn't even need to touch her. Gazing was enough. Her vagina was widening. I could sense that. She wanted me with a tornado's force.

"I dare you," I whispered.

Celeste's eyes shifted to Izzie. She wasn't through with her yet.

20. SHAKE

Times Square Mayhem

MY AIR SCREEN showed a pleasure aircraft over Harlem. I'd seen things like that a million times: looked like a thick saucer, with swimming pools open to the sky, cocktail bars, jacuzzies, saunas. But this one was weird. There were no people in plush spa robes peering down at the city like frickin' gods on Mount Olympus. A little door opened in its underbelly. A long metal rectangle dropped out, falling directly down to the sidewalk in front of the Morelli mansion. A very targeted coffin delivery.

I made the police surveillance recording on my air screen split in two, with one half showing military aircraft arriving in seconds, chasing the pleasure 'craft across the sky. It was no use; that was the official word. The thing was too fast and just disappeared.

In the other feed, the plain-clothed cops guarding Nadia's mansion ran toward the coffin, which had cracked on impact. Cheeta raced outside bristling with outrage, then Nadia tottered out wearing old-fashioned high heels with furry pom-poms. She collapsed on her knees.

Cheeta helped her up. They clung to each other as a swarm of police and FBI detectives collected. Must have been fifty cars full of them. The coffin was inspected, then broken apart to reveal something wrapped in a dirty sheet and duct tape. An emergency team carefully scissored it away, revealing the senator's gruesome face. Neither woman looked like they could stand a second longer, like they wanted to tear apart the world.

I'd gotten the recordings from our inside FBI guy, Mikhail. The "incident" had happened the day before. I switched to a closer view of the senator's corpse. Sure, I'd seen his misery in the holo message that Cheeta shared, but the cadaver was even more grisly and gaunt—bearded face pocked with scabbed sores, shrunken to a skull covered in skin. It didn't seem possible, during my first seconds of shock, that this was the legendary politician millions of people had voted for, who was fiercely righteous in his attempts to expose the truth, to help the Chav. The guy that had saved Cheeta when she was a homeless kid.

When they cut away the fabric some more, they discovered a piece of paper in the senator's hand. One of the cops scanned it and passed it to Nadia. The writing wasn't visible in the recording, but Mikhail had clued me in. There were just four words: "This could be you." There was no doubt about what the threat meant: if Nadia or anyone around her revealed any information about The Fist, that's what would happen. Nadia let the note flutter toward the sidewalk. A detective snatched it.

The diva didn't shriek. It was worse than that, the way she paled and walked blindly back in the house, helped along by her bot, Petunia. Cheeta dealt with the detectives' questions, fists clenched at her sides, chin jutting out defiantly. News reporter drones formed a thick cloud, hovering as close as they dared.

Celeste's words came back to me: *"He's beyond the point of no return, Madame Vice President. Physically. Mentally."* God only knew what was happening now to my sister, Tristan, and that old man, Mercury.

A bell rang, and my mind came back to the present, standing in my Hudson Yards apartment. Memere was at the door looking burnt around the edges and weaving a little.

There was no need to ask how many times she'd watched that holo. Lost count, like me. Of course.

She'd forgotten to eat over the last day. So I made her sit down and had the foodster make her a yogurt parfait.

Her eyes stared into the distance as she slowly ate. "There's something that I don't think I ever told you."

"What?"

"When Izzie was inside me, a little sparky sprite growing and growing, I had these dreams, every night. Huge clouds of butterflies were all around me, in colors and patterns that took my breath away. Black and white figure eights, tiger stripes of violet and peacock-blue swirls. And one always came, a silver queen larger than any other, the size of an eagle. And I followed it through a rain forest. I would have gone anywhere with it. And when my baby was born, I could see the silver butterfly in her eyes, whenever she looked at me. You saw that, right?"

"Not exactly," I whispered. But in the strange world of Izzie, butterfly eyes made sense.

"I keep reminding myself of how she sees possibilities in people like no one else can—how any space she enters becomes brilliant and filled with a kind of energized promise. How could I regret having her? No matter how much havoc surrounds her." Worry deepened in Memere's eyes. It wasn't very hard to guess why.

"What they did to Miles won't happen to them," I said, convincing myself for the hundredth time, as well as her. "Izzie's worth too much alive. So is Tris. *But it will happen to us, if we let out any intel about The Fist—not that we had anything. Yet.*

"What's our next move?"

I sipped my tepid coffee. "I'm not sure. Jarat and Luscious are trying to figure it out. So's Mikhail. And I can't get anyone to answer at the Morelli place. Which doesn't surprise me."

Reporters were barraging Nadia and Cheeta. And now there were the renewed plans for Miles' memorial services in New York and Washington. Dealing with that was probably taking a lot of time.

Then there was the humiliation and rage factors. Some of the most popular talk shows on Nuhope had turned into RDA love fests. And they were featuring comic bits about the coffin bombing down on the sidewalk. People couldn't get enough of them, according to the audience research I pulled up. Thank God we weren't there anymore.

Memere brushed some hair off my forehead. "You did what you could."

"What do you mean?"

"Spying on Celeste Sidhar as long as you did." After that damned alarm had gone off in Celeste's office, I'd raced out of there. No one had caught me. No DirecWep infrared beams tried to fry me. But next time, if there ever was one, I probably wouldn't be so lucky. She was forewarned. Jarat had insisted that it was too dangerous for me to continue, and I'd agreed.

I poured her a cup of coffee. "I can't believe that she's in line to take your old job."

"I can." Memere took a sip. "I wonder how she'll torque the content that Nuhope churns out even more than it already is."

"If that's possible." It wasn't just the talk shows. The news unit was now spewing segments that featured false evidence about Independent party politicos embroiled in one scandal or another. Social media stories claimed that the Chav were rising up to pillage the Elite and Middle homes, rape their daughters and sons. All that on top of pieces about the impending attack from a warring exoplanet and reruns of Izzie's scary and insanely viral message with the prez and veep.

What my sister had said left everything else in the dust,

when it came to mind-twisting power. Hardly anyone had the strength of mind to question her despite the warnings from Ginseng, the ex-Nuhope news chief. It felt like the world was imploding.

"We need another move *now*," Memere said.

"Cheeta is key to all this," I said. She knew stuff that she wasn't telling us. I was sure of it. "Fuck it. I'm going to Sugar Hill."

I DECIDED TO walk the 102 blocks between my place and the Morelli mansion. Needed to work off some tightly wound energy. Speeding North on Broadway, my mind was already at Nadia's front door, imagining a heated conversation with the cops as I tried to convince them to let me inside. I'd sent Cheeta a message: "Coming to see you." But all bets were off, whether she'd let me in, or talk.

I weaved my way through the crowds around the Times Square's thrill rides—rollercoasters, jackhammer drops, gigantic Ferris wheel, kids laughing at gigantic holos of cartoon characters dancing down the street.

A stream of piercing yellow light stopped me cold. It was coming off the skyscrapers, flaring wider and wider. That wasn't normal. Everyone on the street was stunned as the lights transformed into wallscape recordings, all of them the same. A field of daisies and bright green leaves fluttered in a light breeze.

And there was my sister—healthy, beaming as she walked among the flowers, wearing a white T-shirt and pants. Coppery wildfire hair, lips slightly puffed like she'd just finished making love for hours.

"Hello my people. Just wanted to let you know I'm

thinking about all of you," she said, voice so vulnerable and low. "I mean, what happened to Senator Morelli was just off the cray-cray charts. I keep wondering what Chav group was responsible for that. How can anyone let them get away with it? That's what I want to know. Thank God we have leaders like President Pavlarona and Vice President Newton to lead us through these insane times."

"Why, thank you, my dear," said Tippi, as she came into view wearing a perky blue suit. Wanza was right behind her in a red caftan.

"It's not just Morelli's death that's getting to me," Izzie said to them. "I mean, how can anyone sleep, thinking about that exoplanet sending an asteroid to spy on us before they invade!"

"Yes, that is very serious," the president said.

"But are you really sure that aliens are about to attack?" Izzie asked her. "It sounds like a sci-fi show or something."

"Oh yes. I wish it was just a hoax. But this is real. I've brought someone along to explain all that."

A distinguished man with a brush cut stepped into frame. "Madame President, Vice President, thank you for inviting me to be here."

"Izabel, please meet Rance Dillroy, the U.A.'s Secretary of Defense," Tippi said.

"Let me take a crack at your question, Ms. Ellington," Dillroy said. "Make no mistake. There is irrefutable proof that within the next month, Earth will undergo a catastrophic invasion, unless we act swiftly."

"But how?" Izzie said.

"The great nations on Earth must pull together under one government. We must act in unison, under one command. Because if we don't, we court the very real possibility of mass annihilation. Every day, every minute counts."

"But why do you say that—one unified government? Can't we do some kind of United Nations move?"

"That won't work. The only way to move quickly, once the attack is eminent, is to have one leader calling the shots. Speed is absolutely essential. There can't be any drawn-out debate," Dillroy said. "The U.A. stands above every other superpower on Earth when it comes to leadership and enough resources. We can make that happen."

"And if I may interject," Wanza said, "the leaders of the other great superpower nations are aware of this. There are, of course, lots of debates occurring right now. But they will all come around. Because if they fail to do so, the people of their great nations will force them to act. Our lives, all our lives, are at stake."

"Well put, Theowanza," Tippi said. "And thank you for joining us, Rance. I'm afraid we'll have to leave it here. There's so much to be done."

My sister waved to everyone watching as the three leaders moved out of view. "Bye-bye! Till next time."

The wallscape recordings shrank into yellow sizzling balls and disappeared. A shocked hush fell over Times Square. Even the thrill rides had stopped. I'd never seen that happen before.

It was astounding, that the U.A.'s high command would try and take over leadership of the world because of an impending invasion that was totally faked. And the idea that any Chav group would abduct and murder Morelli was bullshit. The only way all of this could seem believable to anyone was because a Charismite was casting her manipulative powers in that recording. My freaking sister was making it all very, very real!

I felt sick, like I'd never been sick in my life. Suddenly the silence was gone, replaced by a roaring frenzy from the crowd. People stampeded in several directions at once. They were out for blood, Chav blood.

The assaults began on a Chav boy here, an old woman there. The boiling, vicious energy kept escalating. Screams of vengeance and terror rose. I sped away, making sure that my ID data notified everyone that I was an Elite. My hand-tailored suit was a big clue, but that dark blotchy face of mine was like a "kick me" sign. Someone pushed me hard, and I slammed into the concrete sidewalk. A thug hurled a trash bin at me that had to be about ninety pounds. I rolled out of the way just in time. People raced over and around my prone body. I dragged myself up, willing myself to keep moving.

A kid, maybe three years old, face covered with grime and utterly terrified yelled, "Daddy! Daddy!" A thug with a bat was heading directly for him. I managed to scoop up the boy just in time. I carried him over to the side of a building so we couldn't be hit from behind, making more data available so people would get that I was an Elite.

"Do you see him? Do you see your Daddy?"

"NOOOO! DADDY, DADDY!"

I hoisted the kid to my shoulders, and he was able to look above the heads and search for his father. But nothing. After a while, I had to put him down, then lift him up after some recovery time. We did it again and again. And as the packed crowd grew less dense, and the sunlight dimmed, my hope faded. Maybe the man, whoever he was, had been killed. Maybe he'd given up on finding his kid.

A ragged man barreled towards us, face lit with relief and joy. After making sure they really did belong to one another, and brushing off the father's thanks, I continued north on Broadway, then west along 70th Street, then north again along West End Avenue, with its more historic, residential apartment buildings.

By the time I reached Morningside Heights, it was night. I found an alcove beside a towering concrete building and took a break. A few glimmers of light were visible in the sky. Somewhere out in oblivion, the *Space Ace* crew was working hard, jockeys zooming toward the Mars. *Not your crew. That's all gone.* A pang rose up in me. Nuhope had always felt like home. But it wasn't the same place, by a long shot. And I had no idea what to do with myself, from a job perspective. Nothing I thought of felt right.

I pulled up views on my mobile of what was happening all over the planet. Izzie's message with the prez and veep seemed to have gone everywhere. There were recordings of people on the streets in Moscow, Beijing, London, Santiago, Cape Town, all in a frenzy. There was nothing I could do about any of it.

Luscious must be crazy with frustration up in Pompey Hollow, dying to send out her own message to counteract all this. But her Charismite powers were far weaker than Izzie's. Even if she Juiced herself up more, any message she made would be easily denied by yet another message featuring Izzie—or maybe Tristan. And The Fist would try even harder to attack the dome and snatch her.

Making my way into Harlem, I filtered through side streets where pockets of antique brownstones still survived. And before long, I was on the Morelli's street, Convent Avenue. It was swarming with security mag-levs and armed soldiers. Two massive female soldiers blocked me at the Morelli front gate.

I was about to deliver my rehearsed plea when Cheeta burst out the doorway. "The fuck in here!" she shouted at me, motioning the guards to let me though, dark hair straggling around her pointy-chinned face.

In the foyer, the quiet calm and venerable old furnishings seemed strange, given the chaos I'd just been through. Cheeta looked really upset. Of course she'd heard Izzie's message. Who hadn't? A portrait of Miles hung on the wall—ten or twenty years younger, face full and flushed with energy, dark eyes gazing out at me. His eerie presence in the room seemed so real.

From another part of the house, Nadia's cracked voice suddenly stabbed out an old blues tune, which was really dark. "She sings that all the frickin' time. Drives me bongo," Cheeta said.

We climbed one set of stairs, then another and another, each one narrower than the last as we headed toward the top of the house. Cheeta's scent reached me in a way it hadn't before—a floral smoky musk. I could barely resist touching her. It was impossible not to imagine her boyishly feminine body under her T-shirt and shorts.

She pivoted around, suspicious. "What?"

I thought fast. "The music. It's gone."

"Yeah. Great, eh?"

Cheeta opened a simple wooden door, and we stepped into a shabby attic room with an angled ceiling and a wrought-iron bed off in one corner. Two rocking chairs with saggy seats and a steamer trunk were in front of a simple fireplace.

A blurry memory teased me. The sound of kids and a mahogany-voiced woman barking commands, rough and loving. My biological mama, from ages ago. Couldn't bring it into focus. A fist of pain pushed up through my throat. As much as I was already stunned—by what happened in Times Square—this threw me even more.

"Earth to Shakespear!" Cheeta's eyes were feathery black.

"Sorry. What?"

"Say hello to my girl LiZee." She nodded at a long orange and black salamander gazing at me lazily from the edge of a round window. "She won't do nothin' unless you got worms."

"No chance of that."

"I know this place ain't much."

Thought about telling her how it made me feel, but the moment didn't seem right. "If I ever need a set location for a show about a crazy old aunt, this is exactly where I'll come."

"Shows like that are so boring."

"Not for certain demos."

"Like what?"

We each took a rocking chair. "Probably Middle women in the twenty-five to fifty-four age group from the center of United America who drink a lot of booze, favor heavy perfume, and are deep in debt. Plus, older non-binary men who live in the Upper Pacific Treasure Zone and buy a ton of pet food."

"God damn. How do you know they like crazy aunt shit?"

"Research on past shows. Kind of goes with the producer gig."

"Nothing I'd ever want." Cheeta lit up a joint, looking me over. "Did somebody jump you?"

"Not exactly."

She handed me the doobie. "We'll keep going 'til you're less freaked."

I gave it a long pull, then passed it back. "You must need it too."

Cheeta shrugged like she was too tough for that—even though she had to know I'd see through it, then took another hit.

"Listen," I said. "You've got to understand something about Izzie and those messages. She would never say any of that, if she was in her right mind."

"I know. Shouldn't have dissed her at the Ellingtons'."

"They're going to keep using her and using her. And God only knows what they have planned for Tris and your friend Mercury."

The salamander leaped down and crawled to the fireplace hearth. "So you came here to put the squeeze on me for deets?" Cheeta asked.

I took another drag. "I got respect for the whole keeping-a-secret thing. Done my share of it. But there comes a time when you hurt too many people if you don't open up. To the right person. Like me."

Cheeta smiled like I was a friend that just told a joke that was kind of lame but touching—not some guy that she was forced to deal with. Which is how it had seemed before. But then, something changed on her face. She threw down a shade over a dusty round window. "Get on the bed."

"What?"

"Just do it."

"Why?"

"Nobody's screwing nobody around here, okay?"

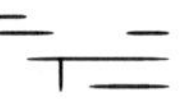

I'VE BEEN AROUND the block about a million times when it comes to metaverses. I studied them, helped design a mess of them. But this place Cheeta took me into didn't throw off the regular sensations. No daring adventures and mysteries, no comedic entertainment or ultra-hip chat rooms. None of that.

At first, it just seemed industrial; that's the only word to describe it. Red-orange infinite void, and an actual smell like… like… bleach, or ozone. Cheeta hardened her grip on my hand. She was doing it in the real world, but I could sure feel it in there.

"Jesus! Would you ease up?"

"Just don't let go."

"I'm not…" A transparent globe-like thing hurtled towards

us out of nowhere. "What the…" Cheeta yanked us off to one side. Another ball, then another, emerged. A whole cosmos of spheres, with colors flashing off their surfaces. Cheeta swerved us in one direction and then another to avoid them.

"It's not like they'd hurt us, but you don't want to open up the wrong ones," she said.

I was about to ask her about that when faces became visible in some of the nearby bubbles. A twerp with lights on the ends of his hair spikes was saying: "I'm tellin' ya, she'll hurt us."

Old granny cackling: "Well, butter my butt and call it a biscuit. That is so wrong!"

Dour fashionista: "It made me look like a clown on acid! I am going to hurt that designer."

Cheeta looked at my confusion. "They're messages. And they're trapped, okay?"

"In here?"

"Yeah. When you open them up, most turn out to be nothing."

"So junk mail?"

"Yeah. I started calling this place the Universe of Lost Messages. It turns out, some of them were created for me—but only a few."

That begged about a million frickin' questions, but before I could ask any, she shouted, "Cheeta LaVera! Cheeta Lucida LaVera!"

"What are you—"

"Calling the ones that are meant for me." Nothing happened. She became more and more agitated, shouting her name again and again.

"Maybe we should come back another time," I finally said.

"No. We're not done!" she snapped, then softened. "Tell you what. I'll take a break. Call out your own name."

So I shouted "Shakespear Cardinale." Nothing happened.

"Shake!" Cheeta yelled. "Shake Cardinale!" A huge cloud formed off to the right, in the far distance. As it grew closer, it looked like it was filled with a zillion stars. When it came even closer, they turned into fizzy little things like carbonated water, then closer still, countless bubbles—a lot more densely packed than any of the ones we'd been seeing. There was no way to move fast enough to avoid impact. The spheres exploded around us.

Some old guy was mixing a cocktail: "Shake it twice…"

A poodle dancing on its hind legs as a woman sang: "Shake it up, Shake it up…"

Stringy old weatherman: "Shakes from the massive earthquake could be felt throughout…"

This was getting us nowhere. "Shakespear Donatono Cardinale!" I roared.

Everything froze. It was like the name was drawing a blank with the whole Universe. Cheeta shot me a withering look. "Donatono?"

"Wasn't my call." Memere did that to me.

She laughed. "You poor bastard."

I didn't think it was that bad and was about to say so when Cheeta's eyes went wide.

Someone's voice dripped out, "Shakespear Donatono Cardinale. *Mon Cherie.*" An earthquake tremor went through me. Only one person had ever made my name sound like a rare liqueur. I followed Cheeta's stare and saw a bubble throwing off fuchsia light, with a certain sweet face inside. Zahra!

Never had as much fun; never laughed quite so hard; never had such awful arguments with anyone but Zahra. Never felt so dead, that day we split apart. *Of all the messages to find, this has to be the one?*

"This can't be real," I said.

"Don't be a wuss."

"What?" *Me, a coward?*

"Hold out your hand. You have to cup it." She watched as I managed to get Zahra's bubble on my palm. "Now squeeze it."

So I did. And there it was: a holo of my old flame. I'd met her at a Parisian party long ago—shaggy brown hair nearly covering her flirty chocolate eyes. Petite frame, long coppery legs.

"I know it's been about a trillion minutes, Shakespear Donatono Cardinale. *Mon Cherie*," Zahra said soulfully. "Didn't expect to hear from me, *non*? But I had to. Because now I can see things clearly."

She drew closer. "All those fights that we had—my questions about how close you are to Izabel—God, they were terrible. And how it stung me when I bought you that expensive gold ring that you put in a drawer and pretended to lose. Because it wasn't your taste. It embarrassed you to wear it. Oh, I know you would argue about that. *Mais c'est vrai.* And now, looking back, I realize that everything you did came down to one thing. Proving that you weren't just some Chav charity case, that you're more amazing, more intelligent than any Elite out there—that you deserved every promotion. And everything that didn't feed your ego got left behind. *Comme moi.*"

A man came up behind her, put his arms around her. Maroon velvet jacket, blonde hair brushing the top of his white shirt collar, drowsy eyes in alignment with her own, gazing out. "*Je te pardonne. Et au revoir, pour toujours*," she said.

The holo was sucked back into the bubble and soared away. Anger roiled through me. She never had been a reliable witness to our shared history. Hoped she got rid of that drug addiction and all the self-destruction that went with it. And that ring was frickin' ugly.

I didn't like Cheeta's curious look. "Yeah, I'm a cad," I said. Fuck her, if that's what she thought.

Her eyes narrowed, watching the bubble turn into a tiny dot far away. "I don't trust that bish."

It seemed like we were in there for hours, not that there was any real sense of time. The place grew on me, weirdly enough. It had this sense of mysterious, majestic infinity, despite the crazy bubble heads. Cheeta kept calling out names: her own, Nadia, Mercury, Miles, Tristan, Isabel. But nothing happened for what felt like a very long time. But then a gleaming, blue-tinged ball swooped in from a long distance, and as it grew closer, a familiar face emerged: Mercury!

"There you are!" Cheeta said under her breath, then groped for a red icon trailing behind us, which I'd barely noticed before.

The old man was shaking with fear. There were monitors behind him, all dark, except for one, with long strings of letters, numbers, and characters. "Miles Morelli is really bad off," he said. So it must have been old.

"They're making more Charismites. And something else." He looked around to make sure he was still safe. "There's one thing about this Universe place you got to be aware of. Downtown. I didn't make that part right. Needs a lot of work. But it might be the answer to everything, if it doesn't eat you up alive."

It sounded like somebody was pounding on a kettledrum—until I realized it was my heart. What did he mean by "more Charismites"? What the hell was Downtown? Swirling static that looked like a wave of water washed Mercury away. Then he came back. "Shoulda tol' you that before." He came closer to the screen. "Don't for—"

The message came to an abrupt end. Cheeta pushed at the

red circle again, and it was only then that she realized it had never recorded at all. “AGAIN?! FUCKING AGAIN!”

She probably would have continued a swarm of curses if we hadn’t seen something hurtling toward us. Not a bubble. There were strange spikes on it that became arms and legs as it grew closer. “*Mierda*!” Cheeta said.

Celeste! There was no doubt. She was focused on the far distance, looking obsessive and crazed. We tried to hide ourselves behind a bubble cluster, but she turned and saw us, screaming, kicking her legs to swim-fly in our direction. Her arms reached out, ready to strangle us, claw us.

This was bad. Really bad.

21. LUSCIOUS

The Only Way

MY MIND WAS on a warpath-from-hell after the Morelli casket drop and Izzie's second message. Jarat was the same way. Things were bad enough already, with the kids in some kind of Goddamned secret prison, but those two new things really tipped us over the edge. We couldn't think straight. But that couldn't go on.

I waited for us to calm down a smidge before I laid a big idea on Jarat about what we should do next. As a warm-up, I had him do what he loved: straddle my naked body on the massage table, work on my back. "Now this, *this* is an all-time top reason why I love you," I said. "OUCH. Chris' awmighty." The muscle knot he was working on near my waist was a motherfucker.

"Sorry, love. Breathe into it. You know what to do."

I let the air in, blew it out. And just like that, the pain eased up. "Fact is, if anybody ever asked me to prioritize the type of person to fall in love with, I'd tell 'em to look out for the massage therapist possibilities—even if they're an ex-therapist like you."

"Anybody ever ask you that?"

"Nope."

"I thought you were into my other vocation."

"Saboteur of all things Nuhope?"

"Uh huh."

That was back in the day. Before Petra got her sea legs and took complete control of the place. Before we settled down in Pompey and had our Tristan.

"OW! Criminy, Jarat!"

He moved away from an evil spot below my shoulder blades, ran his hand down my body and nudged his hard cock on my butt. It was a good sign that he was calming down. Had to believe that if Jarat were to make a "love list" about me, the thrill of having sex with a Charismite would be up at the top, even though my Juice intake was pretty low now.

After all the pleasuring, Jarat went to sleep on the sofa with his head in my lap. I looked at the wall screen that showed the worl' outside. The view swept all the way down our hill, past the transparent walls on the dome and on into Pompey. It meant everything to me, that town, the place where I was raised. I'd kept up the project that I started with my gram—helping the poor folk so they had a decent shelter from the rising heat and could irrigate the veggie and alfalfa fields. Did everything on the Q.T., not that people didn't guess.

What would become of Pompey when I went away for good? A pang rose up from my heart. *Couldn't think about that now. Couldn't.*

Tristan was what counted. So many times he and I had walked through the fields and woods in the biodome—so thick and green in our climate-controlled system. I taught him all I knew about nature, and by the time he was thirteen, he was teaching me—about all he felt inside the animals, and all he'd learned about them on the OuterNet. His life wasn't over yet. Wouldn't let that happen. It was all up to me. I knew that.

Jarat roused himself. And I scrounged around the quick freeze and fixed us this concoction we loved: chilled vodka, lime juice, a touch of maple syrup, and ice. Then I waited until he took a few sips before starting in. "So what do you see happenin' next, Hon?" I asked innocently.

He groaned. "And I thought this afternoon was about trying to forget everything for a little bit."

"You think it's possible?"

"Did you take extra Juice? Because I feel like some mental arm-twisting is about to take place."

"No darlin'. I want you clear-eyed. I'm not trying to take advantage."

Jarat straightened up more, on guard. "It involves you again. Doesn't it?" *Like Petra's party.* Of course he guessed that, and it really steamed him up. "If you think you can show yourself out in the world a second time without—"

"Let them."

"What? Take you?"

"Yeah."

"Love it. What a plan! Give The Fist control of three Charismites instead of two."

"Not if we do it right."

His face was rage red. "There is nothing *right* about that!"

"You gotta hear me out all the way. First, we need a reason for me to go somewhere on the outside."

"Like what?"

"I'll get to it later. I'm sure they'll have spies all around me. But if I see one, I'll pretend not to notice. And when they snatch me, you and Shake will follow behind in ghost mode. And we'll find out where the kids are."

"That is, by far, the worst plan I've ever heard of."

"I know it's an awful risk. But we've got to find the kids before anything else happens. And since nobody's got a handle on where they are, I really think that I'm the only way."

He got up and left. I could see him on the monitors outside.

He was using an axe to hack up an old tree stump. It was like he wanted to murder it. Then he stormed out into the far field and let out a long howl at the top of his lungs. When he came back down to the bunker, I gave him some space, working in the hothouse, transplanting some begonias.

After a while, I came into the sitting room in my dirty dungarees. He stared at me dead on and said, "You realize that I'm addicted to you."

"Yeah." He meant "addicted" literally. The Juice had done that to him, over all the years we'd been together. It wasn't a regular love situation. If I disappeared, there would be withdrawal issues, and it would be super tough. "But we stand a chance that won't happen. We really do. And if it does, if I don't come back, you can get over it."

Maybe it would be better for him, not to be so tied to me. I'd held him back, living in Pompey all these years. He'd never admit it, but I'd always felt that was true.

He turned away so I couldn't see his pain. "How can I live with myself if I let this happen to you?"

I put my middle up to his back and wrapped my arms around his chest. Feeling his body was the purest form of bliss. Losing him would be brutal for me too. But still: "How can we live with ourselves if we don't do this?"

He sighed. "What have you cooked up?"

22. CHEETA

Big Reveal in The Bronx

AS CELESTE LUNGED for Shake and me in the Universe, I punched the black square. Bam! We were back in my room. I let go of his hand and rolled off the bed, trying to find my balance. His hair was shocked out like an electrocuted anime character. He coughed long and hard, flicking the hand I'd gripped as he tried to get back his circulation. "Were you trying to break my bones?" he asked.

"Sorry. Didn't want to lose you."

"I would have held on!" He got softer as his focus shifted to someplace far, far away, like a space explorer that could never go back to just walking on the Earth. It was easy to guess that he wanted to return to that Universe just as fast as I'd brought us out—even if Celeste was in there, even though I gripped him so hard. I'd given him the same addiction I'd had from the first time that lens sent me in there.

"Did you ever see the Sidhar woman in there before?"

"No. Guess it was just a matter of time, with Mercury in her prison. How long could he keep something like the Universe a secret?"

"Wonder how long she's been roaming around."

"The way she looked so freaked out… I bet it was one of the first times she went in there."

He stumbled over to a rocking chair and collapsed. "So The Fist is using Izabel and Tristan to make more Charismites. This is going to get a whole lot worse."

"We got some plays left."

He looked at me sharply. "Like what?"

"What if Mercury was in front of that monitor with all that gobbledygook coding on it for a reason. Maybe that's a clue. Why the hell can't I get that recorded! Pisses me so bad."

"So you'll go back in again and find it. You will," Shake said. "What did he mean by Downtown?"

"I don't know. And there's the other thing."

"What?"

I played him another message I'd recorded, the one where the senator sounded so crazy and kept saying "She red."

It took Shake a minute to recover, seeing Miles that way, knowing what happened after that. "What he said makes sense to you?"

I'd already showed Shake some stuff that I never intended. Might as well keep spilling the beans. "There was this bot that Miles and I built together. We called it Diana. Sometimes it looked like a little girl and sometimes like a woman. Does this transformation thing."

"Why would a VIP like the senator spend time making that?"

If somebody had asked me that two months before, I would have said that it was because we loved being together, and we loved puzzling out robotics stuff. Especially me. It was our time together. No one else's. But now… "I don't think it's a coincidence that the bot took off like a bat out of hell the day Miles disappeared."

"So it knows stuff."

"Maybe. I think Miles was trying to tell me something about it with the 'She red,' given its hair color."

"But he said 'she,' not 'it.'"

"Yeah, he always did that with Diana. It's extra special."

I made us some green tea, which always steadied things after I was in the Universe. When I handed Shake his cup, he looked confused. "Why build a bot that does that girl-woman transformation thing?" he asked. "It's got to be a lot more complex and expensive to do that."

"Miles never gave me a straight answer. It was his idea—and frickin' hard to put together."

Shake stared into the air. "It's hiding something."

"I think so."

"And you don't know where it is?"

"Right. But I've seen it around, walking down the street in little-kid mode. Sometimes it stops on a street corner, just far enough away that the guards don't get agitated. And it just kind of stares at the house. I think it sees me, up here in the window. Then the thing takes off."

"Can you communicate with it?"

"Message delivery is always blocked. And tracking it doesn't get me very far." I flipped on my air screen and pulled up a satellite surveillance recording. It showed the little girl bot flitting down hilly 145th Street, then along the broad sidewalks of Lenox Avenue. Diana was so fast and slight, zigzagging among the street walkers. The camera completely lost track of it around 133rd Street. Every other surveillance holo showing Lenox at that time was completely useless, too.

It was getting late, and Shake needed to push off. Just as I was letting him out the front door, he suddenly turned back, looking embarrassed. "About that message from Zahra—you know, my ex-friend."

"Forget it."

"I don't want you to think…"

Didn't know how to take his tender look. "I already knew you're an asshole."

"What a relief."

PETUNIA DELIVERED SOME *arroz con pollo* to my room. But I didn't get down much. Talking with Shake had washed an old memory back to me. It was from about a year before. Miles and I were building Diana down in the cellar—away from Nadia. Back then, she hated me, and the bot too.

"It's not a *she*," I told Miles. "It's an *it*."

"Not to me. I just can't think of her as purely a machine."

The scent of old dirt eked through the chilly stone walls, and Miles' head nearly scraped the rough ceiling beams. The people that built that mansion back in the 1800s would have peed their pants, to see a humanoid like Diana dead center in that space. I was working on the flubber. It's this material with nano-scale macromolecular porosity that would make Diana's facial expressions seem really human. Getting it to work right was so damned hard, but I was almost there.

Miles was grinning at me. "So I've got some robotic pronoun issues."

"Hey, you're the one that forked over all the dough for Diana, so I guess you can call it anything."

"That's one way to think about it, Mutt." I rolled my eyes at that. He was teasing me with the "mutt" thing; I knew. But I didn't exactly love it. Would have called him on it, but he darkened all of a sudden and said, "You're going to be okay, no matter what."

"What are you talking about?"

"Yeah, I guess that does sound random. I'm talking about college, and whether you ever go."

"Who said I wanted to do that?"

"You will. Someday. But even if something happens… I know your mind, how you work out little things that would try the patience of most people. And you figure out huge things, like this bot."

That made me proud. But now, I had to wonder if he was worried that he was going to get in awful trouble. And I'd need to figure out how to save him. Maybe he'd even suspected that I might need to find Diana one day. I clamped down on the sobs coming up my throat. Had to stay calm. *Where the hell was that damned bot?*

I wrapped up in the green-striped comforter and rocked in a chair before the dead fireplace, breathing in the black smell. Shake's empty tea cup was still on the steamer trunk. Wished he was still there. The guy was growing on me, even though he was way too fancy.

Nah. I wasn't even going to go there.

My mobile buzzed. It was him. Shit. *We were thinking about each other at exactly the same time?* On the air screen, Shake's hair was all messed up, like he was still recovering from the Universe. He didn't even bother with a hello. "Do you think we could kill her in that Universe?" Celeste. Didn't need to ask what he was talking about. "I'm thinking strangulation, but I'm not picky."

"I like the way your mind works. But it's virtual."

"Not virtual like anybody's ever seen."

"Point. But we don't know how different. And if we could kill her in there, that would mean she could kill us."

"Point. All the more reason for you to take me back in there. Two against one. Give it a think."

"Right." It did feel good, to have somebody else with me in that damned Universe.

MY HEAD WAS crowded with too much stuff over the next few days. First the Washington memorial service for Miles, then the New York one, which was two days later. Big, honkin' receptions after each one.

It was hard to stay focused during all the speeches by three ex-U.A. presidents, a Supreme Court justice, three congresspeople, and even a few common folk that Miles had helped out along the way. Colin had everyone laughing through their tears when he spoke at the National Cathedral ceremony. He was at Nadia's side for each one. It made my skin crawl, the way he was sucking up. Was he one of The Fist? I kept looking around the pews, wondering how many Fist a-holes were there.

On the night after the New York memorial it took me a while to doze off. Tried not to think about the burial the next day at Woodlawn Cemetery in the Bronx. The Morellis had a family plot there, so Miles' ashes were going to have a lot of company. I was half asleep when my mobile pinged. The little girl bot sprang up on my air screen.

"It's about time," I snarled.

"Meet me at 145th and Lenox, northeast corner."

"*Now*?" It was 2 AM and a miserable cold rain was pounding down. The bot's holo vanished. *Great.* Five minutes later, I stuck my head out the front door. It was like some giant up in the sky was pouring out water from a humungous pitcher down onto New York. The plain-clothed cops on duty looked at me like I was a bad joke.

"We've been through this. No!" one of them said.

"I know, I know. But if I don't take a walk and burn off some anxiety, I'm never gonna get through this day."

"There's a treadmill. Use it."

"That ain't doing shit for me. It's bad. *Really bad*." Hated to pretend-cry, but that's all I had.

They knew I'd been homeless, that I knew how to look tough and use a knife, which I had in my pocket. Plus, since that attack outside the FBI, I'd learned how to kick box. I kept up the argument until they handed me a big black umbrella and called the sharp shooters, barely visible on the roofs across the street. "Hey! We're letting her pass." All the *café con leches* and *café negros* that I'd had Petunia deliver were paying off.

Had to hold the umbrella nearly vertical in front of my face as the wind and rain battered against it. I turned right on Convent Avenue, then down 145th to the corner with Lenox. Wasn't nobody on the northeast corner, but I could feel eyes on me from someplace nearby. With my back to a temporary wall thrown up to protect a large construction site, I scoped the sex worker bots and their johns in long souped-up hover-limos. Three sopping-wet nightclub trollers weaved by, then circled back looking confused. Sorry-ass addicts huddled under the eaves of a chem store that wouldn't open for hours.

The rain got under the umbrella no matter how I angled it. And even though my parka was repellent and had internal heating controls, water trickled under the edges of the hood and ran down my neck. I cursed Diana over and over, waiting a whole half hour before a message appeared on my air screen: "Look behind you." I swiveled around.

The humanoid was in the back of a black hovercraft, door thrown open for me. I got inside. Couldn't stop staring at that face I'd worked so hard on, golden flubber skin set off by a black body suit. The bot was so finely detailed, so human-like, except for its eyes. They were too transparent—haunted twin pools of hard tech. Should have tweaked that.

"I never programmed you to be such a fucking pain in the ass," I said.

Diana just gave me a mysterious little smile. Really wanted

to slap it. "According to my estimates, you will not be missed by Nadia until 8 AM. We will conclude by 7:24."

The car glided east about ten feet above the street, then straight up the Harlem River. Water churned below us, throwing off light reflections from the high-rise buildings in Queens on the other side. A lacey white dinosaur, the Macombs Dam Bridge, flew by, then the turnoffs for the George Washington, and we went into an industrial section of The Bronx.

The car stopped before a deserted construction site, wedged in between two disintegrating road ramps that old-timey wheeled cars once used. Diana got out and slipped through a break in the metal fence. I followed her to a nearly completed building, which was nothing special.

We went into a giant, empty lobby. "Welcome back," the glowing marble walls said softly.

An elevator shot us upward. Diana stretched out, becoming woman-shaped, nearly six feet tall, the black body suit lengthening over its curvaceous form, blonde-red hair darkening. As irritated as I was by the secrecy, it made me proud that I'd been able to make it do that. We stepped into a vacant, dark space that went on much further than I could see.

"This is where you stay?" I asked.

"Where I'm stored, yes. The building developers are friends of the senator—were friends." Diana's voice had lengthened along with her body; it was warmly musical.

"So why am I here?"

"Watch this." Trails of light streamed from her eyes and collected into a holo, showing the senator at his desk. The way he looked—the dark worry on his face, the sharp-angled blue suit—was how he'd been that last morning, before he disappeared. I squeezed back a lump in my throat. Had. To. Focus.

"Cheeta," Miles said. "I've asked Diana to show this to you in the event of my passing. She's been instructed to remain hidden and to find you if that happens. I've conducted a huge investigation in secret over the last year. I intend to share it with the Senate subcommittee that's focused on The Fist, but if you're seeing me now, it means that didn't happen. I've managed to find out the names of every corporate executive who is a member of that cabal, and every bribe they've paid government officials. The list of people involved is substantial: judges, congresspeople, the president and vice president—city and state politicians as well.

"Workers have suffered because of abysmal conditions in offices and industrial facilities. Poor people struggling to stay alive have received far less government support than they should have. Climate disasters are much worse because of the money that has changed hands between The Fist and corrupt officials. And the end result? Corporate profits have soared to obscene levels.

"Diana holds copies of all my findings. It's inside of her, every last detail. You need to make sure this information is released to the world. Don't let anyone stop you. This must come out!"

The holo became two streaks of light again and streamed back inside Diana's eyes. It felt like the towering building was crumbling, that everything around me was falling. But nothing had changed, except me. The bot handed me a cup of water. "This will make you feel better."

Seemed like a good idea. I took some gulps, looking over the huge empty room, which was becoming more visible in the pre-dawn light coming from huge windows. A large black box was up against one wall. My mind grew clearer the more I drank. There was a slightly sour taste to the water, but not bad. "What's in this?" I asked.

"Something that helps when humans are in shock."

Good call. "Show me what you're hiding."

The bot splayed out its fingers, and a stream of icons for hundreds and hundreds of holos arced out from them into the air. The header of each one contained a name. Some I'd never heard of. Others I recognized from my work with Miles—congresspeople, judges, diplomats. Then came the names of corporate titans that had done the bribing, all members of The Fist. These were the people who had taken Miles—taken Mercury, Izabel, and Tristan. These were the ones who *killed* Miles. "Behind each name is all the information Miles discovered."

"He found out all of this by himself?" I asked.

Diana smiled. "He had me." She walked into the big black box, and it sealed shut like a bank vault.

I got back in the elevator. The bot's car was waiting outside.

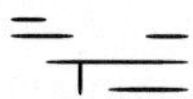

IT TOOK ALL my will power not to say anything to Nadia later that morning. It wouldn't have been good to drop that info bomb before the burial. That evening, I found her in Miles' study, staring down a tunnel of hopelessness. Her grand, rose velvet bathrobe spilled out around her. All her wrinkles had wrinkles on top of them. She looked like she wanted to kill anybody, everybody. But then she saw me. An awful misery took over her face. "Tell me about your mother."

Hadn't expected that. "What do you want to know?"

"Did there ever come a time when you remembered even the littlest thing she did without needing to push it away because it hurt too much?"

"No," I whispered.

Then I told her.

23. SHAKE

Zzzzish!

THERE WAS SO much going on, we decided the best way to talk everything out was in-person. Nadia rode up to Pompey with Memere and me. When we arrived, Mikhail was outside with Jarat. It was the first time Nadia had met the FBI guy, and they assessed each other quietly as we watched another car zip up the long dirt road and land on the lawn. Cheeta stepped out, tough as ever, and then a humanoid with reddish blonde hair, about four feet tall. Would have looked like an exact replica of a little kid if it weren't for the transparent eyes, working, working, working as it took us all in.

Nadia clutched the back of a lawn chair, staring at the bot. "Bloody hell."

"What?" Petra asked.

"God's sake, why would Miles replicate his own sister?"

"Wow. He did?" Cheeta said. "He showed me some pictures of what he was going for, but I didn't know we were doing *that.*"

The humanoid had a piping voice: "She died at four. A two-inch growth in the cerebellum and lesions on her lungs and spine. Couldn't be reversed."

Nadia let out a huff. "You're not the bot I've seen."

Diana lengthened into a really hot full-grown woman type. "Is this what you're looking for?" it said more deeply. Nadia's face curdled with jealousy.

Mikhail whistled in admiration. "That's quite the hat trick. Don't see that type of humanoid very often." He held out a hand and introduced himself to Cheeta, who was beaming.

"Mind if I take a peek at its controls, sometime?" Jarat asked her.

"Sure."

We headed down into the bunker, where Lush had been cooking up a storm. I practically attacked the fried fish—crunchy crust, moist and succulent inside—along with collard greens and the sweetest sliced tomatoes.

The Charismite trailed her fingers along Jarat's neck as she passed behind him with a dish of mac 'n cheese. A look washed over him, like she'd given him a shot of courage. It was a pretty good bet that they had some plan in the works. Diana had reverted to little-girl mode and was watching them curiously, too.

Mikhail put down his fork, face darkening. "I know we're all here to figure what we're going to do next. And I absolutely want to help where I can. But my wings have been clipped. I won't be able to provide protection the way I did at that party." Jarat and I traded a look. It wasn't a huge surprise, since four of the bots Mikhail "borrowed" from FBI's Washington offices to protect us at Memere's bash had been badly damaged—and he wasn't supposed to access any of them to begin with. But without his added protection, things could get considerably more dangerous, depending on what plan we put in place.

"I'm sorry we got you in trouble," Memere said gravely.

"I got *myself* in trouble. But anything I can do besides the muscle, I'm on it."

We took a break before dessert with mugs of hot cinnamon tea, and Cheeta gave us a Diana demonstration. The humanoid swept its left hand before us, and hundreds of holos emerged in a carousel, each one about six inches square and labeled with a name. "Some of them are members of The Fist, and some are the people they've bribed," Diana said.

"Lovely," Memere said. "Go slowly, now. I want to see all the snakes up close."

As the holo cards circled, Petra identified five members of Nuhope's board of directors. They were all C-suite execs at various Fortune 100 companies. Three were supposedly die-hard members of the Independent party. The Fist revelations kept coming, one secretly funded politician followed by another—more and more corporate execs. It was a horror show, the kind where the main character's body is opened up and it's full of crawling roaches.

"There is nothing I'd like better than run a stake through each one's mouth and out through their behinds. Then I'd rotisserie the lot over a fire for eternity," Nadia said.

"Yes! Exactly," Memere said.

"Where did you find all this intel?" Mikhail asked the bot.

The humanoid's cold, clear eyes were amused. "I scraped information in dark files the senator obtained. Then I worked at speeds a thousand times more rapid than most analytical tools available today."

"Remind me to stay on its good side," I whispered to Cheeta, who snorted a laugh.

"We should know more about Celeste, all the chinks in her armor. Can it work on that?" Jarat asked Cheeta.

"We're on it. Those assassins don't scare me. I'm going to start dropping names of who's in The Fist on the OuterNet with all the background intel. The longer they hold onto our people, the more names I send."

"Blackmail, pure and simple," I said. How many politicos would get ousted when the scandal broke? How many corporate fat cats?

Nadia got up from the table abruptly, agitated. "This is where Cheeta and I beg to differ. We've been arguing about it rather vociferously." She poured out some Pinot Grigio. Cheeta glared at her, then knifed into her food a little too hard.

Nadia gave her a compassionate glance. "Dear girl! Everyone! Please understand. We all want to get everyone out of that prison before there's any more death, or children." Her voice was heavy with worry. Everyone knew about the Charismite babies that Mercury had revealed in his message. What havoc would they create? Could we contain them? Sure hadn't worked with Izabel.

The diva continued: "No matter what, all of the information about The Fist has got to be made public. Not just a few names dribbled out now and then. We've got to wait until a time when we can release all of them, completely. It's what Miles died for."

"We'll get the rest of them out when everyone's safe!" Cheeta said.

Lush put a hand on Cheeta's own. "I like your plan a whole lot, darlin'. And you make some good points too, Nadia. But there's something else that Jarat and I want us to try." She gave everyone a gap-toothed grin, flirtatious dimples showing. Her husband didn't look entirely eager about whatever she was going to say. "How about I dish up some apple pie first?"

Like we could possibly say "no" to anything she suggested.

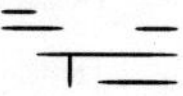

I WAS BACK in New York getting ready to execute Lush's secret plan when an old friend popped up on my air screen. "Hey, Patch Man. You know what sucks more than you getting fired? You kissed me off too!"

"Never, Phineas! Why would I do that? And why the heck are you calling me? Aren't you in the middle of a race?

"If you listened to the news that doesn't pertain to your fucked-up situation, then you'd know I quit."

"What?!" The people who were in charge of *Space Ace* now must have flipped out.

"They were making me say RDA political crap from a goddamned script! That ain't me."

"They let you out of your contract?"

"Exercised a clause. My lawyer got me cut loose. Now I'm working as a consultant for Tseng. In the racing division."

"They're lucky. Nobody flies higher or faster than you."

"You got it. It ain't braggin' if it's true." I only heard him with half an ear as he went on: "Never thought I'd love this kinda test stuff… cryogenic energy… multi-purpose…" I changed into some flying gear as I listened in private mode. My adrenaline was off the charts, thinking about what I was about to do. Barely registered that he was pitching me with a show idea.

"Hey!" Phin finally said. "What's with the dead silence? Don't you have anything to say?"

"Sorry. Can we take this up later?"

"There's a giant opportunity here, and I'm not waiting on you forever."

"Got it."

Half an hour later, I was inside the Morelli mansion in ghost mode. We'd decided to stage our operation there because there were so many eyes around—sharpshooters and guards, of course. But we were counting on some sleaze-bag Fist spies too. I sprinted upstairs to Cheeta's room.

She was staring out the window. I signaled the device and became visible again. "Hey."

She swung around. "*Jesucristo*!"

"I've just been here a minute. Don't want you to think I've been spying."

"I didn't." Her dark eyes had a sweet longing in them. "Can I try that someday?"

"If Jarat lets me, sure."

"Hey Petunia," she called.

The matronly bot popped up on her screen. "At your service!"

"You see Shake come in?"

"Only a slight change in the air current and slushing sound five minutes ago."

"The front door was closed," I said. "Had to go through it. But the cops hardly noticed."

"Must ring off," Petunia said. "Colin Steward is with Nadia."

"What's he doing here?" Cheeta said.

I went downstairs in invisible mode and followed the mangled music to a sitting room. Miles' former chief of staff was in an easy chair listening to Nadia, who was at the piano. I sat on the floor beneath a red and black spattered Jackson Pollock painting and realized that Nadia was warbling something from the dusty old American Songbook playlist. Her voice was flat, then on key, then scraped upwards.

I have to hand it to Steward: didn't even wince. He had on this preppy-looking suit, and his right foot was turned in. Wanted to bet his sandy hair had been slicked the same way since boarding school. But he'd definitely come off well on camera.

The song ended, and he clapped long and hard. "You're getting a lot better! Before long, you'll be ready for the stage."

"What a macabre idea," Nadia said.

"Then why are your practicing?"

"Because it keeps me from murdering someone." Nadia smiled like a cannibal. "To what do I owe this unexpected visit?"

"I just wanted to see how you're doing, and to say how sorry I am, that I haven't been more, uh, supportive."

"That's quite alright."

Jarat's voice whispered in my mobile: "Showtime." That meant he was in ghost mode, stepping out of a car with Luscious in front of the mansion. I could hear Petunia in the foyer talking to the guards.

"Let's make it another time," Nadia said.

"Are you sure you s—" Colin froze, eyes like huge question marks. The air in the room went hyper-clear.

Nadia smiled at Colin's incredulous look as Petunia showed Luscious into the room. The Charismite's magnetism was so strong. Had to wonder how much extra Juice she'd taken. The hair on my arms was standing on end. And more body parts were active than I wanted. *She's like your frickin' aunt!* I told myself. *Calm the fuck down.*

Lush's coppery hair billowed out around her shoulders as she glided toward Nadia. She was wearing a knee-length satin-silver dress that softly outlined her curves. The two women embraced like two waifs lost at sea. And as they pulled away from each other, the diva was washed in a glow. Lush's dreamy eyes became startled as she pretended to catch sight of Colin for the first time. "Oh! Who is this yummy creature?"

Colin approached, barely stopping himself from kissing her as he introduced himself. Lush went blank, then smiled broadly. It was jarring, how she was dissembling—this woman who had always seemed plainly honest. "I know about you! The senator's main guy or something, right?"

"Or something," Nadia said ruefully. After about five minutes of Colin's excited babbling, she nearly pushed him out the door, and he finally took off.

Silence.

"Shake?" Lush whispered.

"Yeah. Here."

"Me too." Jarat's voice placed him right beside his wife.

Nadia's eyes were haunted with fear. "I'm so sorry that all of you have to do this."

The Charismite smoothed out the fake fur trim on Nadia's robe. "Are you kidding? This is gonna be better than sex."

"What?" Jarat said.

"Well, almost, Babes."

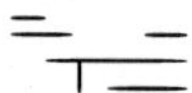

JARAT FOLLOWED IN ghost mode as his wife went to their car. I raced to my waiting hover bike around the corner in a secluded alleyway where no one would see the machine disappear, which happened as soon as I straddled the seat. It was light enough for me to do that, whereas the Ellington car stayed visible, too heavy to be affected by Jarat's "condition." Didn't take long for me to catch up with them, flying at two-thousand feet, higher than usual.

"Something's happening," Cheeta's voice whispered from my mobile. "Military-type 'craft moving up the coast. This ain't no drill, the speed they're going."

Jarat's voice came in: "How many?"

"Five."

Within three minutes we hurtled past Poughkeepsie, heading due north.

"They're over Philly," Cheeta said.

"Yeee ha!" Lush shouted.

Five minutes later, we passed Albany, then seared the air above Lake George. "Now!" Cheeta said. Tiny silver dots in the gray sky turned into four fighter aircraft flanking a helicopter.

They circled the Ellington's mag-lev, which hung a sharp left and headed west.

BAM.

A missile blasted the car's backside. The mag-lev sputtered badly, flames twisting out. I tailed the burning car, heart pounding, waiting, waiting. Finally the Charismite bailed out in a parachute. Jarat's voice whispered in my ear. "Falling with my love." Must have activated his parachute, too.

"This is da bomb," Lush laughed.

A laser beam from one of the aircraft sliced through her parachute's cords. A hatch yawned open in the helicopter's belly, and Lush was sucked inside. I redirected my bike to tail it, flying faster and faster. Slamming the brakes, I flew over the handlebars directly onto the back of the chopper. I landed between the big blades slicing the air on top and the smaller ones on the tail. It seemed like a very lucky break, but the relief only lasted a split second as my body slipped. I prepared to meet death. But I managed to grasp a flat metal band that circled the helicopter's exoskeleton. There was just enough space for my fingers to fit around it. Slowly, very carefully, I managed to climb up the band and then hoist my legs over the back of the chopper, straddling the metal body.

I knew my hoverbike was hurtling toward the ground, although I was too terrified to look down. The auto controls I'd preset would give my ride a soft landing. At least, that was the plan. Why the fuck did I ever think I could do something like this? I *produced* shows with stuff like this in them. That was *it.*

Through my mobile I heard Lush: "Where are you taking me?"

Thank God. That meant Jarat had managed to get sucked inside and was giving me a soundtrack. Cheeta must be getting it, too.

"A safe place," a hard voice said. Female. Military grade.

"You attacked my ride! What kind of fucked up—"

"You're going to be okay, ma'am. Nothing to worry about."

Time went by—how much, I didn't know. Riding the chopper was taking all my concentration. The sun was in my eyes, had to be flying west. "Where are we?" I whispered to Cheeta.

"Nearing Omaha. You okay?"

"Yeah," I lied.

Cheeta said something else.

"What?"

"You're doing this!" Yeah, right.

Inside, the commando's dead voice again: "Where's your husband, ma'am?"

"Home, I guess."

"Uh-huh. Clear the space everybody. Here we go."

There was a heart-rending scream. Jarat! Hardly recognized him. They must be using infrared, right inside the aircraft. And there was little doubt that DirecWep gun had fired into his invisible body. *Was he burnt up? Dead?*

Do not let him down. Keep on this. Find Izzie, find Tristan. Had to. Had to!

Long red beams fired out of two aircrafts alongside the chopper, streaking through clouds, searching until…

ZZZZISH!

24. LUSCIOUS

Full of the Devil

A MEMORY. EARLY morning. Call of a blue jay searching for his mate came from the bedroom holo screen, showing mist on the field outside our house. So few jays left; this one so lonely. Jarat lay beside me, my heart. The stubble on his face was bristly silver, hazel eyes hard and sexy as he turned to me. Silver black hair like a ship back from the Arctic.

He slid two fingers down my face. "We got now."

Another memory, from later that day: Jarat's invisible body outlined by an infrared beam in the helicopter, screaming as a seven-foot humanoid fired a DirecWep into his gut. The giant SWOOSH as my husband slipped through the wall and out into the sky. Where Shake must be, somewhere. Other aircraft alongside the chopper firing again and again. Awful cries. From Jarat? Shake?

Each blast killed me inside. All the while, this military commando watched me coldly. My Juiced-up state didn't do nothing, 'cause it was a humanoid. The creep got on its air screen. Must have been talking to the other aircraft. "Find the bodies. Confiscate that invisible tech."

A soft tinkle came back in response. They might be able to find them. But it would be a whole lot harder to do that if the ghost gizmos were activated and if Jarat and Shake found a good place to hide.

Then again, I was probably fooling myself. How could they

survive? *You killed them with this lame-brain plan. You did this!*

The bot in charge and two other humanoids came at me with an injector tube. I raged and raged, screaming, biting, kicking as they tried to control me. Chems stabbed into my chest.

I went out. And now I was… where?

The cold stream of air up my nose had some kind of chemical in it. Reminded me of the spacecraft I'd been in long ago, when I went up above the worl' and space danced. Was I in an airship? Where were we going? Opened my eyes and blinked hard. There was some kind of Goddamned Alice in Wonderland thing going on. Spindly yellow lamps, turquoise walls, and cushy rose-colored furniture.

I sat up, taking in the four tall posts on each corner of the bed I'd been lying on, silky coral-colored duvet. Slipped my legs over the side. As I stood, it hit me: no pain anywhere, despite getting banged around by those bots. And I was wearing a black cotton-ish V-necked top, baggy drawstring pants. Who put those on me? There was a carafe of water, tinted blue, on a side table. And I was doggone thirsty. So I poured out some into this glass that looked like cut crystal. Tasted normal, but that didn't mean anything.

"Just a few vitamins inside to help you recover," a flowery voice said. I swung around. A woman in the middle of the room. I'd seen enough images of Celeste Sidhar to recognize the dark eyebrows like wings above dark eyes that spoke of ancestors from the Indian subcontinent. She was too far away for me to see the defect in them, but I knew it must be there. Her long, sweeping skirt was a video screen pattern of diamonds, sapphires, and emeralds, constantly moving. Made me dizzy.

"Sorry for the rough handling," she said, arranging herself on a love seat. "I'd hoped it wouldn't come to that."

I smiled like honey. "Where's my son? And Izabel?"

A door sparkled open on the far wall. "Right here, Ma." Tristan glided through behind a servant-type bot. My son was wearing loose satiny clothes, top unbuttoned to show his chest—like a sleazy nightclub crooner. Gliding? On air slippers? Was this really my timid child?

"Don't worry. Everything's great with me. And Izzie, too. Right?" Tris gave Celeste an adoring look.

"Really quite remarkable, what Izabel is doing." Celeste could barely control her hands, itching to get him in bed. His gaze licked her face like a lollipop. They'd had sex many, many times; I could tell. He ran a hand up Celeste's thigh, and she swatted it playfully. "You're embarrassing me."

"Sorry." Tristan smiled wickedly. He got up and gave me a careless hug. *Really? Was that how he felt?* "So glad you're here, Ma." I looked closely into his eyes, trying to sense that this was just an act. But nothing. Tried not to panic.

Celeste was reading me. "I'm sorry, really sorry about what happened to your husband and that other intruder. Was that your friend Shakespear? They really left us no choice."

Tristan looked shattered. "Christ, Ma. What were you all thinking?"

Kept my voice gentle. "What happened to them? You know, don't you?"

"I'm sorry," Celeste said, like her heart was breaking. "They—didn't make it."

No. Wouldn't believe that. It was stupid to even to ask. Tristan looked at her like she was a freakin' sun goddess or something. Wasn't any sadness in him at all. His own father dead or maimed or who knew what—and Shake, who was like a close cousin!

"Tell you what. Why don't we show her?" Celeste said.

"That? Now?" Tristan said.

"Yes. She's ready."

"I don't know about that." What were they talking about? Did they have Jarat and Shake's bodies somewhere?

Celeste fondled his face. "Darling, let's give her a little happiness." Relief shot through me. She couldn't have them and say that.

They led me down this ugly green tube-like hall, then down another, and another. Turned left, left, left, right, on and on around the corners. The curved floor bounced a little under my feet, like thick sneaker padding. Celeste got ahead of us a little, and Tristan grabbed my hand, kissed me on the cheek apologetically. I itched to swat him. Dipping his dick in that evil woman when I was ready to slit my wrists with worry for weeks! His own Da dead, if what they said was true. *Or not.*

A zing of wild energy hit me… like Tris and Izz long ago. Mercury had told us in the message about babies. But I wasn't feeling just one or two.

"Steady now," Tristan whispered.

Let me at them!

Celeste stopped at one section of a green tube that would have looked like all the others, if it wasn't for the vibrations. She hand signaled some commands that sparkled open the wall. Inside, the room was so red and bright that I couldn't get my eyes to work right at first.

"DADDY! DADDY!" Out of the deep areas of the room came the sound of running feet. A little boy headed straight into Tris's arms. Then another, and another. Adorable little Charismites hugged him as he laughed and laughed. Wait. These weren't babies. Maybe two years old. That sure didn't make sense. Why were they so grown?

"Hello!" Halfway down the huge room, Izabel was holding

a child, hand protecting the whorl of blonde hair, the small head glowing with invisible light. Izzie was an angel, a Madonna. She got up and walked toward me.

"Now calm down. Calm down!" Tris shouted at the kids, who all looked so excited to see me.

One of them had eyes blue and green as living worl's; another had tiger-gold orbs, like mine; another set were aqua and silver. They looked sharp-minded, full of the devil. Wasn't no doubt they were all brothers and sisters despite their differences, all tiny versions of Izzie, Tris, Jarat, me, and my dead friend Dove Brown, who was Izzie's biological dad. Fuck a goddamned duck!

"Say hello to Grandma Luscious!" Tris said.

Three of them rushed me, wrapping their arms around my middle. More were ready to pile on. Izzie walked up with the one in her arms, "Look, Sweetness. This is your grandmother." Then she pecked me on the cheek. Felt like my whole worl' was snapping out from under my feet.

Tristan grinned. "Celeste gave the kids this stuff that makes them mature really fast. How long will it be before they're adult?"

"Before you know it!" Celeste said.

Poor things. So innocent, making me drunk with their thrill. Were Izzie and Tris completely brainwashed? How come they were so happy? Couldn't let all these kids be trained by that she-wolf and the rest of The Fist. How did they plan to use them? Wouldn't let anything happen to them. Couldn't.

They were my grandchiles!

25. CHEETA

Hellfire on Earth

DIDN'T USE MUCH media after Lush, Jarat, and Shake disappeared. Knew it would make me crazier than I already was. *Dangerous* crazy. Petunia gave me the basics of what was going on: that second Izabel message was playing all over the place. A massive number of people thought that Tippi and Wanza should control the world. Which was whacked, but that's how powerful the Izzie propaganda was.

Some of the Tippi lunatics had shot and killed the president of the Supreme Africa-Mideast Federation. There'd been an army of humanoids to protect him, but that wasn't enough. He and Miles had been so tight. Met him three times.

While that was going on, there were riots in the Commonwealth of Asia and Republic of Europe as people tried to get the top leaders to step down. Armies of government bots slammed down on the protesters. Half a million people were either dead or wounded. The rulers were forced into seclusion. The heads of two smaller nations, Australia and Israel, were in hiding, too.

"I don't frickin' care if Izabel is a prisoner. Don't care if she isn't in charge of her own mouth. I hate on her something fierce," I told LiZee.

My alarm buzzed. Time for a meeting. I went into Mikhail's virtual chat room. It seemed kind of empty, with just Nadia, Petra, the FBI guy, and me there.

Mikhail showed us some military-grade holos of the attack on Lush's car. The airships that snatched her blazed across the sky and just seemed to disappear around the Seattle Treasure Zone. "There's got to be other feeds of that, but I've been locked out of accessing them," he said. "Anybody heard from Jarat and Shake?"

"Nothing. Complete silence," Petra said. "Why in hell did we let Lush do that? We never should have agreed to that idea." *No shit.* Were Jarat and Shake dead? What would The Fist do next, with three adult Charismites and God only knew how many jacked-up kids?

We'll never win. Never, ever stop them. Tried not to think that, but it was frickin' hard. I brought up the idea I'd had before: the one about releasing The Fist intel that was stored inside Diana—exposing more and more about the group's secret control of political leaders. Maybe they'd get so scared they'd give up the prisoners.

"They'd eat their own young before they let those Charismites go," Mikhail said.

"Then we might as well release all the names at once," I said.

"That won't work either. If you push every member of The Fist off a cliff, you can be sure those Charismites are going with them."

"I will not let this be the end. I will not!" Petra said.

"You got an idea about that?" I asked.

Petra had these beady dark eyes, but she didn't say nothin'. Maybe she hadn't figured it out, but I sure knew my move. If there was a message in that Universe that could help us get everybody out of that prison, then I was sure as *chingada* going to find it!

I FLY-SWAM AROUND the bubbles for a long time, calling out all the names that mattered. Tried to find the bubble with the soldier that had the baby, too, just in case I could get more on him. *Nada*. And no signs of that bish Celeste. I breast-stroked so far into the orange, way past where I'd ever gone, shouting and shouting.

Nothing.

Faint thrumming caught at my ear. What was that? I moved closer. Music! And not just any music. My very favorite song, this fly tune from NoQuest, with a kind of retro hip-hop beat: "Papa Don't Love." What the hellz? Was there a message from NoQuest in there? I'd love to find that! I swerved past a mountain of bubbles—giggling, cooing, whispering faces inside.

This dark red area of the Universe came into view. Reminded me of smog or smoke, only it had a shape—a giant disc that looked miles long, and parts of it curling and curling in little circles. Felt like the smoke was pulling me forward, so gentle, and the music was coming from in there. I went with the flow at first. But the red sucked me faster and faster, spinning me around like a tornado with no wind, a whirlpool without water. Thousands of bubbles spun by, bursting open, people holos stretched like rubber bands as they swooped down into the funnel, big as an inverted mountain—crying, laughing, shrieking.

I backstroked and kicked hard. But I couldn't do nothing to get away from that vortex, swirling faster and faster, the music morphing into clicking icicles. Groped behind me for the black "stop" button. It jerked away wildly. I couldn't stretch far enough to punch it, no matter how I tried.

Felt like I had electric skin, like a million insects were stinging me with fire, all over my arms, legs, torso, face, tongue.

I hurtled down, down, into the center.

"Goddamnit!" I yanked so hard toward that black square that I thought I'd dislocate my shoulder. Jabbed it something good.

And then.

And then.

Back in my bed. Gulped for air, wailed long and hard. Petunia rushed in and scanned my body. My heart was beating like crazy. But after a while, it calmed down, and the stinging feeling on my skin went away. So the bot went back downstairs.

Something niggled at my brain—something Mercury had said. I contacted Diana on the private darknet connection we'd set up. Nobody else could get to the humanoid but me. I told it what happened, then asked: "What's the word 'downtown' mean to you—other than a part of a city?"

Diana's fingers sparkled as the answers materialized. "Downtown is a section of the Milky Way. In the center. Filled with supernova remnants, neutron stars, black holes."

Fucking Mercury. He couldn't have just come out and said, 'Stay away from the goddamned red place?" That would have taken like two seconds.

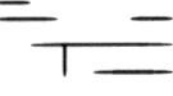

THE DAY SHAPE-SHIFTED by. About nine that night, Nadia burst in shrieking like she'd just won a ga-zillion Americos. "Darling!" she said. Which was weird. We weren't exactly on "darling" terms. "Wait until you see this!"

She pulled up a holo of this trans chick with cheeks so chiseled they looked like some kind of cliff. Didn't need to be told who she was. "Hello! I'm Ginseng Childe, the undercover lover of any news story that the main media just can't get right. And I have a treat for you today." The camera view widened, and there sat our friend, looking a lot more posh than I'd ever seen her—silver hair slicked back, black chainmail dress.

"Petra Cardinale. Former CEO of Nuhope. But you may know her best as the mother of Izabel Cardinale. Welcome!"

"Hello there. I also have a son. Shakespear, who used to be one of Nuhope's most successful producers." Petra shared a recording of Shake, walking with her outside Nuhope, surrounded by cheering staffers. I'd seen it before, from when they got booted out of Nuhope.

"He dreamed up *Space Ace*, right?"

"Among many other shows that attracted gargantuan audiences. He's missing too. So is Luscious Melada Ellington and her husband Jarat Ellington."

"Wait. What? Luscious is a freaking legend! Do you know what happened to them?"

"They tried to save Izabel. I believe Luscious was abducted. Shake and Jarat are either imprisoned, or dead."

"Wow. You need to unpack some things here. First, why did they feel they needed to save Izzie? She said in her message she was just taking some time away."

"It's a lie. She was most definitely abducted, and she's being used as a very powerful propaganda weapon." The camera closed in as Petra swallowed hard. "There's something I need to explain to all of you—to the whole world. Izabel Cardinale is not who you think. My daughter is what's known as a Charismite. She has powers of persuasion that go far beyond what any human is capable of doing naturally. Similar to Luscious."

"I knew Luscious when she was at Nuhope," Ginseng said. "Never forget how she outed herself—that confession when she told everyone that she could sway their minds to think red is white, white is green, *anything*."

"Izabel can do the same thing as Luscious. My daughter is

being used by a secret organization known as The Fist, which controls much of the U.A. government. The same organization that tortured, then assassinated Senator Morelli."

"You're sure about that?"

"Absolutely. The Fist is forcing Izabel to deliver the messages that are making everyone crazy with fear. She's being used as a tool to promote the agenda of the U.A.'s president and vice president."

"So, that asteroid. The one Izabel talked about in her message. Do you believe it was sent by a warring exoplanet? Is that part of what she said real?"

"No. It's a hoax, plain and simple."

"Like I reported before."

"Precisely. No scientific organization based in another country has been allowed to review NASA's analysis of the asteroid, and the Department of Defense has offered no solid evidence either. No activity has been reported on the surface of Kepler-22b. But Izabel's powers of persuasion are so incredibly strong that her messages are convincing everyone that Tippi Pavlarona and Theowanza Newton should govern all territories on Earth."

Ginseng frowned, mouth in a tight line. "I need to understand something. Why did you wait to tell us about Izabel's special powers until now? When you were at Nuhope, you put your daughter in shows in order to attract massive numbers of people, to make that company a bloody fortune. She was manipulating people. You knew what she was doing."

Petra let out a puff of air. "You have to understand. She was bursting at the seams to perform. That's all she really wanted in life. She wasn't hurting anyone. She didn't appear in any commercials, at all. And no political messages. She was making her fans happy, entertaining them, showering them with love.

That's how Shakespear and I both thought about it. And we knew that if the world at large knew what she was capable of—well, she probably would have been abducted a lot sooner than she already was. Or possibly killed."

"So what are we supposed to do with this information?"

Petra looked directly at the camera, as if looking at every person watching. "Understand the facts. You are being manipulated by very, very powerful forces through Izabel. The world has already been invaded. Not by some unknown warring planet. By Tippi Pavlarona, Theowanza Newton, and the puppet masters behind them—members of The Fist. And you may hear messages from Luscious and Tristan next. Force yourselves not to listen to any of them. Keep away from Nuhope's content and every other source of media controlled by the U.A. government."

"Well, that eliminates about two-thirds of all the content available—if not more," Ginseng said.

"Not your reports, right? And as you say, there are others, too. Go back to the message from Luscious delivered to us all, so long ago." Petra flipped her air screen, and the old recording showed up, of Lush about twenty years before looking hotter than hot, saying: "Love everyone you can, every place and animal on Earth and whatever's out there on all the other planets. And if you can't love some of them, just pray for them. Pray for the rest."

The message had turned everybody's head around at the time, made them more peaceful and kinder than they'd ever been—for a while. Especially the Elites and Middles. At least, that's what I heard. It happened before I was born. But over the years, the message had been buried under layers of other ones that probably would have been about ten-thousand miles deep, if there was a way to stack them up. Some people still replayed what Lush had said, but not enough to really change the way people acted or thought much anymore.

The camera view switched back to Petra. "We've got to calm the whole world down. Search out the truth. Avoid media that's harmful. And if you know anything about where any of these missing people are, please, please contact me. The future of this planet, of our sanity, depends on it."

Ginseng closed out the interview with a hot-tip address for anybody who had clues, and the news report disappeared.

Nadia shook her head, sighing. "A valiant attempt. But I don't know that will do any good. People are already so convinced. The Fist will counter with something."

I did a major social media blitz, reposting Ginseng and Petra's interview. We had to do everything to spread it wide and spread it fast. Nadia was off the grid, but Mikhail told me he was doing the same thing, using a secret alias. I didn't get to sleep until four the next morning. About 10 AM, I was woken up by an extremely sexy voice coming from my mobile. The guy that showed up on my air screen was around eighteen and seemed so different than the holos his parents had shown me. The naïve boy had turned into a real hunk, with these intense velvet blue eyes.

"Hi. My name's Tristan Ellington," he said in a voice that was like some smoky blend of booze. Wanted to grab him, kiss him, take him to bed, KILL him. "You may have heard of my mother, Luscious. You know, the one that tweaked so many heads way back when?"

"Of course they remember me," said Luscious, dancing into view. She gave her son a kiss on the cheek. Her eyes were different—the brown color swirled with gold flecks, so hot. "We just wanted you to know that no matter what you might have heard, we are living the good life. Just had to get away, things were getting so nuts!"

"That's right. And that asteroid was definitely a scout from Kepler-22b. NASA's scientists have indisputable proof."

Lush flashed a smile. "After that interview with Petra Cardinale, I can't blame anyone if they have doubts. But people are smart. They'll get that she was just spewing a bunch of lies."

"Exactly," Tristan said. "Which was why she was pushed out of Nuhope."

"And that was long overdue! But there's something else we got to think about now. Things need to change. We've got to stop all the violence, all over the world. For those of you who aren't in the U.A., I've got an extra special message: back off from the folks who run your countries. I get that you must be really unhappy with them. Because we need one group of supreme leaders on Earth right now. And you know who they should be."

Tristan shrugged. "Tippi and Wanza, of course."

"Of course. Give your rulers a chance to calm down, to see how they can work with Tippi and Wanza to make sure our planet defends itself in the best ways possible. Because if we don't come together, well…"

"Let's not go there, Ma. People are scared enough already."

"You're right, Son. Well, that's about it."

"Bye-Bye!" Tristan said. The two beaming Charismites vanished.

Nadia was screaming down on the first floor. Her voice had never gotten all the way up to the attic before. That's how loud it was. I paced the floor, more and more upset. Goddamned Universe! It had to give me *something*.

26. SHAKE

Hairbrained and Jacked Up

THE SUN SNEAKED down through cascades of parched leaves, creating a flutter of shadows on the hard-packed ground and six green and brown splotched tents that were home to the Finch family—and now Jarat and me. The forest was a shadow of its former state, before the temperature went nuts. But its scruffy beauty still gave cover to a Chav encampment that was so far back in the wilderness, near the Niobrara River in Nebraska, that hardly anybody knew it existed. There were four adults, who looked like they were in their twenties and thirties, along with six kids and an older woman they called Gramma—although I got the impression that the designation had more to do with love than biology.

The Finches took the whole idea of "ferociously independent" to the max. They led a renegade existence that didn't involve paying onerous taxes, and if any authority figured out where they were living, they just picked up camp and moved. Two of them, Janae and her husband Dontrez, had a rock star reputation in a hush-hush kind of way, though I realize that sounds like an oxymoron. Farmers loved them, because they knew how to hack into the controls of agricultural equipment and do repairs for a fraction of what the authorized dealers charged. They traveled throughout the county to do their "fuck you" magic on the machines.

Another member of the group, Leroy, was the one who

rescued Jarat, who had landed in some bushes on the edge of a field. Leroy was hunting when he heard a giant thump. He went into fight mode, sure that he was about to confront one of the logging thieves that chopped down trees on the Finch's territory. But Jarat grew visible when Leroy wasn't looking, and he convinced the Chav he was harmless.

Of course, Jarat didn't tell Leroy the full story about how he got there. When the Fist aircraft had captured Lush, Jarat managed to collapse his parachute and get inside the 'craft behind his wife—after which he was discovered, attacked, and blasted into the sky. His stomach wounds were not half as bad as they might have been if he hadn't been wearing protective body gear. But they were no joke. After the ejection, he managed to get the parachute open and floated, invisibly, down to the ground.

It was a softer landing than what I'd gone through—by a long shot. When I was on the airship's backside, a DirecWep sliced through my body armor and sauteed my left shoulder. Then my parachute didn't fully activate. Sure, it was better than plummeting in pure freefall. Instead of that kiss of death, two of my ribs snapped when I slammed into the ground. Gritting my teeth, I stayed in invisible mode, watching the occasional coyote and wolf from my resting spot under some bushes. They were crazy to find the wounded animal they smelled but couldn't see.

After a while, I found enough strength to walk slowly through the wilderness. The pain was so bad that it left me dizzy, and I was parched, too. There was no way to signal anyone on a mobile; both Jarat and I had ditched ours before we went on the mission. The wrong people could have tracked us. Even mobiles with fake identities were too risky. Finally, I collapsed.

By the time Leroy and Dontrez walked by me a day later, I was just strong enough to make myself visible. Jarat had urged them to do a search.

Leroy's petit wife, Khloe, was tasked with helping our broken bodies recover. She worked busily along, but her eyes were really hostile. "Christ!" I winced when she wound a bandage around my shoulder and arm pit too tightly.

"Okay, *okay*." She loosened up the strips of cloth and walked away impatiently.

Leroy was digging a new patch of garden nearby and slowly walked over, sitting down cross-legged beside us. His face was narrow at the jawline, eyes very sensitive, with an animal wisdom. "She's different than you think."

"Oh yeah? What do we think?" Jarat asked.

"You tell me."

"We know better than to insult our doctor," I said.

Leroy picked up a stick and peeled away the bark. "When she was younger, she lived in Kansas City. Worked as a doctor's assistant—this dude that had experimented with all kinds of natural medicines. That's why she knows so much."

"Yeah, that salve she's been using on us is amaz," I said. She'd also given Jarat some syrup to drink that was helping his stomach heal.

"Yeah. It's what she learned from the doc. Anyway, this rich dude patient started stalking her. She had to keep watching her back every time she went home. One night he grabbed her, forced her into a dark park, and stuck the barrel of a gun up her."

"Jesus! That's brutal!"

Leroy wrapped the bark around his fist like he wanted to strangle the asshole. "Didn't go off, but it damaged her inside. She took off without telling anybody. Ended up near here half starved. We're okay, her and me. But liking men doesn't come natural."

"Thanks for explaining," Jarat said. Leroy picked up his shovel and got back to digging.

Khloe's cold edge reminded me of Cheeta, back when we'd first met. It had always felt like there was something behind it, other than a personality clash. Which still might be there to an extent, even though she took me into that bizarre Universe. Strange person. Where was she now? Did she go back in? And did she spot Celeste again? We needed to get out of Nebraska and find all the prisoners, *yesterday.* But that wasn't going to happen until we gained more strength.

"Oh. That's new." Jarat stared at the mug of goat milk he'd been sipping. "Didn't know he liked it."

"He?"

"Jewles." Oh, right. The kid whose brain had been transplanted into Jarat's skull. Small traces of Jewles' memories surfaced every now and then. Jarat doubled over, groaning. "Shit. My stomach doesn't like it." Not only was his belly a hellhole, but the grimness on his face, ever since I'd first seen him in Nebraska, told me he was in hardcore anxiety mode—about his wife and son along with Izzie, and the need to get back home. But I sensed there was something more. He wouldn't open up unless I got him in the right mood. Knew that from experience.

An opening came a few hours later when we were watching the news with Dontrez, using his mobile connection to the BaseNet—which was more restrictive than the OuterNet. That's what most Chav could access. There was a segment on a group of technologists testing some equipment in weather extremes—Antarctica and the Sahara Desert. Wasn't all that interesting to me, but Jarat perked up.

I waited for Dontrez to close down the screen and walk off. "There's a theory I want to run by you," I said.

"Yeah?"

"I'm guessing that even though Lush went almost completely off the Juice for years, you have an addiction to her—not just love."

He turned growly. "So what?"

Two screaming boys raced past Gramma. She grabbed a baseball and threw it, popping one of them in the back. It must have hurt bad, but he didn't scream, just walked off with the other kids through the trees.

I kept going: "It's bad enough for me, not being around Izz. But it's got to be a helluva lot worse for you without Lush and Tris."

"Nah." Jarat stood up. "Only like somebody ripped out my heart and lungs. And if I don't find them I'll die." He walked away.

Two days later, the BaseNet transmitted Ginseng Childe's interview with Memere. It made the Finches wildly confused and frightened, to hear what Izzie's own mother had to say about her. Everybody in the camp was a huge fan of my sister. Jarat and I didn't explain our connections. In fact, we hadn't told them much of anything, and they didn't ask much. Guess it takes a renegade not to question another renegade's story too closely.

Then came Tristan and Lush's holo message. It was so clear that the Charismites' minds had been altered—the way they bent the truth like some kind of evil funhouse mirror—just like Izzie had. Sure, I was extremely agitated by it, but Jarat was off-the-wall apoplectic.

A WEEK LATER, we gave the Finches as much paper cash as we could. Khloe stuffed some of her medicine in our pockets. And we trekked back out into civilization, taking a trail through the woods. Thirteen miles later, we came to a station where long-haul trucks recharged. We plied a driver with more of the money and hitched a ride to Detroit, then used the last of our Americos to proposition another trucker. She let us off on Manhattan's Eleventh Avenue.

Jarat's hair, which had always been scraggily, was wildly out of control, and I didn't even want to know what mine looked like. The sun had darkened us, and we were so bedraggled and smelly that the idea we were Elites, let alone Jarat Ellington and Shakespear Cardinale, would have seemed like a long stretch to most people that knew us.

"Coming with?" I asked. Jarat knew I was headed to Memere's place.

He looked haunted. The overpowering need to find Lush and Tristan was getting worse. "I'm going to stop by a Theseus friend." The one that had helped him heal after other attacks around twenty years ago, he explained. Lived on Sutton Place.

"Okay," I said. "I know it's a risk, but I'm probably going to get a new lens with a fake I.D. Gotta get connected."

"Same. Don't worry if you can't reach me for a few days."

"Going back to Pompey?"

"Nope." He took off before I could quiz him. Okay. I could deal.

The sun was nearly down by the time I reached my childhood home in ghost mode. After the Nebraska wilderness, the 19th century townhouse looked so *normal* and alien, all at the same time. Elegant white wooden molding around the doors and windows accented the red brick facade; window boxes full of straw flowers and trailing green vines, valiantly thriving despite the intense heat.

A small private militia stood guard. I waited for someone to open the front door so I could slip inside without that damned slurping sound. Two hours went by before Memere came out in a maroon dress, eyes flashing with whatever was on her agenda. "Might want to stick around," I whispered in her ear.

She froze. I could sense her heart racing, her barely curbed cry. The guards looked curiously at her odd expression. "Bloody hell! I've got the wrong day for that dinner!" She went back inside, leaving just enough time for me to get in before shutting the door. We walked down the hall away from the front windows, on into the living room, and I materialized. She looked at me with teary relief, exclaiming about my dirty still-fragile state. Would have hugged me too, if I hadn't warned her about my broken ribs, which were still healing.

Her faithful bot Geoff whisked in. Tiny lights whirred behind its round black eyes. "Crikey. Glad you're back from the walkabout. But you smell like a horse with diarrhea."

They listened to a short version of what had happened in Nebraska as Geoff inspected my ribs and shoulder wound. After I cleaned up, it rebandaged them and added some pain meds that were stronger than Khloe's.

I went off for a nap. It was past midnight by the time I came back downstairs, wearing some clothes that I'd found in my old bedroom closet and a new mobile lens with a fake I.D. that Memere had kept handy in case I showed up. Geoff had whipped up a dinner of trout almandine in whiskey sauce along with a caramelized mélange of red peppers, parsnips, Chinese eggplant, and zucchini—which it knew I loved.

As I gave them more details about the Nebraska adventure, there was something in my mother's expression that was like a secret hurt. I fished around as casually as possible. "Did you get a lot of flak after the interview with Ginseng?"

"Eh. I've seen worse."

"What about the new company? How's it coming along?"

"Not bad, if you go for rotting corpses."

Ouch! Her worried eyes made me think that something else was bugging her. "How's Nadia and Cheeta?"

Score! Memere placed her fork and knife in an X on the bone-china plate, lacquered blue fingernails set off by the white. "It's better that you see." She contacted Nadia. The two of them had developed a secret code, so that anyone hacking their mobiles wouldn't know what was going on. The message "For fuck's sake, when are you going to start singing again?" actually meant "They're back!"

Nadia shot back with: "Never. Quit bothering me," which actually meant "Get the hell over here!" Turned out that 2 AM visits were as good as broad daylight for Nadia.

This called for an incognito traveling plan. It would look strange for Memere's car to travel to Nadia's at that hour. Instead, I took her hand, and we both went invisible.

"Wowza! It's even more thrilling than I remembered," she said.

"Ready?" I asked Geoff.

The humanoid opened the front door wide. "What the hell are you doing?" it said to the two guards puffing at smoking sticks in the yard. "It would be easy as shit to get past the two of you."

As the guards gave Geoff a piece of their minds, Memere and I slipped outside without a slurp. We wandered over to Madison and hired a cab from a turnstile on a deserted street corner. It took off, looking completely empty, as if it had been hired remotely and was on its way to pick someone up. We arrived at the Morelli mansion a few minutes later. Memere alerted Nadia we were outside with another coded message. Almost immediately, Petunia emerged and offered the guards some deep chocolate cupcakes, and we followed the bot inside.

Nadia glided toward us in a festive robe with feather trim. “I’m beyond elation!” she said, voice much stronger than I’d last heard it. “Fetch some cocktails, Petunia love. What would you like?” We voted unanimously for scotch, and Petunia bustled around to get it as we went into a salon. The place felt empty. Cheeta’s absence was mystifying as the minutes ticked by and our glasses were nearly drained.

“Is she upstairs?” I finally asked.

“In a manner of speaking,” Nadia said sadly. “Take a splash more for fortitude and then I’ll take you up.”

We climbed up three sets of stairs to Cheeta’s kingdom. The Fire Salamander’s tiny black eyes were riveted on her mistress’s head poking out of the bed covers. Cheeta’s eyes were open, but vacant. Easy to figure out what she was doing.

“How long has she been in there?” I asked.

“Two days.” I let out a string of expletives. Nadia wrung her hands. “I considered popping out the lens to make her come back. But I don’t know if it would work. And even if it did, she might kill me.”

That did make sense. “Okay. I’m going to give something a try.” I spread out on the bed beside Cheeta, wincing from the pain in my ribs, and felt for her hand. Her fingers seemed oddly delicate, more feminine than they ever had before. “It’s me,” I whispered. “I’m back. Let me in.”

At first, nothing happened. I listened to the faint sound of her breath, waiting. Her fingers squeezed my own. There was a soft pull, then a yank as she sucked me into the Universe.

THE ORANGE VOID seemed more brilliantly lit than I remembered; had to squint my eyes at first. Bubbleheads floated by. The murmuring faces looked as if they were so anxious to get out, dying to have somebody burst them.

Cheeta was even more wild-haired than usual, filled with a kind of crazed obsession. And miraculously, all my gnawing pain was gone. The relief was stunning. At least, until she snapped: "What the fuck took you so long?"

"It's so touching, your delight that I actually survived death."

She smiled sadly. "Sorry. My brain gets kind of whacked-out in here. And there's this." I suddenly realized that she was cupping a bubble. The face inside made me feel like I was in a plummeting elevator: Mercury, looking like a walking cadaver. He was in a dirty little room—no monitors in sight.

"This doesn't look like the one that got away," I said.

"No. It's different. I'm afraid I'll lose it—that the recording won't work. And what he's saying is like a foreign language." She squeezed the bubble.

Terror radiated from Mercury's every molecule as his holo popped out. "Morelli getting weaker and weaker. Won't be long before they kill him."

I looked at Cheeta. There wasn't any foreign language. This was an old message, with old information. "Just fucking listen!" she snapped.

Mercury went on: "Did you see the code on that monitor in the message I sent before? It keeps switching, but it always comes back to one sequence and keeps on it for a long time: Star percent ampersand algebra. No. No. Start again: star star percent ampersand allegra dot dot dot." It took Mercury fifteen minutes, just to go through the gibberish one time—at least, it felt like fifteen minutes. Cheeta reran the message and hit the red record button. She did that over and over, just to make sure she had multiple copies. I tried to memorize the string of code too as a backup, but it was really complex. Eventually, Cheeta let the holo disappear, sucking back in the bubble. It floated away.

"You've been in here two days," I said. She was astounded at first, then shrugged it off. "Seen Celeste?"

"Yeah. A long ways away. She didn't spot me. Looked like she was calling out names. Couldn't hear what. But bubbles came at her, and she opened them up and threw them all away. Every message that came at her was probably junk."

"So, she figured out how to do that."

"It ain't like mastering inorganic chemistry."

"Which she's probably already done." A bubble zoomed toward us—the head of a white-haired punk with a snarling video tattoo on his forehead. I yanked Cheeta off to one side.

Even though bubbles like that were so nutso, I couldn't help but admire the magnificent quality of this strange cosmos, the towering collections of brilliantly lit bubbles, the mottled areas of the void where the tangerine color was rippled with blues and greens. Not that I was going to mention it. We weren't in a frickin' art gallery, and we had too much other stuff on our minds.

"I figured out something new about this place. See that?" she said, looking behind herself. I followed her gaze to a small, faint star icon with seven points. "When I fooled around with it, I realized that's what Mercury used to send messages. You can record something, hit that star, and it puts a bubble around the message."

"Huh."

"It's just a good-to-know thing, at least for now. Want to get the hell out of here?"

AS SOON AS we came out of the Universe, the pain in my shoulder started clawing me again. Cheeta stirred on the bed beside me. Nadia and Petra were collapsed in the rocking chairs, fast asleep. Petunia and LiZee were frozen in place, staring at us. The salamander flicked her black and orange tail and scurried over, head popping up on Cheeta's side of the bed.

I groaned, and the ladies woke up with a start. Memere was beside herself. "Shakespear Cardinale! If you don't tell us what's going on, I will have you fired into the goddamned sun!"

"She will have my complete and undivided assistance if you two don't explain everything!" Nadia said.

She had clued Memere in on the Universe, so we didn't need to start from scratch. But they were both so insistent that Cheeta said, "Christ. Give us a second! Other people need to hear about this too." Once we got our bearings, she pulled up Diana and Mikhail on her air screen, using a darknet connection.

"We're not going to be able to reach Jarat," I said, adding that he was going to be offline for a few days. Memere frowned at that.

"Jarat can take care of himself," Mikhail said. "Let's focus on what we got."

Cheeta pulled up Mercury's message, and everyone listened to his strange code. Diana went to work, trying to find a match. She had the results in a few seconds: nothing.

"Let's try something else," Mikhail said. "There are some new geographic coordinate systems that the Department of Defense has been testing. Wouldn't surprise me if The Fist is using one of them." Mikhail wasn't supposed to have access to that info, but as he explained: "The more they keep me out of stuff, the more ways I find to get it." After half an hour of trial and error, he cracked the DOD's security code and fed Diana intel on about thirty different test trials.

Diana found a match with a system code named VelvetCursor and translated Mercury's coordinates. "If my calculations are correct, then they're southeast of the Honolulu Treasure Zone." The bot flipped to a satellite view of the spot in real time. Nothing but water. Not a vessel in sight.

"How deep is the Pacific there?" Petra asked.

"Four-thousand-two-hundred-fifty-two meters, around two-point-six miles. Part of an ocean zone known as The Abyss."

How comforting! "How far below the surface can we detect anything?"

"There are micro-cameras all through the oceans that track objects, even in extremely deep zones like The Abyss. But none of them are in this area. No cabled camera platforms around the Hawaiian islands are monitoring it either. And there are no sonar-detection records."

"An aquatic void, as such," I said. "Maybe that's on purpose."

"Must make it easy for Celeste to come and go," Mikhail said.

"Mercury said that the code was constant for long stretches. But sometimes it changed," Cheeta said. "So maybe the prison itself is a submersible."

"Makes sense," Mikhail said.

"Are you sure you can't send some bot operatives out there?" Nadia asked sweetly.

"Sorry. I may be able to crack through security walls, but when it comes to bots, no can do."

"Ballz!" Nadia said. "I fucking *hate* this!"

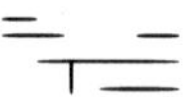

I WASN'T GOOD at waiting for some shift, some new idea about how we could get to that prison. None of us were. In the days that followed, I stayed hidden at Memere's place. It should have felt luxurious after camping in Nebraska—with all the sleep, good food, and Geoff's medical attentions. But I was impatient and bored, which led to a gnawing belief that even if we somehow managed to rescue everyone and nail The Fist, my life was directionless. What was I going to do with myself, if everything got back to some semblance of normal? Then again, what the hell was normal?

My funk ended one morning when I was nursing a cup of coffee, eyes boring a hole through a back window with a view of the enclosed courtyard. The flowers were heavy with humid heat. A shrub gyrated madly, and a man walked through the greenery wearing the kind of jacket reserved for polar expeditions. There was a gray cast to his skin, and he looked extremely thin.

Jarat! He'd slurped through the back wall. After the joyous excitement of his arrival was thoroughly enjoyed, Memere gave him a piece of her mind for taking off for parts unknown. He watched her fondly as he devoured the cheddar and tomato omelet Geoff had whipped up, along with a few slices of crusty bread and some Côtes du Rhône.

"Remember Dr. Kwak?" he asked.

"Who could forget a name like that? Poor man," Memere said. The scientist who invented the digital masking system that allowed Celeste to disguise her appearance.

"I have it. His tech."

"What? How? You found him?" I asked.

He nodded "yes" as he munched some bread. "In Antarctica."

"You went to *Antarctica*?"

"Thus the ridiculous jacket," Memere said.

Jarat jogged my memory about something that happened when we were chillin' with the Finches out in Nebraska: the news spot about scientists working in the Antarctic tundra and the Sahara, testing out equipment in weather extremes. Then he paused to take a sip of wine. "Lovely. A '35?"

"Yes, darling, but go on before I kill you," Memere said.

"I knew from the research I'd done that he was a real workaholic. I always figured that if he wasn't killed and just disappeared, he'd look for a job that was somehow related to what he loved. But if he was evading Celeste, he'd need to keep a low profile—go someplace where no one would find him easily. It was a wild hunch that he'd be testing that equipment, but I decided to check it out."

After Jarat had recovered a bit with his friend on Sutton Place, he had traveled to a station in the Sahara where the scientists were working, snooping around in ghost mode. But there weren't any signs of Kwak, masked or unmasked. So he headed to Antarctica and hung out for a couple of days within an encampment. Just two tech dudes were there, and neither of them detected Jarat while he was around.

There wasn't any signs of Kwak, at first. "But then one of the techies checked in with someone else on his mobile. He had it in audio-only mode. The voice on the other end sounded vaguely like the voice recordings I'd found of Kwak when I did my research. And he was working at an even more remote location." Jarat hiked across bare, rocky wasteland for two days, getting lost again and again. But finally he spotted a tent. "Somebody came out of it, and based on some pictures I'd found of Kwak, he was a perfect match."

"So he wasn't wearing the masking tech?" Memere asked.

"No. He was so completely alone; didn't need to. He was spooked when I revealed myself, needless to say. Took some convincing to make him believe I wasn't out to get him."

I poured out some wine for myself and topped off Jarat's glass. "How much did you pay him for the tech?"

“Nothing. When I told him what Celeste was up to, and how we’re trying to fight back, he didn’t want anything. He can’t stand her.”

“Huh.” That’s all I had in me: huh. But over the next few hours, sections of my thoughts dislodged and moved around—icebergs in a choppy sea, too slippery and jagged to fit together. Until I came up with one hairbrained scheme.

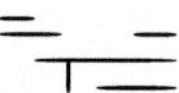

IF THE PLAN I cooked up was ever going to work, then Cheeta would need to tell everybody in the inner circle about the Universe. She got the logic. That wasn’t a problem. But it wasn’t easy for her to unstick the secret from her brain even more than it already was. After a while, she got on board.

We waited until Jarat caught some badly needed sleep. Then the whole group met up at Nadia’s place—including Mikhail, in holo form. Everybody was suitably dumbstruck when she described the Universe—that is, the people that didn’t already know about it. And there were some “ah ha’s” as Mercury’s involvement in this whole mess came fully to light. Nobody was thrilled to hear about our near run-in with Celeste from in there.

“Actually, I’m glad we saw her. That could help solve this entire mess,” I said.

Jarat gleamed with curiosity. “How’s that?”

“There was something that Cheeta and I noticed when we saw Celeste. She was really intent on finding a message.”

“Yeah,” Cheeta said. “It made me wonder if she thought one was missing, or that she was hoping for one.”

I went on: “Say we use Dr. Kwak’s cloaking technology to impersonate someone that Celeste knows—someone that she'd find upsetting, someone that maybe she doesn't expect to hear from. Then we record a message from this person and use the white-star recording function that Cheeta found in the Universe to encase it in a bubble."

Cheeta's face lit up with glee. "And when she gets our fake message, she'll go ape shit."

"Exactly."

Memere raised an eyebrow. "Outside of amusing ourselves with her reaction, what are you going for here?"

"Maybe Celeste is so distracted by the fake message that Cheeta and I can attack her—make sure she doesn't get out of that Universe until she tells us how we can get into the prison. Then we go on a rescue mission."

"That's ludicrous! How do we get to the middle of the Pacific undetected? How do we get under nearly three bloody miles of water?" Nadia said.

"Wait. Hear me out." The room went quiet, and I kept talking.

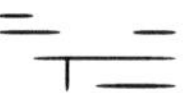

AFTER A LOT of arguing, everyone got on my rickety train. It didn't take long to settle on the people who might upset Celeste the most: her own dead parents, Asrushi and Nintin Sidhar, speaking from beyond the grave, as such. But what would they say that would really push her off the deep end? To figure that out, Cheeta sent the bot Diana on a mission to mine the zillion pieces of content and data that had collected on the Net over the last thirty years.

Diana presented its findings to us on Cheeta's screen from the safety of its Bronx hideaway. First, it pulled up old holos of the mother, Asrushi. The more I saw shots of her, the more

I realized that Celeste had grown up to look nearly identical. Would have been a dead ringer if Celeste put on some weight and switched out her high-end look for the stuffy suits that Asrushi favored.

Like a lot of Elites, Asrushi never needed to work at a paying job. Instead, she had starred in a self-produced cooking show for fans of Indian cuisine. We watched a few episodes.

"Just a little smidge of mango, just a little smidge," Asrushi said in a lilting cadence, putting together her own version of chicken biryani.

"Ugh! That looks slimy," Nadia said, looking at the overripe fruit in Asrushi's hand.

"What's that in the background?" I asked.

"The Sidhar's back patio. They lived in Europe's British Treasure Zone, and their property overlooked the coast of Dover," Diana said.

Celeste's dad, Nintin, was a real worker bee, not that it was necessary. Chemical engineering was his jam. He was quite tall and conservatively dressed. In profile, his face was nearly flat; no cheekbones to speak of, just a small nose. And he seemed buried under a million heavy thoughts in every image that Diana found.

There were tons of surveillance holos and social posts showing young Celeste at an Elite boarding school, Horatio Academy of Arts & Sciences. She gave off this tranquil, flawless look—which wasn't a big surprise, given how she looked now. No one received higher marks in science and math classes. No one scored more soccer goals. No one else was voted as the most likely to become prime minister of the European Republic—or the next great superstar actress. Apparently she was quite the little performer. Again, no surprise.

"I bet she had a lot of enemies," Memere commented,

popping a chocolate-covered dried cherry in her mouth.

Diana, who was in childlike form, shrugged its little shoulders. "She had other problems. There's a ninety-eight percent probability that Celeste and her father adored each other, and a ninety-five percent probability that there was no love between Celeste and her mother."

"You analyze love?" Jarat asked.

"Correct. Through facial tells and body language in every image where they were together. Which may explain why Asrushi wanted to send Celeste here." Diana pulled up a longshot view of a drab building in barren surroundings, save for a few artificial palm trees. A dying tropical forest fringed the background.

"Which particular hell is that?" I asked.

"A reform school in what was once part of the Amazon Rainforest. Designed to smooth out the edges of rebellious offspring."

"If her father loved her, why would he agree to put her in a place like that?"

"His wife manipulated him easily enough. But Celeste never actually went there."

Nadia kept babbling under her breath, and we all tried to ignore her as Diana gave us some more Sidhar family history. Just before Celeste was due to arrive at the school, her parents took a little vacation to the Asian Commonwealth's Thai province. They had a condo in Phuket. Asrushi spent a lot of time in the markets, scouting out rare mushrooms and other delicacies. One mushroom variety she favored looked nearly identical to another that was poisonous. There was a bit of a mix-up, and she served the lethal kind in a dish for dinner one night. That's what a Thai coroner concluded, after conducting an autopsy that analyzed the content of the couple's digestive tracts.

Celeste was in London when both parents died—which made me wonder how she killed them, if that's what she did.

"An assistant was traveling with the parents at the time—a woman who was completely absolved of any crime," Diana said.

"Do you think Celeste and the assistant plotted this?" I asked.

"Probability is twenty percent based on all known holos of the two of them together," it said. Couldn't nail Celeste with that kind of number.

"It doesn't matter if Celeste offed her parents or not. We've got all we need to work with," Memere said. She was ready to charge, like a racehorse at the starting gate—or a woman who had birthed a thousand shows over decades and was hatching a brand new one right there in real time. Her adrenalin was contagious. And right then, it nearly lifted me off the floor.

My rush was interrupted by Nadia, who was mumbling even more loudly. Cheeta fought past it. "So we make a message from Asrushi?"

"That's right. We've got plenty of material to work with."

The diva's mumbling got even louder. Memere gave her an annoyed glance. "Are you having a bloody fit?"

Nadia turned to her with affected charm, speaking in a British-Indian accent. "Just a little smidge of mango, just a smidge." She twirled her outstretched fingers, exactly like Asrushi's gesture.

"That's totally jacked up. Let's fucking nail the bish," Cheeta said.

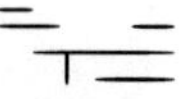

WE WALKED AROUND Nadia like she was a masterpiece of sculptured art. The masking technology made her look like a duplicate of Celeste's mother, in a boxy little pink suit and high heeled air shoes. Everybody whistled and clapped. Jarat's eyebrows were like thunder, taking in the praise for his masking handiwork. But he looked pretty weak, living so many days without Lush. The trip to Antarctica and his still-healing injuries weren't doing him any favors, either.

Mikhail had traveled up from Washington for the grand unveiling. And his eyes were gleaming. "Explain this tech to me."

"It uses something called acoustic levitation—and this." Jarat pulled a pea-sized ball out of his pocket. "Ultrasound is employed to duplicate solid objects or holograms, then this ball vibrates at extremely high rates so that it creates what's known as persistence of vision, which manifests as a volumetric display—a holographic camouflage."

"Yes, I have one in my own pocket," Nadia said, mimicking Asrushi's voice.

"Given that this is going in a holo message, I assume we don't need to worry about how the skin looks under a microscope," Mikhail said, referring to the gangly golden strings he'd zeroed in on before, when analyzing the masking technique.

"That's right."

Mikhail turned to me. "What's your idea about how to get down to the submersible that's holding everybody?"

"Not quite ready to share."

He shook his head at my plastered smile as if to say *frickin' amateur*. "If you don't have something solid, this whole plan is worthless."

"Just give me a little more time." We pressed forward, despite everyone's skepticism. I placed the call I'd rehearsed in my head over and over, the one that could make all the difference. Once again, like the three other times I'd tried, nobody picked up.

But I was convinced I'd get through, eventually.

There was other stuff to do. I put on my proverbial director's hat and coached Nadia as she worked to get Asrushi's odd turns of phrase and gestures spot on. Cheeta watched me with a kind of amused respect. "You should do this for a living," she said when I stopped a minute to drink some water.

"Ha ha. Maybe I don't want to anymore."

"Maybe you're a rich mixed-up boy."

"You got me there," I said lightly. Didn't want her to realize how that was a little too on the nose. I could tell she wanted to ask me more about it, but Memere came to the rescue, calling Cheeta over to the corner where she was working on the script. Cheeta gave her some thoughts.

While that was going on, Jarat adjusted the ultrasound and volumetric display system so that the replication of Asrushi was more exact.

"Do you think that all the masked people who were involved in the abductions were Celeste?" I asked him.

"Who knows? But most of them had that fleck of imperfection in their eyes, just like her," Jarat said. "My guess is, she's too much of a control freak to leave the impersonations to anyone else. It's possible that she used a voice box when she turned herself into the guy that Izzie brought home."

"Makes sense."

"So what about that little transportation issue?" Jarat asked.

Once more with feeling. I placed a call again to the only person I knew that could help. And this time, he picked up.

"Patch Man! Where we drinkin' tonight?"

"Wish I could. But I got this idea I want to talk to you about."

THE ENERGY IN Cheeta's attic intensified with a sense of scary hope as everything came together. Nadia gave us a command performance, which Cheeta captured in a recording. It was showtime. I spread out beside her on the bed. Doubts rushed up and grabbed me by the throat.

"What is wrong with you?" she whispered.

I looked around. Everyone else was busy finding a seat—not paying attention to us. "Just that I'm getting us into one helluva hail-Mary-pass situation."

"That's just coming to you now?"

"Of course not. But it's getting to me."

"Let's just go poke at her, okay? See what happens."

"Right. No sweat." She rolled her eyes at my sarcasm. How could I just poke at this when my sister's life was on the line? And Luscious, Tristan, and Mercury's lives? Some baby Charismites probably needed saving, too. How the hell were we going to deal with *them*? Cheeta gave me a fierce look. I could deal. I sure as hell *would* deal.

Everyone else went quiet, watching us. I found Cheeta's hand. A band of hope surged through me. And we were sucked into the Universe.

27. TRISTAN

The Sex God

NEVER THOUGHT I'D want to kill myself. But it was hard to think of anything else, after that message with Ma—when Celeste used a fog of drugs to make us so pliable that we'd say anything on that teleprompter.

Now I knew firsthand what Izzie had gone through, why she was so crippled and dark inside. Sometimes when she handed me a coffee cup—or when I brushed past her going through the narrow doorway into our bathroom—I was filled with the sickness that she still felt about what was happening. But after we found the kids, she started to change. She was obsessed with the chubby bodies and laughing faces.

When she sat in one of the chairs in our room—hair increasingly uncolored, light brown roots longer and longer—she tended to hum. I was struck by the translucent quality of her skin, like opals. And I knew her mind was with the children, feeding them, playing with them, bathing them. She didn't need to tell me that she was hoping that somehow we'd all be saved—that the kids would find some kind of happy, harmless way of living in the greater world. Not that it had worked out for the two of us. Not that we'd ever get out of this place.

One day, she caught me brooding. "Stop looking like that!" she said.

"Like what?"

"Keep your funky-ass mood to yourself." I laughed at her,

because what else was there to do? But she turned serious. "Do not leave me, Tristan. Do not."

I worked at changing my head. And after a while, memories of a little creature helped me figure out how to do that. Back home, I'd studied crab spiders in the garden. They grew to about half an inch, with eight eyes. Their four front legs were longer than the ones in the back. They skittered in any direction and changed color from yellow to pink when they perched on the roses, waiting to kill insects that were sometimes much larger than they were, like grasshoppers. Their venom took care of the disparity.

I had my own ways of changing, my own venom—the poison of lust and love. A molten sensuality rose up when I fixated on Celeste now. The more I had sex with her, the more addicted she became. She *needed* me in her saffron-colored chambers—even though she convinced herself that I would not control her. She thought she was protected because she knew what I was.

It was good that she didn't understand—that it was only a matter of time before I weakened her enough. That's what I tried to fix on. She had her spider bots. But I could be a spider, too.

The sex with Celeste grew more impassioned and frenzied. I kept building up my body with push-ups, squats, and lunges. Clothes were left in the room that Izzie and I shared: shirts tight across my increasingly muscular chest, pants emphasizing my small waist and powerful legs.

Izabel and Ma watched me transform with a wry cunning. "My son the sex god," Ma said. I saw her every day in the nursery when Darrel took us there.

"Baby boy's all grown up." Izzie teased. I tried to sense some jealousy in her, some distress that someone else was taking me down, not her. But to her, sex was about as important as sampling appetizers—something easy that came and went. Still, there were small moments when she looked at me with ironic regret. It perfumed the air and then disappeared so quickly. We were both human aphrodisiacs. And we would probably die in this place without ever making love.

When I talked to Izzie and Ma now, it was mostly about the kids. But sometimes, when the children were sleeping and we were together in the nursery, Ma told us about what had happened out in the real world—all they'd done to find us, the whole story about the asteroid and the coming power struggle with another planet. She was sure that was fake.

As Ma talked, the memory of what she and I were forced to say in that message rushed back to me even more clearly. I relived the beetle-like cameras trained on us. Celeste had stood by the teleprompter, directing us. We didn't have the mental strength to fight any of it, to feel anything but complete and utter surrender to what she wanted us to do.

The kids were also really disturbing. "I don't like what's happening to them—the whole age acceleration thing," Ma said, hoisting a little auburn-haired girl named Willow back into her transparent-walled bed. "I'd sure like to know what kind of drug Celeste put them on."

"I'll see if I can get her to tell me," I said. "How old do they look now?" Izz and I were so clueless about kids.

"You were both abducted about… what was it? Six weeks ago?" It was hard for us to know, without mobiles. But we took her word for it. "These chillens look to be maybe three."

I watched them change every day; it sent chills through me. After a while, Ma said they reminded her of four-year-olds. At the rate they were growing, it wouldn't take long for them to become young adults.

Some of them were a little goofy, others extremely sharp—in an innocent kind of way. Any company would have paid an incredible amount of money to have one of those little Charismites as an influencer. And the kids would only grow more powerfully persuasive with time. Companies like Nuhope would do anything—the frickin' RDA would do anything—to have human tools like that in their arsenal.

"Hey, Sex God. Tend to the stink," Ma said, handing me a diaper and a red-haired boy named Cal. "There's five others right behind him."

"Can't you give me something else to do?"

Ma glared. "Sure. After you earn your daddy stripes doin' the tough stuff."

"I don't want to earn any stripes. I don't want to have anything to do with them!"

"They can't help who they are any more than you can."

"They are *weapons*. That's all they'll ever be."

"Go ahead, Son. Teach them what it's like to be hated. That way they'll become even bigger weapons. But maybe, just maybe if we *eventually* show them what's important, they stand a chance when we get back out in the real world."

I snickered. There wasn't going to be any "back out."

Ma read my face and grew even angrier. "All this time, your father and everybody else has been searching and searching for you and Izz. Your father risked everyth—" She swallowed hard, refusing to be scared.

It wrung my heart out, seeing her like that. "I know, Ma. And I'm grateful. I am." I'd already tried to find out from Celeste if she really knew whether Da and Shake were dead. And it was pretty clear she didn't.

"If your father is alive still, and Shake, and everyone else, then they'll find us," Ma said. "Mercury has fed them stuff that will help. You know that. Maybe he's still doing that."

It hurt, to think what might be going on with Mercury now. His eye had been such a bloody mess when they scraped out his lens. Even before that, his legs had been bad. How else was he suffering? I couldn't sense him. He was too far away, and it didn't seem safe for me to go outside and visit him in the quiet moments. Since Celeste had changed the door codes, I only went out into the corridors when they took us to the nursery or I was led to Celeste's private quarters. I'd figured out what the new code sequence was; Darrel wasn't careful enough when it signaled the walls to open. For all we knew, Celeste had fixed the glitch with the security cameras, and they were going 24/7 in the halls now. Sneaking out might lead to massive trauma.

Given all we had to worry about, the least I could do was make Ma happy. I turned Cal on his back, taking off his soiled diaper.

Izzie came up to me with Aleesha in her arms. The little girl had baby-fine blonde hair and the same startled gray eyes as Izz. "See, Honey?" Izzie said to her. "He's so good at that. *He's so good*." Her eyes were lakes of fiery energy as she gazed at me, whispering: "You can do this. You know that, right?"

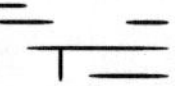

I COULD BE like that little crab spider. Had to keep reminding myself of that as I rehearsed exactly what to do. It filled me with dread, what might happen if the whole thing went wrong. But finally, a silent click went off in my head. I was ready, couldn't wait any longer.

Just like always, Darrel escorted me through the green tubes to Celeste's suite and signaled the wall to open. The bot had this disapproving way of saying, "I'll be back in a few hours."

Inside, everything was artificially serene. Vivid yellow walls accented white cabinetry. Usually, the bank of monitors on one wall was dark. But this time, the air screens revealed various views of the prison. I could see Ma feeding a raven-haired boy; Izzie teaching three other kids how to sing; blinking equipment in what appeared to be a control room. A hallway view showed three spider bots crawling sluggishly across a ceiling. Mercury was on his dirty pallet, suffering badly, I had no doubt. A patch covered his damaged eye. He seemed to be silently talking to someone, some vision. Was he hallucinating? How long could he live like that?

"Hello there," purred a familiar voice. I put a big cold stone over my anguish and pivoted around smiling—couldn't have looked more turned on by the long rose-colored shawl playfully revealing parts of Celeste's naked breasts and the black hair shaved to a small patch over her vulva. My touch sent ecstatic quivers through her. My kiss could have melted the most emotionless human.

Had to make this work. Had to.

She fell back onto an air bed. It was hard, pretending that I didn't despise her, that I was beyond excited to lick her, bite her, throb her. I made her orgasm six times and beg for breath before we peeled away from each other.

We finished a bottle of Bordeaux and started another, nibbling on some caviar and crème fraiche on toast. I pretended to doze off, and Celeste got up, barely in control of her balance. Just before she disappeared into the bathroom, she snapped her fingers in an elaborate pattern to turn on the camera surveillance system in her suite so that Darrel could monitor my activities. She never wanted the bot to see us when we were having sex.

I'd memorized those snaps on earlier visits. As soon as she left—before the system had fully kicked in—I turned it back off. Would Darrel pick up on that? I forgot to breathe, waiting for an attack. But nothing. Silence.

Celeste came back out, and I watched her through the barest of cracks in my eyelids. She tipped her head back and gasped just a little as she inserted Mercury's lens, then sat on an air chair, motionless. She was comfortable enough, being around me now, to do that when she thought I was sleeping. The lens seemed to send her into a trance, a state where she no longer saw me or any of her real surroundings.

I could have strangled her. It would be so easy to crush her windpipe. But it was against everything in my being, to kill anyone. What was beyond this prison? Mercury had told me he guessed we were on the ocean floor. How was he going to do anything?

28. CHEETA

Mean Mango Mumsy

THE UNIVERSE VIBRATED like a silent rattlesnake, so bright it made our eyes hurt at first. Bubble people looked desperate to make us pop out their holos—silly, slick, full of confessions, all at the same time.

"All right," I yelled to Shake. "Let's find that *puta*."

A rope of energy coiled between our connected hands, like our souls were talking to each other. My heart kept thumping to the tune of "It's real. That's how you feel." Which was just stupid. Had to stay focused. I did a one-armed breast stroke, faster and faster. "Are you going to help me with this?"

Shake snapped out of a daze and put his one free arm to work, too. At first, we couldn't do nothing together, but finally we moved in one direction, faster than the regular float speed. The bubble voices got louder and louder.

"Nobody guessed what I stole."… "Don't you dare talk smack about my wig."… "It's like asking a chicken to make a chicken salad sandwich."… "I knifed him. It was me! *Me*!"

Shake tried to drag me to a stop. "Did you hear—"

"No! Not now!"

Time went infinite. I started to wonder if this was going to be like before, when I was in there for days. Shake didn't complain about how far I was steering us, at least not out loud.

Then I saw it: the dark red area, shaped like a gigantic disc. The closer we got, the more it seemed like it was about a thousand miles long. Shake didn't realize that I was up to something.

He said, "I got an idea, once we get on the other side of this cataclysmic disaster."

"Like that's gonna happen."

"Let's say there's a miracle."

"Okay. There's a miracle."

"Once we get out of this, I think we can make a ton of money by duping that lens of yours and giving people access to this place."

The red was like boiling steam, *bloody* steam, and really close now. I fought my nerves, did not want to get sucked in there. It was sending out this *thump thump* bass twang. You could barely hear it. Wasn't that band NoQuest this time. Something else.

Shake was clueless, which was okay. No sense getting freaked unless it was necessary. He started imitating a promo announcer: "Come to the Universe. Find messages from that old girlfriend you can't quite forget."

"Like that chick in Paris?" *Twangy thump, thump.*

"Hmmm. No. We've got to figure out a way to weed out the… Wait." His face lit up. "Hear that? It's the theme to *Space Ace*."

"Really?" The disc was pulling at us, just a little. "Do this." I back stroked, and he did too, but red coils fingered out of the mass, coming straight toward us, and he was seeing them.

"What's th—"

BANG. The coils lunged at us quick as snakes. Music turned into screechy rumbling. Thousands of bubbles tornado-ed at us, past us. Ear-splitting voices—screams, cries, raucous laughter, a vomit of words too fast to understand. The electric prickles on my skin seemed even worse than the first time I was in there.

We were sucked toward the deep, throbbing core. Thousands of bubbles sucked into the center, exploding, disappearing.

Shake panicked, cursing the prickles like he wanted to murder somebody. He reached behind us, hitting wildly at the black exit square over and over. But it was always just out of reach. I tried so hard to get us out of there.

We tumbled around painfully for what felt like days. Time was so slippery in that place. But little by little, we fought our way back toward the edge, and the vacuum strength weakened. Not that we could exactly relax, with that gravitational pull trying to suck us back in.

Shake looked at me suspiciously. "You knew about that place, didn't you?"

"We got a little closer than I planned."

"*Planned?*"

"It's called Downtown."

"*What?*"

"Downtown. Remember? Mercury talked about it in a message."

"You couldn't even forewarn me ABOUT THAT FUCKING PURGATORY?"

"Honest to God, I thought I could keep us safe. I just wanted to show you how this could make things less of a 'Hail Mary Pass.'"

He understood then, in one shocked second. "Oh. You want to throw Celeste in there."

"It's a thought."

He smirked like that was the worse idea he'd ever heard.

That pissed me off. "You think we can just sneak up on her when she sees her mother's message and hold her until somebody finds the goddamned prison? And how the hell are you going to know when that happens? If we can get her inside

Downtown, it would solve everything!"

He knew I had a point. But he still said, "Ha! Like we won't get sucked back inside like cat fur in a vacuum nozzle!"

After a while, I didn't feel like killing him. And the cat-fur bit kinda made me want to laugh. But I wasn't un-pissed enough to give him that. Even though I knew he wanted to laugh too, probably in hysteria.

We floated around the Universe so long after that it felt like we could have died in the real world by then. A hundred years could have passed. Maybe they'd buried us, and we'd turned into fossils or something. Like I said: it was a slippery situation.

Then we saw it: a black speck in the distance. Could have been some kind of giant insect. We swam-flew closer, keeping behind some bubbles, peeking out just long enough to keep track. After a while, we could see it definitely was human-shaped. Maybe one of the bubble heads had popped out? Maybe somebody else had figured a way to get in there?

No. As we got closer, the shape became Celeste, arms and legs splayed out. She was calling out her own name.

"Shit!" Shake whispered. "We're too far away from Downtown!"

"Look behind you."

He turned and saw the tiny glittering red spot, like a poisonous ruby, in the distance. Its soft rumbling sent shrill fear through every nerve in my body. Shake was right: getting Celeste in there without getting caught ourselves was going to be tough. Celeste glanced in our direction, and we ducked behind a bubble just in time, barely peering out. Her eyes latched onto Downtown. It sure looked like she didn't know what to make of it. Then she looked away, calling out her name.

We moved closer, keeping behind her, watching roiling red Downtown, waiting to strike when we got close enough.

My heart was beating something fierce. Shake looked pretty scared, too.

It came to me, what we needed to do. I whispered, "Izabel, Tristan, Luscious, Mercury. Izabel, Tristan, Luscious, Mercury." Over and over I chanted the names, and pretty soon, Shake was saying them too. Our voices were too soft for Celeste to hear. We moved from one cluster of bubbles to the next, keeping out of sight. Would she kill us in that Universe? Would we look like comatose idiots to everybody in my attic room? Would she see us, bail out of the Universe, and move that frickin' prison someplace where we'd never find it?

"Izabel, Tristan, Luscious, Mercury. Izabel, Tristan, Luscious, Mercury." They weren't just words anymore. Courage rippled through me, stronger and stronger, turning into titanium down my middle. And I could feel it in Shake, too. It was all or nothing. *No. All. It was all. Wasn't going to be no "nothing." Wouldn't let it be.*

Shake grinned wildly. "Hit it!"

I jabbed the white star and out sprang the bubble we'd made, a little larger and bluer than any of the others. Inside, we could see Nadia cloaked in Asrushi's face. Would Celeste realize it was fake?

The bish was still calling her own name, and the bubble responded, slowly soaring toward her. She turned and gasped at the sight of it, gliding faster and faster toward her. We floated even nearer, still hiding. Celeste was fixed on the flashes of sapphire light surrounding her mother. The sphere picked up speed, flying like a hovertrain directly toward her face. She screamed, trying to swerve off to one side.

POW! POW! POW! POW!

It was a lot louder than what an average bubble sounded like when it popped. But there wasn't time for Celeste to think about that as her dead mother sprang out in that square-shaped suit the color of pink digestive pills.

"Hello. Asrushi Sidhar here. This message is for the MI6, the Asian Commonwealth police—anyone and everyone who investigated my supposed death twenty-two years ago. But most of all, it's for the person who thought she murdered me: my daughter, Celeste Sidhar."

"What?!" Celeste shrieked.

Asrushi picked up a mango, tearing at the skin. "It's been an amazing ride, this last couple of decades, living out my life in anonymity. I'd grown so tired of my turn as a celebrity at the time that my manipulative daughter plotted to kill me along with her father, Nintin. She always accused me of being a mean mumsy. But I never would have guessed she'd do that to Nintin. Oh well."

Celeste reeled backward in panic. But Asrushi's holo moved in closer. "When my personal assistant confessed that Celeste had hired her to poison us, we worked out a deal. Nintin was... Well, let's just say I was ready to let him go. Such a depressing person. He really needed to be put out of his misery. With a little instruction from me and enough money for a very luxurious retirement, she was sufficiently incentivized to change the plan just a wee bit. Managed to find a person in the fish market that looked enough like me to kill. Just a smidge of the poison did the trick."

Celeste swatted at the Asrushi holo. It whisked away, still talking. "Now, you might be thinking, 'Asrushi, you adorable, sweet thing. Why on Earth would you suddenly make this heinous accusation? Whyever did you wait? Your fans have mourned your tragic passing for so long. Well, you know that old saw about revenge best served cold? It certainly seemed so much more delicious to make Celeste's crime known when it would be the most humiliating. And my spies are telling me that she's on the verge of becoming the new CEO of… Now, what was that? Oh, right! The most powerful media company on the planet! Nuhope!"

"No, no!" Celeste screamed.

Asrushi pointed her finger directly at Celeste, who swung her arms wildly, trying to swim backwards in the void. But the holo of her mother kept coming forward, larger and larger, the size of a monstrous elephant. "*J'accuse*, Celeste Sidhar! May you rot in the most insufferable state of humiliation known to humankind. Ta-ta!"

With a little pop sound, Asrushi sucked back into the bubble, and it drifted away.

Celeste searched the bubbles around her with an insane rage, trying to spot us, just far enough away from the boiling red Downtown not to get sucked inside. "Well, that was certainly entertaining," she purred. "That idiot Dr. Kwak must have sold you the camouflage tech. Who did you get to play Asrushi? That cow Nadia Morelli?"

Shake yanked us both out of hiding. "Wassa matter? Does the truth hurt too much?"

"That isn't the truth. Not even a speck."

"We're going to drop that message in the inbox of a whole lot of journos and detectives," I said.

"That is, unless you give up the Charismites and Mercury," Shake said.

Celeste opened her wide, dark-stained mouth, howling a laugh. "Isn't that rich? The son of a failed media tycoon tries to smear the woman who's about to replace her. You and your weakling mother will be buried under a manure pile of shame when I expose what you're doing."

"No way! Because your ass is fried!" I yelled.

Shake got quieter. "Unless. Unless! Tell us where they are. Release the prisoners and this all goes away."

We came closer to her, and Celeste backed up, eyes watery, nearer to Downtown. "But you guessed wrong. There wasn't any need to kill my parents, because my father did that all by himself."

"Cut the crocodile tears. There's nobody here you can fool," Shake said.

"I would never, ever kill my father. He was dearer to me than my own life."

"Bullshit!" I said.

Celeste backed up some more. "My mother had an insane plan to send me away to an awful school. He knew it would kill me. She was toxic, TOXIC, for both of us. So he arranged a mercy killing. Merciful for him and me. But he wasn't supposed to kill himself. That wasn't the plan. You have it all wrong! You will regret this!" She reached for the black square behind her, ready to bail, but she was too close to Downtown. The square was too shaky-slippery to jab.

"Let them go!" Shake shouted.

"Never! I will have Nadia Morelli's house carpet-bombed. That's where your real bodies are. I know. You'll be vaporized, along with everyone else."

We grabbed her around the neck with our free hands and gripped her tighter and tighter. And when she went limp, we pushed her straight into the red tornado.

29. TRISTAN

Ready to Move

I'D BEEN AROUND Celeste enough to know that when she was wearing Mercury's lens, she'd be in the trance for some time. When she came out, she was always disoriented, more vulnerable. That's when my persuasive powers would really tip her over the edge. I brewed some coffee in her kitchen, took a shower, becoming as alert and sober as possible. I was drying myself off when a gagging, hocking sound sent me racing back into the other room. Celeste was spasming violently, face tinged blue, desperate unseeing eyes.

I ran my hand down her convulsing body. Instantly, my system mirrored her—throat badly constricted, heart palpitating, nerves registering intense panic. I was fading, fading into unconsciousness as I continued to search. No foreign objects or tumors inside her esophagus or lungs. No abnormalities in her other organs. Her right hand reached out, as if she wanted to push something with her index finger that wasn't there. *Why?* Just before I was going to black out, I tore my hand away.

Celeste's suite was still, except for the sound of her desperate gasps. How long would it take Darrel to realize that the security system had been turned off for an unusually long time—that something was seriously wrong? If he found her like this, he'd have me punished. All the adult prisoners might suffer, violently.

Adrenalin surged through me. Mercury. Had to get to him, even though it was so risky. I put my ear against the outside wall and heard shuffling, very faint. Probably in another corridor. I quickly made the hand signals that opened the wall and sped down the tubes. Left, left, right, two more rights, then left. I wasn't sure how to get to Mercury's room from Celeste's. Never had started from that point.

Laughter drifted from far away. The kids. I knew how to get to Mercury from the nursery. I followed the sound, which grew louder and louder. SLAM. Right in my jaw. I fell backwards into the green wall, knees buckling. Darrel yanked me to my feet, its mouth opening wide, wider, full of steel teeth. The bot lunged to take a chunk out of my neck. I punched it in the torso. Stepping on its foot as a counterweight, and with more strength than I knew was possible, I ripped its head off, then threw it down the hall. The bot's body lumbered around blindly, neck full of wiring. I slammed it again and again until it crashed to the floor and stopped moving.

There was no sound of the spider bots scampering on the other side of the ceiling. So far. It wouldn't last; that seemed sure. I crept silently to the nursery and opened the wall. Izzie and Ma gaped at me, in shock. "You're bleeding," Izzie said. I looked down in surprise. My shirt was covered in red.

"I'm okay." The story of what happened spilled out quickly, just enough. It all seemed hopeless. What had I gotten us into?

Ma looked at me in exasperation. "Wipe that look off your face."

"What look?"

"Of course you don't know what the hell is going to happen. Just keep goin'. Take me to Mercury. I'll get him up and at 'em." It might make sense. Her female energy could get him moving faster than mine would, if he was able to move at all.

Izzie watched Ma stuff some cookies in a pocket. "I could go."

"I know, Sugar," Ma said, grabbing the thermos she always kept with her. "But you saw how he looked at me. He's in my fan base. Get the kids ready."

"For what?"

"Anything!"

Ma and I raced to Mercury's room. Inside, the stench of sweat, piss, and vomit was overpowering. The old man's one uncovered eye shone out in the dim light, jaundice yellow. A few days before I'd sensed a tumor in his gall bladder when I ran a hand over his middle. His face was riddled with pain. Beside his pallet was a plate of putrid beans and a cup half-filled with water.

His gaze latched onto Ma's halo of golden hair, her gap-toothed grin. He burned with her invisible god-like shimmer.

"Take this." She cradled his head in her arms and lifted the thermos, filled with honeyed green tea, to his lips. "Just a sip."

"No," he rasped, but he couldn't resist. Ma guided the liquid down his throat, made him take small bites of a cookie. But mostly, she was touching him, transferring her radiance. He turned to me. "Tell me."

"Celeste is wearing your lens. It seems like she's strangling."

"Tol' you." Mercury looked into the distance, past the walls, out into the world that must still be there. Who was he talking to? He looked back at me. "Any of those freak-show bots know about all this?"

"Darrel. But I took care of him. Security's turned off in her suite."

"Help me up." I pulled one of his stick-like arms, and he came bolt upright more quickly than I expected. His breath heaved up, liquid rattling in his lungs. I could feel it unsettling in my own chest. Ma helped him take another sip of tea. "Knew the girl would do something."

"Izzie?"

"Cheeta."

I had no idea who he was talking about, but Ma said, "Oh yeah. That girl's really something."

Mercury nodded in agreement. "If we ever get out of here, you're probably gonna owe her big. I believe she just drove ol' Celeste into Downtown." He read our confusion. "Don't worry about it now. I gotta get to the control room. And I figured out where they keep some explosives. That should come in handy."

Ma and I traded an alarmed look. What was he thinking? There was no time to quiz him. We just had to trust he wasn't crazy, that whatever he was planning could work. I took one of his skeletal hands, helping him to his feet. We went through the wall, and I started to follow them down the hall. Mercury waved at me wildly. "Take care of Celeste. Cross her over the finish line. And get ready to move!"

30. CHEETA

Blowing Off the Roof

I COULDN'T STOP coughing after we got out of the Universe. Shake heaved in huge gulps of air beside me. Swinging off the bed, my legs nearly buckled. Jarat rushed over and guided me to a chair. Never had such a bad reaction. Then again, never tried to strangle anybody, inside the Universe or out. Shook my hands hard, trying to get the circulation back. I'd squeezed them something fierce in the real world at the same time I was trying to hold onto Shake and choke that satanic woman. Shake smoothed one hand over the other in little nursing strokes, like he was going through the same thing.

"Good glory and the heavens beyond! Thank God you're back!" Nadia said, looking even more of a wreck than usual.

Petra wasn't much better. She threw her arms out in a wide V, and Shake came into them. "I don't think my heart is working anymore," she said. "I used up all the beats."

"How long have we been gone?" Shake asked.

"Thirty-four hours and five minutes," Jarat said, studying us like a scientist *and* a cave man. He hadn't changed his look after hanging out in the Nebraska forests and then freaking Antarctica.

"We fucked that bish up something good," I said.

"She's not dead?" Nadia asked.

"If she isn't, she's very, er, busy," Shake said. Everyone was dying to know what he meant by that, but Jarat wanted to get

Mikhail in on the convo before we said anything more.

It was a shocker when the FBI guy showed up on screen. Before he always seemed to have a sign that read "tired-out loser" stuck on his pasty skin. Now, light from sparky blue water bounced off his face. Never thought somebody like him would ever do *tan*. But he was. Didn't even know he could grin, but that's what he was doing—so wide we could see his teeth, which looked like the chompers of a monster cuddle toy. A baseball cap pushed his big ears out to the sides. Everybody wanted to know what was up with all that.

"I'll get into it," he said. "Let the kids go first."

Kids. Okay. Shake and I took turns explaining how we vice-gripped Celeste's neck and forced her deep into the Downtown hell pit. There was no way to avoid getting sucked in too, and we plunged around in the bubble tornado, gritting our teeth at the feeling of electric fire ants all over our skin. After a while, we found enough combined strength to fly-swim our way out. And as soon as we were far enough away from Downtown for the black exit icon to stop jerking around, I gave it a hard jab, bringing us back to my attic room.

"Even if we didn't kill her, it could take her a long time to get out of there," I said.

"But we don't know," Shake said. "Maybe ten years, maybe two minutes."

"An optimistically negative assessment if there ever was one," said Petra.

Jarat looked at her wryly. "Realistic, for short."

"I think I know where her physical body might be," Mikhail said, pulling up a screen-share of an underwater holo. A fish-like metal structure loomed in the darkness, completely immobile. Cold light from a long line of square port holes stabbed through the murky water. A readout in one corner showed the view was in real time. That was where Miles had died, where Mercury was now. And Luscious, Izzie, and Tristan.

Evil. Pure evil. Hate didn't begin to describe what was raging in me.

Mikhail started from the beginning. We already knew that he couldn't send FBI bot operatives anywhere. So he decided to go on vacation. To the Maui Treasure Zone. In disguise as a paunchy, gasbag tourist who just happened to know where to buy black market aquatic micro-drones with cameras.

"State of the art gizmos. Sonar, ray-tracing, you name it—nothing can detect them," Mikhail said.

"You did all this on your own dime?" Petra asked.

"Nope. Tapped into some Theseus funds."

Jarat grinned at that. Theseus was this underground group that Mikhail and Jarat belonged to—a real bad-boy rebel org back in the day, but way under the radar now.

After he did the black market shopping, Mikhail hired a sport-fishing hover-boat and hydroplaned to a location that matched Mercury's geocoding. Then he dropped the micro-drones, which drifted down toward the sea bed. He'd been watching their camera feeds from the comfort of a hotel room ever since—including what we were looking at now.

"I've seen a couple of places like this before," Mikhail said. "Private jails that are usually run by black market cartels in the South China Sea and the Caribbean. Even went aboard one once during a drug-ring bust. Usually they're run by one person who comes and goes at various times, overseeing a crew of bots. If that one person is in trouble, it can throw off the whole operation."

Over the last week, the giant sub surfaced just one time. It connected with a ship that recharged the sub's solar power. Mikhail's drones also picked up shots of a humanoid and several spider bots carrying supplies from the ship into the sub. "Nothing's happened since then, at least nothing that I can detect."

"Never let a good crisis go to waste," Shake said.

"You came up with that?" I asked.

"Naw. Somebody named Churchill."

Petra rolled her eyes. "But we don't know if Celeste was actually down there when she got pushed into Downtown—or if she's still there, right?"

"Correct," Mikhail said. "But no matter where she is, the prison is probably in a state of emergency, given that Celeste controls the place and she's been thrown into… what did you call it?"

"Downtown," I said.

"I want to bet there are other members of The Fist that are watching over that operation remotely. If they sense there's any kind of trouble, they're going to pay a visit," Jarat said. "We've got to get to that prison *now*. It may already be too late."

Shake looked at Mikhail: "You met with my friend yet?"

"Yeah. That racer really knows his way around a liquor cabinet."

"*And* how to take some calculated risks."

Petra gave Shake a stunned look. "Phineas?"

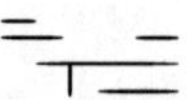

IT DIDN'T TAKE Jarat and Shake long to get ready. They needed to meet the Phin guy at his place outside the San Diego Treasure Zone. Shake couldn't believe I didn't want to go. "You realize this is dangerous. Plus, Phin is this really hot racing star."

It was kind of cute, the way he was baiting me. "Eh! He's gotta be over thirty-five. Ancient. Plus, you don't need me. I'd get in the way."

He looked like somebody'd splashed him with a drink. "Oh."

"What do you mean, 'Oh?'"

"You think I can't figure this out?" He glanced at his mother and Nadia. "The three of you look like Macbeth's witches stirring a goddamned cauldron."

"Ah, the old play by that writer you were named after," Nadia said to Shakespear. "I sang in Verdi's version a few times. Never a fan."

He tried not to show how bugged that made him, but I knew how to read him now. Nadia scraped her eyes away like she couldn't have cared less. Which was so like her.

"Whatever you do, don't get caught," Shake said to me, letting out a tender laugh. Sort of like the senator used to do. But not fatherly. Brotherly? Didn't know what.

Maybe he was about to get killed. Maybe this would be the last time I'd ever see him. And yeah, we'd done crazy stuff in the Universe, but this time, this time we were one-hundred percent real world, with super real shit going on. I tried to swallow the lump in my throat. "Get the hell out of here."

ABOUT AN HOUR later, Nadia, Petra, and I stepped into the gigantic, raw space where Diana was hidden. Nadia had morphed from her regular old hag look to a somebody that could take your breath away, if you were into older babes. But she looked really nervous as she straightened the shoulder straps of her long red gown. It was made out of two layers of transparent material sandwiching red fluid that sparkled up and down the length of her.

This was the glamor puss that Miles had fallen for, whose name was always on his lips, every day I was with him. Even after she'd turned into a resentful, jealous bish, he never stopped seeing who she really was, underneath. Petra had worked on the look that Nadia was sporting now. She knew a bunch of makeup and body-enhancing tricks.

"You're a freaking magician," I said to Petra, making her laugh.

Nadia rehearsed a song with despair, wandering off across the long open floor. Her voice cracked again and again. It was pathetic, and she knew it. She cowered beneath her hopelessness on a little stool, tears streaming.

Diana started toward her with a glass of water, but Petra called the bot softly, and it pivoted over to us, athletic and graceful in its adult state. Petra's eyes glittered, still on Nadia. "I'll handle it." She took the glass and walked over to the diva, sitting on the stool beside her.

It was super easy to see why Nadia would be stressed. It wasn't just the singing-voice issue. If she didn't make a big impact—and if The Fist used the Charismites to send out another message—the whole thing would fall flat. We were counting on Shake, Mikhail, and Jarat to save the Charismites before something like that happened! But even if that rescue mission went completely bust, we had to do this. Because what else did we have?

I got close enough to hear Petra and Nadia talking without them noticing. The diva stared at the mirror on her air screen, trying to push her makeup back into place. "I'm ruining everything!"

"Did I ever tell you about my father?" Petra asked. Nadia shook her head no. "I called him Dab. He couldn't understand me, in so many ways. But no one *wanted* to understand me more than he did. And whenever things went to hell, he was the one I talked to. He was the one that brought me together with Shake when he lost his whole family. That little boy saved miserable little me as much as I saved him. Dab knew that would happen, in his bones. And now, even though he's been gone so long, I still talk to my Dab. Sometimes he seems to change everything inside me when I do that. And I've come to believe that the dead are with us, if we try to sense them. They can generate power in us, when we've lost—well, whatever it is we need."

Nadia spat out, "I don't believe in that spirit-world fluff."

"Suit yourself. But you can believe this: what Miles discovered? Nothing is going to stop me from getting it out. If you don't do this, I will."

"Me too!" I said, then muttered under my breath "fucking wuss" just loud enough for Nadia to hear. Petra and I walked away. Nadia's eyes were shooting laser knives in my back. Petra give me a secret wink.

My mobile buzzed. Ginseng Childe's holo appeared before me. "It's 8:45!"

We'd told her we'd be ready by 8. "Yeah, I know. Frickin' prima donna. What can I say?" No sense getting into deets.

"Well I hope she gets it together soon!" Ginseng said. Since Nuhope kicked her out, the journo had attracted a big base of followers. Within minutes, those followers would repost the holo again and again. And in a couple of hours a huge chunk of the entire world would see it. At least, that's what we hoped.

I glanced over at Nadia. A holo of the senator was on her air screen. It was from a trip they'd taken to Rome. Miles' hair was blowing in five directions, and he was wearing a rose polo shirt damp with sweat from the blistering day. Nadia's eyes locked on the strength in his eyes, and huge breaths burst out of her. Her chest expanded like the sails of a great yacht as she swept toward Petra and me.

"Alright! Let's blow the roof off the world!" she said.

"That's what I'm talkin' 'bout!" I yelled.

We got calm and took our positions. Diana and Petra stood on either side of me as my air-screen camera focused on a black wall. I pushed the record button as Petra said, "And action. Three, two, one."

Diana's mouth opened, but instead of the bot's usual voice, a tinkling piano sound came out, like a musical conversation. The train of Nadia's red dress rippled behind her as she moved into camera view, a queen dragon opening its wings. Her breasts heaved with a pent-up longing, then she seemed to throw it away with a toss of her head. All of her nervousness was gone. The air tingled with excitement and calm, all at once.

Nadia gazed at my face. So many memories were packed in that look—the awfulness, strangeness, love we'd both felt. We were bonded like the strongest glue ever invented, probably forever.

Her eyes shifted to the camera. "Good evening, everyone. I'm Nadia Morelli." Her rusty-pipe rasp was controlled, with velvet underneath. "This is my first public performance in about five years. So I hope you'll indulge me if I sound a bit raw. I decided that it was time for me to come back out into the world, but not as the singer you once knew. You see, my voice is so changed. I've always loved the blues, from the time I was a little girl. And now, now there's no better sound, for me."

She walked a little closer to the camera screen. "My late husband, Senator Miles Morelli, wrote the lyrics to the song I'm performing. Though he didn't think of the words in a musical way. He uncovered a long list of names, of people you might be very familiar with. All of them, every last one, is either a member of a secret group of corporate titans, The Fist, or they are politicians who have been bribed to become its puppets. My husband was tortured and killed because he wanted to expose them all, for what they are. He died so that you could hear this."

Diana's arms spread out wide, and the little holographic cards emerged with all the intel that she and the senator had uncovered. They went by in a slow carousel off camera, like a teleprompter. The bot's piano voice ruffled between four notes, over and over, with the thrill of a drum roll. And I could imagine the audience gasping as a gigantic holo smoked up behind Nadia: the face of the U.A.'s vice president, Theawanza Newton.

Nadia sang out all the ugliness: how the veep secretly pocketed millions of Americos from the largest air polluter on the planet. Wanza's face was replaced by others: corporate CEOs, judges, congresspeople, media personalities, in a long daisy chain of connections. She sprinkled in facts about false promises in campaign speeches, corrupt court hearings, news-show lies. And at the same time, Diana fed Ginseng extra facts from the cards, in real time, to relay even more info out into the world.

Nadia's rough voice bounced out every name in the database, and she saved the best parts for last. First came Celeste Sidhar, who had abducted two of the biggest legends on the planet—Luscious and Izabel—and killed one of the greatest senators of all time, Miles. Then came the face of President Pavlarona with secret intel about her jacked-up plan to gain control of all the world's great nations by faking a goddamned alien invasion.

The whole time Nadia was singing, I imagined that a billion mobile pings about her were going all over the world… that The Fist people were sending out screaming messages denying everything… that massive investigations would take place… that other news people would turn on Wanza and Tippi like attack dogs. The truth we sent out was that solid, that strong.

But maybe none of that was happening. Or if some of it did, it didn't matter because the Charismites were still twisting everybody's brains. We didn't know.

31. SHAKE

Into The Abyss

THE RENTED CAB zoomed us across the country in ninety minutes flat. Jarat and I came out of ghost mode as it coasted through a private security field and landed outside a lavish home with a view of the Pacific so perfect that it didn't seem real—until Phineas stepped out the front door.

His impish, weathered face beamed. "It's about time, Patch Man. God! Jarat Ellington! I've been a fan of yours since I was a kid."

Jarat got a little red faced. "I don't know why."

"Legendary rebel? Come on, man. Own it!"

I coughed. There was no time for this. "You got something to show us?"

"Allow me to blow your mind." Phineas led us to a white barn. Inside, dust motes whorled like fireflies in the light of two high windows, circling around a 'craft that looked like some kind of mishmash—as if its designers couldn't decide they wanted to build. It was about forty feet long, and the hull was shaped like a dolphin. Two wings on either side were folded into a box-like configuration.

"What we have here is the Tseng SeaQueen 8A4," Phin said. "Runs on cryogenic hydrogen. Flies above land at blazing speeds, *and* it skims across water with up to fourteen-foot waves, *plus* it's a submersible."

"How far down does it go?" Jarat asked.

"As far as we want."

"Sweet."

"Yeah. It's epic! Total triathlon show material, Shake. You know, once your mother gets her newco up and running. We get a few of these puppies racing around the worl' and it'll pull in some amazing demos!"

"If we get through this, we'll talk."

"If? We better. I just got this as a loaner for three days. Told the big girls and boys at Tseng I wanted to do a few test runs on my own. So I can't wreck it."

Jarat shot me a wary look. "That's the plan."

Phin didn't seem too concerned; he was already back to his pitch. "The other thing I love about it is the anti-surveillance-tracking software in the skin along with some pretty colors." He activated a control panel on his mobile, and the SeaQueen's silver exterior turned mottled shades of brown and yellow, like the space we were standing in. "Matches its environment. Which is a bitch, if you're racing against one of these things. But that's just going to sex-up the show I'm talking about."

"How many people can it carry?" I asked.

"Ten. You have any idea how many we're picking up?"

"Hopefully four adults and some babies."

"Babies!" Phin's face blanched, like dealing with kids was terrifying.

"We don't know how many."

The racer recovered easily enough. "Well, let's crack on, lads."

The sun was already down by the time we started zooming over the Pacific at ten-thousand feet. The luxurious interior was geared toward pleasure excursions, but it seared the sky faster than anything I'd ever been in. Phin's triathlon show concept suddenly seemed like a killer idea. That flitted through my head for about two seconds before it was overpowered by thoughts about whatever lay dead. We were all pretty tense.

"The prison sub should have a port on its side that we can connect to and enter from there," Phin said. "The prison is too far below for scuba diving, but there's gear for that in the closets by the loo. We might need to use it to up near the surface. You know how to dive?"

Jarat said he did, but that wasn't my jam. Tried not to feel like a wuss.

The SeaQueen dropped altitude and hydroplaned a few feet above the Pacific. Its lights picked up endless iron-gray waves, spiking up with primeval power. As we came within a few miles of our target, a pinprick of light glinted in the distance. Drawing closer, we could make out a sport-fishing boat. Mikhail was on deck, hands in his pockets, still wearing the cap and a T-shirt with the words "Maui Is Wowie" encircled with red hearts. He sure put the ug in "ugly *turista*."

Mikhail clamored up the SeaQueen's ladder, gave us some fist bumps, then stripped down to scuba gear. His aging, out-of-shape body seemed a little problematic for a dip in the drink.

"Where's your cane?" Jarat asked.

"No need. I used some extra pharmas."

"I don't mean to be feckin' rude but are your sure you're up for this?" asked Phin.

Mikhail raised his chin defiantly. "I'm doing it."

The SeaQueen dropped straight down. I watched the sonar readout as five hundred meters flew by. "We're in the Twilight Zone," Phin said. "Runs down to a thousand meters." Tiny fish shone like confetti, their bioluminescence turning them into multicolored neon squiggles in the velvety blackness. It felt like my mind was exploding: to have been in the orange Universe just a short while ago, and now in these surreal surroundings.

We dropped to a mile below sea level, then two miles, and

before long we were in The Abyssal Zone, better known as The Abyss. The cabin was freezing now. We could see our breath, which left water beads on the wall. "Two tons of pressure per square inch out there," Phin said.

What the hell would happen to a human body, swimming this far below? Hoped none of the prisoners had tried to escape into that. Something huge drifted by, too far away and vague for me to make out—except for its gaping maw. Nope. Definitely didn't want to go out there.

Phin pulled a lever, and the SeaQueen changed direction, gliding parallel to the sea floor. "We're 2.3 miles below," Phin said. He eyed the sonar readout. "Still no other visitors around."

"You sure about that?" I asked. After all, wouldn't the bots in Celeste's prison have alerted someone that she was in trouble—*if* she was actually there, and *if* she was still in Downtown and couldn't get back to the real world? Didn't relish the idea of an attack.

Phin shrugged. "Even if there were, this baby's hard to track."

"I wouldn't count on that," Mikhail said. "The Fist has deep military sources, and it's probably got a lot of tricks up its sleeve." Not that he looked at all worried.

We moved from half a mile away from our target to one-thousand four-hundred feet. Dead ahead, a long line of cold white lights emerged in the black. The facility looked enormous, filled with unwitnessed cruelty. *Lush, Tristan, Izzie, and Mercury. Lush, Tristan, Izzie, and Mercury.* That's where they were, right now. My heart hammered with optimism and dread.

The control board flashed, and a piercing buzz cut the air. "Here comes somebody," Phin said. Way off in the distance: a powerful light slashed through the darkness, aiming straight for the prison. Then it landed right on top of the massive structure.

What the hell could we do now without getting killed? Just then, something white shot out from the side of the prison. What the—

BOOM! The SeaQueen was thrown violently backwards. Huge shards of metal battered the exterior. My teeth clenched so hard my jaw hurt.

"Jesus, Mary, and Joe," Phin roared. Our ride was probably getting scratched up—if not more than that.

We ascended through the debris, all of us hoping desperately that the white we'd seen hurtling off the side of that sub was some kind of prisoner escape. Dawn was breaking above as we drew closer to the surface, the water so intensely blue it was almost an emotion, like entering heaven might be, if it existed. Who knew?

We surfaced into the air and scanned the waves in all directions, desperate for clues about what just happened. Nothing. No other vessel surfaced. "Crap. Whoever took off must have got caught in the blast," Mikhail said.

"Nope," Jarat said. "Look." We tracked his gaze to a small sub just popping out of the water. It was made of some thick semi-transparent substance and filled with light. We could see the vague shape of people inside. A hatch opened and my sister's head popped through. I let out a shout.

As we came alongside the sub and Izzie climbed out further, we realized she was carrying two kids. Not babies. Kids! Phin dropped the gangway, and Izz climbed aboard the SeaQueen. Then Lush emerged, beaming her gap-toothed smile as she carried two more children across the narrow plank. Behind her was a stud-licious guy that turned out to be Tristan, carefully guiding a fragile figure: the strange old man from the messages, Mercury.

Two more little faces peered out from inside the little sub.

Six kids!? Each one bewitched us.

Jarat was in shock. I grinned. "Congratulations, Granddad." He scrambled across the gangway to get the last two out.

32. TRISTAN

Rules? What Rules?

GOLDEN DUST DRIFTED through the air—on leaves, veggies in the garden, the koi pond, and in the doors of my family's home. So I was told.

"You really don't see any sparkles?" Cheeta asked. She was in the lawn chair next to my own, lowering her sunglasses to shoot me a seductive look.

"Nope. None of us Charismites can sense that part of what we're doing. Although it's kind of unusual. I guess because there's so many of us in one place."

She tilted her head back to soak in the brightness of the sky beyond the transparent dome. "The way you all are making me feel is *intense*."

"I get it." Of course Mercury, Nadia, and Cheeta would feel the euphoria that Charismites gave off. But even the inner circle—Da, Shake, and Petra—were on a high. They were used to dealing with a few Charismites at a time, but freaking nine of us were together there: Lush, Izzie, me, and the six kids. They all felt hyper alive.

A few weeks had gone by since we all settled in the biosphere. The world beyond us was full of seismic change. News reports about our escape and Nadia's performance had gone nuts. Ma, Izzie, and I amplified the diva's song even more in messages. And we sent out others that retracted everything we'd been forced to say in that prison.

A slew of politicians and corporate tycoons were trying to save themselves, denying all the evidence they were connected to The Fist—that they had anything to do with our abduction and the senator's death. But the more the public and reporters looked into Senator Morelli's findings, the more it became clear that none of the accused would be saved from public humiliation and financial destruction. There were calls for Congressional hearings, but a lot had to be sorted out on that front because so many of the lawmakers were involved in the corruption.

The secretary of defense gave a press conference, confessing that there was no evidence of an approaching Kepler-22b invasion. The once-wildly-popular idea that the disgraced leaders of the U.A.—Tippi and Wanza—should lead the world had fizzled away.

And Celeste? We were pretty sure she'd been killed. Sometimes those final panicked minutes in the prison came back to me like a horrendous nightmare: how Mercury hobbled so painfully through the halls to show us where the explosives were stored, then where we could get into the mini sub on the side of the prison. He'd figured that all out, before Celeste slammed down on him so hard.

We were all terrified, loading the kids inside that sub, worrying that Mercury wouldn't survive this. But somehow we escaped, just as Fist commandos landed on top of the prison and the explosives went off.

Now, none of us wanted to leave the Ellington compound. We'd arrived there in a state of near collapse. Everyone needed the rest, to hold onto the feeling that no one could attack us, no one could snatch *anyone* here. Da had fortified the place with much stronger materials and defensive weaponry than ever before, with help from Mikhail. When word surfaced within the FBI about what Mikhail had done, while on vacation, the agency forgave his indiscretions and granted him access to highly classified security resources to help Jarat protect the biodome.

Izzie danced out of the house in a tattered dress, flame-colored hair flying. Behind her came five of our kids doing little goofy-joy dances—blonde heads, curly tops, poofs of fine black hair. Nadia burst out the door in a filmy purple dress and pranced down the lawn behind them, bellowing a song that vibrated far and wide. The merrymakers joined hands, dancing together in a giddy circle.

Cheeta's eyes fixed on Izzie. I knew she was turned on by her as much as me. Kind of felt sorry for her, getting our vibes from both sides. Shake pushed through the screen door and let it bang shut on purpose. Cheeta jumped, and he flashed a glare at her that came and went instantaneously. She turned all innocent, smiling back. Something was going on between them, and I wasn't sure exactly what. Maybe they didn't know, either. Shake headed to the picnic table with a caprese salad and olive bread.

The door shot open again, and Petra bolted toward the fish pond. "Hey! What did I tell you?" she shouted. "Do not drink that water!" Cal lifted up his soaking wet head of red hair, giggling like his grandma was the funniest person alive. Don't know if anybody ever thought of Petra that way before, and I could tell she loved it. Crouching down, she opened her arms in a wide V, and he ran into them, soaking her. Not that it mattered. She was heady with love for him, for all her grandchildren.

Nadia broke off from the dancing circle and came puffing up the hill. She sank into a chair beside Cheeta, gazing at the kids down below. "How old are they now?"

"About three months," I said. They all looked to be about seven.

An acid look took over her. "At this rate, they'll be geriatric before you know it."

"Not if I can help it," Da said. He came out the screen door like a gunslinger, with a pitcher of sangria in one fist and a pitcher of milk in the other. "I'm working on a fix. Tweaking the chems Lush takes when she's sauced up." He made his way down to the table.

"Well, I hope you figure it out soon!" Nadia sang. He turned around to give her the stink eye.

Mercury came around the corner of the house with Ma, who was holding one of his arms as they took halting steps together. He adored her with one shiny black eye. The other was covered in a patch. I'd felt into his body several times over the last few weeks and suspected that the eye would heal eventually, but he'd never fully recover from the bot attacks and the torture, no matter what we did to help.

"Now don't you even think about leaving here," Ma said to him.

"No ma'am. Not directly."

"Don't make me crank up my voodoo! You want to retire? Well this is the best place to do it."

"There's this cabin in the Sierras. We got to get there." I knew he meant his wife with that "we," even though she was gone.

"We'll build a cabin for you right here, Honey. You'd be doing us a favor. We kind of need another gramps."

"Plus, you can tell me more about the Universe," Cheeta said. "I know you got more going on in there than I figured out."

Mercury chuckled. "Oh, you know pretty much all you need to. Although Downtown could use a little tweak."

"Ya think?!" Seemed like the two of them had a formed a real mutual admiration society. And the way Ma was working on Mercury, I got the sense that maybe the idea of that cabin under our dome might grow on him.

We heaped the table with fried chicken, three kinds of salad, collard greens, and Ma's world-class rhubarb custard pie. Long past sunset, Nadia and Izzie sang softly together as we lingered under the tree, lulled by the food, drinks, and a sense of unshakeable happiness, even though it would get shook—life being what it is. Finally Izzie and I roused ourselves and took the kids off to bed.

Later, as we started downstairs, Izzie ran a hand down my back. The full surge of our attraction flared up. It was so easy to surface, now that we had birth control, now that we were no longer gripped with terror. It had nothing to do with being Charismites and everything to do with being human.

We stood at a window, looking down at the others still under the tree—so much love there. "That metaverse, it's not about lost messages. Cheeta gave it the wrong name," Izzie said.

"I won't tell her you said that."

"No, don't. But between you and me, it's the Universe of Finding—finding what people need to pay attention to. Might even find things they don't know they need."

"Or what they think is impossible."

"Yeah, like that." We melted into a long, epic kiss. Ancient legends could have fit inside it. Eventually, we made our way down to the table. Petra was saying, "So how do we raise the kids? How do we make sure they're protected but lead full lives?"

"Good question. Don't think we really got that part right before," Ma said, glancing at Izzie and me. "Not to say I don't love the 2.0 versions."

"Yeah, well we love you too, Lil Ms. 1.0," Izzie said. Ma

gave her a grin.

"Don't forget: we're the parents. We'll decide about the kids," I said.

"Fair enough," Da said. "What's the plan?"

Izzie turned her high beams on him. "That has to do with you." Could he come up with some kind of anti-Charismite solution? That's what we both wanted to know.

"What? In addition to slowing down your kids' biological clock?" he teased. "What do you think I am, some kind of miracle short order cook?"

"Uh, yeah," Izzie said, making him laugh. She always wrapped Da around her little finger.

"Matter of fact, I've been working on something for years. But it isn't there yet." Was it a chemical? Some kind of tech? He told us we'd have to wait and see. If he could figure out a way to tamp down our effect on people, it sure would make life a lot simpler for the kids, and help me to get trained as a doctor, bringing physicians and medical instructors into the biodome without making them completely obsessed. From there, maybe we could build a medical facility.

Izzie and I had dreamed about going out into the world with our kids as quietly as we could when they were older, traveling to the poorest parts of the world to help people. Maybe some of the kids would be healers. Maybe they'd become builders, teachers, other types of workers—inspiring others to launch their own relief efforts.

In the end, we had to throw that idea away. Just because we'd blown the lid off The Fist didn't mean there weren't a lot of bad actors out there in the world that would try to use us. At least for now, we needed the biodome's protection. It wasn't what Izzie had wanted, staying there, but when the kids emerged, it changed everything. She was obsessed with raising them, and determined to keep them safe.

That's why she'd come up with another idea. Izzie gazed at Mercury. "You're such a master metaverse designer. I think you should build a new one. Tris and I could move around in it, and Lush too. And maybe the kids someday."

"If it worked out, we'd spotlight the work that people are doing all over the world to help the poor or make the Earth a better place in other ways," I said.

Mercury's one uncovered eye lit up. "I think you got something there."

"Oh hellz, yeah," Ma said. "I want in on that."

Petra's brain was on fire, too. "We could put some camera crews out into the field to capture what people are up to, then you all serve as the hosts from the safety of the biodome. That could have a real snowball effect. The more that people see how to get involved, the more ideas could pop up."

"Whoa! Sure it's a good idea, but it sounds so damned educational. Where's the fun? Where's the entertainment?" Shake said. "There should be something more. Izzie, I know you could think of *something*."

"Sure. I'll gets some friends involved."

"And of course this metaverse would just *have* to be part of your newco," Shake teased his mother.

"*Our* newco. Owned by all of us right here."

"Oh, no. I have my own repertoire of ideas to work on," Nadia said mysteriously. Although it was easy to guess she was planning some kind of music comeback. But I had a feeling she'd put on a show in our new metaverse, too, with a little persuading.

"I've got something else going on, too," Cheeta said.

We talked way into the night, debating everything in conversations that went heated and comical by turns. Nothing was decided. Everything was out there before us, uncertain. But not one of us was afraid—not after what we'd been through. It's like we'd been given an inoculation against fear that might last a long time.

I woke up the next morning with a throbbing ache near my left scapula. I managed to get up without waking Izzie. The pain grew more intense as I neared the pond. A dove was thrashing on the ground. One of its wings was broken. I picked it up very gently, brought it to the shed, wrapped the wing with tape, then put the bird in an old metal carrier. I'd need to watch over it for a few weeks before releasing it.

When I came back to the house, Ma was teaching Cal and his sister Willa how to play poker on the porch. Nadia stood over Ma's shoulder, watching how they laid down the cards. "You can't do that! It's against the rules!" the diva said.

"Rules? What rules?" Ma said. "We don't worry about little things like that."

I went into the kitchen for some water. Out the back window, Cheeta was staring at all the greenery like she was on some kind of strange planet and still couldn't get used to it. Shake sauntered up to her. Neither of them saw me.

"So how old are you?" he asked her.

She looked him over in surprise. "Seventeen."

"I'm twenty-three."

"Congratulations." She was laughing inside at him.

He didn't seem to care. "And you're—what did you call it—flexible?"

"You got a problem with that?"

"Nope. But I'll tell you what: I got a problem if you don't go to college."

"If there's time."

"Make it. You can still do other things." Like go back into

the Universe. Had to be what he meant.

"Yeah. Guess so," Cheeta said.

"Mind if I come? I mean, no promises. But maybe I could help."

"With what?"

"Deliver other messages. The ones that count."

"You've got the new company to worry about."

"We'll see how that goes. But the Universe—it's calling to me, you know? It feels like what I need to do, find those messages. Even though it's whacked-out, sometimes it looks—well, magnificent, even sublime."

"What!?"

"Never mind. The point is, we should give it a shot. And I could help keep you out of Downtown if Mercury doesn't come up with a fix."

Cheeta snorted. "Yeah. Right."

They were a total mismatch: the scratchy haired girl-woman in rumpled black clothes; my big-brother friend with the posh edge. And yet somehow, they kind of interlocked.

"C'mon. Let's do it. Right now. Maybe we'll even get back in time for dinner," Shake said.

"Okay. I want to see this sublime thingy." Cheeta pulled a mobile lens out of a little carrying case in her pocket and slipped it on. They lay down next to each other in the grass. Shake's hand folded over hers. And then their minds were gone.

ACKNOWLEDGMENTS

WHEN I STARTED covering the media industry as a journalist, it became addictive. Chronicling the changes within corporations that entertain and inform us—and influence what we think and do—became a passion. And I love the surprises, when smaller companies upend the status quo. As with the first book in this series, *The Juice*, that journalism work inspired my vision for *Universe*, and what huge media companies might be like decades from today. I am grateful for all the assignments I've received over the years, keeping me financially afloat and deepening my understanding of the business.

Several people were huge champions to the *Universe of Lost Messages* cause. Among them were colleagues who read through a draft that contained a lot of scraggily edges that needed to be reconsidered or smoothed out—kind of like Cheeta LaVera's hair. So I'm sending a huge airship of thanks to Jenna Zark, Barbara Vaccaro, Haley Sive, Larry Maness, and Jan Kimbrough. The editor, Jonathan Oliver, followed behind the beta readers when the book was nearly done, becoming a crucial sounding board. I'm deeply flattered by his encouragement and glowing assessment of this novel.

Two singers, Michael Rogers and Virginia Pluth Walker, gave me an understanding of the intense passion and training that goes into performing in great opera houses and what it would be like to leave that world behind. That was critical, because I knew very little about opera singers when the character Nadia Morelli suddenly barged into my imagination and would not be denied. If it hadn't been for Krista Van Lewen Rogers, I never would have received Virginia and Michael's invaluable insights. So thank you, Krista!

My understanding of what would happen if an asteroid with strange properties landed in the Sonoran Desert also owes much to Al Feinberg, a media specialist at NASA. He helped me obtain answers to questions from Jeffrey J.E. Hayes, a discipline scientist within NASA's Space Operations Mission Directorate. Jeffrey helped me add an extra layer of credibility with humor and insight.

I'd also like to thank Brian Dewey for the reality check on how email messages get retransmitted in server farms. And the Dorland Mountain Arts residency program gave me much needed space and time to work on this novel, as it did with *The Juice*.

I'm also deeply thankful that the publisher Gwen Gades of Dragon Moon Press, who chose to champion both books in the Charismite series: *The Juice* and *Universe*. She took a gamble on my work, and I'll never forget that.

The biggest guiding star in my universe is David Chachere, my husband, who passed away about a month after *The Juice* was published in 2021. The enthusiasm he expressed for my work stays with me. And it uplifts me in moments of despair and doubt. This led to the creation of Mercury's dead wife, Tavee, whom I named after David's grandmother. (Although her name is spelled differently.) Unlike Mercury, I don't have imaginary conversations with my dear one. But there are times when I sense David's presence.

New York City, December 2023

About the Author

Janet Stilson writes novels, short stories, and scripts that largely fall in the grounded sci-fi and fantasy genres and illuminate the human condition in provocative ways. Her work has been selected to be part of the Writers' Lab for Women, which is funded by Meryl Streep and Nicole Kidman. And it has also appeared in *Asimov's* magazine.

As a journalist, Janet got her "chops" at the storied showbiz bible *Variety*. She has traveled the world, chronicling the business of media and entertainment. That work inspired both *Universe of Lost Messages* and her first novel, *The Juice*, which received rave reviews. *Publishers Weekly* wrote: "Stilson debuts with an energetic vision of a dystopian near-future America … This cyberpunk adventure delivers plenty of future tech and social commentary to please genre fans."

Janet lives in The Bronx, which is a world away from her childhood home: Franklin, a gorgeous upstate New York village. Cars pass through Franklin in almost the blink of an eye, and she hopes it stays that way.

Find out more about Janet and subscribe to her newsletter by visiting janetstilson.com.

Made in United States
North Haven, CT
21 December 2024

62795732R00243